RES...R
JAMES GRIPPANDO
AND
THE PARDON

"*T*he Pardon arrives with the pistol-shot crack
of a gavel cutting through a courtroom."
Tampa Tribune

"*G*rippando writes in nail-biting style."
Larry King, *USA Today*

"*P*owerful. . . . I read *The Pardon* in one sitting—
one exciting night of thrills and chills."
New York Times bestselling author
James Patterson

"*C*hilling. . . . Grippando ratchets the tension up
every few pages. *The Pardon* is a promising,
cleverly plotted, and taut first novel."
Booklist

"*J*ames Grippando is a very inventive and
ingenious storyteller."
New York Times bestselling author
Nelson DeMille

"*[T*he Pardon] takes us into the seamy side of
Florida law, politics and murder. . . . Grippando
writes about what he knows and it's good."
Sunday Oklahoman

By James Grippando

Forthcoming

And for Young Adults

*A Jack Swyteck Novel
†Also featuring FBI Agent Andie Henning

JAMES GRIPPANDO

the pardon

THE FIRST JACK SWYTECK NOVEL

HARPER

An Imprint of HarperCollinsPublishers

This is a work of fiction. Names, characters, places, and incidents are products of the author's imagination or are used fictitiously and are not to be construed as real. Any resemblance to actual events, locales, organizations, or persons, living or dead, is entirely coincidental.

HARPER

An Imprint of HarperCollins*Publishers*
10 East 53rd Street
New York, New York 10022-5299

Copyright © 1994 by James Grippando
Author photo © Monica Hopkins Photography
ISBN 978-0-06-202448-0

First Harper premium printing: July 2011
First Harper mass market printing: December 2007
First Avon Books mass market printing: May 2002
First HarperPaperbacks printing: November 1995
First HarperCollins hardcover printing: September 1994

Printed in the United States of America

Visit Harper paperbacks on the World Wide Web at www.harpercollins.com

10 9 8 7 6 5 4 3 2 1

To my parents

Acknowledgments

•

I am indebted to a great many people who helped make this dream come true.

A very warm thank-you to my first readers—Carlos Sires, James C. Cunningham, Jr., Terri Pepper, Denise Gordon, and Jerry Houlihan—who were good enough friends to suffer through the truly rough drafts. Jerry was a special help. His advice and courtroom instincts proved as invaluable to me as a writer as they were to me as a young lawyer. Thanks also to James W. Hall, Deputy Sheriff and Search and Rescue Coordinator in Yakima County, Washington, for his law-enforcement expertise.

From the very start, I had the extremely good fortune of dealing with the best in the book business. Special thanks to my literary agents, Artie and Richard Pine, for patiently waiting until I got it right, and for running—and howling—like the wolves when they knew we had something. I am equally grateful to Joan Sanger, whom I met through Artie, and whose editorial guidance helped turn an outline into a novel. And Rick Horgan, my editor, was an amazing teacher. He has left his mark not just on the book, but on the writer as well. Rick is one of the many reasons I am eternally thankful for the backing of a publisher of the quality and repute of Harper-Collins.

Thanks also to the lawyers, paralegals, secretaries, and staff at Steel Hector & Davis for their support and enthusiasm. I'm happy to say I've spent the last ten years working with friends and colleagues who are rightfully proud of what they do for a living.

Finally, my deepest gratitude goes to my wife, Tiffany, and to my family. Without your love, prayers, and encouragement, I would still be just talking about writing a book.

the
pardon

Part One

October 1992

Prologue

•

The vigil had begun at dusk, and it would last all night. Clouds had moved in after midnight, blocking out the full moon. It was as if heaven had closed its omniscient eye in sorrow or just plain indifference. Another six hours of darkness and waiting, and the red morning sun would rise over the pine trees and palms of northeast Florida. Then, at precisely 7:00 A.M., Raul Fernandez would be put to death.

Crowds gathered along the chain-link fence surrounding the state's largest maximum-security penitentiary. Silence and a few glowing lights emanated from the boxy three-story building across the compound, a human warehouse of useless parts and broken spirits. Armed guards paced in their lookout towers, silhouettes in the occasional sweep of a searchlight. Not as many onlookers gathered tonight as in the old days, back when Florida's executions had been front-page news rather than a blip next to the weather forecast. Even so, the usual shouting had erupted when the black hearse that would carry out the corpse arrived. The loudest spectators were hooting and hollering from the backs of their pickup trucks, chugging their long-neck Budweisers and brandishing banners that proclaimed GO SPARKY, the nickname death-penalty supporters had affectionately given "the chair."

The victim's parents peered through the chain-link fence with quiet determination, searching only for retribution, there being no justice or meaning in the slashing of their daughter's throat. Across the road, candles burned and guitars strummed as the names of John Lennon and Joan Baez were invoked by former flower children of a caring generation, their worried faces wrinkled with age and the weight of the world's problems. Beside a cluster of nuns kneeling in prayer, supporters from Miami's "Little Havana" neighborhood shouted in their native Spanish, *"Raul es inocente, inocente!"*

Behind the penitentiary's brick walls and barred windows, Raul Fernandez had just finished his last meal—a bucket of honey-glazed chicken wings with extra mashed potatoes—and he was about to pay his last visit to the prison barber. Escorted by armed correction officers in starched beige-and-brown uniforms, he took a seat in a worn leather barber's chair that was nearly as uncomfortable as the boxy wooden throne on which he was scheduled to die. The guards strapped him in and assumed their posts—one by the door, the other at the prisoner's side.

"Barber'll be here in a minute," said one of the guards. "Just sit tight."

Fernandez sat rigidly and waited, as if he expected the electricity to flow at any moment. His bloodshot eyes squinted beneath the harsh glare as the bright white lights overhead reflected off the white walls of painted cinder block and the white tile floors. He allowed himself a moment of bitter irony as he noticed that even the guards were white.

All was white, in fact, except the man scheduled to die. Fernandez was one of the thousands of Cuban refugees who'd landed in Miami during the Mariel boat lift of 1980. Within a year he was arrested for first-degree murder. The jury convicted him in less time than it had taken the young victim to choke on her own blood. The judge sentenced him to die in the electric chair, and after a decade of appeals, his time had come.

"Mornin', Bud," said the big guard who'd posted himself at the door.

The prisoner watched tentatively as a potbellied barber with cauliflower ears and a self-inflicted marine-style haircut entered the room. His movements were slow and methodical. He seemed to enjoy the fact that for Fernandez every moment was like an eternity. He stood before his captive customer and smirked, his trusty electric shaver in one hand and, in the other, a big plastic cup of the thickest-looking tea Fernandez had ever seen.

"Right on time," said the barber through his tobacco-stained teeth. He spat his brown slime into his cup, placed it on the counter, and took a good look at Fernandez. "Oh, yeah," he wheezed, "you look just like you does on the TV," he said, pronouncing *TV* as if it rhymed with *Stevie*.

Fernandez sat stone-faced in the chair, ignoring the remark.

"Got a special on the Louis Armstrong look today," the barber said as he switched on his shaver.

Curly black hair fell to the floor as the whining razor transformed the prisoner's thick mop to a stubble that glistened with nervous beads of sweat. At the proper moment, the guards lifted Fernandez's pant legs, and the barber shaved around the ankles. That done, the prisoner was ready to be plugged in at both ends, his bald head and bare ankles serving as human sockets for the surge of kilovolts that would sear his skin, boil his blood, and snuff out his life.

The barber took a step back to admire his handiwork. "Now, ain't that a sharp-lookin' haircut," he said. "Comes with a lifetime guarantee too."

The guards snickered as Fernandez clenched his fists.

A quick knock on the door broke the tension. The big guard's keys tinkled as he opened the door. Raul strained to hear the mumbling, but he couldn't make out what was being said. Finally, the guard turned to him, looking annoyed.

"Fernandez, you got a phone call. It's your lawyer."

Raul's head snapped up at the news.

"Let's go," ordered the guard as he took the prisoner by the arm.

Fernandez popped from the chair.

"Slow down!" said the guard.

Fernandez knew the drill. He extended his arms, and the guard cuffed his wrists. Then he fell to his knees so the other guard could shackle his ankles from behind. He rose slowly but impatiently, and as quickly as his chains and armed escorts would let him travel, he passed through the door and headed down the hallway. In a minute, he was in the small recessed booth where prisoners took calls from their lawyers. It had a diamond-shaped window on the door that allowed the guards to watch but not hear the privileged conversation.

"What'd they say, man?"

There was a pause on the other end of the line, which didn't bode well.

"I'm sorry, Raul," said his attorney.

"No!" He banged his fist on the counter. "This can't be! I'm innocent! I'm *innocent!*" He took several short, angry breaths as his wild eyes scanned the little booth, searching for a way out.

The lawyer continued in a low, calm voice. "I promised you I wouldn't sugarcoat it, Raul. The fact is, we've done absolutely everything we can in the courts. It couldn't be worse. Not only did the Supreme Court deny your request for a stay of execution, but they've issued an order that prevents any other court in the country from giving you a stay."

"Why? I want to know *why*, damn it!"

"The court didn't say why—it doesn't have to," his lawyer answered.

"Then *you* tell me! *Somebody* tell me why this is happening to me!"

The line was silent.

Fernandez brought his hand to his head in disbelief, but the strange feeling of his baldness only reinforced what he'd just heard. "There has . . . some way . . . look, we've gotta stop this," he said, his voice quivering. "We've been here before, you and me. Do like the last time. File another appeal, or a writ or a motion or whatever the hell you lawyers call those things. Just buy me some *time*. And do it like quick, man. They already shaved my fucking hair off!"

His lawyer sighed so loudly that the line crackled.

"Come on," said Fernandez in desperation. "There has to be *something* you can do."

"There may be one thing," his lawyer said without enthusiasm.

"Yeah, baby!" He came to life, fists clenched for one more round.

"It's a billion-to-one shot," the lawyer said, reeling in his client's overreaction. "I *may* have found a new angle on this. I'm going to ask the governor to commute your sentence. But I won't mislead you. You need to prepare for the worst. Remember, the governor is the man who signed your death warrant. He's not likely to scale it back to life imprisonment. You understand what I'm saying?"

Fernandez closed his eyes tightly and swallowed his fear, but he didn't give up hope. "I understand, man, I really do. But go for it. Just go for it. And thank you, man. Thank you and God bless you," he added as he hung up the phone.

He took a deep breath and checked the clock on the wall. Eight minutes after two. Just five hours left to live.

1
.

It was 5:00 A.M. and Governor Harold Swyteck had finally fallen asleep on the daybed. Rest was always elusive on execution nights, which would have been news to anyone who'd heard the governor on numerous occasions emphasizing the need to evict "those holdover tenants" on Florida's overcrowded death row. A former cop and state legislator, Harry Swyteck had campaigned for governor on a law-and-order platform that prescribed more prisons, longer sentences, and more executions as a swift and certain cure for a runaway crime rate. After sweeping into office by a comfortable margin, he'd delivered immediately on his campaign promise, signing his first death warrant on inauguration day in January 1991. In the ensuing twenty-one months, more death warrants had received the governor's John Hancock than in the previous two administrations combined.

At twenty minutes past five, a shrill ring interrupted the governor's slumber. Instinctively, Harry reached out to swat the alarm clock, but it wasn't there. The ringing continued.

"The phone," his wife grumbled from across the room, snug in their bed.

The governor shook himself to full consciousness, realized he was in the daybed, and then started at the blinking red light on the security phone beside his empty half of the four-poster bed.

He stubbed his toe against the bed as he made his way toward the receiver. "Dammit! What is it?"

"Governor," came the reply, "this is security."

"I *know* who you are, Mel. What's the emergency?"

The guard shifted uncomfortably at his post, the way anyone would who'd just woken his boss before sunrise. "Sir, there's someone here who wants to see you. It's about the execution."

The governor gritted his teeth, trying hard not to misdirect the anger of a stubbed toe and a sleepless night toward the man who guarded his safety. "Mel—please. You can't be waking me up every time a last-minute plea lands on my doorstep. We have channels for these things. That's why I have counsel. Call *them*. Now, good—"

"Sir," he gently interrupted, "I—I understand your reaction, sir. But this one, I think, is different. Says he has information that will convince you Fernandez is innocent."

"Who is it this time?" Harry asked with a roll of his eyes. "His mother? Some friend of the family?"

"No, sir, he . . . well, he says he's your son."

The governor was suddenly wide awake. "Send

him in," he said, then hung up the phone. He checked the clock. Almost five-thirty. Just ninety minutes left. *One hell of a time for your first visit to the mansion, son.*

Jack Swyteck stood stiffly on the covered front porch, not sure how to read the sullen expression on his father's face.

"Well, well," the governor said, standing in the open doorway in his monogrammed burgundy bathrobe. Jack was the governor's twenty-six-year-old son, his only offspring. Jack's mother had died a few hours after his birth. Try as he might, Harold had never quite forgiven his son for that.

"I'm here on business," Jack said quickly. "All I need is ten minutes."

The governor stared coolly across the threshold at Jack, who with the same dark, penetrating eyes was plainly his father's son. Tonight he wore faded blue jeans, a brown leather aviator's jacket, and matching boots. His rugged, broad-shouldered appearance could have made him an instant heartthrob as a country singer, though with his perfect diction and Yale law degree he was anything but country. His father had looked much the same in his twenties, and at fifty-three he was still lean and barrel-chested. He'd graduated from the University of Florida, class of '65—a savvy sabre-fencer who'd turned street cop, then politician. The governor was a man who could take your best shot, bounce right back, and hand you your head if you let your guard down. His son was always on guard.

"Come in," Harry said.

Jack entered the foyer, shut the door behind him, and followed his father down the main hall. The rooms were smaller than Jack had expected—elegant but simple, with high coffered ceilings and floors of oak and inlaid mahogany. Period antiques, silk Persian rugs, and crystal chandeliers were the principal furnishings. The art was original and reflected Florida's history.

"Sit down," said the governor as they stepped into the library at the end of the hall.

The dark-paneled library reminded Jack of the house in which he'd grown up. He sat in a leather armchair before the stone fireplace, his crossed legs fully extended and his boots propped up irreverently on the head of a big Alaskan brown bear that his father had years ago stopped in its tracks and turned into a rug. The governor looked away, containing his impulse to tell his son to sit up straight. He stepped behind the big oak bar and filled his old-fashioned glass with ice cubes.

Jack did a double take. He thought his father had given up hard liquor—then again, this was the first time he'd seen him as *Governor* Swyteck. "Do you have to drink? Like I said, this is business."

The governor shot him a glance, then reached for the Chivas and filled his glass to the brim. "And *this*"—he raised his glass—"is *none* of your business. Cheers." He took a long sip.

Jack just watched, telling himself to focus on the reason he was there.

"So," the governor said, smacking his lips. "I can't

really remember the last time we even spoke, let alone saw each other. How long has it been this time?"

Jack shrugged. "Two, two and a half years."

"Since your law-school graduation, wasn't it?"

"No"—Jack's expression betrayed the faintest of smiles—"since I told you I was taking a job with the Freedom Institute."

"Ah, yes, the Freedom Institute." Harry Swyteck rolled his eyes. "The place where lawyers measure success by turning murderers, rapists, and robbers back onto the street. The place where bleeding-heart liberals can defend the guilty and be insufferably sanctimonious about it, because they don't take a fee from the vermin they defend." His look soured. "The *one* place you knew it would absolutely kill me to see you work."

Jack held on tightly to the arm of the chair. "I didn't come here to replow old ground."

"I'm sure you didn't. It's much the same old story, anyway. Granted, this last time the rift grew a little wider between us. But in the final analysis, this one will shake out no differently than the other times you've cut me out of your life. You'll never recognize that all I ever wanted is what's best for you."

Jack was about to comment on his father's presumed infallibility, but was distracted by something on the bookshelf. It was an old photograph of the two of them, together on a deep-sea fishing trip, in one of their too-few happy moments. *Lay in to me first chance you get, Father, but you have that picture up there for all to see, don't you?*

"Look," Jack said, "I know we have things to talk about. But now's not the time. I didn't come here for that."

"I know. You came because Raul Fernandez is scheduled to die in the electric chair in"—the governor looked at his watch—"about eighty minutes."

"I came because he is innocent."

"Twelve jurors didn't think so, Jack."

"They didn't hear the whole story."

"They heard enough to convict him after deliberating for less than twenty minutes. I've known juries to take longer deciding who's going to be foreman."

"Will you just *listen* to me," Jack snapped. "Please, Father"—he tried a more civil tone—"listen to me."

The governor refilled his glass. "All right," he said. "I'm listening."

Jack leaned forward. "About five hours ago, a man called me and said he had to see me—in confidence, as a client. He wouldn't give me his name, but he said it was life and death, so I agreed to meet him. He showed up at my office ten minutes later wearing a ski mask. At first I thought he was going to rob me, but it turned out he just wanted to talk about the Fernandez case. So that's what we did—talked." He paused, focusing his eyes directly on his father's. "And in less than five minutes he had me convinced that Raul Fernandez is innocent."

The governor looked skeptical. "And just what did this mysterious man of the night tell you?"

"I can't say."

"Why not?"

"I told you: He agreed to speak to me only in

confidence, as a client. I've never seen his face, and I doubt that I'll ever see him again, but technically I'm his lawyer—or at least I was for that conversation. Anyway, everything he told me is protected by attorney-client privilege. I can't divulge any of it without his approval. And he won't let me repeat a word."

"Then what are you doing here?"

Jack gave him a sobering look. "Because an innocent man is going to die in the electric chair unless you stop the Fernandez execution right now."

The governor slowly crossed the room, a glass in one hand and an open bottle of scotch in the other. He sat in the matching arm chair, facing Jack. "And I'll ask you one more time: How do you *know* Fernandez is innocent?"

"How do I *know*?" Jack's reddening face conveyed total exasperation. "Why is it that you *always* want more than I can give? My flying up here in the middle of the night isn't enough for you? My telling you everything I legally and ethically can tell you just isn't enough?"

"All I'm saying is that I need *proof*. I can't just stay an execution based on . . . on *nothing*, really."

"My word is worth nothing, then," Jack translated.

"In this setting, yes—that's the way it has to be. In this context, you're a lawyer, and I'm the governor."

"No—in this context, I'm a witness, and you're a murderer. Because you're going to put Fernandez to death. And I *know* he's innocent."

"*How* do you know?"

"Because I met the *real* killer tonight. He confessed to me. He did more than confess: He *showed* me something that proves he's the killer."

"And what was that?" the governor asked, genuinely interested.

"I *can't* tell you," Jack said. He felt his frustration rising. "I've already said more than I can under the attorney-client privilege."

The governor nestled into his chair, flashing a thin, paternalistic smile. "You're being a little naive, don't you think? You have to put these last-minute pleas in context. Fernandez is a convicted killer. He and everyone who knows him is desperate. You can't take anything they say at face value. This so-called client who showed up at your door is undoubtedly a cousin or brother or street friend of Raul Fernandez's, and he'll do anything to stop the execution."

"You don't *know* that!"

The governor sighed heavily, his eyes cast downward. "You're right." He brought his hands to his temples and began rubbing them. "We never know for certain. I suppose that's why I've taken to *this*," he said as he reached over and lifted the bottle of scotch. "But the cold reality is that I campaigned as the law-and-order governor. I made the death penalty the central issue in the election. I promised to carry it out with vigor, and at the time I meant what I said. Now that I'm here, it's not quite so easy to sign my name to a death warrant. You've seen them before—ominous-looking documents, with their black border and embossed state seal. But have you ever really *read* what they say? Believe me, I have." His voice trailed off. "That kind of power can get to a man, if you let it. Hell," he scoffed and sipped his drink, "and doctors think *they're* God."

Jack was silent, surprised by this rare look into his father's conscience and not quite sure what to say. "That's all the more reason to listen to me," he said. "To make sure it's not a mistake."

"This is no mistake, Jack. Don't you see? What you're *not* saying is as significant as what you're saying. You won't breach the attorney-client privilege, not even to persuade me to change my mind about the execution. I respect that, Jack. But you have to respect me, too. I have rules. I have obligations, just like you do. Mine are to the people who elected me—and who expect me to honor my campaign promises."

"It's not the same thing."

"That's true," he agreed. "It's not the same. That's why, when you leave here tonight, I don't want you to blame yourself for anything. You did the best you could. Now it's up to me to make a decision. And *I'm* making it. I don't believe Raul Fernandez is innocent. But if *you* believe it, I don't want you feeling responsible for his death."

Jack looked into his father's eyes. He knew the man was reaching out—that he was looking for something from his son, some reciprocal acknowledgment that Jack didn't blame *him*, either, for doing *his* job. Harold Swyteck wanted absolution, forgiveness—a pardon.

Jack glanced away. He would not—could not—allow the moment to weaken his resolve. "Don't worry, Father, I won't blame myself. It's like you always used to tell me: We're all responsible for our own actions. If an innocent man dies in the electric chair, you're the governor. You're responsible. You're the one to blame."

Jack's words struck a nerve. The governor's face flushed red with fury as every conciliatory sentiment drained away. "There is *no one* to blame," he declared. "No one but Fernandez himself. You're being played for a sucker. Fernandez and his buddy are *using* you. Why do you think this character didn't tell you his name or even show you his face?"

"Because he doesn't want to get caught," Jack answered, "but he doesn't want an innocent man to die."

"A *killer*—especially one guilty of this sort of savagery—doesn't want an innocent man to die?" Harry Swyteck shook his head condescendingly. "It's ironic, Jack"—he spoke out of anger now—"but sometimes you almost make me glad your mother never lived to see what a thick-headed son she brought into the world."

Jack quickly rose from his chair. "I don't have to take this crap from you."

"I'm your *father!*" Harry blustered. "You'll take whatever I—"

"No! I'll take *nothing* from you. I've never asked for anything. And I don't *want* anything. *Ever.*" He stormed toward the door.

"Wait!" the governor shouted, freezing him in his tracks. Jack turned around slowly and glared at his father. "Listen to me, young man. Fernandez is going to be executed this morning, because I don't believe any of this nonsense about his being innocent.

No more than I believed the eleventh-hour story from the last 'innocent man' we executed—the one who claimed it was only an accident that he stabbed his girlfriend"—he paused, so furious he was out of breath—"twenty-one times."

"You've become an incredibly narrow-minded old man," Jack said.

The governor stood stoically at the bar. "Get out, Jack. Get out of my house."

Jack turned and marched down the hall, his boots punishing the mansion's hard wooden floor. He threw the front door open, then stopped at the tinkling sound of his father filling his empty scotch glass with ice cubes. "Drink up, Governor!" his voice echoed in the hallway. "Do us all a favor, and drink yourself to death."

He slammed the door and left.

2.

Death was just minutes away for Raul Fernandez. He sat on the edge of the bunk in his cell, shoulders slumped, bald head bowed, and hands folded between his knees. Father José Ramirez, a Roman Catholic priest, was at the prisoner's side, dressed all in black save for his white hair and Roman collar. Rosary beads were draped over one knee, an open Bible rested on the other. He was looking at Fernandez with concern, almost desperation, as he tried once more to cleanse the man's soul.

"Murder is a mortal sin, Raul," he said. "Heaven holds no place for those who die without confessing their mortal sins. In John, chapter twenty, Jesus tells his disciples: 'Whose sins you forgive are forgiven them, and whose sins you hold bound are held bound.' Let me hear your sins, Raul. So that you may be forgiven them."

Fernandez looked him directly in the eye. "Father," he said with all the sincerity he could muster, "right now, I have nothing to lose by telling you the truth. And I'm telling you this: I have nothing to confess."

Father Ramirez showed no expression, though a chill went down his spine. He flinched only at the sound of the key jiggling in the iron door.

"It's time," announced the guard. A team of two stepped inside the cell to escort Fernandez. Father Ramirez rose from his chair, blessed the prisoner with the sign of the cross, and then stepped aside. Fernandez did not budge from his bunk.

"Let's go," ordered the guard.

"Give him a minute," said the priest.

The guard stepped briskly toward the prisoner. "We don't have a minute."

Fernandez suddenly sprung from his chair, burrowing his shoulder into the lead guard's belly. They tumbled to the floor. "I'm innocent!" he cried, his arms flailing. A barrage of blows from the other guard's blackjack battered his back and shoulders, stunning the prisoner into near paralysis.

"You crazy son of a bitch!" cried the fallen guard, forcing Fernandez onto his belly. "Cuff him!" he shouted to his partner. Together they pinned his arms behind his back, then cuffed the wrists and ankles.

"I'm innocent," Fernandez whimpered, his face pressing on the cement floor. "I'm *innocent!*"

"The hell with this," said the guard who'd just wrestled with the condemned man. He snatched a leather strap from his pocket and gagged the prisoner, fastening it tightly around the back of his head.

Father Ramirez looked on in horror as the guards lifted Fernandez to his feet. He was still groggy from the blows, so they shook him to revive him. The law required that a condemned man be fully conscious and alert to his impending death. Each guard grabbed an arm, and together they led him out of the cell.

The priest was pensive and disturbed as he followed the procession down the brightly lit hallway. He'd seen many death-row inmates, but none was the fighter this one was. Certainly, none had so strongly proclaimed his innocence.

They stopped at the end of the hall and waited as the execution chamber's iron door slid open automatically. The guards then handed the prisoner over to two attendants inside who specialized in executions. They moved quickly and efficiently as precious seconds ticked away on the wall clock. Fernandez was strapped into the heavy oak chair. Electrodes were fastened to his shaved head and ankles. The gag was removed from his mouth and replaced with a steel bit.

All was quiet, save for the hum of the bright fluorescent lights overhead. Fernandez sat stiffly in his chair. The guards brought the black hood down over his face, then took their places along the gray-green walls. The venetian blinds opened, exposing the prisoner to three dozen witnesses on the dark side of the glass wall. A few reporters stirred. An assistant state attorney looked on impassively. The victim's uncle—the only relative of the young girl in attendance—took a deep breath. All eyes except the prisoner's turned toward the clock. His were hidden behind the hood and a tight leather band that would keep his eyeballs from bursting when the current flowed.

Father Ramirez stepped into the dark seating area and joined the audience. The guard at the door raised his eyebrows. "You really gonna watch this one, padre?" he asked quietly.

"You know I never watch," said the priest.

"There's a first time for everything."

"Yes," said Ramirez. "There is, indeed. And if my instincts are correct, let's hope this is the *last* time you kill an innocent man." Then he closed his eyes and retreated into prayer.

The guard looked away. The priest's words had been pointed, but the guard shook them off, taking the proverbial common man's comfort in the fact that *he* wasn't killing anyone. It was Governor Harold Swyteck who'd signed the man's death warrant. It was someone else who would flip the switch.

At that moment, the second hand swept by its highest point, the warden gave the signal, and lights dimmed throughout the prison as twenty-five hundred volts surged into the prisoner's body. Fernandez lunged forward with the force of a head-on collision, his back arching and his skin smoking and sizzling. His jaws clenched the steel bit so tightly his teeth shattered. His fingers pried into the oak armrests with such effort that his bones snapped.

A second quick jolt went right to his heart.

A third made sure the job was done.

It had taken a little more than a minute—the last and longest sixty-seven seconds of this thirty-five-year-old's life. An exhaust fan came on, sucking out the stench. A physician stepped forward, placed a stethoscope on the prisoner's chest, and listened.

"He's dead," pronounced the doctor.

Father Ramirez sighed with sorrow as he opened his eyes, then lowered his head and blessed himself with the sign of the cross. "May God forgive us," he said under his breath, "as He receives the innocent."

Part Two

July 1994

3

Eddy Goss was on trial for an act of violence so unusual that it amazed even him. He'd first noticed the girl when she was walking home from school one night in her drill-team uniform. At the time, he thought she must be sixteen. She had the kind of looks he liked—long blond hair that cascaded over her shoulders, a nice, curvy shape, and most important of all, no makeup. He liked that fresh look. It told him he would be the first.

By the time he'd caught up to her, she'd known something was wrong. He was sure of that. She'd started looking over her shoulder and walking faster. He guessed she must have been really scared—too scared to react—because it took him only a few seconds to force her into his Ford Pinto. About five miles out of town, in a thick stand of pines far from the main highway, he held a knife to her throat and warned her to do everything he asked. Naturally, she agreed. What choice did she have? She hiked up her skirt, pulled off her panty hose—all the drill-team members at Senior High had to wear nude hose, he knew—and sat perfectly still as Eddy probed her vagina with his fingers. But then she started crying—great wracking sobs that made him furious. He hated it when they cried. So he wrapped the nylon around her neck—and pulled. And pulled. He pulled so hard that he finally did it: He actually severed her vertebrae and decapitated her. *Son of a bitch!*

Eddy Goss was on trial for his proudest accomplishment. And his lawyer was Jack Swyteck.

"All rise!" the bailiff shouted as the jury returned from its deliberations. Quietly, they shuffled in. A nursing student. A bus driver. A janitor. Five blacks, two Jews. Four men, eight women. Seven blue collars, two professionals, three who didn't fit a mold. It didn't matter how Jack categorized them anymore. Individual votes were no longer important; their collective mind had been made up. They divided themselves into two rows of six, stood before their Naugahyde chairs, and cast their eyes into "the wishing well," as Jack called it, that empty, stagelike area before the judge and jury where lawyers who defended the guilty pitched their penny-ante arguments and then hoped for the best.

Jack swallowed hard as he strained to read their faces. Experience made him appear calm, though the adrenaline was flowing on this final day of a trial that had been front-page news for more than a month. He looked much the same now as he had two years ago, save for the healthy cynicism in his eye and a touch of gray in his hair that made him look as though he were more than just four years out of law school. Jack buttoned his pinstripe suit, then glanced quickly at his client, standing stiffly beside him. *What a piece of work.*

"Be seated," said the silver-haired judge to an over-crowded courtroom.

Defendant Eddy Goss watched with dark, deep-set eyes as the jurors took their seats. His expression had the intensity of a soldier dismantling a land mine. He had huge hands—the hands of a strangler, the prosecutor had been quick to point out—and nails that were bitten halfway down to the cuticle. His prominent jaw and big shiny forehead gave him a menacing look that made it easy to imagine him committing the crime of which he was accused. Today he seemed aloof, Jack thought, as if he were enjoying this.

Indeed, that had been Jack's impression of Goss four months ago, when Jack had watched a video-tape of his client bragging about the grisly murder to police investigators. It was supposed to be an open-and-shut case: The prosecutor had a video-taped confession. But the jury never saw it. Jack had kept it out of evidence.

"Has the jury reached a verdict?" asked the judge.

"We have," announced the forewoman.

Spectators slid to the edge of their seats. Whirling paddle fans stirred the silence overhead. The written verdict passed from jury to judge.

It doesn't matter what the verdict is, Jack tried to convince himself. He had served the system, served justice. As he stood there, watching the judge hand the paper back to the clerk, he thought of all those homilies he'd been handed in law school—how every citizen had a right to the best defense, how the rights of the innocent would be trampled if not for lawyers who vindicated those rights in defense of the guilty. Back then it had all sounded so noble, but reality had a way of raining on your parade. Here he was, defending someone who wasn't even *sorry* for what he had done. And the jury had found him . . .

"Not guilty."

"Noooooo!" screamed the victim's sister, setting off a wave of anger that rocked the courtroom.

Jack closed his eyes tightly; it was a painful victory.

"Order!" shouted the judge, banging his gavel to calm a packed crowd that had erupted in hysteria. Insults, glares, and wadded paper continued to fly across the room, all directed at Jack Swyteck and the scum he'd defended.

"Order!"

"You'll get yours, Goss!" shouted a friend of the dead girl's family. "You too, Swyteck."

Jack looked at the ceiling, tried to block it all out.

"Hope *you* can sleep tonight," an angry prosecutor muttered to him on her way out.

Jack reached deep inside for a response, but he found nothing. He just turned away and did what he supposed was the socially acceptable thing. He didn't congratulate Eddy Goss or shake his hand. Instead, he packed up his trial bag and glanced to his right.

Goss was staring at him, a satisfied smirk on his face. "Can I have your business card, Mr. Swyteck?" asked Goss, his head cocked and his hands planted smugly on his hips. "Just so I know who to call—next time."

Suddenly, it was as if Jack were looking not just at Goss, but at all the remorseless criminals he had defended over the years. He stepped up to Goss and spoke right into his face. "Listen, you son of a bitch," he whispered, "there'd better not *be* a next time. Because if there is, not only will I *not* represent you, but I will personally make sure that you get a class-A fuck-up for an attorney. And don't think the son of the governor can't pull it off. You understand me?"

Goss's smirk faded, and his eyes narrowed with contempt. "Nobody threatens me, Swyteck."

"I just did."

Goss curled his lip with disdain. "Now you've done it. Now you've hurt my feelings. I don't know if I can forgive you for that, Swyteck. But I do know this," he said, leaning forward. "Someday—someday soon, Jack Swyteck is gonna *beg* me to forgive him." Goss pulled back, his dark eyes boring into Jack's. "*Beg* me."

Jack tried not to flinch, but those eyes were getting to him. "You know nothing about forgiveness, Goss," he said finally, then turned and walked away. He headed down the aisle, scuffed leather briefcase in hand, feeling very alone as he pushed his way through the angry and disgusted crowd, toward the carved mahogany doors marked EXIT.

"There he goes, ladies and gentlemen," Goss shouted over the crowd, waving his arms like a circus master. "My *ex*-best friend, Jack Swyteck."

Jack ignored him, as did everyone else. The crowd was looking at the lawyer.

"Asshole!" a stranger jeered at Jack.

"Creep!" said another.

Jack's eyes swept around, catching a volley of glares from the spectators. He suddenly knew what it meant, literally, to *represent* someone. He represented Eddy Goss the way a flag represented a country, the way suffering represented Satan. "There he is!" reporters shouted as Jack emerged from the bustling courtroom, elbow-to-elbow with a rush of spectators. In the lobby, another crowd waited for him in front of the elevators, armed with cameras and microphones.

"Mr. Swyteck!" cried the reporters over the general crowd noise. In an instant microphones were in his face, making forward progress impossible. "Your reaction? . . . your client do now? . . . say to the victim's family?" The questions ran together.

Jack was sandwiched between the crowd pressing from behind and the reporters pressing forward. He'd never get out of here with just a curt "No comment." He stopped, paused for a moment, and said: "I believe that the only way to characterize today's verdict is to call it a victory for the system. *Our* system, which requires the prosecutor to *prove* that the accused is guilty beyond a reasonable—"

Shrill screams suddenly filled the lobby, as a geyser of red erupted from the crowd, drenching Jack. The panic continued as more of the thick liquid splattered Jack and everyone around him.

He was stunned for a moment, uncomprehending. He wiped the red substance from around his eyes—was it blood or some kind of paint?—and said nothing as it traced ruby-red rivulets down his pants onto the floor.

"It's on you, Swyteck," his symbolic assailant hollered from somewhere in the crowd. "Her blood is on you!"

4
.

Jack drove home topless in every sense of the word. His blood-soaked shirt and suit coat were stuffed in the back of his '73 Mustang convertible, and the top was rolled back to air the stench. It was a bizarre ending, but the press *had* been predicting an acquittal, and the prospect of a not-guilty verdict had apparently angered someone enough to arm himself with bags of some thick red liquid—the same way animal-rights extremists sometimes ambushed fur-coated women on the streets of New York. He wondered again what kind of ammunition had been used. Animal blood? Human blood infected with AIDS? He cringed at the thought of the photo and headline that would appear in the next day's tabloids: "Jack Swyteck—Bleeding Liberal." *Shit, does it get any worse than this?*

It was after dark by the time he got home. He noticed immediately that there was no red Pontiac in the driveway, which meant his girlfriend, Cindy Paige, wouldn't be there to listen to the day's events.

His girlfriend. He wondered if he was kidding himself about that. Things hadn't been the best between them lately. The story she'd handed him about staying with her friend Gina for a few days "to help her with some problems she's been having" was starting to sound like just an excuse to get out from under all the baggage he'd been carrying these past few months. Hell, he couldn't blame her. When he wasn't up to his eyeballs in work, he was having these dialogues with himself, questioning where his life was going. And most of the time he left Cindy on the outside looking in.

"Hey, boy," said Jack as his hairy best friend attacked him on the porch, planting his bearlike paws on his master's chest and greeting him nose to cold nose. His name was Thursday, for the day Jack, Cindy, and her five-year-old niece picked him up from the pound and saved him from being put to sleep—the most deserving prisoner he'd ever kept from dying. He was definitely part Lab, but mostly a product of the canine melting pot. His expressive, chocolate-brown eyes made him an excellent communicator—and at the moment, the eyes were screaming, "I'm hungry."

"Looks like you have a case of the munchies," Jack said, gently pushing him away as he entered the house. He went to the kitchen and filled the dog's bowl with Puppy Chow, then dug the pizza-bones appetizer out of the refrigerator. Cindy never ate the crust or the pepperoni. She saved them for Thursday.

He set the bowl on the floor and watched the dog dig in.

Fortunately, the blood—or whatever it was— washed off easily in the shower. As he toweled himself dry, Jack could hear Thursday pushing his empty bowl across the kitchen floor with his nose. Jack smiled and pulled on his boxer shorts. Then he went to the bedroom and sat on the edge of the king-size bed. His eyes scanned the room, finally coming to rest on a framed photograph of Cindy that stood on the nightstand. In it she was standing on a rock along some mountain trail they'd hiked together in Utah. She had a big, happy smile on her face, and the summer wind was tossing her honey-blond hair. It was his favorite picture of her, because it captured so many of the qualities that made her special. At first glance, anyone would be struck by her beautiful face and great body. But for Jack, it was Cindy's eyes and her smile that told the whole story.

On impulse, he reached for the phone. He frowned when Gina Terisi's machine picked up: "I'm sorry I can't come to the phone right now . . ." said the recorded message.

"Cindy, call me," he said. "Miss you," he added, and put the receiver down. He fell back on the bed, closed his eyes, and began to relax for the first time in more than a day. But he was disturbed as he realized that Gina would get the message first and convince Cindy he was pining away for her. Well, he was, wasn't he?

Idly, he flipped on the TV and began channel-surfing, searching for any station that didn't have something to say about the acquittal of Eddy Goss. He fixed on MTV. Two mangy-looking rockers were banging on their guitars while getting their faces licked by a Cindy Crawford look-alike.

He switched off the set, nestled his head in the pillow, and lay in the darkness. But he couldn't sleep. He looked straight ahead, over the tops of his toes, staring at the television on the dresser. There was nothing he wanted to watch. But as the day's ugly events played out in his mind, there was one thing he suddenly *had* to watch.

He rolled out of bed, grabbed his briefcase, and popped it open, quickly finding what he was looking for, even in the darkness. He switched on the television and VCR, shoved in the cassette, and sat on the edge of the bed, waiting. There was a screen full of snow, a few rolling blips, and then . . .

"My name is Eddy Goss," said the man on the screen, speaking stiffly into a police video camera. Goss's normally flat and stringy hair was a tangled, greasy mess. He looked and undoubtedly smelled as if he'd been sleeping under a bridge all week, dressed in dirty Levi's, unlaced tennis shoes, and a yellow-white undershirt, torn at the V and stained with underarm sweat. He sat smugly in the metal folding chair, exuding a punk's confidence, his arms folded tightly. Four long and fresh red scratches ran along his neck. The date and time, 11:04 P.M., March 12— four and a half months ago—flashed in the corner of the screen.

"I live at four-oh-nine East Adams Street," Goss continued, "apartment two-seventeen."

The camera drew back to show the suspect, seated at the end of the long conference table, and an older man seated on the side, to Goss's right. The man appeared to be in his late sixties, gray-haired, with a hawk nose that supported his black-rimmed glasses.

"Mr. Goss," said the man, "I'm Detective Lonzo Stafford. With me, behind the camera, is Detective Jamahl Bradley. You understand, son, that you have the right to remain silent. You have the right—"

Jack hit the remote, fast-forwarding to the part he'd seen at least a hundred times before. Visible in the frame now was a different Goss, more animated, boasting like a proud father.

". . . I killed the little prick tease," Goss said with a carefree shrug.

Jack stopped the tape, rewound, and listened again, as if flogging himself.

". . . I killed the little prick tease," he heard one more time. Just the way thousands of other people had heard it—with expletive deleted—and were probably hearing it again tonight, on the television news. The tape rolled on, and Jack closed his eyes and listened as Goss described the deed in grisly detail. The car ride to the woods. The knife at the young girl's throat. The tears that had stemmed his vulgar attempts at gentle caresses. The struggle that had ensued. And finally, pulling the nylon tight around the girl's neck . . .

Jack sighed, keeping his eyes closed. The tape continued, but there was only silence. Even the police interrogators, it seemed, had needed to catch their breath. Had they been allowed to hear it, a jury probably would have reacted the same way. But he'd prevented that. He'd kept the entire videotape out of evidence by arguing that Goss's constitutional rights had been violated—that his confession had been involuntary. The police hadn't beaten it out of him with a rubber hose. They hadn't even threatened him. "They tricked him," Jack had argued, relying on one questionable remark by a seasoned detective who so desperately wanted to nail Goss that he pushed it a little too far—though the detective had still played good odds, knowing from experience that only the most liberal judge would condemn his tactics.

"We don't want to know if you did it," Detective Stafford had assured Goss. "We just want you to show us where Kerry's body is, so we can give her a decent Christian burial." That was all the ammunition Jack had needed. "They induced a confession by playing on my client's conscience!" he'd argued to the judge. "They appealed to his religious convictions. A Christian burial speech is patently illegal, Your Honor."

No one was more surprised than Jack when the judge bought the argument. The confession was ruled inadmissible. The jury never saw the videotape. They acquitted a guilty man. And the miscarriage of justice was clear. *Nice going, Swyteck.*

He hit the eject button on his VCR and tossed the confession aside, disgusted at himself and what he did for a living. He grabbed another cassette from the case beside the television, pushed *To Kill a Mockingbird* into his VCR, and for the fifteenth time since joining the Freedom Institute, watched Gregory Peck defend the innocent.

Peck's Atticus Finch had just launched into his peroration when a shrill ringing startled Jack from a state of half sleep.

He snatched up the telephone, hoping to hear Cindy's voice. For a few moments, though, all he heard was silence. Finally, a surly voice came over the line. "Swyteck?" it asked.

Jack didn't move. The voice seemed vaguely familiar, but it also seemed raspy and disguised. He waited. And finally came the brief, sobering message.

"A killer is on the loose tonight, Swyteck. A killer is on the loose."

Jack gripped the receiver tighter. "Who's there?"

Again, there was only silence.

"Who's there? Who are you?" Jack waited, but heard only the sound of his own erratic breathing. Then, finally . . .

"Sleep tight," was the cool reply. The phone clicked, and then came the dial tone.

5

G overnor Harold Swyteck jogged down a wood-
chip jogging path. He muttered a soft curse
as he reflected on the political repercussions of
Jack's victory the previous day. The governor and
his advisers had been speculating for weeks on how
the trial might affect his bid for re-election. They
figured a few tough anticrime speeches would probably counter Jack's involvement. Never, however,
had they figured he'd actually win an acquittal. Had
they considered it, they might have had a comeback
when the media issued its hourly reports that it was
indeed the governor's son who'd gotten a confessed
killer off on a technicality.

"Damn it all!" Harry blurted with another husky
breath, his arms pumping to a quicker cadence. As
his legs surged forward he felt his anger building. It
was a father's anger, tinged more with disappointment than with vitriol.

The governor struggled to maintain his pace. Since
the Fernandez execution, he'd taken up jogging and

sworn off the booze. In some twelve hundred days in office, he'd jogged about as many miles and thought about that one disturbing night at least as many times, wishing he'd just listened to his son and stopped the execution—if only for a few days, long enough to investigate Jack's story. Jogging gave him a chance to reflect on events and feelings without yielding to the urge to confide. His advisers pleaded with him about security, but he avoided escorts, except late at night or in big cities. "If some crazy is gunning for me," he'd always say, "he won't come looking on a back road for some guy in frumpy jogging sweats and a baseball cap." So far, he'd been right.

Harry slowed as he neared a cluster of sprawling oak trees and royal poincianas that marked the halfway point of his route. He reminded himself of the rules: The first half of his run was for venting anger; the second was reserved for positive thoughts.

"My fellow Floridians," he silently intoned as he reached his halfway marker, jogging beneath the fire-orange canopy of a royal poinciana. He could feel his attitude changing. His troubles were falling behind him; this morning's speech and throngs of loyal supporters were looming ahead. In just a few hours he would officially launch his re-election campaign.

". . . in this election, you have a choice," the speech continued in his mind. But his feet went out from under him, and he found himself sprawled on the ground, his right elbow and knee skinned and bleeding. At first he thought he'd tripped over something, but as he looked behind him a dark blur raced out from the shadow of a huge old oak and pounced on top of him, knocking him flat again. Their bodies locked together as they tumbled down a steep ravine along the deserted jogging path. They landed hard amid the tangled weeds and cattails beside a scummy green canal. The governor quickly reached in his pocket for his electronic pager to alert security, but before his finger could hit the red button, his attacker knocked the wind out of him with a fist to the solar plexus. In a split second, Harry was flat on his belly, his face pushed into the dirt.

"Heh!" the governor gasped, his head moving just enough to the side to allow his mouth to work. But a cold steel blade was at his throat before he could utter another word.

"Don't move," the man ordered.

Harry froze, his body trembling as he forced himself to remain facedown and perfectly still. His right cheek was pressed to the ground, but out of the corner of his left eye he could see a bruiser of a body sitting on his kidneys. Its sheer weight nearly prevented him from breathing, let alone moving. It was a man, he presumed. The voice was deep; the hands covered by black leather gloves were very large. The features, however, were indiscernible. He wore camouflaged marine fatigues, and his face was covered by a ski mask.

"Well, what do we have here," the man taunted in a thick, raspy voice. "Mr. Big-Time Politician out for his morning jog."

The governor clenched his fists, not to defend himself but to bring his fear under control. All was silent, except for a sucking sound the man made when he breathed. He must have been drooling from the wads of cotton or whatever he had in his mouth to disguise his voice.

"Hey, Governor," the attacker said, mocking him now with a friendly tone. "I hear you politicians like to deal. Well, here's one for you, my man. How about I give you proof that Raul Fernandez was innocent?"

Raul Fernandez? Harry started at the name. His mind ran in a dozen different directions, trying to make sense of why that name was being dredged up now.

"And in exchange for me being such a stand-up guy," the attacker continued, "for saving this big-time job of yours by not letting it slip that you and Junior killed an innocent man, you give me some money. A shitload of it."

The governor remained silent.

The man squeezed the back of Harry's neck, as if the knife were not already commanding enough attention. "Or maybe you prefer I just have a conversation with the newspapers."

The governor forced himself to put his fear aside long enough to ask a question. "What do you want from me?"

"There's a drugstore at the corner of Tenth and Monroe—Albert's. Be at the pay phone out front. Noon, Thursday. Alone. And don't even think about calling the cops. If you do, I go right to the newspapers. You hear what I'm saying?"

The governor swallowed hard. "Yes," he replied.

The man pushed the governor's face into the ground and sprung to his feet. "Before you even twitch a finger, count to a hundred, out loud, nice and slow. *Now.*"

"One, two," Harry counted off, listening carefully as the man's footsteps faded into the distance. He lay still until he reached thirty, when he figured it was safe to move. Then he quickly rolled over and snatched the transmitter from his pocket. If he pushed the red button, security would be there in less than a minute. But he hesitated. What would he tell them? That some thug had threatened to reveal he'd executed an innocent man?

He tucked the transmitter into his pocket, still thinking. His attacker had warned him: Alert security and the Fernandez story goes straight to the media. Would that really be so disastrous? No question, it would be bad, but inside he felt an even deeper fear. That the attacker *wouldn't* go to the newspapers. That if he didn't show up at Albert's, he'd never hear from the man again. And he'd never know the truth about Fernandez.

He cast a forlorn look over the weeds, toward the thick woods where his attacker had disappeared. Tenth and Monroe was a crowded intersection—a very public and safe place. It wasn't like a face-to-face meeting in a dark alley. Hell, if the guy'd wanted to kill him, he'd be dead already. The decision was clear.

"Noon," he said aloud, confirming their telephone conference. "Tomorrow."

6

G rateful for smart lawyers and legal loopholes, Eddy Goss was back on the streets of Miami, following the familiar cracked sidewalk to his favorite hangout. It was in a desolate part of town, where women stood alone on street corners to pay for their hundred-dollar-a-day crack habit and married men drove slowly by to satisfy their twenty-dollar urges. Goss, however, always avoided the women, ignoring their blunt offers of a quick "up and down." He would pass right by them on his way to the bright yellow building with no windows and huge black triple X's covering the length of the door. Inside, the windowless walls were lined with cellophane-wrapped magazines sitting in floor-to-ceiling racks. Goss liked the magazines because the girls were always so much prettier than the women on the street.

He moved around the adult bookstore like he owned the place, familiar with every rack. He liked the way the materials were organized. Oral sex on the east wall. Group sex on the west. If he wanted messy sex, the south wall was the place. His favorite was the back wall, the place for those who liked really young girls.

"You buying anything?" asked the very fat man seated by the cash register behind the counter.

"Huh?" Goss responded, realizing that the man was talking to him.

The man rolled his eyes as his dirty, stubby fingers shoved an overstuffed sandwich into his mouth. "I said," he repeated with his mouth full, bits of lettuce and mayonnaise stuck in his straggly salt-and-pepper beard, "are you gonna buy anything, asshole?"

Goss shoved a magazine entitled *Pixie Vixens* back into the rack. "I'm just lookin' around."

"Well, an hour and a fucking half is long enough to look. Out, pal."

Goss stood rigidly, his furor-filled eyes locked in an intense stare-down. At first the clerk's expression was tough, but after a few seconds he seemed to lose heart. Just three weeks on the job and already he'd seen hundreds of weirdos in the shop. No one, however, had *ever* looked at him with such bone-chilling contempt.

"Do you know who you're talking to?" Goss seethed.

The clerk swallowed hard. "I don't care who—"

"I'm Eddy Goss."

The clerk froze. He'd seen the news coverage on television, and suddenly the face was familiar.

Goss took a couple of steps forward, toward the bin in the center of the room that was full of plastic dildos and other adult paraphernalia. He stopped short and stared at the clerk. "*I'm* Eddy Goss," he said, as if there were no need to say more. Then, with a quick jerk of his hand he sent an armful of merchandise sailing across the store.

The barrage of paraphernalia galvanized the clerk. Instinctively, he reached under the counter and came up with a pistol aimed at Goss. "Get outta here," his voice trembled. "Or I'm gonna blow your fucking head off!"

Goss scoffed and shook his head.

"You got ten seconds!" the clerk warned.

Goss just glared at him.

The clerk shifted his weight nervously. His arms strained to hold the pistol out in front of him. Beads of sweat began building on his brow, and the gun started shaking. "I'm not foolin', asshole!"

Goss was unshaken, convinced that this clerk didn't have the nerve to shoot him. But he'd had enough of this place for one day. "I'm outta here," he said as he headed for the door and stepped outside.

The sun had been shining brightly when he'd arrived at the bookstore, but it was overcast now, and dusk was near. He was hungry and thirsty, so he cut through the parking lot to the 7-Eleven next door. The store was empty, except for the Haitian clerk behind the counter. Goss opened a pack of Twinkies on his way down the aisle and stuffed them into his mouth as he reached the coolers in the back. He opened the glass doors, tossed the Twinkie wrapper behind the cold six-packs, and grabbed himself a tall can of malt liquor. He paid the clerk for the drink and left. He checked over his shoulder to see if the man was looking. He wasn't, so he grabbed a newspaper from the stand. He tucked it under his arm and headed down the dimly lit alley that led to the back of the store. He chugged down his malt liquor and threw the empty can onto the pavement. He found a secluded spot behind the store, by the Dumpster, and sat on some plastic bread crates beside a tall wooden fence that offered plenty of privacy. It was time.

Goss tore into the paper and pitched the sports, classifieds, and other useless sections onto the ground until he found something suitable—a Victoria's Secret special advertising pullout. He flipped the pages until he found the right girl, one with a particularly demure expression, then he spread the pullout on the ground at his feet. He hurriedly unzipped his pants, spit into the palm of his hand, and reached down between his legs. His eyes narrowed to slits as he imagined himself on top of the girl. His breathing became deeper and more rushed as his hand moved rhythmically back and forth.

"Fucking bitches," he gasped as his body jerked violently. He closed his eyes completely, then a second later opened them and inspected his handiwork. *Son of a bitch.*

Slowly he stood up and zipped his fly, towering over the smeared pictures on the ground. He reached inside his pocket and tossed down something tiny that landed with a tick on the wet surface. It was a seed. A chrysanthemum seed.

"My card," said Goss with a quick, sinister laugh.

7

Governor Swyteck woke at six o'clock Thursday morning. As he showered and shaved, his wife, Agnes, lay awake in bed, exhausted after a night spent tossing and turning. Harold Swyteck was not a man who kept secrets from his wife. Yesterday he'd fabricated a story about a bad fall to explain his disheveled appearance to his security guards. But he told his wife the truth—as much out of concern for her safety as out of a need to be honest.

Agnes listlessly flipped on the television with her remote, tuning in to the local "News at Sunrise." Harry was in it again, this time appearing with a group of ministers, priests, and rabbis who were endorsing his candidacy. As her husband gratefully acknowledged the clergy's words of praise, she felt a surge of pride, but then her thoughts returned to what he'd told her the previous evening.

Agnes had always feared that a lifetime of public service could put her Harry in danger—that eventually one of his enemies might do something more than just threaten. But her fear gave way to more complicated feelings when Harry told her that this particular attacker had special knowledge about the Fernandez case. Agnes knew all too well how her husband had anguished over the decision not to grant a stay of execution—how he'd second-guessed the clarity of his own judgment. She understood her husband's pain. She shared it. Not just because there was no way to know whether the right decision had been made, but because of Jack.

She'd pretty much botched it as a stepmother. She knew that. She'd tried to reach out to her stepson countless times, but there was nothing left but to accept the reality of his bitterness. She might have had a fighting chance of winning his love but for a low moment twenty-three years before. It had happened the day that her doctor broke the news that she and Harry would never have children, and the awful truth had caused her to reach for the bottle.

She'd been too drunk to pick Jack up after kindergarten, so a neighbor had dropped him off. Jack came in quietly through the back door, making a conscious effort to avoid his new "mother," whom he still didn't trust.

"Jack," Agnes had muttered as her eyes popped open. Her tongue was thick as frozen molasses. "Come here, sweetie."

Jack tried to scoot past her, but Agnes reached out and managed to grab him by the back of his britches as he passed. She wrapped her arms around him in an awkward embrace and mashed her lips against his cheek. "Give Mommy a big hug," she said, stinking of her gin martini. He struggled to get out of her grip, but Agnes squeezed him tighter. "Don't you want to give Mommy a hug?" she asked.

"No," he grimaced. "And you're not my mommy!"

Resentment flared within her. She pushed little Jack off her lap but held him tightly by the wrist, so he couldn't go anywhere. "Don't you *dare* talk to me that way," she scolded. Then she slapped him across the face. The boy burst into tears as he struggled to get loose, but Agnes wouldn't release him.

"Let me go, you're hurting me."

"Hurt is the only thing you understand, young man. You don't appreciate anything else. I'm the one who changed your dirty diapers. I'm the one who . . . who"—she struggled to find the words—"lost sleep with all your crying in the night. Not your mother. *I* did it. *I'm* your mother. I'm all you've *got!*"

"You're *not* my mommy. My mommy's in heaven!"

Agnes didn't know where the ugly words were coming from, but she couldn't stop them. "Your mother isn't dead, you little brat. She just didn't *want* you!"

Jack's hands trembled as he stared at his stepmother. "That's a lie!" he cried. "A lie, lie, lie! That's all it is! That's—"

". . . the news at sunrise," The anchorman's voice drew Agnes out of her past. "From all of us at channel seven, have a great day."

Agnes hit the off button as she returned from her memories. The governor stepped from the bathroom, dressed and ready to take his phone call at the corner of Tenth and Monroe, ready to find out the truth about Raul Fernandez. However, last night he'd promised his wife that he wouldn't go without her blessing. She'd promised to sleep on it. As he stood at the foot of the bed, adjusting his necktie, she knew it was time for her to give him an answer.

"Well?" he asked.

Agnes sighed. It wasn't an easy decision. Even taking a phone call could be dangerous. The man *did* have a knife. But if this was a way to ease Harry's pain, a way to fix the rupture between her husband and her stepson, she couldn't stand in his way.

"Don't you dare take any chances, Harry Swyteck."

The governor smiled appreciatively, then came to her and kissed her on the lips. "I'll call you when it's over. And don't worry—I'm the original Chicken Little, remember?"

Agnes nodded but without conviction. In the beginning of their marriage, when Harry had been on the police force, such assurances were offered on a daily basis. It was her knowledge of her husband's innate bravery that worried her so much.

He pulled away, then stopped as he reached the door. "But if I don't call by one—"

"Don't say it, Harry," she said, eyes glassy now with tears. "Don't even think it."

He nodded slowly. "I'll call you," he promised. Then he was out the door.

More out of an ingrained sense of obligation than passion for his work, Jack put on jeans and a polo shirt—typical summer attire at the Freedom Institute—gave Thursday a friendly pat on the rump, and headed out the door. In the car he brooded on whether he would tender his resignation. When he arrived at nine o'clock, he still hadn't come to a decision. It was his first day back in the office in almost three weeks, since the Goss trial had begun. He stood in the foyer, taking a hard look at the place where he'd worked for the past four years. The reception area was little more than a hallway. Bright fluorescent lighting showed every stain on the indoor-outdoor carpet. A few unmatched chairs lined the bare white walls. An oversized metal desk was at the end of the hall. It belonged to the pregnant woman who served as both the Institute's receptionist and only secretary. Behind her were four windowless offices, one for each of the lawyers. Beyond that was a vintage sixties kitchen, where the lawyers did everything from interviewing witnesses to eating their bagged lunches.

"Victory!" chorused Jack's colleagues as he stepped into the kitchen. All three of the Institute's other lawyers were smiling widely and assuming a celebratory stance around the Formica-topped table. There was Brian, a suntanned and sandy-haired outdoor type who moved as smoothly in court as he did on water skis. And Eve, the resident jokester who helped everyone keep sanity, the only woman Jack had ever known to smoke a pipe. And Neil Goderich, who'd lost his ponytail since establishing the Institute twenty-eight years ago, but who still wore his shirt collar unbuttoned beneath his tie—not just to be casual, but because his neck had swollen more than an inch since he last bought a new dress shirt.

The home team cheered as they broke out a six-dollar bottle of cold duck and popped the cork.

"Congratulations!" said Neil as he filled four coffee-stained mugs.

They raised their cups in unison, and Jack smiled at their celebration; although he didn't share the festive mood, he appreciated the gesture. He considered them all friends. At his first interview four years ago he'd learned they were down-to-earth people who believed in themselves and their principles. They were honest enough to tell even the son of a prominent politician that anything "politically correct" was a walking oxymoron. It was the strength of their collective character that made it hard for Jack to leave. But suddenly, he knew the time had come.

"Excellent job!" said Neil, a sentiment echoed by the others.

"Thank you," said Jack, hoping to stem any further backslapping. "I really appreciate this. But . . . as long as everyone's here, I might as well take this chance to tell you." He looked at them and sighed. "Guys, Eddy Goss was my last case. I'm leaving the Institute."

That took the fizz right out of their cold duck.

Jack placed his cup on the table, turned, and quietly headed toward his office, leaving them staring at one another. The announcement had been awkward, but he didn't feel like explaining. With no other job offer in hand, he was having a hard time explaining it to himself.

He spent a couple of hours packing up his things, going through old files. At eleven o'clock Neil Goderich appeared in his doorway.

"When you first came here," Neil began, "we honestly wondered if you'd ever fit in."

Jack picked up some books, placed them in a box. "I wondered the same thing."

Neil smiled sadly, like a parent sending a kid off to college. He took a seat on the edge of Jack's desk, beside a stack of packed boxes. "We never would have hired your type," he said as he stroked his salt-and-pepper beard. "You had 'big greedy law firm' written all over your résumé. Someone who clearly valued principal and interest over interest in one's principles."

"Then why'd you hire me?"

Neil smiled wryly. "Because you were the son of Harold Swyteck. And I could think of no better way to piss off the future law-and-order governor than to have his son come work for a long-haired leftover from a lost generation."

It was Jack's turn to smile. "So you put up with me for the same reason I put up with you."

"I suspected that was why you were here," he said, then turned serious. "You were tired of doing everything your old man said you *should* do. The Institute was as far off the beaten path as you could get."

Jack fell silent. He and Neil had never spoken about his father, and Neil's unflattering perception of the relationship was more than a little disturbing.

Neil leaned forward and folded his hands, the way he always did when he was speaking on the level. "Look, Jack. I read the papers. I watch TV. I know you're catching hell about Goss, and I know the bad press can't be doing the governor's campaign any good. Maybe you feel guilty about that . . . maybe your old man is even pressuring you to leave us. I don't know, and that's none of my business. But this much is my business: You've got what it takes, Jack. You're an incredibly talented lawyer. And deep down, I know you're not like all those people out there who are perfectly content to put up with poverty and drugs and homelessness and all the other problems that turn children into criminals, so long as the criminal justice system allows them revenge. The Freedom Institute deprives them of that revenge—of *their* sense of 'justice.' But we are doing the right thing here. *You've* done the right thing."

Jack looked away, then sighed. He had never been as sure about right and wrong as Neil was, though there had indeed been times when he saw the higher purpose, when he actually believed that each acquittal reaffirmed the rights of all people. But it took more than vision to defend the likes of Eddy Goss day after day. It took passion—the kind of passion that started revolutions. Jack had felt that passion only once in his life: the night his father had executed Raul Fernandez. But that was different. Fernandez had been innocent.

"I'm sorry, Neil. But the lofty goals just don't drive me anymore. Maybe I wouldn't be leaving if I'd defended just *one* murderer who was sorry for what he'd done. Not innocent, mind you. Just sorry. Someone who saw a not-guilty verdict as a second chance at life, rather than another chance to kill. Instead, I got clients like Eddy Goss. I hate to disappoint you, but I just can't stay here anymore. If I did, I'd be nothing but a hypocrite."

Neil nodded, not in agreement but in understanding. "I *am* disappointed," he said, "but not in you." He rose from the edge of the desk and shook Jack's hand. "The door's open, Jack. If ever you change your mind."

"Thanks."

"Got time for lunch today?"

Jack checked his watch. Almost eleven-thirty. He had no official plans, but right now he figured he needed a stronger dose of good cheer than Neil could provide. "I'd like a rain check on that, okay?"

"Sure thing," Neil said, giving him a mock salute as he turned and left.

Ten minutes later, Jack's thoughts were on Cindy as he walked toward his car, weighed down with three of the ten boxes he'd packed. He'd still had no return call from her. Which meant either she hadn't gotten his messages or she was sending him a message of her own.

He thought back to the last night they'd been together, how she'd told him she was going over to her best friend Gina's to console her. The story might have been believable if it had been anyone but Gina—a woman to whom the adjective *needy* didn't apply. Certainly Jack had never thought of her that way, and he knew her quite well. It was through her that he'd met Cindy. Fourteen months ago, a mutual friend had fixed him up on a blind date with Gina. It was their first and only. She'd kept Jack waiting in her living room nearly an hour while she got ready. Cindy was Gina's roommate back then, and she kept Jack entertained while he waited. He and Cindy clicked. Boy, did they click. He spent the rest of the evening with Gina just trying to find out about Cindy, and Cindy was the only woman he'd dated ever since. At first, Gina had seemed upset by the turn of events. But as he and Cindy became more serious, Gina came to accept it.

He checked the traffic at the curb, waited for the light to change, then started across the boulevard toward the Institute's parking lot. He was still wrapped up in his thoughts and struggling under the weight of the boxes when he noticed a car rolling through the red light. He picked up his pace to get out of the way, but the car increased its speed. Suddenly, it swerved sharply in his direction. He dove from the street to the sidewalk to keep from getting run over. As he tumbled to the concrete, he caught a glimpse of the retreating car. The first letter on the license plate was a Z. In Florida, that meant it was a rental.

His heart was in his throat. He couldn't stop shaking. He looked to see if there were any witnesses, but he saw no one. The Freedom Institute wasn't in a neighborhood where many people strolled the sidewalks. He remained on the ground for a moment, trying to sort out whether it was an accident, some street gang's initiation rite, just another crazy driver—or something else. He didn't want to be paranoid, but it was hard to dismiss the event as an accident. He picked himself up, then froze as he thought he heard a phone ringing. He listened carefully. It was *his* phone, a cheap but reliable car phone he'd installed at Neil Goderich's insistence, just in case his twenty-year-old Mustang happened to leave him stranded in one of those questionable areas that were breeding grounds for Freedom Institute clientele.

He looked around. He was still alone. The phone kept ringing. He walked to his car, disengaged the alarm with the button on his key chain, and opened the door. The phone must have rung twenty times. Finally, he picked up.

"Hello," he answered.

"Swyteck?"

Jack exhaled. It was that voice—that raspy, disguised voice on his home telephone two nights ago.

"Who is this?"

There was no answer.

"Who is this?"

"You let the killer loose. *You're* the one who let him go."

"What do you *want* from me?"

There was a long pause, an audible sigh, and then the response: "Stop the killer, Swyteck. I *dare* you."

"What—" Jack started to say. But he was too late. The line clicked, and they were disconnected.

8

At 11:40 A.M. Harry Swyteck put on his seer-sucker jacket, exited the capitol building through the rear entrance, and headed to Albert's Pharmacy at the busy intersection of Tenth Street and Monroe. The bright morning sun promised another insufferable afternoon, but the air wasn't yet completely saturated with the summer humidity that would bring the inevitable three o'clock shower. It was the perfect time of day to hit the streets, press the flesh, and do some grass-roots campaigning.

He reached the drugstore a few minutes before noon, masking his anxiety with campaign smiles and occasional handshakes along the way. Albert's was a corner pharmacy that hadn't changed in forty years, selling everything from hemorrhoidal ointment to three-alarm chili. Most important for the governor's purposes, though, it was one of the few places in town that still offered the privacy of a good old-fashioned phone booth out front. Harry wondered if his attacker had that in mind when he selected it.

"Mornin', Governor," came a friendly greeting. It was seventy-nine-year-old Mr. Albert, sweeping up in front of his store.

"Morning," Harry said, smiling. "Great day to be out, isn't it?"

Mr. Albert wiped the sweat from his brow. "I suppose," he said as he retreated back inside. Harry felt that he, too, should be on his way. But he couldn't go anywhere until his phone call came—and, above all, he couldn't arouse suspicion by hanging around in front of a drugstore. So he stepped inside the booth and tucked the receiver under his chin, giving the appearance that he was deeply engaged in private conversation. He casually rested his hand on the cradle, concealing from passersby that he was pressing the disconnect button. He checked the time on a bank marquee down the block. Exactly twelve o'clock. He was suddenly very nervous—not about taking the call, but about the possibility that it wouldn't come at all. To his quick relief, the phone rang, and he immediately released the disconnect button.

"I'm here," he said into the phone.

"So you are, my man." There was still that thick sucking sound to the man's speech. "Let's make this quick."

"Don't worry, I'm not tracing the call."

The man seemed to scoff. "I'm not worried at all. You're not about to call in the cops."

Harry bristled, annoyed that the caller had him figured for an easy mark. "How can you be so sure?"

"Because I can read you like a book. I saw the way your eyes lit up when I told you I had information about Fernandez. You've been thinking about that one for a while, haven't you?"

The governor listened carefully as pedestrians and cars buzzed by outside the booth. It disturbed him that this stranger understood him so well—this stranger who spoke like a punk but had the insight of a shrink. *Part of his disguise*, he figured. "What's your proposal?" he asked.

"Simple. I'll give you the evidence. The same evidence I showed your son two years ago, so you can see with your own eyes it was *me* who slit the bitch's throat. All you gotta do is come up with the cash."

Harry's mind was reeling. *This* was the man who had visited Jack the night of the Fernandez execution? Could he be on the level—could he really be the killer?

"Wait a minute, you're saying *you* killed that young girl?"

"You need a hearing aid, old man? That's exactly what I'm saying."

The governor felt as if a deep chasm were opening up in front of him and he was plummeting downward with no end in sight. It took a few seconds to collect himself. "You said something about money?"

"Ten thousand. Unmarked fifties."

"How do I get it to you?" he asked, though he could hardly believe he was actually negotiating. "And how do I get this evidence you claim you have?"

"Just bring the money to Bayfront Park in Miami. Go to where the carriage rides start, by the big statue of Christopher Columbus. Get in the white carriage with the red velvet seats. The driver's an old nigger named Calvin. Get the nine P.M. ride. When you get to the amphitheater, he'll stop for a break and get himself an iced tea from the roach-coach señorita with the big tits. When he does, check under your seat on the right-hand side. The seat cushion flips up, and there's storage space underneath. You'll find a shoe box and a note. Leave the money, take the box, read the note—and do *exactly* as it says. Got it?"

"What if the carriage driver doesn't stop?"

"He'll stop, if you get the nine o'clock ride. You can set a fucking clock by him. He always stops."

"I can't just go for a carriage ride with a sack full of money."

"You can—and you *will*."

The governor quickly sensed the nonnegotiability of the terms. "I'll need a little time. When do you want it?"

"Saturday night. And like I said: Take the nine o'clock ride. Gotta go, my man. I don't think you're tracing the call, but just in case you are, my seventy seconds is about up."

The governor heard a click on the other end of the line. Slowly he placed the receiver back in the cradle, then took a deep breath. He worried about getting in deeper, but he had to be certain that what this man was telling him was the truth. He didn't know what he'd do once he confirmed it, how he'd be able to live with himself or explain it to Jack, but he had to be certain.

Besides, it could be worse. Paying a single dime to this low-life would be too much, but the truth was that ten thousand dollars would not devastate his and Agnes's finances. The man could easily have asked for much more.

He wondered why the man *hadn't* asked for more. He was taking quite a risk exposing himself like this. Why not go for the big payday? Unless he was playing a different game altogether, one Harry couldn't even begin to fathom.

Somehow the possibility of that filled him with an even deeper dread.

9

"To my good buddy, Jack," said Crazy Mike Mannon, proprietor of Mike's Bikes and Jack Swyteck's best friend. He raised a bottle of Michelob. "May you come to your senses and never find another job as a lawyer."

Jack smiled, then tipped back his Amstel and took a long pull. After a day of phone calls to friends about potential job openings, he'd let Mike talk him into dinner on South Beach. A couple of beers and cheeseburgers at a sidewalk cafe sounded good.

They enjoyed the ocean breezes and watched bronzed bodies on roller blades weave in and out of bright-red convertibles, classic Corvettes, and fat-tired jeeps blaring reggae and Cuban salsa. By eight o'clock the sun had gone down and everything trendy, sexy, and borderline illegal was parading down Ocean Drive beneath colorful neon hues.

"Whoa," said Mike as a deeply tanned blonde with a seriously plunging neckline sent a ripple of whiplash through the cafe.

Jack smiled with amusement. Mike was one of those guys who was forever on the make—a frat boy stuck in a man's body. Even so, he had an irrepressible spirit that most people found charming. He had a way of not taking life too seriously, of following his own desires and not worrying about what others thought or said. Jack envied him for that.

"You know, Mike, there's an orthopedic surgeon over at Jackson Memorial who would love to see your X rays. She's doing a paper on swivel heads."

"Easy for you to be so pious, Mr. Monogamous. But some of us don't go to bed every night with Cindy Paige."

"Yeah, well," Jack said, looking away, "I'm beginning to wonder how much longer that's going to last."

"Uh-oh. Trouble in Camelot. That's okay, I'll find a honey for you, too. How about that one?" Mike said, nodding at a leather-clad bodybuilder with spiked burgundy hair.

"Perfect. She looks like the type who'd go for a guy without a job. And if she seems undecided, I'll just mention that some maniac wants to turn me into roadkill."

Mike gave him an assessing look. "Any new theories about that car thing yesterday?"

"Your guess is still as good as mine," Jack said, shrugging. "I suppose it could be Goss having fun with me. This 'killer on the loose' stuff is his style. But I'm not sure he has the attention span. First the phone call three days ago. Now this. It's a real campaign. Someone is obviously furious about the verdict."

Mike's head swiveled to follow two halter-topped women who'd emerged from the ladies' room. "Maybe you should call the cops."

Jack smiled. "The Miami Police Department would like nothing better than to hear Jack Swyteck is being hassled. They'd probably offer the guy the key to the city. I don't think the cops are an option right now."

"Well, you watch your back," Mike said with emphasis. He grinned. "You might even want to consider a new line of work—you know, greeting-card salesman or something."

Jack nodded. Maybe Mike had a point. Maybe he did need a clean break—even a move to another state. Away from Goss, and out of the shadow of his father, for whom the best was never enough, and Cindy who was always pushing him to open up. Hell, why *couldn't* he open up? Everyone else in America was unloading their thoughts. You couldn't turn on a talk show these days without watching someone turn his guts inside out in front of the camera.

"Hey, Mike," Jack asked, his mind drifting. "Do you get along with your family—you know, do you chew the fat regularly with your mom and dad?"

Mannon had made eye contact with some woman in tight purple capri pants. "Huh," he said, refocusing on Jack. "Oh, family . . . well, yeah, you know. My mom and I talk. It's mostly her that does the ear-bending. Always wants to know when I'm going to get married and give her grandchildren."

"And your dad?"

"We get along." He smiled, but with a hint of sadness. "When I was a kid, we were real tight. Horsed around, went to the Hurricanes games. We took the boat down toward Elliot Key nearly every weekend. Came back with our limit every time, it seemed." He paused. "After I got out of school, though, it was more formal—you know, brisk handshake and 'how's the business going, son?' That sort of thing. But we're always there for each other."

Jack thought of that picture he'd seen on his father's bookshelf the night of the Fernandez execution. Deep-sea fishing. Just the two of them.

"Waiter," he called out. "Two more over here, please."

Driving back from South Beach at 1:45 that Saturday morning, Cindy leaned over, turned off the A.C. in Gina's car, and opened her window to let in some warmer air.

"Why'd you do that?" Gina said petulantly.

"Because it's getting cold in here."

"I like the cold air. It keeps me awake—especially after I've had a few drinks. Besides, these pants I'm wearing are hot."

Cindy looked over at her girlfriend. Oh, they were hot all right, but not in a thermal sense. The clingy black spandex molded Gina's body perfectly—a body that could get her anything from dinner at world-class restaurants to full service at self-service gas stations. She was gorgeous, and she worked at it, still striving at age twenty-four for "the fresh look" that had earned her a thousand dollars a week as a sixteen-year-old model.

They'd first met six years ago in college, two eighteen-year-old opposites who were thrown together by the administrative fiat of dorm-room assignments. Cindy was the more serious student; Gina, the more serious partyer. For the better part of a semester they simply put up with each other. Then late one Saturday night Gina came back to their room in tears. It took until dawn, but Cindy finally convinced her that no college professor, no matter how good a lover, was worth a fifth of bourbon and a bottle of sleeping pills. Cindy was the only person who ever learned that a man had pushed Gina Terisi to the edge. A friendship grew out of that night's conversation, and over the years Cindy had witnessed the slaughter of countless innocent men who came along later and paid for the sins of Gina's first and only "true love." Cindy knew that the predatory Gina wasn't the real Gina; but it was hard convincing others who hadn't seen her at her most vulnerable.

"Have you ever driven a car with your eyes closed?" Gina asked.

"Can't say I have," said Cindy as she fiddled with the buttons on the car radio trying to find something she liked.

"I have. Sometimes when I see there's a car coming at me, I get this feeling that I want to hold the wheel steady, close my eyes, and wait for that *whoooooooosh* sound as the car whizzes by."

Cindy rolled her eyes. "Just drive, Gina."

Gina made a face. "You're in one hell of a mood."

"Sorry. I guess I don't feel like I should be out

partying tonight. I'm having second thoughts about telling Jack I want to break up."

"We've been over this a hundred times, Cindy—you're getting out of that relationship."

Cindy blinked. "It's just that we were so close. We were even talking about making it permanent."

"Which means that I rescued you without a moment to spare. Believe me, it's no accident that the word *married* rhymes with *buried*," she said, mashing the pronunciation. "Life's no dress rehearsal, okay? Find some excitement without standing on the sidelines and living your life through me. You've got a great opportunity right in front of you. It's not every twenty-five-year-old photographer who gets hired by the Italian Consulate to go traveling around Italy taking pictures for a trade brochure. Jump on it. If you don't—if you stay behind because you think you're gonna lose Jack—you'll end up hating him for it someday."

"Maybe," Cindy said. "But that doesn't mean I have to dump him. I could just tell him that the time apart will give us both a chance to decide whether our relationship should be permanent or not."

"Just *stop it*, will you? You've been living with Jack for months. After that much time, you either know it's right or it's wrong. And if you're still saying you're trying to make up your mind—believe me, it ain't right."

"It felt right at times."

"That was a long time ago. I know you, Cindy. And I know you've been unhappy with Jack for months.

Here's a guy who claims to be talking about 'making things permanent,' yet half the time he won't even give you a hint of what's *really* on his mind. And whatever the hell this big secret is that keeps him from talking to his big-shot father is too weird. I think he has a screw loose."

"There's nothing wrong with Jack," Cindy said defensively. "I just think the way his mother died and how his family handled all these problems has him confused about a lot of things."

"Fine. So while he sorts it all out, you go have yourself a ball in Italy."

"I don't know—"

"Well," Gina huffed, "do what you want then. But it's a moot point, anyway. Once Jack hears who your traveling companion will be, it'll be over between you two anyway."

Cindy didn't answer. Gina had a point, but she didn't want to think about that right now. She just listened to the radio for a few minutes, until the early-morning jazz gave way to the local news at 2:00 A.M. The lead story was still Eddy Goss.

". . . the confessed killer," said the newscaster, "who was acquitted by a jury Tuesday afternoon on first-degree murder charges." This report was about Detective Lonzo Stafford's diligent efforts to link Goss to at least two other murders, to get him off the streets so that, according to Stafford, "Goss will never kill again."

Cindy and Gina both pretended not to listen, though neither had the other one fooled. Jack's involvement in the Goss case had brought this killer a little too close to home. Cindy thought of Jack, probably by himself, back at the house. Gina thought of Eddy Goss. Out there. Somewhere.

Gina steered her champagne-colored BMW, a gift from her latest disappointed suitor, into her private townhouse community, a collection of twenty lushly landscaped units facing the bay. Gina could never have afforded waterfront property on her salary as an interior designer, so she "leased" this place from an extremely wealthy and married Venezuelan businessman who, as Gina once kidded, "comes about three times a year, all in one night, to collect the rent."

Cindy's car was parked in Gina's garage, so Gina parked in a guest space across the lot. They stepped tentatively from the car with the disquieting newscast about Eddy Goss still fresh in their minds.

"Nothing like a killer on the loose to make a marathon out of a two-minute walk to the front door," Cindy half-joked as they briskly crossed the empty parking lot.

"Yeah," Gina replied, her nervous laughter ringing flat and hollow in the stillness of the dark night. She ran up the front steps two at a time. Cindy trailed behind, moving not quite as fast in heels as her long-legged friend. The porch light was on and the front door was locked, just the way they'd left it. Gina fumbled through her cosmetic-packed purse for her key and poked awkwardly at the lock. Finally, she found the slot and pushed the key home. With two quick turns she unlocked the dead bolt, then turned the knob and leaned into the door, opening it—but just a foot, as her body jerked to an unexpected halt. The door caught on the inside chain.

They froze as they realized they couldn't possibly have gotten out of the townhouse had *they* put the chain on the door.

Gina glanced at the clay pot on the porch that hid her extra key—a spare only a few people knew about. The pot had been moved.

Before Gina could back away, the door slammed shut, pushing her back and spilling the contents of her purse onto the porch.

Panic gripped the two women as they grabbed for each other. When they heard the chain coming off the door, they screamed in unison as they raced down the stairs. Gina led the way, kicking off her shoes and negotiating the steps like a steeplechase racer. Cindy's left heel caught on the bottom step, and she tumbled to the sidewalk.

"Gina, help!" she cried, sprawled out on her hands and knees. But her friend never looked back.

"Gina!"

10

·

"H ey!" Jack shouted as the door flew open at the top of the steps. "Hey! It's me!"

Gina kept running, but Cindy stopped and looked up from the foot of the stairs. "Jack?" she called out as she picked herself up from the sidewalk.

Jack waved from the top of the stairs. "It's okay. It's just me."

"You son of a bitch!" Gina shouted on her way back from the parking lot. "What the hell are you doing here?"

Good question, thought Jack. Back at the bar, he'd yielded to Mike's urging and switched from beers to Bahama Mamas. And in no time flat he was feeling the effects of the grain alcohol. He rarely drank hard liquor, so when he did, it went straight to his head. Rather than kill someone trying to drive all the way home, he'd stopped at Gina's, hoping to find Cindy.

"I don't know *what* I'm doing here," he said with a shrug, speaking to himself more than anyone else. Then he looked at Cindy. "Sorry, guess I had a little too much to drink. I just wanted to talk to you, find out what was going on with us."

"Jack," Cindy sighed, "this is not the place—"

"I just want to *talk*, Cindy. You owe me at least that." As he spoke he wobbled slightly and used the railing to regain his balance.

Cindy struggled. Seeing Jack made her regret the way she'd handled their problem. "I'm not sure I *can* talk—at least tonight. I honestly haven't made up my—"

"Her mind *is* made up," Gina contradicted. "Forget it, Jack. She's leaving you. Like it or not, she's a better person without you. Just let her go."

Cindy shot an exasperated look at her friend.

Jack was suddenly embarrassed by the spectacle he was making of himself.

"Just forget it," he said as he shook his head and then started down the stairs.

Cindy hesitated a moment, then moved to stop him. "No, you're right, we do need to talk. Let me get my car keys. We can talk at home."

He looked back at Gina, then turned to Cindy. "You're sure?"

She gave a quick nod, avoiding his eyes. "Go ahead, get in your car. I'll follow."

There is no line more palpable than the one that runs down the middle of the bed. The room may be dark. The eyes may be shut. But it is there, silent testament to the deep division that can separate a couple.

The line between Jack and Cindy began to emerge as they drove from Gina's in separate cars, parked in their driveway, and headed into the house single file. It became more pronounced as they undressed in silence, and by the time they tucked themselves into their respective corners of the king-size mattress, it was the Berlin Wall born again. Jack knew they had to talk, but after a night of drinking, he was afraid of what he might say. He played it safe. He flipped off the light, mumbled a clipped "night," and pretended to be asleep, though it was actually hours before his troubled mind finally let his body rest.

Cindy didn't try to keep him up, but she couldn't fall asleep either. She was thinking of how he'd asked her to move in with him, almost ten months ago. He'd covered her eyes with his hands and led her to his bedroom, and when he took his hands away she saw little yellow ribbons tied to the handles on half the dresser drawers, marking the empty ones. "Those are yours," he'd told her. Now, lying in their bed, she closed her eyes and thought of yellow ribbons—ribbons and lace and streamers. As her thoughts melted into sleep, the last waking image was of a room decorated for a party. A lavish party with hundreds of guests. Instinctively, she knew that it was important Jack be there, but when she looked for him, when she called out his name, no one answered.

"Jack," she whispered barely three hours later as the heat from the morning sun warmed her forehead. The sound of her own voice speaking in a dream woke her, and she rolled over onto her side. "Jack," she said, nudging his shoulder. "We need to talk."

"Huh?" Jack rubbed his eyes and turned to face her. He stole a look at the alarm clock and saw that it was just 7:00 A.M.

"Be back in a second," he said as he slid to the side of the bed, stood up, then sat right back down. "Whoa," he groaned, feeling the first throb of a hangover so massive that had someone suggested amputation as the only cure, he might have considered it. He sighed, resigning himself to remaining seated. "Listen," he said as he glanced over his shoulder at Cindy, "I'm sorry about last night, okay?"

Cindy sat up, then hesitated, deciding whether to cross the line between them. It was strange, but after ten months of living with him, she suddenly felt uncomfortable about Jack, sitting there in his striped underwear, and about herself, wearing only an oversized T-shirt.

"I'm sorry too," she said as she slid tentatively across the bed. She sat on the edge, beside him, though she kept her distance. "But it's not enough just to exchange apologies. We need to talk. I've been giving this a lot of thought."

"Giving *what* a lot of thought?"

She grimaced. "I've been offered a photo shoot for the Italian Trade Consulate. In Italy."

He smiled, relieved it was good news. "That's fantastic, absolutely terrific," he said as he reached out and squeezed her hand. "That's the kind of thing you've always dreamed about. Why didn't you tell me before?"

"Because I'd have to leave right away—and it'll take me away for three or four months."

He shrugged it off. "We can survive that."

"That's just it," she said, averting her eyes. "I'm not so sure we can."

"What do you mean?" he asked, his smile fading.

She sighed. "What I mean is, we have problems, Jack. And the problem isn't really *us*. It's something inside you that for some reason you just won't share."

He looked away. She was right. The problem *was* inside him.

"We've been over this before," he said. "I mope—get in these lousy moods. A lot of it's work—the job I do." He thought for a second of telling her he'd quit the Freedom Institute, but decided that being jobless wouldn't help his case. "But I'm dealing with it."

"There's just something that makes you unable or unwilling to communicate and expose yourself emotionally. I can't just dismiss it. As long as we've been together, you've been completely incapable of reaching out to your own father and solving whatever it is that keeps you two apart. It worries me that you handle relationship problems that way. It worries me so much that I took the Goss trial as an opportunity to get away from you for a few days. To think about us . . . whether we have a future. I honestly wasn't sure how I was going to leave it. Whether I'd say, 'Let's just go our separate ways' or 'I still love you, I'll phone and write and see you when I get back from Europe.'"

"And you were going to make that decision by yourself?" he asked, now somewhat annoyed. "I was just supposed to go along with whatever you announced?"

"No, I knew we had to talk, but it just wasn't that easy. It gets a little more complicated."

"In what way?"

She looked at her toes. "I'm not going alone," she said sheepishly. "It's me and Chet."

His mouth opened, but the words wouldn't come. "Chet," he finally uttered. Chet was Cindy's old boss at Image Maker Studios, her first employer out of college—and the man in her life before Jack had come along. Jack felt sick.

"It's not what you think," Cindy said. "It's purely professional—"

"Why are you doing it this way?" he asked, ignoring her explanation. "Do you think I'm gonna go over the edge if you just tell me the truth and dump me? I won't, don't worry. I'm stronger than that. For the past month, every time I turn on the nightly news or read a newspaper, it's one story after another about confessed killer Eddy Goss and his lawyer, Jack Swyteck—always mentioned in the same sentence, always in the same disgusted tone. I walk down the street, and people I know avoid me. I walk down the other side of the street, and people I've never even *seen* spit at me. Lately, it's been worse." He thought of his near rundown just two days ago. "But you know what? I'm gonna come out of this okay. I'm gonna beat it. If I have to do it without you, that's your choice. But doing it without your pity—that's *my* choice."

"I'm not pitying you. And I'm not leaving you. Can't you just accept what I'm telling you as my honest feelings and be honest with me about your own feelings?"

"I've never lied to you about my feelings."

"But you never *tell* me anything, either. That bothers me. Sometimes I think it's me. Maybe it's my fault. I don't know. Gina thinks it's just the way you are, because of the way you and your father—"

"What the hell does Gina know about my father?"

She swallowed hard. She knew she'd slipped. He was shaking his head, and his fists were clenched. "Did you tell her the things I told you?"

"Gina's my best friend. We talk. We tell each other the important things in our lives."

"Damn it, Cindy!" he shouted as he sprung from the bed. "You don't tell her *anything* I tell you about me and my father. How could you be so fucking insensitive!"

Cindy's hands trembled as her nails dug into the mattress. "Don't talk to me that way," she said firmly, "or I'm leaving right this second."

"You're leaving anyway," he said. "Don't you think I can see that? You're going to Italy with the boss you used to sleep with. You're out with Gina till two in the morning, checking out guys and prowling the nightclubs—"

"That's not what we were—"

"Oh, bullshit!" His emotions had run away so completely that he'd forgotten his own whereabouts the night before. "You're not hanging with Mother Teresa, you know. Hell, I've had more meaningful conversations with tollbooth attendants than Gina's had with half the men she's slept with."

"I'm not Gina. And besides, Gina's not that way. Just stop it, Jack."

"Stop what?" he said, raising his voice another level. "Stop looking behind what this is really all about? Stop taking the fun out of Cindy and Gina's excellent adventure?"

She sat rigidly on the side of the bed, too hurt to speak.

He charged toward the bedroom door. "You want to go?" he asked sharply, flinging the door open. "Go."

She looked up, tears welling in her eyes.

"Go *on*," he ordered. "Get outta here!"

She still didn't move.

He moved his head from side to side, looking frantically about the room for some way to release months or maybe even years of pent-up anger that Cindy hadn't caused but was now the unfortunate recipient of. He darted toward the bureau and snatched the snapshots of them she'd tucked into the wood frame around the mirror—their memories.

"Jack!"

"There," he said as he ripped one to pieces.

"Don't do that!"

"You're leaving," he said as he took the picture of them taken in Freeport from his stack.

She jumped up and dashed for the walk-in closet. He jumped in front of her.

"I need to get some clothes!"

"Nope," he said, holding another photo before her eyes. "You're leaving right now. Go back to Gina— your confidante."

"Stop it!"

He ripped the entire stack in half.

"Jack!" She grabbed her car keys and headed for the door, wearing only her T-shirt. She stopped in the doorway and said tearfully, "I didn't want it to turn out this way."

He scoffed. "Now you sound like the scum I defend."

Her face reddened, ready to burst with tears or erupt with anger. "You *are* the scum you defend!" she screamed, then raced out of the house.

11

A t eight-thirty that Saturday evening, Harry Swyteck parked his rented Buick beneath one of the countless fifty-foot palm trees that line Biscayne Boulevard, Miami's main north-south artery. The governor was alone, as he'd promised his blackmailer. It was a few minutes past sunset, and the streetlights had just blinked on. Harry sighed at the impending darkness. As if he didn't already have enough to worry about, now he had to carry around ten thousand dollars in cash in Miami after dark. He checked the locks on his briefcase and stepped quickly from the car, then scurried across six lanes of traffic to the east side of the boulevard, following the sidewalk into the park.

Bayfront Park was Miami's green space between bustling city streets and the sailboats on Biscayne Bay. Granite, glass, and marble towers lit up the Miami skyline to the south and west of the park. Across the bay toward South Miami Beach the lights of Caribbean-bound cruise ships glittered like a string of floating pearls. Cool summer breezes blew off the bay from the east, carrying with them the soothing sound of rolling waves breaking against the shoreline. At the north end of the park was Bayside Marketplace, an indoor-outdoor collection of shops, restaurants, and bars, and the starting place for the horse-and-buggy rides through the park that were favored by tourists.

Tonight it was Governor Swyteck's turn to take a carriage ride. He hoped to blend in as a tourist, which was the reason for his white sailing pants, plaid madras shirt and Marlins baseball cap. But the leather briefcase made him feel conspicuous. He bought a stuffed animal from one of the cart vendors, just to get hold of the paper shopping bag, and stuck the briefcase in the bag. Now his outfit was complete: He didn't *look* at all like a governor, and that was the whole idea—though he did have a plan in case anyone recognized him. "Another stop on my grass-roots campaign trail," he'd say, and they'd probably buy it. Four years ago he'd manned a McDonald's drivethrough, taught phonics to first-graders, and worked other one-day jobs—all just to look like a regular Joe.

"Carriage ride?" one of the drivers called out as he reached the staging area.

"Uh—I'm thinking about it," Harry replied.

"Forty bucks for the half hour," the driver said, but the governor wasn't listening. He was trying to figure out which of the half dozen carriages belonged to Calvin, the man he'd been told to hire for the nine o'clock ride. By process of elimination he zoomed in on a sparkling white carriage with red velvet seats, pulled by an Appaloosa with donkeylike ears poking through an old straw hat. The governor felt nervous as he approached the wiry old black driver, but he told himself once again that he had to see this mission through. Sensing he was being watched, he looked one way, then the other, but could see nothing out of the ordinary.

"Are you Calvin?" he asked, looking up at the driver.

"Yessuh," he replied. Calvin was in his eighties, a relic of old Miami, when the city was "My-amma" and truly part of the South. He had frosty white hair and the callous hands of a man who had worked hard all his life. He seemed exaggeratedly deferential, making Harry feel momentarily guilty for his race and the way this old codger must have been treated as a young man.

"I'd like to take a little ride," said the governor as he handed up two twenty-dollar bills.

"Yessuh," said Calvin as he checked his watch. "Fair warnin' for you, though: You're my nine o'clock ride. I always stop at the concession stand on my nine o'clock ride. Get myself an iced tea."

"That's fine," said the governor as he climbed aboard. *I wouldn't have it any other way.*

Calvin made a clicking sound with his mouth and gave the reins a little tug. His horse pulled away from the rail and started toward the waterfront, as if on automatic pilot, while the governor looked on with amusement as the animal navigated the route. "How long you been doing this, Calvin?"

"Lot longer than you been guvnuh, suh."

So much for anonymity.

The journey began at the towering bronze statue of Christopher Columbus and headed south along the shoreline. Palm trees and musicians playing saxophones and guitars lined the wide pedestrian walkway of white coral rock, the south Florida version of a quaint cobblestone street. Calvin played tour guide as they rolled down the walkway. He was a veritable history book on wheels when it came to the park and its past, talking about how they had filled in the bay to build it in 1924 and how the sea had tried to reclaim it in the hurricane of 1926. He spoke from memory and years of practice, but he was clearly putting a little more emotion into it for his distinguished guest. The governor listened politely, but he was fading in and out, trying to remain focused on the purpose of his trip. His anxiety heightened as the carriage curled around the spewing fountain and headed west, away from the brightly lit walkway along the water to the interior of the park, where palm trees and live oaks cast shadows beneath street lamps that were becoming fewer and farther between. As they reached the amphitheater, the carriage slowed up, just as Calvin had warned and the blackmailer had said it would.

"Whoa," Calvin said gently to his horse, bringing the carriage to a halt. He turned and faced the governor. "Now, this is what I call the dark side of my tour, sir. For it was right here, where the old bandstand used to be, in the year of our Lord nineteen hundred and thirty-three, that President-Elect Franklin Delano Roosevelt addressed a crowd of fifteen thousand people. Amidst that huge crowd there stood one very angry young man—a man who doctors would later describe as a highly intelligent psychopath with pet schemes and morbid emotions that ran in conflict with the established order of society. That disturbed young man stood patiently atop a park bench until the president finished his speech, then took out his revolver and fired over the crowd at the dignitaries onstage, intending to kill Mr. Roosevelt. The president escaped unhurt, but five innocent people were shot. The most seriously injured was Anton Cermak, the distinguished mayor of Chicago, who, before he died, told the president, 'I'm glad it was me, instead of you.'"

Calvin saw the expression on the governor's face, then looked down apologetically. "Didn't mean to frighten you, Guvnuh. I always tell that story to all my passengers, not just to politicians. Just a part of our history, that's all."

"That's quite all right," he said, trying to ignore the chill running down his spine. But he wondered if his blackmailer knew that Calvin did indeed tell this story to all his passengers. Maybe that was the reason he had selected this particular carriage ride for the exchange. It was certainly possible—the man had apparently been planning this for two years, since the Fernandez execution. The governor suddenly wanted to hear more. "So, Calvin," he said casually, "I imagine this assassination must have been pretty big news back in '33."

"Oh, sure. Was front-page news for about a month or so, as I recall."

"What happened to the assassin?"

Calvin widened his eyes and raised his bushy white eyebrows. "I don't mean no disrespect, sir. But this man pulled out a pistol in front of fifteen thousand people, fired six shots at the president of the United States, wounded five people and done killed the mayor of Chicago. They dragged him into court, where he proceeded to tell the world that his only regret was that he didn't get Mr. Roosevelt. And to top it all off, the man begged the judge to give him the chair. Now whatchoo think they done to that fool?"

"Executed him," he said quietly.

"*Course* they executed him. Four days after they laid Mayor Cermak's dead body in the ground they done did execute him. Swift justice was what we had back then. Not like we got these days. All these lawyers we got now, hemmin' and hawin' and flappin' their jaws. Appealin' this and delayin' that. Anyhow," Calvin said with a sigh, "that's enough bellyachin'. I'm gonna let Daisy rest a spell and get myself a nice iced tea. Somethin' for you, Guvnuh?"

"No, thank you, Calvin. I'll wait here." Harry watched the old man hobble over to the concession stand, and he began to wonder about this whole curious arrangement. Was the blackmailer revealing his deeper, darker side—the "morbid emotions that ran at conflict with the established order of society?" Could he be *that* clever, that he had purposefully sent the governor to this old tour guide who in his own melodramatic way could make so painfully obvious the difference between the relatively easy capital cases and the unbearably difficult ones, between a man who boasts of his crime all the way to the electric chair and a man who proclaims his innocence to the end—between a crazed political assassin and someone like Raul Fernandez? Or maybe the message was less subtle, less philosophical. Maybe he was simply telling the governor that the very site of Florida's most famous political assassination was about to be the site of its next political assassination—tonight.

Harry glanced nervously toward Calvin, who was smiling and chatting with the concessionaire, an attractive young Hispanic woman whose shapely appearance alone explained the regularity of Calvin's nine o'clock stops. He pulled the carriage blanket over his lap, even though it was seventy-five degrees outside, so as to hide his movements. Then he touched the edge of the red velvet seat cushion beside him and got ready to lift it off. His heart began to race as he suddenly wondered whether a pistol-wielding madman would leap from the darkness or a bomb would explode when he lifted the carriage seat, writing the final chapter to Calvin's history lesson. He took a deep breath and pulled up. The seat popped out, just as his blackmailer had said it would. No explosion. No rattlesnakes inside. He checked over his shoulder to make sure no one was looking. Again he sensed he was being watched. But he saw nothing. He looked down to see what was beneath the seat.

Inside the little cubbyhole was a brown shoe box, with a note on the side: "Leave the money. Take the box." There was no signature. Only this warning: "I'm watching you."

The governor didn't dare turn his head to look around. He opened the briefcase in his shopping bag, emptied two stacks of crisp fifty-dollar bills under the seat, stuffed the shoe box into his bag, and put the seat cover back in place.

Calvin returned a few minutes later, and the ride back to Bayside Marketplace took only a few minutes more, though it seemed like an eternity. Harry thanked Calvin for the ride and quickly retraced his steps across the busy street to his car. As soon as he was behind the wheel, he set the shopping bag on the front seat beside him and took a deep breath, relieved that no one had stopped him. He turned on the ignition, but before he could pull into traffic he was startled by a short, high-pitched ring. It stopped, and then started up again. It seemed to emanate from the box inside the shopping bag. He took the shoe box from the bag and unfastened the tape on the lid. The shrill ringing continued. He flipped off the top and found a portable phone inside, resting on top of a sealed white envelope. He switched on the "talk" button and pressed the phone to his ear.

"It's in the envelope," came the familiar, thickly disguised voice.

The governor shuddered. Of course it would be him, but he was disturbed by the voice nonetheless. "What's in the envelope?"

"You have to ask, Governor?" came the reply. "I have your money, and you've got the proof it was me, not Raul, who killed the girl. That was our deal, wasn't it?"

The governor was silent.

"*Was* that our deal, Governor?"

"Yes, I suppose so."

"Good," said the caller in a calmer voice. "Now open the envelope. Just open it. Don't take anything out."

Harry tucked the phone under his chin and unsealed the envelope. "It's open."

"There's two photographs inside, both of the girl Raul got the chair for. Take out the one on the left."

The governor removed the snapshot from the envelope and froze. It was a photo of a teenage girl from her bare breasts up. She was lying on her back with her shoulders pinned behind her, as if her hands were bound tightly behind her back. A red bandanna gagged her mouth. The long blade of a knife pressed against her throat. Her blood-shot eyes stared up helplessly at her killer. The rest of her face was puffy and bruised from unmerciful beatings.

"You see it, my man?"

"Yes," his voice trembled.

"That's real fear in those eyes. You can't fake that. Sometimes I wish I'd videotaped it. But no need, really. I play it over and over again in my mind. It's like a movie. I call it 'The Taming of Vanessa.' Vanessa was her name, you know. It's nice to know their name. Makes it all more real."

The photograph shook in the governor's hand as his whole body was overcome by fear and disgust.

"Take out the next picture," said the caller.

Harry closed his eyes and sighed. It would have been difficult to look under any circumstances, but it was doubly painful now, realizing that Raul Fernandez was not responsible for this girl's death. The enormity of the governor's mistake was beginning to sink in, and all at once he was filled with self-loathing. "I've seen enough," he said quietly.

"Look at the next one. Look what I did with the knife."

"I said I've seen enough," Harry said firmly as he shoved the photo back into the envelope. "You've got your money, you monster. Just take it. That was our deal. Take it, keep your mouth shut, and don't ever call me again."

The caller chuckled with amusement. "Harry, Harry—that's not how the game is played. We're just getting started, you and me. Next installment's in a few days."

"I'm not paying you another cent."

"Such conviction. I guess you still can't feel that noose around your neck. Here, give *this* a listen."

The governor pressed the phone closer to his ear, straining to hear every sound. There was a click, then static, then a clicking sound again—and then a voice he clearly recognized as his own: *"You've got your money, you monster. Just take it. That was our deal. Take it, keep your mouth shut, and don't ever call me again."*

Another click, and the caller was back on the line. "It's all on tape, my man. You, the esteemed Governor Harold Swyteck, bribing an admitted killer to keep his mouth shut to save your own political skin. Every word of it's on tape—and ready to go to the newspapers."

"You wouldn't—"

"I *would*. So consider your piddling ten grand as

nothing more than a down payment. Because you're gonna take another ten thousand dollars to four-oh-nine East Adams Street, Miami, apartment two-seventeen. Be there at four A.M., August second. Not a minute before, not a minute after. The door will be open. Leave it right on the kitchen table. Be good, my man."

"You son of a—" the governor started to say, but the caller was gone. A wave of panic overcame him. He pitched the phone and the envelope into the box beside him, holding his head in his hands as a deep pit of nausea swelled in his stomach. "You idiot," he groaned aloud, sinking in his car seat. But it wasn't just his own stupidity that had him shaking. It was the whole night that sent a current of fear coursing through him. The "history lesson" in the park, the photographs of the young girl, the tape recording in the car—and, most of all, the dawning realization that in this confrontation with a cold-blooded killer, he was clearly overmatched.

12
·

Jack Swyteck bent low to avoid the doorway arch as he carried the last stack of boxes into the house. Behind him, carelessly flicking ashes from a fat cigar and obviously enjoying his friend's huffing and puffing, was Mike Mannon.

"I do believe you're out of shape," Mike needled.

"Excuse me, Mr. Schwarzenegger, but I didn't notice you setting any weight-lifting records today. And get that stink-rod out of my house."

Mike shrugged and blew a thick cloud of smoke at Jack. "Not my job to lift. You said you needed wheels because your 'stang was in the shop. You *didn't* say I had to play donkey."

"Well, I guess that's about it," Jack said, surveying his office haul. "God knows why I went back to get all this stuff, but I suppose it'll come in handy one of these days when I find a new job."

Mike looked down at the stack of legal volumes poking out of the biggest carton. "Yeah," he said,

"McDonald's crew chiefs find frequent reason to cite legal precedent."

"I'll remember that, Mannon, next time some collection agency's breathing down your deadbeat neck." Jack smiled bitterly. "Hell, what am I saying. I'll probably *be* the guy breathing down your neck. That's about the extent of my options in this town until this Goss thing blows over."

"Ah, don't sell yourself short, old boy. One of those big law firms can always use an unscrupulous man like you."

Jack gave a short laugh, then turned serious. "Sure you can't hang out for a while?"

"Nah, got to get back to the shop. It takes Lenny about two and a half hours to create a major crisis." He looked at his watch. "One should be brewing about now."

"Okay, then," Jack said, following him out the door. He looked down to see Thursday wriggling through his legs with a bookend in his mouth. "Hey, give me that," Jack said, reaching down and patting his head. He called out after Mike, who was walking down the wood-chip path. "Thanks for the help."

"No problem," Mike said, turning around. He gave a short wave as Thursday bounded after him and nipped at his heels. In a few seconds the car had pulled away from the curb, and Jack was left alone with his thoughts.

He closed the door and headed to the living room. The sofa felt good as he fell back onto it and propped his feet on the hassock. He looked around. Emptiness—a lot of emptiness. Sitting there, it seemed as if he were the only occupant of a grand hotel. Why had he ever bought such a huge house? Cindy once told him that as a girl she'd dreamed of living in a mansion. Sharing a small apartment with her parents and three brothers probably had something to do with it.

There he went again. Thinking of her. Ever since yesterday morning, when he'd made such an ass of himself and insisted she leave, he couldn't get her out of his mind. For perhaps the thousandth time since watching her go, he marveled at his stupidity. Deep down, he'd been worried that her relationship with Chet might be starting up again, and what did he do but drive her into his arms.

Brilliant move, Swyteck. Jack was tempted to call her, plead for forgiveness, but some inner voice told him he needed to get his life together—that he was too much at loose ends these days. For now, he stalled.

He had been reduced to counting the motes of dust that swirled in a shaft of sunlight when the phone rang. Cindy, maybe? His face darkened as he considered that it could be the guy who was hassling him. He decided to let the machine pick up.

"Jack," came a woman's voice. But it wasn't Cindy. "This is your—" she began, then stopped. "This is Agnes."

He felt a rush of emotion, of which most was confusion. He hadn't heard Agnes's voice since law school. She sounded worried, but he resisted the urge to pick up.

"I can't be specific, Jack, but there's something going on in your father's life right now that I think you should know about. He's not sick—I mean, your father is definitely healthy. I don't mean to worry you about that. But please call him. And don't tell him I asked you to do it. It's important."

He sat upright, not sure of what to make of the message. He couldn't remember the last time his stepmother had phoned him, but her voice had temporarily taken his mind off Cindy. He *had* caught the slip at the beginning of the message—Agnes's almost saying the words "your mother." Brooding on that phrase, he felt himself drifting back, to when he was five years old . . .

"Your mother isn't dead, she just didn't want you!"

"You're a liar!" Jack screamed as he ran from the family room, leaving his stepmother alone with her gin martini. Tears streamed down his face as he reached his room, slammed the door, and dove into the bed. He *knew* his real mother was dead. Agnes had to be lying when he said his real mother didn't want him. He buried his face in the pillow and cried. After a minute or two he rolled over and stared up at the ceiling. He was thinking about how he could prove to Agnes that she was wrong. At the age of five, he was planning his first case.

He rolled off the bed and went to the door. He peered out and heard the television in the family room. It was less than fifteen feet to his parents' room. As he approached the closed white door, he looked over his shoulder. There'd be big trouble if he were caught. But he went in anyway.

At the far corner of the room, he pulled out the

bottom drawer of the Queen Anne highboy. It was his father's drawer. Jack had first rummaged through it two months earlier, searching for some after-shave he could slap on his face after having "borrowed" his father's electric razor. He hadn't found the after-shave. But tucked beneath the T-shirts and underwear, he *had* found a box. It was a jewelry box, burl maple with fancy, engraved silver initials that Jack couldn't read. The initials were his mother's. His *real* mother's.

As he had that day two months earlier, he lifted the box and opened it. Quickly, he lifted out the top tray of jewelry to reveal the compartment below. There it was. A heavy brass crucifix, concave on the back, the way cookie dough curved when it stuck to the rolling pin, he thought, only not as much. The first time he'd seen the crucifix, the concave back had completely perplexed him. He'd never seen one like that. So, after swearing his grandmother to secrecy, he'd told her about his discovery, and she'd explained the strange shape. It was the crucifix that had lain flat atop the rounded lid of his mother's coffin. His mother was dead, and this was the proof.

He removed the crucifix and put the jewelry box back in the drawer. Squeezing his physical evidence tightly, he left the bedroom and walked determinedly down the hall.

He saw his stepmother on the couch. "You're a liar!" he called out.

Agnes slowly raised her aching head to see Jack standing in the doorway.

He brandished the crucifix from across the room. "See," he said smartly, "my mother's in heaven. You're a liar!"

"Come here, Jack."

He froze.

"Come here!" she shouted.

He swallowed hard, took one timid step back, then turned and ran. "Jack!" she shouted as he scampered down the hall.

He darted into his parents' room, pulled open the drawer to the highboy, and tried to stuff the crucifix back into the box. But Agnes grabbed his arm before he could close the box. "What is *that?*" she demanded.

He stared up at her with fright in his eyes. She saw the initials on the box, and her face was flush with anger. He cringed, waiting for the blow to fall, but when he looked at her again, she seemed lost in thought. "Go to your room," she said distractedly. Once he'd stepped into the hallway, she pulled the door shut . . .

The sound of screeching tires jarred Jack back into the present. He went to the window and parted the curtain. The heavy foliage in the front yard obscured his view of the street, but he thought he saw some movement in the lengthening shadows by the side of the garage.

He got up from the sofa and went to the front door. Outside, the wind was picking up, whipping the palm fronds against the house. He looked around but saw nothing. Slowly, he began walking toward the garage. He felt apprehensive, unsettled. That incident the other day as he was leaving work . . . Agnes's call . . . and now the sound of a car peeling out . . .

He walked along the side of the garage, then in back, squinting in the half-light. Nothing. He doubled around to the front, and that's when he saw Thursday. The dog was struggling to get on all fours, but his legs buckled and he fell on his side.

"Thursday!" Jack rushed to him and cradled his head, then quickly ran his hand along the dog's body to check for wounds. The dog whimpered softly at his master's touch. Red foam was coming from his mouth.

Jack looked around, panicky. No car. *Shit*. Then he remembered. Jeff Zebert, four doors down, was a vet. "Hold on, boy," Jack said. He gathered him up and started running.

Less than thirty seconds later, he was striding up the Zeberts' walkway. Jeff was in the front yard, watering his shrubs. "I've got an emergency here!" Jack called out breathlessly. "It's Thursday," he said. "I think he got into something, poisoned himself."

Jeff dropped the hose. "Do you know what it might have been?"

"Could be anything—here, take a look," Jack said, holding his pet out for the doctor's examination.

The vet glanced quickly at the dog, then instructed Jack to put him on the picnic table. He ran into the house. When he returned, he washed some solution down Thursday's throat with the hose.

"C'mon, boy," Jack said desperately. Thursday lifted his head a few inches, reacting to Jack's voice.

He finally managed to bring something up, but it looked mostly like blood. Jeff tried the hose again, but got no reaction. The animal's paws had stopped shaking. Suddenly, his whimpering stopped and his chest stilled. There was only the sound of running water. Jack looked at the vet.

"I'm sorry, Jack."

Jack couldn't speak, just looked away. Jeff gave him a moment, then touched him on the shoulder. "There's nothing we could have done."

"I shouldn't have left him running around alone. I should have—"

"Jack, really. Don't blame yourself. I don't think it was some poison he just happened to come in contact with. Looks like somebody fed him about a pound of raw hamburger—with two pounds of glass mixed in. Poor guy about swallowed it whole."

"What—" Jack said, disbelieving. Then it began to click into place. "That sick bastard."

"Who?"

"Huh? Oh, nothing. I . . . I just can't believe it that someone would do this."

"Listen," Jeff said, "Why don't you leave him with me. I'll bring him in tomorrow morning and take care of it."

Jack nodded reluctantly. "Thanks." He stared down at Thursday, gave him a last pat on the head, and headed for home. As he walked the gravel path between the two houses, trying to maintain his self-control, it seemed like his whole life was spiraling downward—that he'd entered a dark tunnel and completely lost his bearings. He wondered when—or if—it would end.

He'd been in the house only a few minutes when the phone rang. He was seized with cold fury as he recalled how he'd nearly been run over outside the Freedom Institute, and then gotten a call a few seconds later. He snatched up the phone.

"Listen, you son of a bitch—"

"Jack, it's Jeff," said the vet.

Jack swallowed back his anger. "Sorry. I thought—"

"No problem. I just wanted you to know. After you left, I took a closer look at that stuff Thursday expelled from his stomach. There's not just glass in the meat. There's seeds too. Some kind of flower seeds, it looks like. I don't know if they're poisonous or not, but it was still the glass that killed your dog. I just thought I should mention it."

Jack nodded with comprehension. But he didn't share his thoughts with the vet. "Thanks, Jeff. Maybe it'll help me get a lead on the guy. I'll let you know if I turn up anything."

He hung up the phone. The seeds gave him a lead all right. In fact, they pointed right at Eddy Goss. Jack's most notorious client had explained the meaning of the seeds in Jack's very first in-depth consultation with him. The two of them had been locked alone in a dimly lit, high-security conference room at the county jail, about twelve hours after Goss had confessed on videotape to Detective Lonzo Stafford. Jack had sat passively on one side of the table listening, as his client doted on the details of his crime. Now some of those details—the ones that had earned Goss the nickname "Chrysanthemum Killer"—were coming back.

"Did they find the seed?" Goss asked his lawyer.

Jack lifted his eyes from his yellow notepad, pen in hand, and looked across the table at his client. "The medical examiner found it. It was shoved somewhere beyond her vagina."

Goss sat back in his chair and folded his arms smugly, obviously pleased. "It's a chrysanthemum seed, you know." He arched his eyebrows, as if his lawyer was supposed to see the hidden significance.

Jack just shrugged.

Goss seemed annoyed, almost angry that Jack didn't appreciate his point. "Don't you get it?" Goss asked impatiently.

"No," Jack said with a sigh. "I don't *get* it." *Sigmund Freud wouldn't get you, buddy.*

Goss leaned forward, eager to explain. "Chrysanthemums are the coolest flower in the world, man."

"They remind me of funerals," Jack said.

"Right," Goss answered, pleased that Jack was following along. "Nature *designed* them for funerals. Because funerals are dark, like death. And chrysanthemums love that."

Jack flashed a curious but cautious expression. "What are you talking about?"

Goss warmed to the topic. "The chrysanthemum seed is just really unique. Most flowers bloom when it's warm outside. They love summer and sunshine. But chrysanthemums are different. You plant the seed in the summer, when the ground is nice and warm, but it doesn't do anything. It just sits there. The seed doesn't even start to grow until summer's almost over, when the days get shorter and the nights get cooler. And the cooler and darker it gets, the more the seeds like it. Then, in November—when everything around it's dying, when the ground is getting cold, when the nights are long and the days are cloudy—that's when the big flower pops out."

"So," Jack said warily, "you planted your seed."

"In a warm, dark place," Goss explained. "And that place is going to grow darker and colder every day from now on—until it's the perfect place for my seed to grow."

Jack stared at Goss in stone-faced silence, then scribbled the words "possible insanity defense" on his pad. "How did you learn so much about flowers, Eddy?"

Goss averted his eyes. "When I was a kid in Jersey, there was this man in the neighborhood who had a greenhouse. He grew everything in there," he said with a sly smile. "Me and him used to smoke some of it, too."

"How did you learn about planting the seed? How did you get this idea about planting seeds in a warm, dark place?"

Goss's mouth drew tight. "I don't remember."

"How old were you?"

"Ten or eleven," he said with a shrug.

"And how old was the man?"

"Old . . . not real old."

Jack leaned forward and spoke firmly, but with

understanding. "What did you used to do in there, Eddy? With that man?"

Goss's eyes flared, and his hands started to shake. "I said I don't *remember*. Something wrong with your ears, man?"

"No, I just want you to try to remember—"

"Just get the fuck outta here!" Goss shouted. "Meeting's over. I got nothing more to say."

"Just take it easy—"

"I said, get your ass outta here!"

Jack nodded, then packed up his bag and rose from his chair. "We'll talk again." He turned and stepped toward the locked metal security door.

"Hey," Goss called out.

Jack stopped and looked back at him.

"You're gonna get me out of here, aren't you?"

"I'm going to represent you," Jack said.

Goss narrowed his eyes. "You have to get me outta here." He leaned forward in his chair to press his point. "You *have* to. I have a *lot* more seeds to sow."

As Jack stood in his living room recalling that conversation, the memory still gave him a chill. He sighed, shook his head. If the situation wasn't so serious, he'd laugh at the irony. He'd secured a psychopath's acquittal, only to find himself the man's next target.

But was he really Goss's target? Of his rancor, maybe. But Jack found it hard to believe that Goss would actually do him physical harm. He seemed more comfortable confronting overmatched women and small animals.

He had more than enough to get a restraining

order against Goss, if he wanted one. But he wasn't sure that was the answer. The legal system had failed once before to stop Eddy Goss—thanks to him.

So it was up to Jack to find something that would work, once and for all.

It was just after 11:00 P.M.—bedtime at the governor's mansion. Harry Swyteck was in his pajamas, sitting up in bed against the brass headboard, reading a recent *Florida Trend* magazine article about acquitted killer Eddy Goss. Toward the end of the story, his irritation ripened into anger as the writer delivered a fusillade of criticism against Goss's "argue-anything" lawyer, Jack Swyteck. "They call this *balanced* journalism?" the governor muttered as he threw down the magazine.

A few seconds later, Agnes emerged from the bathroom in her robe and slippers. She stopped at the table by the window and tended to a bouquet of flowers, her back to her husband.

"Thank you for the flowers, Harry," she said, her body blocking his view of the bouquet.

"Huh," said the governor, looking over. He hadn't sent any flowers. Today wasn't a birthday, anniversary, or any other occasion he could think of that called for flowers. But it wasn't inconceivable that in all the campaign commotion he'd forgotten a special day and one of his staff had covered for him. So he just played along. "Oh," he replied, "you're welcome, dear. I hope you like them."

"It's nice to get things for no reason," she said with a sparkle in her eye. "It was so spontaneous of you." Her mouth curled suggestively. Then she stepped away from the table, revealing the bouquet, and the governor went white.

"Keep the bed warm," she said as she disappeared into her walk-in closet, but the governor wasn't listening. His eyes were fixed on the bouquet of big white, pink, and yellow chrysanthemums perched on the table. He rose from the bed and stepped toward the bouquet. The card was still in the holder. Harry's hand trembled as he opened the envelope. It suddenly seemed so obvious: the disguised voice, the threats, the photographs of a gruesome murder, and now the flowers. His mind raced, making a logical link between the "Chrysanthemum Killer," whose weird pathology had been mentioned in the article he'd just been reading, and the blackmailer.

He read the message. Instantly, he knew it was intended for him, not his wife. "You and me forever," it read, "till death do us part."

"Eddy Goss," the governor muttered softly to himself, his voice cracking with fear. *I'm being blackmailed by a psychopath.*

13
•

The following morning, Monday, Jack picked up his Mustang from the garage and went to A&G Alarm Company, where he arranged to have a security system immediately installed in his house. By noon he had new locks on the doors and was thinking about escape plans. He still couldn't bring himself to believe that Goss would try to kill him, but it would be foolish not to take precautions. He imagined the worst-case scenarios—an attack in the middle of the night or an ambush in the parking lot—and planned in advance how he would respond. And he called the telephone company. In two days he'd have a new, unlisted phone number.

But there was one basic precaution he decided not to take. He didn't call the police because he still felt the cops would do little to protect Eddy Goss's lawyer. Besides, he had another idea. That afternoon he bought ammunition for his gun.

It wasn't actually *his* gun. He'd inherited a .38-caliber

pistol from Donna Boyd, an old flame at Yale. Most people didn't know it, but crime was a problem in certain areas of New Haven where many students lived off campus. After Jack's neighbor had been robbed, Donna had refused to sleep over anymore unless Jack kept her gun in the nightstand. Even for an independent-minded Yale coed, she was a bit unconventional. He agreed but took the precaution of signing up for a few shooting lessons at the local range. He didn't want to make a mistake they'd both regret.

As it turned out, the gun stayed in his drawer until after graduation, when he was packing for Miami. By that point, he and Donna had broken up and she'd been bitter enough to leave town without stopping by to pick up her things. A mutual friend said she'd gone to Europe. So Jack had just packed the gun away with her racquet-ball racket and Elvis Costello CD and forgotten about it until now.

Suddenly, he had a use for the gun that had lain in his footlocker for the last six years, last registered in Connecticut, in the name of Donna Boyd.

Jack had never considered violence an answer to anything. But this was something altogether different. This was truly self-defense. Or was it? Deep down, he wondered if he actually hoped Goss would break into his house. As he sat back in the sofa in his living room with the ammunition he'd just purchased, he thought hard about his real motivation for not calling the cops. But the possibility that he was subconsciously looking for a showdown with Goss was ridiculous. Goss was the killer. Not him.

The phone rang. Jack muted the nine o'clock Movie of the Week on TV and snatched it up.

"Have you checked your mail, Jack?" came the familiar voice.

He hesitated. He knew that stalkers thrived on contact, and that any "expert" would have told him just to hang up. But he was nearly certain he knew who it was, and if he could just get him to speak in his normal voice, he'd have confirmation. "This is not *clever*, Goss," Jack goaded. "Knock off the funny voice. I know it's you."

A condescending snicker came over the phone, then a pause—followed by a decided change in tone. "You don't know shit, Swyteck. So just shut up, and check your mail. *Now.*"

Jack blinked hard, frightened by how easily he'd set off the man's temper. "Why?"

"Just check it," the caller ordered. "And take the phone with you. I'll tell you what to look for."

Jack wondered whether it was wise to play along, but he was determined to get to the bottom of this. "All right," he answered, then headed down the hall with his portable phone pressed to his ear. He looked through the window before stepping outside but saw nothing. He opened the front door and stepped onto the porch. "Okay," he said into the phone. "I'm at the box."

"Look inside," the caller ordered.

Cautiously, Jack reached for the lid on the mailbox beside the door. He extended one finger, pried under the lid, and quickly popped it open, jerking his hand back as if he'd just touched molten lava.

"Do you see it, Swyteck?"

Jack stood on his toes and peered inside from a distance, fearful that he was about to see bloody gym shorts or torn panties or some other evidence of Goss's latest handiwork. "There's an envelope," he said, seeing nothing else inside.

"Open it," said the caller.

Jack carefully took the envelope from the box. It was plain white. No return address. No addressee. It had been hand-delivered, which meant the stalker had been on his porch—an unsettling thought. He unfolded the flap and tentatively removed the contents. "What is this?"

"What's it look like?"

He studied the page. "A map." A route had been high-lighted by yellow felt-tip pen.

"Follow it—if you want to know who the killer on the loose is. You *do* want to know, don't you, Swyteck?"

"I already know it's you, Goss. This is a map to your apartment."

"It's a map to the killer on the loose. Be there. Meet him at four-thirty A.M. tonight. And no cops. Or you'll be *very* sorry."

Jack bristled at the sound of the dial tone, then switched off the portable phone. At first it didn't even occur to him to actually go to Goss's apartment. But if Goss were going to kill him, would he do it in his own apartment? Would he *invite* Jack over and give him directions to the scene of the crime? No, he must be up to something else, and Jack's curiosity was piqued.

But it was more than just curiosity. He was thinking of the night two years ago when he'd refused to give his father enough "privileged" information to stop Raul Fernandez's execution. His rigidity had resulted in Raul's death, and he was determined not to make the same mistake again. In dealing with a confessed killer who was continuing his evil ways, he *had* to be more flexible with privileged information.

It was time to issue an ultimatum. Months ago, when he and Goss had been considering an insanity defense, Jack had pumped him for information about his past crimes—some of which included murder. His client had told him plenty. Now it was time to confront Goss and let him know that if he wanted to stay out of the electric chair—if he didn't want a prosecutor to get an anonymous tip about his most perverted secrets—then he'd better change his ways.

He stepped to the window and looked outside. It was getting dark and starting to drizzle. A storm was brewing. If he was going to meet Goss, there was no reason to wait until four-thirty in the morning. In fact, it seemed safer *not* to wait. He started toward the door, then stopped. He went up to the attic, opened his footlocker, and found the .38. Downstairs, he spent several minutes cleaning the gun, then loaded it with bullets.

Just in case.

14

Rain started to fall as Jack pulled his Mustang out of the driveway. The downpour was a continuation of a violent Florida thunderstorm that had flooded city streets that afternoon. The nasty weather didn't bring him down, though. He was determined to get to Goss's as quickly as possible, before he could change his mind. He raced his old eight-cylinder down the expressway at a speed only a fleeing fugitive would have considered safe, exited into a section of town that *no one* considered safe, and screeched to a halt outside Goss's apartment.

The old two-story building stretched nearly a third of the city block. It was bordered on one side by a gas station and on the other by a burned-out shell of an apartment building that some pyromaniac landlord had probably figured could generate more income in fire-insurance proceeds than in rent. Rusty iron security bars covered most of the ground-floor windows, plywood sealed off others, and noisy air conditioners stuck out of a few. Weeds popping up through cracks in the sidewalk were the closest thing to landscaping.

The rain beat loudly on the convertible's canvas top and seeped in where the twenty-year-old rubber window seals had rotted away. Jack jumped out and dashed through water that ran in wide rivulets down the street. He was at the apartment entrance in only fifteen seconds, but that was long enough for the rain to soak his clothes and paste them to his body. Dripping wet, he stepped inside the dimly lit foyer and checked the rows of metal mailboxes recessed into the wall. He had the right place. GOSS, APT 217, read one of them.

He ran up a flight of stairs to a long hallway lined with apartments on either side. It was even darker here than in the foyer, the tenants having stolen most of the bulbs to light their apartments. Spray-painted graffiti covered the walls and doors, forming one continuous mural. Most of the ceiling tiles had been punched out by kids proving how high they could jump. Rainwater leaked in from above and streaked down the water-stained walls, forming little puddles on the musty indoor-outdoor carpet. All was quiet, except for heavy raindrops pounding on the flimsy flat roof.

He started down the hall, checking the numbers on the doors that still had them. His pace quickened as he approached 217, the fifth door on the left. He was convinced that the only way to stop Goss was to threaten him—and to do so in a way that only his own lawyer could. If Goss was to report him to the Florida bar for threatening to reveal a client's secrets, it could end his career. But it didn't matter at this point. The stark contrast between his one tragic failure in the Fernandez case and his string of "successes" in sending men like Goss back onto the streets to prey on an unwary public had weighed on him too long. He'd reached the lowest point of his life.

Jack knocked on the hollow wood door to Goss's apartment, then waited. No one answered, but he refused to believe that Goss wasn't there. He knocked harder, almost banging. Still no answer. "Goss," he said loudly. "I know it's you. Answer the door!"

"Hey!" an angry man shouted from an open apartment doorway down the hall. "It's ten o'clock, man. I got a two-year-old here. Cut the racket."

Jack took a deep breath. He'd been so focused in his pursuit of Goss that he'd acted as if no one else lived in the building. That was a stupid approach, he realized. So he stepped back from the door and slowly headed down the hall, as if to leave. As soon as Goss's neighbor retreated into his apartment, Jack quietly but quickly returned to apartment 217 and turned the knob. It was unlocked. He hesitated and listened for footsteps on the inside. Nothing. He pushed the door open slowly, about a foot, and peered inside. All was dark and quiet. He pushed it open further, about halfway, and stood in the open doorway.

"Goss," he said in a firm voice. Then he waited.

There was no reply, only the sound of heavy tropical rain tapping on the roof and against the window on the other side of the room. Jack swallowed hard. As he saw it, he had two choices. He could turn and walk away, his tail between his legs. If he did, it would only be a matter of time before he got another threat, before the violence escalated further. His other choice—the only *real* choice—was to do something right then.

He discreetly checked the hallway, but saw no one. Then he stared nervously into the dark apartment. He could hear his heart pounding and feel his palms begin to sweat. He took a deep breath and reached deep inside himself for the strength he needed. Slowly and very cautiously, he entered the dark, deathly quiet apartment of Eddy Goss.

"Goss," Jack said again, standing just inside the open door. "It's Swyteck. You and I need to talk, so come on out."

When after a few seconds there was no response, Jack reached out and flipped the light switch by the door. But no lights came on.

A huge bolt of lightning cracked just outside, sending his heart to his throat. The storm was worsening, the heavy rain pelting against the room's only window. Another large bolt struck even closer, bathing the small room in a burst of eerie white light. Jack got a mental snapshot, hastening his eyes' adjustment to the layout of the apartment. The kitchen, dining, and living areas were one continuous room. A ghostly white bed sheet covered the window. Furniture was sparse—he noticed only a beaten-up old couch, a floor lamp, a kitchen table, and one folding chair. The walls were bare, but there were a few plants. Not your ordinary houseplants. These were big and colorful crucifixes, Stars of David, and other tributes to the dead, all made of chrysanthemums and other fresh flowers, apparently stolen by Goss from graves at the local cemetery. Jack felt anger rising in him as he read one pink ribbon inscribed OUR BE-LOVED DAUGHTER. He looked away in disgust, then noticed a door across the room that led to the bed-room. It was open.

Whit-whooooo, came a sudden shrill-pitched whistle from the bedroom, like a catcall at the girls on the beach. Jack coiled, ready for an attack.

Whit-whoooo came the sound again, a little louder this time.

His heart raced. The urge to turn and run was almost irresistible, but his feet refused to retreat. Slowly, he forced one foot in front of the other, sur-prising even himself as he moved closer to the bed-room. He took deliberate, stalking steps, trying to minimize the squeak in his rain-soaked tennis shoes. He stared at the open doorway as he steadily crossed the room, his eyes wide with intense concentration, his every sense alert to what might be inside the bed-room. He flinched slightly as heavy thunder rum-bled in the distance. He halted just two steps away from the open door.

Whit-whooooo came the whistle again.

The whistling spooked Jack, but it was also begin-ning to anger him. The bastard was taunting him. This was all just a game to Goss. And Jack knew the rules by which Goss played his games. He took the loaded gun from his pocket.

"Eddy," he called out. "Cut the game-playing, all right? I just want to talk to you."

Thunder clapped as a flash of lightning filled the room with strobelike light. Jack took a half step forward, and then another. He glanced at the kitchen table beside him. There was a dirty plate with dried ketchup and remnants of Goss's fish-stick dinner. An empty Coke bottle. A fork. And a steak knife. The sight of the knife made Jack glad he had his gun. He raised his weapon to chest level, clutching it with both hands. His hands were shaking, but he wasn't about to stop now. He took the last step and peered inside the bedroom.

A sudden shriek sent Jack flying backward. He saw something—a figure, a shadow, an attacker! But as he took a step back and tried to squeeze off a shot, he lost his balance. He collided with the floor lamp, sending it careening across the carpet. For a second he was on his hands and knees, then he struggled to his feet, panting from the burst of excitement. The fight was over as quickly as it had started. "A stupid cockatoo," he said aloud, but with a sigh of relief.

Whit-whooooo, the bird whistled at him, perched on his pedestal.

Jack flinched, suddenly panicked by what sounded like footsteps in the hall. He didn't want to have to explain himself to someone checking on the noise. He shoved the gun into his pants, ran from the bedroom, and pushed up the window to open it. But it raised only six inches. A nail inside the frame put there by a previous tenant as a crude form of security kept it from opening all the way. Jack's heart raced as he thought he heard the footsteps in the hall getting closer. He quickly scanned the room, grabbed the steak knife from Goss's dinner table, and used it like a claw hammer to work the nail free. At first the nail wouldn't budge, but then it suddenly popped out. As it did, the knife slipped and sliced Jack across the back of his left hand. He was bleeding, but was too scared to feel the pain. He tossed the knife back toward the table and climbed out the open window. He climbed down the rickety fire escape like a middle-schooler on monkey bars, letting himself drop the last ten feet and landing with a splash in an ankle-deep puddle. He ran around the building and back to his car as fast as he could, then pulled away slowly, realizing that the faster he went, the more suspicious he'd look.

As he drove he took several deep breaths, trying to collect himself. He checked the back of his left hand. The cut was fairly deep and still bleeding, but it didn't look like he'd need stitches. He steered with his wounded hand and applied pressure with the other to stop the bleeding.

"Damn," Jack cursed at himself—and at that stupid cockatoo. That bird had scared the hell out of him. It seemed strange that Goss would own a bird—that he'd care about any living creature. But then it made sense as he thought of the bird pecking at his food around the pedestal. Seeds. There had been all kinds of seeds—the seeds of the Chrysanthemum Killer. Jack thought again of Goss's comment: "I still have a lot of seeds to sow."

As he put more distance between himself and Goss's apartment, he re-evaluated the events that had drawn him there—the phone call, the map, the invitation to meet the "killer on the loose." It made him think through Goss's gradual escalation of violence and what might be the logical next step after killing his dog. He was suddenly afraid his instincts had been right. Goss was not luring him to his apartment to kill *him* but, rather, someone else.

"Cindy," Jack said aloud, frantically weighing the possibility. Maybe he was giving Goss too much credit, but on the other hand, this madman could have lured him to his apartment at exactly 4:30 A.M. to make sure Cindy would be alone—so that Goss could sow another seed.

Jack punched the accelerator to the floor and raced toward Gina's apartment, steering with one hand and dialing his car phone with the other. It wasn't even midnight yet, let alone 4:30 A.M., but he was not taking any chances.

"Come on," Jack groaned at the busy signal from Gina's apartment. He tried the number again. It was still busy, so he asked the operator to interrupt. "Yes, it is definitely an emergency," he said firmly.

But Gina refused to let him cut in.

"What do you mean, she won't *let* me?" he asked with disbelief. But the operator gave no explanation.

He switched off the phone and drove even faster, fearing the worst.

15
.

Seven minutes later the Mustang careened over a speed bump and squealed to a stop outside Gina's condominium. Jack jumped out, devoured two steps at a time on the stairway to Gina's front door, and then knocked firmly. He paced frantically until Gina finally opened up.

"Is everything okay?" he asked. "Are you all right?"

Gina stood in the doorway, wearing a tight-fitting white denim mini and a loose red tank top that revealed as much of her breasts as any wandering eye cared to see.

"Where's Cindy?" he demanded.

"Cindy's out."

"Out where?"

Gina made a face. "Out being twisted like a pretzel by a squadron of Chippendale dancers. It's none of your business *where* she is. She's out."

"I have to find her. I think someone may be after her."

"Yeah," Gina scoffed, hands resting on her hips. "*You* are."

Jack stiff-armed the door to keep Gina from shutting it in his face. "I'm not making this up. Ever since the Goss trial ended, someone's been following me—making threats. Some guy with a raspy voice called me and said there was a killer on the loose. He tried to run me over with his car. He killed my dog. And now he might be after Cindy."

Gina's face finally registered concern. "Cindy's safe," she said coolly. "After you two had your little Saturday morning brawl, she decided to catch an earlier flight to Rome. We went by the house this afternoon, while you were out, and cleaned out her closet. Then I dropped her off at the airport. She's on her way to Italy."

"Oh," he said, "that's great." But he didn't feel great. He was relieved that she was safe, but he was having a hard time adjusting to the fact that she was actually gone. Some part of him was wishing he had had one last chance to explain himself to her.

Gina watched as he turned to leave. It amazed her the way Jack looked after Cindy, even after they'd split up. Gina had definitely felt rejected last year, when Jack had dropped her for Cindy after their one blind date. And although Jack and Cindy were both denying it to themselves, she was convinced that the trip to Italy would be the end of their relationship—which only made her wonder, as she'd often wondered before, just what it would take to get Jack to notice *her*.

"And what about me?" she said, arching her eyebrow as he looked back at her quizzically. "What if this lunatic comes looking for Cindy, and I'm here all alone?"

"What do you want me to do?"

"Stay," she said. "Just in case something happens."

His mouth opened, but his speech was on a several-second delay. "I don't think—"

"You think too much, Jack. That's your whole problem. Come on, I'll buy you a drink. Maybe I'll even give you the lowdown on how truly 'professional' Cindy's so-called business trip to Italy is," she said coyly as she stepped back, inviting Jack inside.

He flinched. He wanted to think that she was yanking his chain about Cindy, but her insinuation had the ring of truth—especially since she'd packed up her clothes and left this afternoon without giving him a chance to apologize. In any event, after everything he'd been through over the last week, he saw no harm in not being alone—especially if his company could fill him in on what Cindy was really thinking. "Make it a Scotch," he said. "On the rocks."

Jack followed Gina inside the townhouse, through the foyer and living room. The downstairs was one big room, done in white tile, black lacquer, chrome and glass, with some large abstract acrylic paintings, Persian rugs, and dried flowers for color.

"Here," she said as she tossed him a terrycloth robe. "Let me put those wet clothes in the dryer for you."

He hesitated, even though he *was* soaked.

"Believe me, Jack," she half-kidded, "if I wanted

you out of your clothes, I'd be far less subtle. Now get in there and change before you catch pneumonia."

He retreated into the bathroom and peeled off his wet clothes—which left him with the problem of what to do with the gun in his pants pocket. He didn't want to do any more explaining to Gina. He removed the bullets, wrapped them with the gun in a washcloth, and slid the wad into one of the robe's deep pockets. The knife wound on his left hand had stopped bleeding, so he carefully rinsed away some of the dried blood. He emerged with his hand in his pocket. Gina took his clothes and tossed them into the dryer, then led him to the kitchen.

"You did say Scotch," said Gina.

"Right," he replied. He watched from the bar stool across the kitchen counter as she filled his glass. The kitchen's bright fluorescent lights afforded him a really good look at his ex-girlfriend's best friend. *Gorgeous*, he thought, *absolutely gorgeous*. She had dark, glistening eyes, set off against a smooth olive complexion; he imagined there were no tan lines beneath her tight white miniskirt. Her only flaw was an ever-so-slightly crooked smile, noticeable only because it was accentuated by her bright red lip gloss. The imperfection was enough to have kept her from becoming a teenage supermodel, but Jack didn't see it as an imperfection.

"Here you are," she said as she handed him his glass.

He nodded appreciatively, then downed most of the drink.

"Tough night?" she teased, pouring him a refill.

"Tough month," he quipped.

A gleam came to Gina's eye. "I've got just the thing for you. Let's do Jagermeisters."

"Excuse me?"

"Shots," she said as she lined up a couple of glasses on the counter. "It's just a cordial."

"I don't think—"

"I told you," she interrupted, "you think too much." She poured two shots, more in Jack's glass than hers, then handed him one. "Prost," she said, toasting in German.

Their heads jerked back in unison as they downed the shots.

Gina smiled. "Good start. Have another," she said as she filled his glass.

The second was gone as quickly as the first.

"Whoa," Jack wheezed.

Gina filled his glass again.

"What's in this stuff?" he asked, his throat burning.

"Drink that one. Then I'll tell you."

He hesitated, reminding himself he was there to keep a lid on things. It wouldn't do to be half-in-the-bag if Goss showed up. "Gina, I think I've had enough."

"C'mon," she pouted. "Just one more. Relax"—she looked over her shoulder—"the lock on that door is strong enough to keep the bogeyman out."

It was no use. She raised the shot glass to his lips, and he reluctantly swallowed.

She smirked at the glazed look on his face. "It's from Germany. It's actually illegal in most of this country. Something about the opium in it."

"Opium?" His jaw dropped.

Gina smiled wryly. "You'll be totally shit-faced in about ninety seconds."

He took a deep breath. He was already feeling something considerably more than an ordinary buzz. He grabbed the edge of the counter to keep his bearings. "I've got to go," he said.

She leaned across the counter and looked into his eyes. He blinked and looked away only to get an eyeful of cleavage, which made him shift awkwardly, as if his personal space had been invaded.

"I really should go," he said. But he didn't pull back.

"I know a couple of ways to make you stay," she said slyly.

"Such as?"

"Bribery, for one," she said quietly.

He swallowed hard. "And the other?"

Her eyes slowly narrowed. "Torture!" she said as she grabbed his ribs and pinched hard, laughing as she turned and stepped away.

"Oww!" Jack groaned. It had really hurt, but he knew she was just playing and tried to smile. "Could we maybe stick to bribery?"

"Whatever you want," she whispered as she handed him another Scotch, then directed him toward the living room with a casual wave of her hand. She twisted the dimmer switch, lowering the overhead lighting, then sauntered toward her stereo, walking the way she always did when she knew a man was watching her.

At first he couldn't help but admire the gentle sway

of her curves as she crossed the room. He was certain Gina was coming on to him. And after a month of personal, professional, and public rejection, he was definitely starting to feel too weak, too lonely, and too drunk to put a stop to it, particularly after she'd re-kindled his doubts about the "purely professional" na-ture of Cindy's trip.

"Take a load off," Gina said from behind, knock-ing him onto the couch. She fell in next to him, and they were instantly swallowed by the fabric of her overstuffed couch. She kicked off her shoes and drew her knees up onto the cushion. She scooted closer to Jack, stirred the ice in his drink with her finger, and then licked it off.

She leaned into him, her firm breasts pressing against his arm and her hand falling onto his hip. He suddenly thought of Cindy, which made him tense up.

"What are you, a linebacker?" she grumbled as she gave him a little shove. She reached across his lap, grabbed the remote control from the end table, and flipped on the stereo, preset for Gato Barbieri's "Europa."

"Oh, sorry," he said with a nervous smile, now realizing what all the pushing was about.

"I *love* Gato," she interrupted him. "You like the sax?"

Jack coughed into his drink, thinking she'd said "sex."

"I think it's the sexiest instrument ever invented," she said as she leaned back, clearly enjoying the mood of the music. "Have you ever watched a man play the sax, Jack? I mean *really* watched him, in a jazz bar, late at night? The lighting is always dimmed, just so. The smoke rises in the room in a certain fuzzy way, as if it's all a fantasy. And then the musician makes love to his instrument, his lips pressed to the mouthpiece, his eyes closed tightly while his face displays his every emotion. It's like a man with the confidence, the courage, the balls, or whatever it takes to cry, or to make love or to reveal himself, all at the same time, with the whole world watching. How can they be so free? I don't know how they do it . . . but it affects me deep inside when they do." She leaned toward him and stared deeply into his eyes.

Once again he hesitated. That was the most articulate he had ever known Gina to be. *Bet you've given that little speech a few times before,* he wanted to say.

She moved closer. "Could you do that?" she whispered.

"Could I what?" he played dumb.

"Let yourself go," she answered. "Turn yourself inside out. And enjoy it."

He sighed. There was indeed a woman who made him feel that way, who could strip him down to a desire so intense that he could have stood naked to the world and yet felt like the most powerful man on the planet. Then something happened. It wasn't his fault or hers. It just happened. And nothing had been the same since. "I suppose it depends on who I'm with."

She smiled, only to have her next move interrupted by the shrill ring of the telephone.

Cindy? asked his guilty conscience.

Gina sprang from the couch, snatched up the phone, and carried it to the other side of the room, as far away from Jack as the cord would allow her to travel. She hissed something into the receiver, slammed it down, and walked back toward him, an intense look of desire having replaced the anger in her eyes.

"My old boyfriend," she volunteered as she took her place next to Jack, "Antoine. Guy buys me a BMW and he thinks he owns me for life. He calls whenever he figures I have a date. Kind of pathetic," she shrugged, "but he just doesn't want anyone else to have me."

"Does this Antoine own a gun?" Jack only half-kidded.

The phone rang again. Gina jumped up, angrier than before. She grabbed the phone and threw it at the floor. "Asshole!" she shouted, as if Antoine could hear her. She sighed deeply to collect herself, then returned to Jack and knelt beside him on the couch. "Now," she said softly, "where were we?"

He edged away from her. "I think we were talking about . . . Antoine," he said nervously.

"Antoine," she scoffed. "What I wouldn't give for someone who could make me forget I ever knew a silly *boy* named Antoine."

Their eyes met and held. Jack started to say something, but the clothes dryer buzzed, and he looked away, distracted. "I think I'm ready. I mean, my clothes are ready," he said as he pushed himself up from the couch. His knees shook, the room spun, and he was back on the couch in a split second.

"I don't think you're going anywhere tonight."

"I really should go."

"No way," she said as she jiggled the car keys she'd taken from his pants before tossing them into the dryer. "Friends don't let out-of-town girlfriends' ex-boyfriends drive drunk. You're staying here tonight."

"I—"

"Don't argue," she interrupted him. "It's already after midnight, and your clothes probably aren't even dry yet. I'll sleep in Cindy's bed—too many bad vibes in there for you. You can sleep in mine. Come on," she said as she rose from the couch, pulling him by the elbow.

He wobbled to his feet, drunker than he'd been since college. He knew he couldn't drive, and part of him was glad he couldn't. "All right. I'll stay."

Gina held on to his arm and guided him across the room, toward the stairway. They were both startled as they heard the sudden pulsating noise of the phone off the hook. Together they glanced at the screaming receiver on the floor and then at each other, as if to see whether either would make the move to put it back on the hook. The noise stopped on its own, and they let the phone lie on the floor. No more Antoine. No more interruptions. It was just Jack and Gina. Gina the man-eater. Jack shook his arm loose from her grasp and followed her up the stairs.

"Time for bed," she sang as she led him to her bedroom. The hallway lighting gave the room a warm glow. He sat on the edge of the bed and watched as she turned down the sheets. He wondered how many men had been in Gina's bed. He figured he'd be the first to sleep in it without sleeping *with* her.

"If you need anything, I'm right across the hall."

"Good night," he said.

Gina disappeared into the hallway, leaving the door open. She turned off the hallway light, and Jack was in total darkness. He started to remove his robe, but felt uncomfortable about being naked in Gina's bed, so he left it on. He removed the washcloth containing the gun and the bullets from his pocket and laid it on the nightstand, then crawled between the sheets. His head was buzzing. The shots Gina had poured him would surely give him a splitting headache in the morning, but at least they would speed him toward a deep and much needed sleep. He was nearly gone when a light suddenly flashed in his eyes, stirring him from his rest. It was the hallway light, but it seemed to shine like a flashlight right into his eyes. He raised his head groggily from the pillow and strained to make out the figure in the darkness. Someone was standing in the doorway, the backlighting from the hallway making the image a silhouette.

"I couldn't sleep," Gina's voice cut through the darkness.

He propped himself up on his elbow, his eyes adjusting. She was posing like a pinup, one hand on her hip and the other on the door frame. Her long brown hair was pulled to one side in a bushy ponytail that seemed to flow from her ear like water from a hydrant. A gold hoop earring dangled from the other side. She was naked, except for a silk sash around her waist.

"I need my own bed," she said.

Jack pulled back the covers and stood up, but she was already on him, pushing him gently toward the bed.

"Let me find my own way," she said in a low voice.

He searched for his conscience as his head hit the pillow, but Gina's earlier remarks had him feeling foolish about waiting for Cindy while she traveled around Italy with her old boyfriend, and in his drunken, semidream state he was well beyond resistance. Gina started at the foot of the king-size bed and worked her way up, touching and tasting beneath his robe, demonstrating skills that he had only known as fantasies—until the caresses turned to pain.

"Oww!" Jack withdrew. "That hurt!"

"Oh, come on," Gina smiled playfully, looking up from between his legs. "It's a fine line, isn't it—pleasure and pain?"

"Not *that* fine. I'm gonna have fucking bruises."

"Just relax," she said as she removed his robe. Then she swung her leg over him and sent him into a state of arousal that bordered on the uncontrollable. She was on top of him, but not touching him. She was teasing, tempting, torturing him. She kissed him on the chest, gently pulling his hair with her teeth. He winced at the pain, then felt the pleasure of her gentle kiss around his mouth. In a sudden lucid moment, it flashed through his mind that he hadn't made love to anyone but Cindy in a long time. But this wasn't about making love.

"Tell me," Gina breathed heavily down his neck, her lips touching his as she spoke. "Tell me what you want."

"I want you," he said, caught up in her passion.

She probed and pressed with her fingers, touching him at his center of gravity. "Tell me exactly what you want," she whispered.

"I want to be inside you," he said.

She stared down at him, amused by his euphemism. "I want you to *fuck* me," she said with fire in her eyes, then pressed her body against his and rolled, pulling him on top of her. He entered with a rush, pushing out a horrible month's worth of anger, frustration, and rejection, taking delight in her moans and groans as her long, red nails attacked his back.

Suddenly, Jack froze. "Did you hear that?" he asked quickly, his body completely rigid.

"Hear what?" Gina said with a satisfied smile.

"That thumping noise."

Gina answered with a flick of her tongue. "That's the headboard pounding against the wall, you stud."

"No. It's downstairs."

"Stop it," she said sharply. "Don't do this to me, Jack."

"I'm not fooling around, Gina. Did you lock the front door like you said?"

"Of course."

"And the sliding doors in back?"

"Always locked," she replied, "when the A.C. is on."

"That wouldn't stop Goss—if it is Goss." He slid out from between her thighs. "I know I heard something." He rolled off the bed without a sound, walked cautiously toward the bedroom door, and leaned forward, listening intently. He put the robe back on and took the gun from the nightstand.

"You brought a *gun* into my house," she said angrily.

"Yeah—and aren't you glad I did?"

"No. Please, Jack. No shoot-outs. Just call the police."

"I can't. The phone's off the hook."

Gina grimaced, as if for the first time in her life she regretted her craziness.

He checked the chambers to make sure the gun was fully loaded. It was. "I'll take a look downstairs," he said. "You stay here."

"Don't worry," she assured him.

He opened the door carefully, holding the pistol out in front of him. The hall was dark. The apartment was still. He quietly stepped out and closed the bedroom door. He heard Gina lock it behind him; there was no turning back. He peered down the stairway but saw nothing. He stepped forward and slowly descended the first four steps. From his vantage point he could see most of the downstairs, but none of the kitchen. He noticed the phone on the floor by the couch, still off the hook. He took a few more steps and waited at the bottom of the stairs. He saw nothing, heard nothing, felt only the pounding of his heart. Slowly, he crossed the living room and placed the phone back on the hook. He turned and gasped as he noticed the front door—it was wide open.

He jumped back at a sudden burst of noise from outside. Then he realized it was his car alarm, blasting from the parking lot. Instinctively, he bolted out of the apartment and raced down the steps, leaving the door open behind him. He reached his car and froze as he saw firsthand one of the more obvious reasons that even a twenty-year-old convertible needed an alarm: The black canvas top was in shreds, sliced open from windshield to rear window.

"I can't believe this," Jack said to himself. An instant later his head was snapped around by the sound of a shrill scream from inside Gina's townhouse. He rushed back up the stairs and dashed inside.

"Jack!" Gina cried from upstairs—in Cindy's bedroom.

He led with his gun as he raced up the stairs and burst into the room. Gina stood in her green satin robe, frozen beside Cindy's brass bed. She was alone. He caught his breath and stared. The pink bedspread had been neatly turned down, revealing clean white sheets that were smeared with something bright red and wet that looked like blood. He reached down and touched it.

"Ketchup," Gina said, nodding toward the empty bottle on the floor, which had been taken from her refrigerator.

He cautiously approached Cindy's bed, his gut wrenching as he imagined what might have happened here tonight. He knew better than to touch anything, but he could tell there was something beneath Cindy's pillow—something, he figured, that whoever had been here tonight had wanted him to find. He gently took the corner of the pillowcase between his fingertips. Slowly, with arms fully extended so that he could stand as far away as possible, he raised the pillow.

"Jack," her voice trembled, "what the hell are you doing?"

He ignored her. He kept lifting, slowly, until he saw it. A flower—a chrysanthemum.

"Goss," he said as he lowered the pillow back into place.

Suddenly, the phone rang. Jack's eyes locked with Gina's. Her panicked expression said there was no way she was going to pick up. "Hello," he answered, trying to sound calm.

Four blocks away at a pay phone on the street, a man in torn blue jeans and a yellowed undershirt stood in the murky shadows of a flickering streetlight, pressing the receiver to his ear and covering the mouthpiece with a rag. "You came early to my party," he said accusingly.

Jack took a deep breath. It was the same voice, but the tone was different. The man was breathing heavily, as if he'd been running, and his voice trembled as he spoke.

"You came early, Swyteck. And now I'm *very* angry."

Jack stayed on the line but was unable to speak, paralyzed by the crazed panting of a madman so furious he was gasping for breath. "Please," Jack said, "let's talk."

"I said four-thirty A.M.," he seethed. "And I meant four-thirty A.M. This is your last chance. Be there—at *four-thirty*."

Jack started to say something, but the phone went dead. His hand shook as he hung up.

"What was that?" Gina asked with fear.

He looked at her. "My final invitation," he said.

16

·

Two hours later, Miami was in its deepest phase of sleep, that eerie, silent period just after the last drunk makes it home for the evening and just before the first early bird leaves for work. There was a knocking, then a pounding at the door. Eddy Goss rose from his bed and listened, wondering if he'd really heard something. Another round of pounding told him he wasn't dreaming. He rolled out of bed and paused, letting his eyes adjust to the darkness. He couldn't switch on a light; they'd shut the power off when he failed to pay his last bill. He took small, precarious steps out of his bedroom and toward the door, somewhat leery of answering the knock. He reached under the couch cushion and retrieved his revolver, then pressed his face to the door and looked through the peephole. The bulb hanging outside his apartment was out, and all he could distinguish was a distorted silhouette. He recognized the dark blue police uniform, however, so he tucked the gun away. Convicted felons weren't allowed to have guns. He opened the door and presented himself in the same cocky way he always addressed cops.

His face showed confusion as he stared into the eyes of the man in uniform. "What the hell—" he started to say, but before he could get the next word out, the intruder burst inside the apartment, slammed the door behind him, and shoved Goss against the wall. He had no time to think, no time to fully understand what was happening. In half a second, the look of horror that he'd seen in so many of his own young victims overtook his face as he stared down the marksman's tunnel of death and swallowed two silenced bullets that pierced his cheeks and blew his brains out the back of his skull. He slid to the floor, smearing a bright red streak against the wall and landing with a thud, a twisted heap in a pool of blood. His lifeless body lay in the dark shadow of his executioner. Then the door opened quietly, and in an instant the shadow was gone—down the dimly lit hall, down the stairs, and back onto the street, carried away from the scene and into the night by the lonely echo of worn leather heels pounding on the pavement . . . like just any other beat cop making his rounds.

Part Three

Tuesday, August 2

17

At 5:25 A.M. a frantic 911 call came in to the department. A crimson pool of blood had seeped beneath the closed door to Goss's apartment, staining the hallway's dirty green carpet. A neighbor had spotted it coming home from her night shift at the county hospital. The address she gave to the dispatcher would have been familiar to any homicide detective in the city, with all the publicity the Goss trial had received. Any one of them would have been tickled to see Goss get his due. But the chief of the homicide division knew exactly who should answer the call.

"Jump in your car, Lon," he said as he rushed into the office of Detective Lonzo Stafford. The venetian blinds rattled against the glass door as it swung open. "Sun ain't even up, and I'm about to make your day."

Stafford looked up from the *Miami Herald* sports section spread out on his desk. As usual, he was in his cubicle of an office a full ninety minutes before his 7:00 A.M. shift officially began, sipping coffee and dunking doughnuts. Stafford had been in law enforcement for almost forty-five years, a detective for nearly twenty. He was an ex-marine and a worka-holic who filled nearly all his free time with overtime. Some said he worked longer hours because he'd lost a step with age—that he had to push a little harder to get less satisfactory results, like a magic lamp that had to be rubbed three times to yield one wish. In his prime, however, Lonzo Stafford had been the best homicide detective on the force. He didn't make mistakes. Except one time in forty-five years, and it had been so big that it cost a prosecutor a sure con-viction. He'd played on a murder suspect's con-science during a videotaped interview and induced a confession by giving a "Christian burial speech." He'd botched the case against Eddy Goss. And Lonzo Stafford despised Jack Swyteck for nailing him to the wall with that one.

"Whatchya got for me?" Stafford asked.

"Cold one," the homicide chief replied with a smirk. "Four-oh-nine East Adams Street. Apartment two-seventeen."

A satisfied grin came to Stafford's face as he in-stantly recognized the address. "Praise Jesus," he said, rising from his old Naugahyde chair. "I'm on my way."

"Lon," said the chief as he stepped inside and closed the office door. Stafford was stopped in his tracks by the chief's pointed look. "I know how you felt when that bastard Goss walked. I felt the same way. And I want you to understand that I won't be upset if, just this once, your investigation turns up goose eggs."

Stafford looked back plaintively, without disagreement. The chief turned to leave, then stopped before opening the door. "Actually," he said, sighing, "there's more to it than that. Right after Goss's neighbor called nine-one-one, we got another call. Some guy who didn't want to get involved. Wouldn't leave his name, and he called from a pay phone outside the building so we couldn't trace it back. Claims he saw someone in a police uniform leave apartment two-seventeen—right about the time Goss got blown away."

Stafford raised an eyebrow but said nothing.

"We don't know anything for sure," the chief continued, "but I suppose it's possible that when the jury didn't give Goss what he deserved, one of our men decided to take matters into his own hands. Can't say I'd be terribly shocked if that's what happened. Can't say I'd be terribly disappointed, either. You've been around long enough to know what I'm saying. Your job isn't to catch a killer. It's to kill a rumor."

Stafford smiled wryly. "Second call sounds like a dead end already."

"Good. Now, on your way, Detective. And give my regards to Eddy Goss."

The two men chuckled as they headed out the door together, smiling the way men smile when they're in complete agreement.

"Morning, Lon," Detective Jamahl Bradley said to his partner as he ducked his six-foot-six frame beneath the yellow police tape that spanned the width of the hall outside Goss's apartment. The building had been completely secured, with uniformed police officers standing guard at the staircase and at either end of the hall. The door to apartment 217 was wide open, a yellow tarp draped over the bloody corpse that blocked the entrance. Dawn's eerie glow seeped in through the apartment's only window. All was quiet, save for the occasional squawk and static of a police walkie-talkie.

Stafford glanced at Bradley as he folded his arms across his signature attire: red tie, white shirt and twenty-year-old blue blazer—"the colors," the flag-waving ex-marine liked to say. "About damn time you got here," Stafford grumbled.

Bradley gave him a look that typified the mutual disrespect this young African-American and old Florida cracker outwardly demonstrated toward each other. But their banter belied their true feelings. Deep down, they knew they worked well together, basically liked each other, and, most of all, loved giving each other unmitigated hell. "You're lucky my black ass is here," Bradley snapped back. "Your daughter wouldn't let me out of bed."

A joke like that would normally have drawn a nuclear reaction out of Stafford. But he wasn't listening. The old master was absorbed in details, standing squarely in the open apartment doorway as he peered inside with narrowed, discerning eyes. He'd been on the scene for over an hour already. He needed just one more hard look before turning things over to the department's "lab rats," who would collect blood, fingerprints, fibers, and whatever else they could find.

"Let's go," said Stafford.

"Go?" asked Bradley.

"Yeah," he nodded. "You and me gotta be at Jack Swyteck's house before he turns on the morning news."

Bradley winced with confusion. "What for?"

"Justice," he quipped, the corner of his mouth curling in a wry smile. "I can't wait to see that cocky bastard's expression when I tell him that half his client's ugly face is splattered on the living room wall."

Detective Bradley returned the smile. Like everyone else in the police department, he was familiar with the way Eddy Goss's lawyer had skewered Stafford on the witness stand. "I'll drive," he said.

They left Goss's apartment building at 7:00 A.M., just as rush hour began, but they were headed against traffic. They reached Jack's house in fifteen minutes, pulled into the driveway, and marched up to the front door, Stafford leading the way. The detective gave three loud knocks and waited. There was no answer. Jack's car was in the driveway, though, so he knocked again, louder this time. He listened carefully, then smiled with success as he and his partner heard someone stirring inside.

Jack lumbered out of his bedroom and shuffled through the living room to the door. His eyes were puffy slits, and his hair stuck out in all directions. He wore no shoes and no shirt, only the baggy gray gym shorts he'd slept in. He yawned as he pulled aside the curtain and looked out the window next to the front door. He recognized the beige sedan in the driveway as an unmarked police car, and his brow furrowed with curiosity. Then his curiosity turned to concern as Lonzo Stafford's familiar face appeared in the window. Right behind the crusty old detective was his young black partner, whom Jack recognized from Goss's videotaped confession. Bradley seemed even taller and more formidable in person. He had the thick neck of a weight lifter, and his hair was cropped short on the sides and flat on the top, like a pencil eraser. Jack's heart fluttered as the black detective glanced at the Mustang in the driveway. Fortunately, the top was still down so the slash wasn't visible. Relieved, Jack took the chain off the door and opened it.

"Good morning," Stafford said matter-of-factly.

"It certainly is morning," Jack answered.

"We need to talk."

"What about?" asked Jack.

"You mind if we come in?"

"What's it about?" Jack repeated, this time more firmly.

Stafford showed no expression. "It's about Eddy Goss."

Jack shook his head. "Then we have nothing to talk about. I don't work at the Freedom Institute anymore. I don't represent Goss anymore."

"He's dead," said Stafford.

Jack froze. "What?"

"Goss is dead," he repeated, as if he liked the sound of it. "We found him in his apartment a few hours ago. Somebody killed him."

"Are you sure?"

"I seen a few dead bodies in my day," Stafford said. "I know a homicide when I see one. Now," he arched an eyebrow, "you mind if we come inside for a minute?"

"Sure," said Jack.

"You do mind?" Stafford asked, pretending to have misunderstood.

"No," Jack said, flustered. "I mean, I don't mind."

"Because you don't have to talk—"

"I don't mind," Jack asserted, a little too forcefully. "Come on in," he said as he stepped aside, allowing Stafford and Bradley to pass.

As he entered, Stafford reflected on the irony of the situation. Had a homicide detective shown up at the door of any of Swyteck's clients the night after a murder, Swyteck would have been the first to tell him to get lost. It amazed Stafford how lawyers never seemed to heed their own advice.

"Have a seat," said Jack as he cleared the newspapers off the couch.

Stafford watched him carefully. Jack's movements were jerky, a little nervous. Stafford noted the fresh red scratches on his bare back. *Could have been a woman*, he thought. There was a purple bruise on his ribs, too. *Would have taken a pretty aggressive woman.* And the back of Jack's left hand had a nasty cut—like from a knife. *Not something a woman delivers in ordinary course.*

"That's quite a gash you got there," said Stafford as he and his partner took their seats on the couch.

Jack glanced down, picking up on the detective's

nod at his hand. It suddenly hurt more now than when he'd stabbed himself with the steak knife. It looked worse, too. *Everything* looked worse than it had last night. There was a dead body and two nosy detectives looking for an explanation.

"It's nothing, really," said Jack. "Just a scratch."

"Pretty deep for a scratch," observed Bradley. "More like a puncture."

Jack shifted uneasily, feeling somewhat double-teamed now that Stafford's partner was talking too. He glanced at Stafford, then at Bradley. They seemed to want an explanation. So he gave them one. "Yesterday, I was doing some work on my Mustang," he lied. "I was loosening a really tight nut, you know—one of those ones that gets rusted on real tight. I just pushed and pushed," he said, demonstrating with his left hand. "The wrench slipped, and I cut my hand."

Stafford arched an eyebrow suspiciously. "Didn't know you were a lefty, Jack."

Jack hesitated, measuring his response. "I'm not. But I use both hands."

"You're ambidextrous?" Bradley followed up.

"No, not exactly, but whenever I work on my car I use both hands. One gets tired, I use the other. You know how it is," he smiled nervously, "especially on the really tough nuts."

Stafford gave a slow, exaggerated nod, as if to say, *"You're a fool and a liar, but let's move on."*

"So," said Jack, "you didn't come here to talk about cars."

"No," Stafford agreed. "We're here about Goss. Some routine stuff. Just a few minutes of your time. You mind answering a few questions?"

"Sure," Jack shrugged.

"You do mind?" said Stafford, taunting again.

"No, I don't mind," Jack snapped. The detective took mental note of his agitated tone.

Stafford continued the game. "It's okay, really, if you don't want to talk, Jack. I mean, you don't have to talk to us."

"I know that," Jack said dryly.

Stafford's eyes narrowed. "You have the right, you know, to remain silent."

Jack rolled his eyes.

"You have the right to an attorney," Stafford continued. "If you can't afford an attorney—"

"Are you reading me my rights?" Jack asked. "I mean, for real?"

Stafford's expression was deadly serious.

"Look," said Jack, "I know you guys are just doing your job. But the truth is, nobody is going to be terribly upset if you don't catch the guy who blew away Eddy Goss."

"How'd you know he was shot?"

All expression drained from Jack's face. "I just figured he'd been shot," Jack backpedaled. "I just meant killed, that's all."

Stafford gave him that slow, exaggerated nod again, his old detective's eyes brightening as he pulled a little pad and pen from his inside coat pocket. "You mind if I take a few notes?"

Jack thought for a moment. "I think this has gone far enough."

"That's certainly your right," Stafford said with a shrug. "You don't have to cooperate."

"It's not that I don't want to cooperate."

"Hey," Bradley intervened, as if to calm Jack down. "It's no problem."

Jack swallowed hard, completely unaware of how obvious it was that they'd rattled the hell out of him.

The detectives rose from the couch, and Jack showed them to the door.

"See you again, Jack," Stafford promised.

Jack showed no reaction. He just closed the door as soon as they stepped outside and went to the window, watching as the two detectives walked side-by-side to their car. He looked for some feedback, but they didn't even look at each other until Bradley got behind the wheel and Stafford was in the passenger seat.

"There was a steak knife on the floor at Goss's apartment," said Stafford as his partner backed the car out of the driveway.

Bradley glanced at his passenger, then looked back at the road as he backed into the street. "So?"

Stafford sat in silence, thinking. "Check with forensics for prints. First thing."

"Sure," Bradley shrugged, "no problem."

"Then call the Florida bar. They keep a set of fingerprints on all attorneys. Tell them you need a set for Swyteck."

"Come on, Lon," Bradley groaned. "We had a little fun with the guy in there, playing with the

Miranda rights and the whole bit. But you don't *really* think he killed Goss?"

"You heard me," Stafford snapped. "Check it out."

Bradley sighed and shook his head. "Swyteck, huh?"

Stafford stared at the dashboard. He cracked his window, lit a cigarette, and took a long, satisfying drag. "Swyteck," he confirmed, smoke and disdain pouring from his lips. "Defender of scum."

18

·

The steak knife found in Goss's apartment yielded a nice set of prints, and by the following Monday afternoon Detective Stafford thought they looked even nicer, when Jack Swyteck's prints came from the Florida bar.

"We got a match!" Stafford blurted as he barged into the state attorney's office.

Wilson McCue peered out over the top of his rimless spectacles, his working files spread across the top of his desk. Stafford closed the door behind him and bounded into the room with boyish enthusiasm. "Swyteck's prints are all over the steak knife," he said with a grin.

The prosecutor leaned back in his chair. Had anyone but Lonzo Stafford charged unannounced into his office like this, he would have tossed him out on his tail. But Lonzo Stafford enjoyed a special status—acquired more than half a century ago, when an eleven-year-old Lonnie entered into a pact with an eight-year-old Willie to remain "friends forever, no matter what." As boys they'd hunted in the same fields, fished in the same ponds, and gone to the same school, Lonzo always a couple of steps ahead of Wilson on the time line, but Wilson always a notch higher on the grading curve. Now, at sixty-five, Wilson looked at least seventy-five, even on a good day.

"I want you to convene a grand jury," said Stafford.

The prosecutor coughed his smoker's hack, then lit up a Camel. "What for?"

Stafford snatched the lit cigarette from his friend and smoked it himself, pacing as he spoke. "Because I got a suspect," he replied, "in the murder of Eddy Goss."

"Yeah," McCue scoffed, "so do I. About twelve million of them. Anybody who has seen that animal's videotaped confession is a suspect. Eddy Goss *deserved* to die, and everybody wanted him dead. There ain't a jury in the world that would convict the guy who did the world a favor by blowing Goss's brains out."

Stafford arched an eyebrow. "Unless the guy who did it was the same slick defense lawyer who got him—and others like him—off the hook and back on the street."

McCue was apprehensive. "And I can see the headlines already: 'Republican State Attorney Attacks Democrat Governor's Son.' It'll be ugly, Lon. With the gubernatorial election just three months away, you'd *better* have plenty of ammunition if we're gonna start that war."

Stafford took a drag on his cigarette. "We got plenty," he said, smoke pouring through his nostrils. "We got Swyteck's prints on the handle of a knife we found on the floor. I also had the blade checked. There was blood on the tip. AB negative. Very rare. Same as Swyteck's. Lab found some fish-stick remnants on there, too, which is what the autopsy showed Goss had for dinner. And best of all, the blood came later, after the fish sticks."

"Which means?"

"Which means that on the night Goss was murdered I can place Jack Swyteck in the victim's apartment, after dinner, wielding a steak knife."

"And you got a victim who was shot to death," the prosecutor fired back. "I'd say we need more."

"There is more. Just a few hours after the murder, about seven in the morning, we interviewed Swyteck. This was before he was a suspect. Swyteck came to the door in a pair of gym shorts, right outta bed. Nervous as a cat, he was. Big bruise on his ribs. Looked like a bite mark on his belly. Fresh red scratches on his back. Had an open cut on the back of his left hand, too. It looked like a stab wound, to me and Bradley both. Just to look at him, I'd say he'd been in a pretty recent scuffle."

"And he would say he fell down the stairs."

"Maybe," said Stafford, his voice gathering intensity. "But he's gonna have a hard time explaining how he knew Goss had been shot before we ever told him so."

"What do you mean?"

"I checked with the media. No news reports were out about Goss's murder until almost eight o'clock. We showed up at Swyteck's house at seven, and we told him Goss had been killed—but we didn't tell him how. Swyteck knew he had been shot. He said so. It was a slip of the tongue, I think, but he was talking about a shooting before we were."

McCue listened with interest. "We're getting there," he said. He paused to rub at his temples and think for a second. "Why don't you just arrest him, Lonnie. You know, maybe B and E or something, if all you want to do is rattle his cage?"

Stafford's eyes narrowed with contempt. "I want to do more than rattle him. I want to *convict* his ass."

"Because of what he did to you in the Goss trial?" McCue asked directly.

"Because he's guilty. The fact that I would thoroughly enjoy nailing his ass doesn't change that. I wouldn't tag him or any one of those crusaders at the Freedom Institute just to get even. Swyteck *did* it. I'm convinced of it. He wigged out and blew away his scumbag client. He screwed up—big time. And I want to be the guy who makes him pay."

The prosecutor sighed heavily. "We can't be wrong about this one."

"I'm *not* wrong. And if you'd seen Swyteck's face that morning after the murder like I did, you'd *know* I'm not wrong. I've got a feeling about this one, Wilson. Not some flaky feeling you get when you wake up one morning and read your horoscope. This one's based on a lifetime of police work. And in all the years you've known me, have my instincts ever steered you wrong?"

McCue averted his eyes. He had complete trust in his friend, but the pointed question reminded him that there may very well have been one instance when Lonzo Stafford had steered him wrong—dead wrong. It was a first-degree murder charge that Stafford had built on circumstantial evidence. McCue had gone ahead and prosecuted the case, but by the time it was over, even he was beginning to wonder whether Stafford had tagged the right man. It was academic now, of course. The jury had convicted him. Governor Swyteck had signed his death warrant. The state had put him to death. He was gone. McCue would never forget him, though. His name was Raul Fernandez.

"Let me sleep on it," McCue told his friend.

"What more do you want?"

He shrugged uneasily. "It's just that there are so many people who wanted to see Eddy Goss dead. We need to talk to other suspects. We need to talk to neighbors. You need to make sure there isn't some witness out there, somewhere, who'll gut the whole case by saying they saw somebody running from Goss's apartment with smoke pouring from the barrel of a .38-caliber pistol. Somebody who couldn't possibly be Swyteck. Like a woman, a seven-foot black guy, a friend of one of Goss's victims, or—"

"A cop," Stafford interjected, his tone disdainful. "That call to nine-one-one about the cop being around Goss's apartment has you spooked, doesn't it?"

McCue removed his eyeglasses. "I'm concerned about it, yeah. And so's your boss. That's why he told you about it when he put you on the case."

Stafford shook his head. "You know as well as I do, Wilson, that if it'd really been a cop who'd blown Goss's brains out, he wouldn't have showed up at his apartment wearing a uniform. He would've stopped Goss on the street, shot him in 'self-defense,' and laid a Saturday-night special in his cold, dead hand."

"Maybe," said McCue. "But the fact of the matter is that we're talking about the governor's son here. And we're talking about a first-degree murder charge. I'm not taking *that* case to the grand jury until you've got some good, hard evidence."

Stafford's eyes flared. He looked angry, but he wasn't. He took it as a challenge. "I'm gonna get it," he vowed. "I'm gonna get whatever you need to bring Swyteck down."

McCue nodded. "If it's out there, I'm sure you will."

"It's out there," Stafford replied, his tone very serious. "I know it's out there. Because in here," he thumped his chest, "I *know* Swyteck's guilty." He rose quickly from his chair and started for the door, then shoved his hand in his coat pocket and stopped short, as if he'd suddenly found something. "What the hell's this?" he asked, clearly overacting as he pulled a plastic bag from his pocket.

McCue smiled. He knew his old friend was up to something.

"Well, I'll be damned," said Stafford as he smacked

his hand playfully against his forehead. The Cheshire-cat smile he'd been holding inside was now plastered from ear to ear. "I almost forgot to tell you the best part, Wilson. You see, nobody heard any gunshots at the time of Goss's murder. Doesn't seem possible, really, that nobody hears nothin' in a building like that—unless, of course, the man who plugged Goss had a silencer on his thirty-eight-caliber pistol. Which is why *this* is so important," he said as he raised the plastic evidence bag before the prosecutor's eyes.

"And just what is *this?*"

"A silencer," Stafford said smugly, "for a thirty-eight-caliber pistol."

"Where'd you get it?"

"Underneath the front seat of Jack Swyteck's car."

McCue's eyes widened with interest, then concern. "Hope you had a search warrant?"

"Didn't need one. This came to us via Kaiser Auto Repair—Swyteck's mechanics. Seems our favorite lawyer brings in his Mustang every other day for something—it's a real Rent-A-Wreck. Thursday morning, he leaves his car to get the convertible top fixed. A few hours later, the owner of the shop catches one of his mechanics stealing things from the customers' cars and calls us. One of the cars the grease monkey robbed happened to be Swyteck's. And what do you suppose shows up in the guy's loot?" Stafford gave a huge grin. "One silencer."

"That's a pretty strange coincidence, Lonnie, that some punk was rifling through Swyteck's car. You sure it happened that way?"

"Shop owner will back me up a hundred percent," he said, giving McCue an insider's wink.

McCue sat back in his chair, folding his hands contentedly on his belly. "Lonnie," he said with a power grin, "*now* we're on to something."

19

Y ou had forty-three press calls, Governor," Harry Swyteck's secretary reported, trailing at the heel of the candidate-by-day/governor-by-night as he rushed into his spacious office. "And that's just in the last hour."

"Oh, for Pete's sake," the governor groaned as he tossed his charcoal suit coat onto the couch, loosened his tie, and plopped into the high-back leather chair behind his carved mahogany desk, exhausted. Before the campaign, he found it relaxing to nestle into his position of power between the state and American flags, amidst the brass chandeliers, white coffered ceilings, and big arching windows with red velvet drapes that reminded him he was indeed governor. But now that the campaign was in full swing, the opulent surroundings were stark reminders that he had to be re-elected to keep these trappings of power for another four years. "Who did I insult this time?" he asked, only half kidding.

"No one," his secretary assured him as she placed his hot cup of tea with lemon on his desk. She served without a smile, her expression all business. With her gray hair pulled back and a white silk scarf wrapped tightly around her neck, she had all the warmth of a nun on a vow of silence. When it came to political staffers, however, personality was a small sacrifice for eighteen years of efficiency and undivided loyalty. "I'm sure they're all trying to get the scoop before the six o'clock news," she said, "that's all."

The governor froze as he brought his teacup to his lips. Even after all these years it still bothered him that Paula always seemed to know everything about late-breaking news before he knew *anything* about it. "The scoop on what?" he asked with some trepidation.

Her look was more somber than usual. "Your son, of course."

His trepidation turned to concern. "What about my son?"

"Campbell's on his way up," she said, avoiding the question. "He'll explain."

Moments later the door flew open, and the governor's chief aide, Campbell McSwain, rushed into the office, nearly mowing down Paula on her way out. Campbell was a handsome, thirty-eight-year-old Princeton graduate who looked as if he wouldn't know a blue collar unless it was pinpoint Oxford cloth, but his uncanny ability to portray Harold Swyteck as a regular Joe to the average voter had gone a long way toward winning the election four years ago. Campbell wore his usual Bass loafers, khaki slacks, and a Brooks Brothers blazer over a white polo shirt, but his wide-eyed expression was far less understated.

"Sorry, sir," Campbell said as he gasped for breath. He'd run all the way to the governor's office. "I just got off the phone with the Dade County State Attorney's Office."

"The state attorney?"

"It's your son, sir. Our sources tell us he's the target of a grand jury investigation. He's the prime suspect in the murder of Eddy Goss."

The governor's mouth fell open, as if he'd just been punched in the chest. "Goss is dead? And they think Jack did it? That's preposterous. It's *impossible*. Jack is no murderer. It has to be a mistake."

"Well, whether it's true or not, Governor, this is a terrible setback for us. Until a month ago, no one thought a former state insurance commissioner would be a serious challenge to a popular incumbent like yourself. But he's making a damn good showing. He made quite a name for himself rooting out fraud, and he had the good sense not to push so hard that big business wouldn't open its wallets when the campaigning got under way. The polls have you up by just four points at last tally. *This*, however, could change everything. The press is already pouncing all over it. Forty-three calls, Paula said."

The governor leaned forward in his chair and glared at his aide. "This is my son we're talking about," he said angrily. "We're not talking about bad press, or about points on an opinion poll."

Campbell stood in check. "I'm sorry, Governor," he said quietly. "I mean—it's just that, I know you and your son haven't been close. At least not as long as I've known you. I guess I should have been more sensitive."

The governor rose from his chair, turned, and walked slowly to the floor-to-ceiling window that overlooked the garden in the courtyard. "It's true," he said, speaking as much to himself as to his aide, his voice trailing off as if he were retreating deep into his innermost thoughts. "Jack and I have not been as close as I'd like."

Campbell watched with concern, searching for something to say. "Your son is only a grand jury *target*—a suspect," he said. "The lawyers tell me there's at least a theoretical possibility he might not actually be indicted."

Harry nodded appreciatively at Campbell's attempted consolation. But in his mind he could already see the chilling accusation: "John Lawrence Swyteck did with malice aforethought knowingly commit murder in the first degree." Sometimes he couldn't help wondering if fate meant him to be separated from Jack, if the alignment of the stars foreordained a rift between them. But he knew that was a cop-out, an attempt to deny his own complicity in the shaping of Jack's . . . what were they? Neuroses? Problems? Confusion, certainly. With a deep sense of guilt, Harry thought back to the *first* time his son was accused of murder—when he was five years old . . .

Harry had pulled into the driveway around supper

time and walked briskly up the sidewalk to the front door. He could see his young son peering sadly out the bedroom window as if he were being punished for something. Before Harry had even closed the front door and stepped inside, Agnes was screaming at him about Jack and the crucifix he'd found. Harry tried to calm her, but she was determined to have it out. He rushed to the kitchen and closed the door, so Jack couldn't hear, but the bitter argument continued.

"I told you I didn't want these things in the house anymore," Agnes said. "*I'm* your wife now. Give up the past, Harry. I won't tolerate you having your own little shrine."

"It's not for me. I'm saving them for Jack, when he's old enough to understand."

"I don't believe that for a second," she shouted. "You're not thinking of Jack. You're thinking of yourself. You're living in the past—ever since you took that boy home and left her behind. You won't let go. Admit it, Harry, you hate me for not being her. And you hate your own son for killing her."

"Shut up!" he shouted as he rushed toward her.

"Don't you dare raise a hand to me! It's sick, Harry! And I'm *sick* of it!"

Just outside the kitchen, five-year-old Jack trembled in shock and fear of what he had done to his mother. He'd snuck out of his room and tiptoed down the hallway, finding a spot behind a large spider plant, just outside the kitchen, where his father and stepmother had dug in to do battle. He had wanted to hear the truth—but the truth was more than any five-year-old could handle. He stepped back in a daze, then tripped over the pedestal holding the plant, sending himself and the plant crashing to the floor.

The noise from the hall immediately silenced the argument in the kitchen. Harry rushed out and saw Jack lying on the floor, beside the overturned plant. Their eyes met, but neither one spoke. Harold Swyteck didn't have to ask how much his son had heard. The look on his face told him he'd heard it all. And from that day forward, they'd never looked at each other the same way . . .

"Are you listening to me, sir?" Campbell asked. The governor looked at him blankly. His mind was elsewhere.

"I'm sorry," he said, trying to shake himself loose of his memories. But he was still thinking of Jack. After so many disappointments and regrets, he wanted to help his son. But with their turbulent history, it wouldn't be that simple. Jack would surely rebuff any overtures he made.

"Governor," Campbell interrupted, "obviously this isn't something you want to focus on now. I'm not trying to be insensitive. I do understand that, for all your differences, Jack is still your son. That's really none of my business. It is my business, however, to get you re-elected. And, like it or not, we have to evaluate your son's predicament in political terms. Personal tragedy aside, sir, the simple fact is that if Jack Swyteck loses his trial, Harold Swyteck loses his election. Politically speaking," he said coolly, "*that* is the bottom line."

Harry was angered by Campbell's mercenary view, but he also appreciated the simple logic of his words. Campbell was right: Helping Jack *would* help his campaign. And that was the answer to the problem—a kind of reverse psychology. Jack wouldn't accept help if his father were doing it only for his son. But if the governor were doing it for himself, for his own political reasons, Jack would owe him nothing—not even gratitude. That would be the way he could help Jack— and, more important, be assured that Jack would *let* him.

"You're absolutely right," said the governor, smiling inwardly. "I guess I have no choice but to help my son—any way I can."

20
·

After just a week in Rome, Cindy Paige re-turned to Miami that afternoon. The photo shoot in Italy was officially off. It turned out that Chet had a much more recreational view of their "business" trip than she did—which became clear the moment she found out he'd reserved one hotel room with one king-size bed in each of the cities on their tour. It had hurt to find out that it wasn't her talent with a camera that had landed her the job.

Gina met her at the baggage claim, but she wasn't a very chatty chauffeur on the ride home from the airport. She told Cindy she wasn't feeling very well, and she wasn't. Of all the things Gina had done in her life, she realized now that bedding Jack was the lowest. Somehow it had seemed easy to view Jack as "fair game" the other night, when she'd thought Cindy was jetting off to the Eternal City with her old lover. But her friend's quick return simply con-firmed what Gina had suspected all along: Despite the ugly words Jack and Cindy had exchanged the last time they were together, they were far from through.

When they got back to the townhouse, Gina retreated right to her bedroom. She flopped onto the bed and escaped into a rerun of "Lifestyles of the Rich and Famous."

Cindy left her suitcase by the door and went straight to the kitchen. The so-called snack on the airplane had been about as appetizing as boiled lettuce. She quickly microwaved herself some french fries, then opened the refrigerator in search of ketchup.

"Gina," she called out, "where's the Heinz?"

Gina didn't answer.

"Oh, well," Cindy said, shrugging. Balancing the plate of fries in one hand and a Diet Coke in the other, she headed for the living room. She grabbed the remote control as she sat on the couch and flipped on the television.

The lead story on every local evening-news broadcast was the same. She was just in time to catch the south Florida version, the hometown approach to the breaking story of how, "in a shocking development, the grand jury investigation into the murder of Eddy Goss had now targeted murder suspect Jack Swyteck."

She stared dumbfounded at Jack's face on the television screen, framed by an imposing graphic of the scales of justice. "Oh, my God," she muttered. She punched the buttons on the remote control and flipped frantically from one channel to the next, as if trying to watch them all at once. She couldn't believe it, even after hearing it straight from the mouth of every news anchor in the city. After ten minutes she'd had enough, since coverage on every station had degenerated to "live and exclusive" interviews with virtually every publicity hound in town who claimed to "know" Jack Swyteck. She switched off the set in disgust. Not one of these people knew Jack the way she did. He was no killer.

Her hands were shaking as she sank into the couch. She wasn't sure what to do. Should she just let him know she was back in town—if he needed a friend? She wondered why, indeed, she *was* back in town. Had it really been necessary to call off the photo shoot in Italy? She probably could have laid down a few ground rules with Chet and gotten the job done—unless, of course, her relationship with Jack had subconsciously drawn her back to Miami.

She glanced at the phone. Talking to him wouldn't be good enough. Not after the blowup they'd had when they were last together. She needed to *see* him. She grabbed her purse from the coffee table. "I'll be back later," she shouted up the stairway, then hurried out the door.

The sun had set and the streetlights had popped on by the time Cindy reached Jack's house. Even when she'd lived there, she'd never liked driving up alone after dark. Jack professed to like landscaping, but what he really meant was that he liked foliage of any kind, and lots of it. His "lawn" was a thick blanket of bromeliads, bushy ferns, and practically anything else that didn't look like a weed. Large, bushy palms and leafy ficus trees were scattered everywhere, creating an array of menacing shadows. It was enough to make any twenty-five-year-old blonde in blue denim shorts and sleeveless white shell a bit on edge. At night the scene always made her feel a bit like Dorothy in the land of Oz contending with the talking apple trees.

Anxiety propelled her to the front door in a matter of seconds. The porch light flipped on before she could knock, and the door swung open.

Jack stood in the doorway, looking perplexed. "Cindy, what are you doing here?"

"I saw the story on the news. I thought you might need to talk."

"You're too much," he said, opening his arms. She stepped forward to accept his embrace. "After you left I wanted to call you and tell you how sorry I was, but I felt like such a jerk." He held her tighter and looked into her eyes. "Can you forgive me?"

"Let's try to forget that ever happened," Cindy said. "I felt terrible about what I said, too."

"No, no, you were right," he protested, "I totally lost it. But—" he shook his head in confusion. "What happened with Italy?"

She slipped from his embrace and gave him a look of concern. "That's not nearly as important as what's happening to you."

His spirits soared. Just an hour ago, after having watched the six o'clock news, he'd thought it would be a very long time before he'd ever feel happy again.

"I guess you know all about the grand jury investigation," he said, still not quite believing the turn of circumstances.

She nodded.

"Do I need to tell you I didn't do it?"

She looked into his eyes. "I know you didn't."

He went to embrace her again, but his attention was diverted by a car pulling into his driveway. It was a police car—not one but two in fact. And inside the lead car was Detective Lonzo Stafford.

"I've got to talk to these guys," Jack said to Cindy as he gestured for her to go inside. At first she hesitated, but then she entered the house.

Stafford trudged up the path and took Cindy's place on the porch. His blue blazer was even more wrinkled than usual, his necktie was loosened, and a few extra lines seemed to have appeared in his tired old face. He'd clearly been working some long hours, but the gleam in his gray eyes made it equally clear that he thought his hard work was about to pay off.

"Got a warrant here, my friend. Time for a little search party."

Jack sighed, relieved that it wasn't an arrest warrant. "You won't find a murder weapon here," he assured the detective. For a moment, Jack felt like leading him right to his footlocker and the old .38. A simple ballistics test would prove it wasn't involved in the Goss shooting. But the gun was never registered in Florida, a problem in itself, and possessing it would only prove his familiarity with the same type of weapon the newspapers said had killed Goss. Jack figured the less grist the detective had for wild conjecture, the better.

Stafford glanced over his shoulder to make sure the other officers couldn't hear him. "Do you think

I'm stupid enough to get a warrant to look for a murder weapon?" he asked contemptuously. "Then I'd have to tell the jury we looked for it and didn't find it, wouldn't I, Swyteck? Besides," he said smugly, "I don't need to find the gun. Not since Ballistics determined a silencer was used to kill Goss. Not since that mechanic down at Kaiser pulled a silencer out of your convertible."

"A mechanic did *what?*"

Stafford smiled wryly. "You'll hear all about it soon enough, counselor. Right now," he said with a wink as he flashed the warrant in Jack's face, "baby needs a new pair a' shoes. Reeboks to be exact. You may recall that it was a rainy night when you visited your favorite client. Your footprints are all over the apartment."

Jack fell silent. Things were getting worse by the minute, but he had nothing to gain by sparring with the old detective. "Just get what you came for," he said flatly. "And be on your way."

Stafford signaled back to his team with a jerk of his head. Jamahl Bradley and two other officers filed into the house, heading straight for the master bedroom. Jack followed closely behind, his stomach in knots.

"What's happening?" Cindy asked Jack, her voice trembling as the officers whisked by her in the living room.

Stafford stopped to field the question. "We're gonna prove your boyfriend here was traipsing around Eddy Goss's apartment the night of the murder. That's what's happening, miss." Stafford took another step, then stopped and arched a suggestive eyebrow at Cindy. "You sure you want to sleep here tonight, sweetheart?"

"Shut the hell up, Stafford," Jack snapped.

Stafford just shrugged and continued on toward the bedroom. Jack started to follow but stopped when he saw the look on Cindy's face. He wanted to watch the police conduct their search, just to make sure they stuck to the warrant, but he couldn't let Stafford's remark linger. He had to keep Cindy's trust, so he took her by the hand and led her quickly through the kitchen, into the backyard by the gazebo where they'd be out of earshot.

"Were you really at Goss's apartment the night he was murdered?"

He looked into the middle distance, obviously struggling with what he was about to say. "Listen, Cindy, there are going to be things I won't be able to tell you from here on out. Not because I'm guilty, but because it's possible you may end up being a witness at trial—and the less you know, the better. But I may as well tell you this, because the footprints are going to prove it anyway. Yes, I was there that night. I went to Goss's apartment. But I didn't kill him. I went because of some threats I was getting. Someone was calling me, telling me there was a 'killer on the loose.' And then I was nearly run down, and Thursday—he killed Thursday."

Cindy brought her hand to her mouth. "Oh, my God . . . oh, my God, Jack."

Jack touched her cheek gently to console her. "I figured it was Goss, and sure enough, that day you left for Italy I got a call inviting me to his apartment. He didn't identify himself, but that was just part of the game-playing. I had to confront him, Cindy. But I didn't kill him."

"Are you going to tell the police all that?"

"No way." He laid his hands on her shoulders for emphasis as he spoke. "It's very important that you understand this. We can *never* tell the police about the harassment. Not unless they force us to tell them."

"Why not?"

He sighed. "Right now, they're trying to build a case against me for killing Eddy Goss. I don't know how good it's going to be, but off the top of my head, I can see one glaring weakness: motive. Why would I kill Goss? Without any evidence that Goss was stalking me, all the prosecution can say is that I killed him because I felt guilty about having gotten him acquitted. Their whole case boils down to whether or not a lawyer—a *criminal defense lawyer*—had a guilty conscience. Now, how many jurors would even believe a lawyer actually *has* a conscience, let alone one strong enough to make him into a killer?"

She listened carefully, considering his explanation.

"It's simple," he continued. "If I were to tell the police about the threats I started getting after Goss's trial, I'd be handing them a motive on a silver platter. The moment they find out Goss was after me, that's it. Bingo! They've got a motive. Understand?"

Cindy sighed. She felt like she was going to cry, not so much because of what was happening at the moment, but because she realized that this was all just the beginning of a new and terrible set of events. "Yes," she said quietly, "I understand. Don't worry, Jack. I'm with you."

Jack and Cindy ordered out for Chinese after Stafford left the house. At first they tried to keep the conversation light, but as Jack finished his last spring roll, he turned the discussion in a more serious direction. "I'm sorry we didn't get to talk before you left for Italy—at least to say good-bye."

"More than that needed to be said," Cindy answered. "There's a side of you that always seems cut off from me. And it's not just me—you seem to deal with your father the same way. The whole time I've known you, you've never made an effort to contact him, and he's never called you either."

"I don't blame you for being confused about that."

"It's not about blame, Jack. It's just something you've got to deal with."

He averted his eyes as he fiddled with an empty soy sauce packet. "I've wanted to. Oddly enough, just before this thing got really crazy, my stepmother phoned. Said I should give my father a call. I don't know how to explain it . . . it's absurd, really, but as long as I don't call him, there's hope we'll work things out. If I do take a chance, and there's a blowup, I'm not sure we can ever put the pieces back together. It's like they say, if you take your shot and miss, the dream is over. But if you don't, there's always *someday*."

"C'mon, Jack, you know better than that. You can't trudge along, status quo, hoping things will change. There comes a point when you have to do something.

That's what I did with us. I'm not saying I handled it perfectly, but I had to do something." Her eyes sought his. "You need to know that it was strictly business between me and Chet." She shook her head, rolled her eyes. "It turned out that *he* wanted it to be more, and that's why I came right back home. I didn't feel it was over between us—which is why I told Gina to give you the number at my hotel."

"Gina never gave me a number," said Jack.

"Oh . . ." Cindy looked confused. "She promised me she would. I guess she forgot."

"Yeah," he said skeptically. He'd really allowed Gina to sucker him in. His feelings of guilt were overwhelming.

After they'd cleared the dinner plates, Jack glanced at his watch. They'd been talking longer than he thought. It was nearly eleven-thirty. He asked Cindy if she'd be all right getting back to Gina's.

"I want to stay here tonight," she said, avoiding direct eye contact. "But 'tonight' means just that. No commitments yet, okay?"

"That's fine," he said, his expression showing both gratitude and relief.

Twenty minutes later, Cindy emerged from the bathroom wearing a big football jersey Jack had loaned her to sleep in. She shuffled toward the bed, then paused as she noticed the dresser mirror. "You replaced all the torn snapshots."

"Yeah, I dug out the negatives and made some new prints," he said sheepishly. "I didn't have much of a choice. Every time I looked at the mirror, it reminded me of how awful I was the last time we were together."

She flashed a wide smile. "Come to bed," she said as she led him by the hand.

As he drew back the sheets, thoughts of his impending arrest took the edge off his desire. He looked at Cindy and felt an enormous burden of guilt. She was *so* willing to give him a second chance, *so* willing to support him as he weathered this latest crisis. He wondered how she'd react if she heard that his best shot at an alibi was her own best friend.

21

Stafford and his assistants left Jack's house at about eight o'clock. Jack's tennis shoes were in the lab by eight-thirty. Stafford and his partner hung around the police station for the preliminary results, patiently waiting in the senior detective's office. Stafford was at his desk, still in that faded blue blazer he never seemed to take off, his white shirt collar unbuttoned and wide polyester tie dropped over his chair. He was busying himself smoking cigarettes and straightening out paper clips. Bradley was in the chair beside the window, wadding up yesterday's newspaper into little balls and shooting free throws into the wastebasket in the corner.

The phone rang at ten. "Stafford," the detective answered eagerly, cigarette smoke pouring from his lips as he spoke.

Bradley watched expectantly as his partner nodded and grunted.

"Got him!" Stafford proclaimed as he hung up. He leaned back in his chair and folded his arms smugly across his chest. "Perfect match on the Reeboks. Twenty-seven glorious prints all over the apartment, and even one on the windowsill. Can't say I'm surprised. I knew in my gut Swyteck did it. But I'm pleased as hell we can *prove* it."

Bradley nodded slowly. "Congratulations," he said, though he spoke without heart.

Stafford looked questioningly at his partner. "I would have expected a little more excitement than that, Jamahl."

Bradley hesitated, but there was something he needed to say. "Frankly, Lon, you just seem a little too eager to nail this guy. That's all."

Stafford's eyes flared with anger, but he kept control. "Listen to me," he lectured. "I've been a cop more than forty years, son. I know enough to listen to my instincts. And my instincts say that Jack Swyteck lost his cool after that trial, and he blew Goss away. I know what I'm talking about," he growled, then took a drag from his cigarette. "The system is just a game to these criminal defense lawyers. They don't care about the truth. They'll say or do whatever it takes to win: 'My client ate too many Twinkies,' or 'My client watched too much television.' I've heard it all and I've seen 'em all, and Swyteck ranks up there with the worst. I listened to Eddy Goss confess murder right to my face. Right to my damn *face*. And then I watched Fancy Jack Swyteck convince a jury his client wasn't guilty. That boy made a *fool* out of me. I've watched that son of a bitch do it time and time again. And every time he wins, another killer goes back on the street. Usually it's on a technicality or some flaky defense. And Swyteck's just getting warmed up. He's a tenderfoot. Can you imagine him doing this for the next twenty-five, thirty years?"

Bradley swallowed apprehensively. He knew the dangers of a cop who let the ends justify the means—especially one who seemed out for revenge. "So what are you saying, Lon? Somebody's got to stop him?"

Stafford's expression turned very cold. "No," he snapped. "All I'm saying is that this slick defense lawyer has got himself into deep trouble, and I'm gonna make damn sure he pays for it. So excuse *me* if I seem a little too happy about catchin' myself a killer, okay?"

Bradley nodded slowly. "Okay, chief," he shrugged, seeming to back off. "After all, you *do* have twenty-seven footprints."

"You're damn right I do."

"But don't forget," said Bradley, shooting him a look. "There's still an unidentified footprint right outside the apartment door. We know it's not from Goss. It's not the right shoe size. And we know it's not from Swyteck, either, since he was wearing the Reeboks."

"So what," said Stafford, waving it off. "It's from the janitor or somebody else in the building."

Bradley shook his head. "No, it's not, Lon. That's a very clean print. You can see the insignia on the heel very plainly: two crossed oars. Those are Wiggins wing tips—three-hundred-dollar jobs. There ain't no janitor and nobody in that slum of an apartment building who wears three-hundred-dollar wing tips."

"Look, Jamahl," Stafford grimaced. "We got twenty-seven footprints from Jack Swyteck *inside* the apartment. We got one stray footprint *outside* the apartment. Quit bein' a pain in the ass, will ya?"

Bradley sighed. His doubts weren't alleviated, but he didn't want to provoke his partner. "Maybe you're right," he said as he rose from his chair and stepped toward the door. Then he stopped. "But let me put it to you this way, Lon. Twenty-seven footprints from the same pair of shoes adds up to how many people?"

Stafford shrugged, as if the question were stupid. "One, of course," he said.

"That's right. And no matter how you look at it, one single footprint from a different pair of shoes adds up to what?"

"One person," Stafford answered reluctantly.

"Right," said Bradley, "as in one *other* person. Think about it," he said.

22

·

Sometime after 2:00 A.M. Jack finally fell asleep with Cindy in his arms. He awoke at about ten o'clock, and he smiled at the sight of her sleeping at his side. She looked great even in the morning, he thought. Cindy was the woman he loved, the only woman he really wanted. Her coming back to him was like a dream come true.

He heard a pounding on the front door. He immediately sat upright; he knew who it was. Grand juries normally convened at nine. As much as he'd expected the visit, he still shuddered at the thought that he was no longer just someone the prosecutor had labeled a grand jury "target." If his guess was correct, in the last hour he'd been formally indicted for murder in the first degree.

He jumped out of bed and pulled on khaki slacks and loafers. The pounding continued.

Cindy sat up. "What is it?"

He slipped on a blue oxford shirt, decided against a tie, then spoke in a voice that strained to be upbeat. "I think it's time . . . they probably handed down an indictment." He went to the bureau, checked himself in the mirror, and quickly brushed his hair. He fumbled through his wallet and took out all the pictures and credit cards, leaving only his driver's license, voter's registration, and fifty dollars cash. He shoved the wallet into his back pocket, tucked in his shirt, and took a deep breath. In the mirror he saw Cindy looking at him, and he turned to meet her stare.

"I love you, Jack," she said quietly.

He felt a rush of emotion, which he managed to control, then, smiling a sad smile, said, "I love you, too."

The knocking continued, louder this time.

"It won't be bad," he assured her. "It's not like they're about to lock me up and throw away the key. They'll book me at the station, and then I'll go before the judge, who'll probably release me on bail. I'll be home this afternoon. No sweat." He leaned down and kissed her on the forehead.

She nodded slowly. A tear rolled down her cheek as she watched him turn and disappear into the hallway. Another loud knock, and it was definitely time to go.

"Coming," Jack said as he walked briskly toward the front door. He grabbed the knob, then stopped to collect himself. He was as ready as he'd ever be. Ironically, he'd coolly and calmly counseled scores of clients on how to prepare for arrest, but now he realized that this was one of those events that no amount of preparation could completely smooth over.

Jack swallowed his apprehension and opened the door.

"Manny?" he said with surprise.

"How you doing, Jack?" replied Manuel Cardenal, Florida's preeminent criminal defense lawyer. Jack knew him from the courthouse. *Everyone* knew Manuel Cardenal from the courthouse. He'd started his career twenty years ago as a murder-rape-robbery public defender, making his name defending the guilty. He'd spent the last ten years at the helm of his own law firm, making a fortune defending the wealthy.

"What are *you* doing here?" asked Jack.

"I'm your attorney. Can I come in?"

"Of course."

Manny stepped inside. He wore a blue double-breasted suit, black Italian shoes, and a colorful silk necktie with matching handkerchief showing from the left breast pocket. He stopped to check his reflection in the mirror beside the door and obviously liked what he saw. At forty-three, Manny's life with women was at its peak; younger women still found him handsome, while older women were drawn to his youthfulness. He had a smile that bespoke confidence and experience, yet his eyes sparkled with the vibrancy of a teenage heartthrob. He wore his jet-black hair straight back, no part, as if he were looking into a windstorm. He turned and faced the man in the eye of a real storm.

"I didn't hire you," said Jack. "Not that I wouldn't want to. I just can't *afford* you."

Manny took a seat on the couch. "Sorry for the

short notice, but just this morning your father retained me on your behalf."

"Excuse me?"

"Your father regrets that you have to suffer at his expense."

"At *his* expense?"

Manny nodded. "You're going to have one hell of a day, Jack. If you weren't Harry Swyteck's son, you wouldn't be dragged out of your house in cuffs and carted away in a squad car with the lights flashing. You wouldn't be locked up like a crack dealer pulled off the street and forced to wait in the pen for arraignment. You'd be allowed to surrender yourself and immediately be released on your own recognizance, or at worst for some token signature bond. It's politics," Manny explained, "and your father regrets that."

"Are you saying that the indictment was politically motivated?"

"No. But everything after the indictment will be."

"Great . . . so I'm going to be dragged through the system by my father's political enemies."

"I'm afraid so, Jack. I called the state attorney to see if they'd just let you come in and surrender quietly. No go. They want a spectacle. They want publicity. Your case is already a political football. Your father recognizes that. And he knows that however your case goes, so goes his election."

"Is *that* the reason you're here, Manny? To save my father's election?"

"All I know is what your father told me, Jack."

Jack narrowed his eyes and took a good look at Manny, as if he were searching his face for the truth. "I'm not stupid, Manny. And I know my father. At least I know him well enough to know that this can't be entirely about politics. And I know you, too. I don't believe a man like *you* would get involved in this case if my father didn't genuinely want to help me. So what gives? Why did the two of you have to come up with this little charade to make it look like the governor is doing it not for me, but for his own political gain? Is he too proud or too afraid to tell the truth? Why the hell doesn't he just be my father and *tell* me he wants to help?"

Manny's warm eyes seemed to convey more than he was saying. "Maybe that *is* what he's telling you, Jack."

Jack fell silent. Manny's answer had him thinking.

A loud knock on the door interrupted his thoughts. "Open up!" came the order.

Jack and Manny exchanged glances.

"So, what do you say, Jack? Shall we dance?"

Jack took a deep breath, and a thin smile crept onto his face. "Just don't step on my toes, Cardenal." Then he opened the door.

"Police," said Detective Lonzo Stafford, flashing his badge. Stafford wore his usual blue blazer and an unmistakable smirk. Detective Bradley was at his side. "You're under arrest," Stafford announced with relish, "for the murder of Eddy Goss."

Jack was stiff but composed as he surveyed the situation. Manny appeared to be right about being put through the wringer. It wasn't the low-profile, cooperative approach he'd hoped for. They'd driven up in a patrol car rather than Stafford's unmarked vehicle, and they'd left the lights flashing, a blue swirl of authority in his yard.

A crowd of nosy neighbors and probing reporters gathered at the end of Jack's driveway, just off his property. Jack could hear their collective "there he is" when he appeared in the doorway, followed by a barrage of clicking cameras with telephoto lenses.

"You have the right to remain silent," Jack heard Stafford say, but he wasn't really listening to the Miranda litany until Stafford said to his partner, "Cuff him, Jamahl."

"What?" Jack asked in disbelief.

"Cuff him," Stafford repeated with pleasure.

"Look, Detective. I'm willing to cooperate—"

"Good," Stafford cut him off. "Then cuff his hands in front, instead of behind his back."

Jack knew better than to resist. He obediently stuck his hands out in front of him, and Bradley quickly clamped the steel cuffs around his wrists.

"Let's go for a ride," said Stafford.

Jack stepped onto the porch and turned to close the door. He reached with his right hand, the left one following as the chain pulled it along. He froze as he saw Cindy standing in his bathrobe at the end of the hallway, staring at him and his handcuffs with shock and utter fear.

"Stay by the phone," he called to her, no longer so sure that he'd be coming home that afternoon. She nodded quickly, and he closed the door.

Stafford took Jack's left arm and Bradley took his

right as they led him down the winding wood-chip path to the squad car. Jack said nothing and looked straight ahead. He tried not to look worried or ashamed or, worst of all, guilty. He knew his neighbors were watching and the reporters had their video cameras running. He hoped to God that Cindy wasn't looking out the window.

Manny joined Jack in the backseat and the detectives sat in front. As Detective Bradley steered slowly onto the street, faces and cameras pressed against the car windows, all eager for a peek at the lawyer who'd allegedly killed his client, as if Jack were in the midst of those famous fifteen minutes Andy Warhol had talked about.

Jack was whisked downtown in a matter of minutes, and the crowds came into view a block from the station. Mobs of reporters filled all three tiers of granite steps in front of the Metro-Justice Building, like so many expectant fans in the grandstands.

Jack's gut wrenched. He looked at the crowds, then down at his cuffed hands. "Can't we lose these?" he asked, holding up the cuffs. "This really is *not* necessary."

"Sorry, counselor," Stafford said smugly. "No professional courtesy between defense lawyers and cops."

Jack tried to show no reaction, since he knew it would only please Stafford to elicit one. But he was angry and more than a little scared.

"As soon as we're at the curb," said Stafford, "we're outta here. We won't run, but it won't be a stroll either. Just stay close behind us. Got that, Swyteck?"

Jack remained silent.

"Just shut up and drive," Manny responded.

Bradley punched the accelerator, and in a moment they could see the station with its flock of reporters, photographers, and the just plain curious. The car squealed around the final corner, and Bradley slammed on the brakes. "Here we go!" he shouted.

The detectives popped open the front doors and jumped out of the car, then they threw open Jack's door and pulled him out. Reporters were all over them before Jack could get both feet on the sidewalk. Manny and Stafford each grabbed an elbow and pushed him into the crowd, but the mob pushed back, turning Jack into a pigskin in a lopsided rugby match.

"Outta the way!" Stafford shouted, pushing reporters aside and forging ahead toward the crowded steps, taking the accused killer into custody as the flock assaulted them with flailing hands, wires, and microphones.

"Mr. Swyteck!" someone yelled, "will you represent yourself?"

More arms, more wires, more microphones. *Keep moving*, Jack thought, *just keep moving*.

"Mr. Swyteck!" they shouted, their voices indistinguishable.

Jack had never been so aware of putting one foot in front of the other, but forward progress had never been more important.

"Will the Freedom Institute defend you, Mr. Swyteck?" The reporters' questions kept coming, but Jack and his escorts inched steadily up the granite steps, past the video cameras that taped their every movement.

"Gonna craft another insanity defense, Jack, baby?" a photographer taunted, trying to get Jack to look his way.

Stafford kept them moving forward through the mass of wires, cameras, and bodies. They finally reached the station's bottlenecked entrance, pried themselves away from the heaving crowd, and disappeared from view through the revolving door.

Inside, the steady clatter of a busy station house replaced the mob's raucous din. The station had a thirty-foot ceiling, like a huge bank lobby, but the glass dividers with venetian blinds that sectioned the space into individual offices were only nine feet high, so if seen from the ceiling, the station would have appeared to be a sprawling rat maze. Men and women in dark blue police uniforms whisked by, glancing at Detective Stafford's latest and biggest catch.

Jack and Manny knew the routine. This was where the lawyer left his client behind for fingerprinting and snapshots along the booking assembly line. *In* the front door as a private citizen, *out* the back door as an accused criminal. They'd meet again in the courtroom for arraignment, when Jack would enter his plea.

"See you at the other end of the chute," Manny told his client.

"Let's go," Detective Stafford grumbled.

Manny's look soured. "And Stafford," he said,

catching him just as he started inside. The detective glared back at him.

"If you think Jack Swyteck ripped into you on the stand," Manny warned, "just wait 'til Jack's lawyer rips into your hide."

Stafford was stoic. He turned and hauled Jack away, satisfied that, for now at least, Jack Swyteck was his.

23

That same morning, Governor Harold Swyteck stood tall on a raised dais in the courtyard outside the old legislative chambers, a gray two-story building with arches, columns, and striped-canvas window canopies that provided a nostalgic backdrop. The courtyard was his favorite place for press conferences because of its size—large enough to hold everyone who cared to attend, yet small enough to create a crowded, newsworthy feeling. Clusters of red, white, and blue helium balloons decorated surrounding trees and fences. Above it all, a slickly painted banner read FOUR MORE YEARS—a more inspiring message than either LAWYER TURNS KILLER, SON OF THE GUV WAS GOSS'S LOVER, or the other recent headlines that threatened to send the governor plunging in public-opinion polls.

"Thank you all for coming," Harry Swyteck said after he finished his answer to the final question. Cameras clicked and reporters jostled for position as he stepped away from the lectern, smiling and waving to one side and then the other, flashing his politician's smile and pretending to know everyone.

"One more question, Governor?" came a friendly voice from the crowd.

He returned the smile, expecting a lob at this stage of the game. "All right."

"What about mine?" shouted the one reporter no politician could stomach. It was David Malone, a smooth, good-looking, and notoriously unethical tabloid-television reporter who thrived on scandal. He was the kind of sleazy journalist who, on a slow news night, could take a video camera and microphone into a local tavern and make six drunken loudmouths falling off their bar stools look like the raging nucleus of a community-wide riot on anything from race relations to the Eddy Goss trial. Today, however, Malone didn't have to reach for controversy. All he needed was a few minutes, one-on-one, with Jack Swyteck's father. "You afraid of my questions, Governor?"

Harry cringed inside. Malone had been pushing toward the front of the crowd since the beginning of the press conference, and the governor had simply ignored him. But he couldn't just walk away from someone who had publicly called him chicken. "A quick one," he acquiesced. "What's your question, Mr. Malone?"

Malone's eyes lit up, eager for the opportunity. "Four years ago," he read from his tattered spiral notepad, "you campaigned on a 'two-fisted approach' to

law and order. Specifically, you promised to ensure
that the death penalty was carried out 'with vigor,' I
think were your exact words."

"Do you have a question?"

"My question, sir, is this: Do you intend to keep
that promise in the next term?"

"I've kept all my campaign promises. And will
continue to honor them after I'm re-elected. Thank
you." As he closed he started to move away from the
lectern.

"More specifically," Malone pressed, raising his
voice. "If the jury convicts Jack Swyteck of murder
in the first degree, are you going to sign his death
warrant?"

The governor halted in his tracks. His plastic smile
faded, and his eyes flared with anger. But Malone
waited for an answer. "The answer," said the governor, "is definitely no."

"Why not?"

The governor glared at his interrogator. "Because
Jack is innocent. And I would never execute an innocent man."

"How would you know?"

"I know my son's not a murderer."

"No," said Malone. "I meant, how do you know that
you haven't already executed an innocent man?"

The governor glared menacingly at the reporter,
but his eye twitched nervously. A sign of weakness,
Malone detected.

"First of all," said the governor, "most of them
admitted they were guilty before—"

"Not all of them."

"No, but—"

"What about the ones who didn't confess? What about the ones who went down swinging? What about the guys who swore their innocence to the end?"

"What about Raul Fernandez?" someone shouted from the rear.

The governor went cold. That was a name he hadn't heard since his blackmailer had threatened him—since the death of Eddy Goss. He looked out to see who had asked the question, but the faces in the crowd were indistinguishable.

"What *about* Fernandez?" Malone picked up the question. Heads bowed, as legions of reporters scribbled down the name.

The governor shifted nervously. He was clueless as to who had shouted out Fernandez's name, but he was suspicious of the way Malone's line of questioning had prompted the outburst. "I'm sorry. I'm not going to get into individual cases today, no more than I'm going to discuss my son's individual case. It's just not appropriate. That's all for today," he said as he started toward the exit.

"Governor!" others called out in unison, wishing for a follow-up. But he'd lost his concentration. There would be no more questions. "Thank you," he said with a wave as he exited the stage through a side door, into a private room.

The governor's aide was there to greet him and to close the door on pursuing press. Harry wiped little beads of sweat from his brow, relieved to have the conference behind him.

"Went well, I thought," said Campbell as he handed

his boss a cold drink. The governor chugged down the Coca-Cola but didn't respond. "Except for that little exchange about your son," Campbell added. "I'm telling you, that son of yours is killing you, Governor. We checked the polls again this morning. You've lost another point and—"

Campbell droned on, but Harry had stopped listening. He glanced out the window, strangely amused by the irony. It seemed that Jack was always being accused of killing someone. His father. His client. And a long time ago, on a day Harold Swyteck would never forget—his own mother. It had been nearly a quarter century since Agnes, in a drunken state, had made the accusation, and then added to the boy's confusion by suggesting that Harry reckoned his son accountable. Harry's own role in that ugly interchange had been the worst, however, because he had yet to look Jack in the eye and deny it.

"Jack isn't killing anyone," Harry suddenly objected in a loud voice. Campbell was a bit taken aback. He watched, curious, as the governor seemed to retreat into his thoughts.

"I killed *him*," Harry finally said in a low voice. "By my silence—a long time ago."

Campbell was about to follow up, but the governor quickly changed the subject—to someone he may have *really* killed. "Who was that reporter who yelled out the name of Raul Fernandez?" he asked, trying not to sound too interested.

"I don't know. I sent a security man after him, but he was long gone before anyone really knew what was going on. You want me to follow up on it?"

"*No*," he said, a little too forcefully. The last thing he wanted was someone else poking into this. "It's not worth the trouble," he said in a more reasonable tone. Then he stepped toward the window and sighed. "Could you give me a few minutes, please?"

Campbell nodded. His boss looked like he could use some time alone. "I'll be in the car," he said, then left the room.

Harry lowered himself into a chair. He was still weak in the knees from the pointed Fernandez questions. *Could he be back?* The chrysanthemums had led him to believe that Goss was the blackmailer. And since he hadn't heard from the man since Goss's murder, he had been convinced he was right. But this was too strange for coincidence. It couldn't have been a heckler or someone making a lucky guess who'd shouted out Fernandez's name. And Malone's line of questioning had been deliberate. He trembled at the thought: Not only had his blackmailer returned, but one of Florida's sleaziest television reporters knew something about it.

Don't jump to conclusions, he told himself. Raul Fernandez had been the most controversial execution of his administration. A reporter or a protester didn't have to *know* anything to draw a comparison between the execution of the governor's son and the execution of a man who had proclaimed his innocence to the very end. It wasn't completely outside the realm of possibility that today had been coincidence—that Goss *had* been the extortionist, and that his extortionist was dead. Then it occurred to him that there was a way to find out for sure if it had been Goss.

The first time Harry had been attacked, his assailant had identified himself as the man who confessed to Jack the night of Fernandez's execution. Surely, Jack would know if that very same man was Goss.

Now all he had to do was figure out a way to get Jack to tell him.

24
.

"S tate versus *Swyteck*," the bailiff finally announced, ending Jack's ninety-minute wait in the holding cell. The cavernous courtroom came to life as Manuel Cardenal met his client at the prisoners' side entrance and escorted him across the marble floor to a mahogany podium, where they stood and faced the judge. Clusters of newscasters and curious spectators looked on from the public seating area as Jack passed before them, his head down and eyes forward, the accused murderer of the infamous Eddy Goss. Goss was indeed on Jack's mind. The entire scene was hauntingly reminiscent of the Goss arraignment, when Jack had accompanied the confessed killer to the very same podium to enter his not-guilty plea. Now, as Jack was about to enter his own plea, it was more plain than ever that a simple "not guilty" was no assertion of innocence. Innocence was a moral judgment—a matter of conscience between mortals and their maker. "Not guilty" was a legalistic play on words, the defendant's public affirmation that he would stand on his constitutional right to force the prosecutor to *prove* guilt beyond a reasonable doubt. Manuel Cardenal seemed sensitive to that fine distinction when he entered Jack's plea.

"My client is more than not guilty," Manny announced to the judge. "Jack Swyteck is *innocent*."

The pale old judge peered down from the bench over the top of his bifocals, his wrinkled brow furrowed and bushy white eyebrows raised. He didn't approve of defense lawyers who vouched for the innocence of their clients, but he didn't make an issue of it. "Register a plea of not guilty," he directed the clerk. "And Mr. Cardenal," he said sharply, pointing menacingly with his gavel, "save the speeches for your press conference."

Manny just smiled to himself.

"There's also the issue of bail, Judge," came the deep, gravelly voice from across the room. It was Wilson McCue, the state attorney, wearing his traditional three-piece suit. His pudgy face was nearly as round as his rimless spectacles, and a heavy gold chain from his pocket watch stretched across a bulging belly. Jack knew that the aging state attorney rarely even went to trial anymore, so seeing him at a routine matter like an arraignment was a bit like noticing a semiretired general on the front lines. "The govuhment," McCue continued in his deep drawl, "requests that the court set bail at—"

"I'm quite familiar with the case," the judge interrupted, "and I know the defendant. Mr. Swyteck is no stranger to the criminal courtrooms. Bail is set at one hundred thousand dollars. Next case," he announced with a bang of his gavel.

McCue's mouth hung open momentarily, unaccustomed as he was to such abrupt treatment from anyone, including judges.

"Thank you, Your Honor," said Manny.

Jack moved quickly across the courtroom to the clerk, continuing along the assembly line. Thankfully, the politicians hadn't gotten the judge to deny bail. Now all Jack had to do to get back on the street was pledge his every worldly possession to José Restrepo-Merono, the five-foot-tall, two-hundred-pound Puerto Rican president of "F. Lee Bail-Me, Inc."—the only bail bondsman ever known to have a sense of humor.

Jack returned to the holding cell for another hour or so while Manny's assistant handled the mechanical aspects of posting bail. Late that afternoon he was released, thankful he could spend the night in his own bed. He didn't have a car, since Stafford had driven him to the station. Manny's assistant was supposed to swing by and take Jack home, so he wouldn't have to wait for a taxi while fighting off reporters eager for their shot at eliciting a little quote that might make theirs the breaking story. As it turned out, though, Manny himself showed up at the curb behind the wheel of his Jaguar. The look on his face told Jack he wasn't just playing chauffeur.

"Get in," Manny said solemnly when Jack opened the door.

Jack slid into the passenger seat, and Manny pulled into the late-afternoon traffic.

"I wasn't expecting to see *you*," said Jack.

"Your father called me," Manny replied, as if that were enough to explain his appearance. He looked away from the road, just long enough to read Jack's face. "He told me about Raul Fernandez. I heard all about your request for a stay that night, and his response."

Jack smoldered, but said nothing. Instead, he made a conscious effort to look out the window.

"Okay," he said finally, "so now you know the Swyteck family secret. We not only defend the guilty. We execute the innocent."

Manny steered around the corner, then pulled into a parking space beneath a shady tree. He wanted to look right at his client as he spoke. "I don't know everything, Jack. I only know what your father knows about that night. And he's missing a key piece of information. So we both want to know if there's more to this case than whether Jack Swyteck killed Eddy Goss. He and I *both* want a straight answer from you: Did Raul Fernandez die for Eddy Goss?"

"What?" Jack asked, thoroughly confused.

"The night before Fernandez was executed, was Eddy Goss the guy who came to you and confessed to the murder? Was Raul Fernandez innocent, and Eddy Goss guilty?"

"Where did you dream up—" Jack paused, calmed himself down. "Look, Manny, if my father wants to talk, *I'll* talk to him. Fernandez is between him and me. This has nothing to do with your defending me for the murder of Eddy Goss."

"Wrong, Jack. This could have *everything* to do with the murder of Eddy Goss. Because it bears directly on your motive to kill—or to 'execute'—Eddy Goss. You can't risk letting Wilson McCue flesh out this theory before I do. So answer me, Jack. And I want the truth."

Jack looked Manny right in the eye. "The truth, Manny, is that I didn't kill Eddy Goss. And as far as who it was who came to me the night Fernandez was executed, the honest answer is that I don't know. The guy never gave me his name. He never even showed me his face. But I do know this much: It was *not* Eddy Goss. The eyes are different, the build is different, the voice is different. It's just a *different person*."

Manny took a deep breath and looked away, then gave a quick nod of appreciation. "Thanks, I know this isn't an easy subject for you. And I'm glad you leveled with me."

"Maybe it's time I leveled with my father, too. I think he and I need to talk."

"I'm advising you not to do that, Jack."

"It's kind of a personal decision, don't you think?"

"From a legal standpoint, I am *strongly* advising you not to speak to your father. I don't want you talking to anyone who might jeopardize your ability to take the witness stand in your own defense. And talking to your father is very risky."

"What are you implying?"

Manny measured his words carefully. "Right after I spoke to your father," he began, "I had an uneasy feeling. It was just a feeling, but when you've been doing this as long as I have, you follow your gut. So I went and took another look at the police file."

"And?"

"I wasn't looking for anything in particular. But I noticed that the police report showed an extraneous footprint, right outside Goss's apartment. It wasn't from you, and it wasn't from Eddy Goss. It was from someone else. Now, that's a definite plus for us, because it can help us prove that someone else was at the scene of the crime. But what has me concerned is that the footprint is very clear." He sighed. "It's from a Wiggins wing tip."

Jack's expression went white. He said nothing, but Manny read the message on his face.

"How long has your father worn Wiggins wing tips, Jack?"

"As long as I can remember," he said with disbelief. "But, you can't possibly think my father—"

"I don't know what to think. There was just something about the urgency in your father's voice—his curious tone—that concerns me. I don't know if there's something he's not telling me or what. But I do know this: I don't want my client talking to him. I can't take the risk that he'll confess something to you, and then you won't be able to take the witness stand, for fear you might incriminate your own father. Or, even worse, I don't want you being evasive on the stand because you're trying to protect your father. So until I get to the bottom of this, I want you to stay as far away from him as possible. Can I have your word on that?"

Jack felt sick inside. But he knew Manny was right. A tough judgment call like this one was precisely the reason that lawyers should never represent themselves. He needed someone like Manny to put the personal issues aside and counsel him wisely. "All right," he said with resignation. "I haven't spoken to my father in two years. I can wait a little longer. You have my word."

25

J ack woke the next morning with the memory of his conversation with Manny still vivid. He ran all sorts of hypotheses through his head but was unable to explain why his father would be involved with Goss. It just didn't make sense. He needed to find some answers, and he knew they wouldn't come to him if he sat around the house.

So, after showering and downing a quick cup of coffee, he threw on a jacket and tie and headed for the police station. He arrived at the document section around ten o'clock and asked the clerk to pull the investigative file on *State* v. *Swyteck*. He wanted to see for himself what this business of an "extraneous footprint" was all about.

Only the police, the prosecutor, the defendant, or the defendant's attorney can pull the file in a pending murder case, but Jack had done it so many times as a lawyer with the Freedom Institute that he didn't even have to show his Florida bar card to the clerk behind the counter. He just signed his name in the

registry and filled in his bar number. Out of curiosity, he checked to see who else had been review-
ing his file. Detective Stafford and his assistant, of
course . . . Manny had been there twice, as recently
as yesterday . . . and someone else had been there:
Richard Dressler, an attorney.

He had never heard of any attorney named Richard Dressler, so he checked with the file clerk to see
who he was.

"You putting me on, Mr. Swyteck?" said the young
black woman behind the counter. She had large, al-
mond eyes and straightened black hair with an
orangey-red streak on one side. Other than Jack,
she was the only person in the busy station who wasn't
a cop, and she was the only person he'd ever seen
with ten different glittering works of art on two-inch
fingernails of curling acrylic. "Richard Dressler's a
lawyer," she told Jack, looking at him as if he were
senile. "Said he was *your* lawyer."

Jack was stunned, but he put on his best poker
face. "You know," he shook his head with a smile,
"my lead counsel has so many other young lawyers
helping him on this case, sometimes I can't keep
track of them. Dressler . . ." Jack baited her, as if he
were trying to place the man. "Tall guy—right?"

She just rolled her eyes. "I don't know what he
looked like," she said, fussing with a little ornamental
rhinestone that had loosened from her thumbnail. "I
got five hundred people a day coming through here."

Jack nodded slowly. He definitely wanted to know
more about this Richard Dressler, but the last thing
he wanted to do was make an issue out of it in the

middle of the police station—deep in the heart of enemy territory. He had an idea. "I changed my mind," he said as he slid the file back over the counter to her. "Thanks anyway. I'll check it out later."

"Suit yourself," she said with a shrug.

He left the police station quickly and headed for a pay phone at the corner. He dialed the Florida bar's Attorney Information Service and asked for some basic information on Richard Dressler.

"Mr. Dressler's office is at five-oh-one Kennedy Boulevard, Tampa, Florida," the woman in the records department cheerfully reported.

A hell of a long way from Miami. "And what kind of law does he practice? Does he do criminal defense?"

The woman checked the computer screen before her. "Mr. Dressler is a board-certified real estate attorney. Would you like a listing of criminal defense lawyers in that area, sir?"

"No, thank you. That's all I need." He slowly replaced the receiver and leaned against the phone, totally confused. Why would a real estate attorney from Tampa come three hundred miles to look at a police file in Miami? And why would he pose as Jack's criminal defense lawyer? Jack could think of no reason—at least no *good* reason. He shook his head, then walked back to his car. He started thinking about the extraneous footprint that had drawn him to the police file in the first place. He wondered if Dressler had also been curious about Wiggins wing tips.

26

Harry Swyteck may not have liked the way his campaign manager had phrased it, but if Jack wasn't actually "killing" him, the publicity certainly wasn't doing his campaign any good. It was only August, and the November election was still arguably far enough away to dismiss the plunging public-opinion polls as not the pulse of the people but merely the palpitations of the times. The governor, however, was not one to sit around and wait for things to change. A road trip was in order—one of those whirlwind, statewide tours that would allow him to press the flesh and pick a few wallets in face-to-face meetings with Rotarians, Shriners, and virtually any other group that wanted a breakfast or luncheon speaker.

He finished the first of what would be many fifteen-hour days on the speaking circuit at 9:30 P.M. and retired to his motel room. The Thunderhead Motel was one of those roadside lodges familiar to any traveler who'd been forced to spend the night in some small town where the nicest restaurant was the Denny's across from a bowling alley. It was typical of those long and narrow two-story motels where the rooms on one side faced the parking lot and the rooms on the other faced the algae-stained swimming pool. The rooms facing the parking lot, however, didn't directly abut the rooms facing the pool. An interior service corridor ran through the middle of the building, for use by housekeepers and other hotel employees. That didn't seem very important, unless you also knew that the walls in the corridor were a paper-thin sheet of plaster-board, and that employees sometimes poked holes in them to satisfy their perverse curiosity.

Harry, in his second-floor room, was completely unaware of this as he peeled off his clothes and stepped into the tub for a nice hot shower. The incredibly tacky brown, orange, and yellow floral-print wallpaper made it impossible to detect any holes in the wall that separated the bathroom from the service corridor. In fact, there *was* a small hole right next to the towel rack, which offered a full view of the governor's left profile. Eight inches below that was a larger hole that accommodated the barrel of a .38-caliber revolver pointed directly at the governor's ear.

"Don't move," came a muffled voice from the other side of the bathroom wall.

The governor was both startled and confused by the sound of a strange voice over running water. He froze when he saw the barrel of the gun.

"I'll kill you if you move," came another warning, followed by the cocking of the hammer. "You know I will. You *do* recognize the voice, don't you, my man?"

Goose bumps popped up beneath the soap and lather on the governor's body. He knew the voice all right. "You're still alive?" he said with a mix of fear and wonder. It hadn't been Eddy Goss who was blackmailing him; and it couldn't have been Eddy Goss who confessed to Jack. "Why are you here?"

"Just wanted to make sure you knew it was me who fucked up your press conference, Governor."

Harry swallowed apprehensively. "And what about the reporter—Malone? What does he know?"

"Squat. I just told him Fernandez was innocent. That's all. Just enough to let *you* know I'm serious about going to the press. Didn't show him any proof—*yet*."

The governor trembled. He could barely find the nerve to ask another question, but he had to know: "Did you tell him I received a report that Fernandez was innocent before"—he paused—"before he was executed?"

"No. But I will, my man. Unless you pay up."

"You already have ten thousand."

The scoff was audible even over the sound of the still cascading shower. "You stiffed me on the last installment. You went all the way to Goss's apartment, just like I told you to. I watched you walk right up to the fucking door. And you chickened out. You turned and walked away. You didn't leave my money. And now, with interest and all, I'd say you owe me an even fifty grand."

"Fifty thousand! I don't have—"

"Don't lie to me!" he snapped. "You and that rich society bitch you married have it. And you *will* give it to me. Don't forget, Governor. I still have our last conversation on tape. No money, and the tape goes right to Malone—along with the proof that Fernandez was innocent. You hear me?"

Silenced by fear and utter disbelief that this could be happening to him, the governor stood quietly as the water from the shower pelted his body.

"Do you hear me!"

The governor shifted his eyes slowly toward the gun. "This is the end of it, right? This is the last installment."

"That's why it's fifty grand, my man. I want the whole enchilada in one big bite. So shut the fuck up and listen. Since this is the last one, I want you to buy a big bouquet of flowers—chrysanthemums, to be exact. Get one with a nice big pot. Put the money in the pot. And just for fun, put your shoes in there, too—those Wiggins wing tips you like to wear. This Friday night, seven o'clock, take the whole thing to Memorial Cemetery in Miami. Row twelve, plot two thirty-two in the west quadrant. Leave it right there. It's a flat marker."

"How do I find plot two thirty-two? Who's buried there?"

"It's a new grave. You'll recognize the name on it."

"Eddy Goss?" the governor swallowed his words.

"Raul Fernandez, asshole. Go pay your *respects*."

The barrel of the gun suddenly disappeared through the hole, and the quick footsteps and the slam of a door in the service corridor told the governor that his blackmailer was gone—for now.

27
.

Two hours after Jack had requested his file at the police station and turned up the information about Richard Dressler, he met Manny in his offices for a brainstorming session. Manny knew nothing about Dressler. He'd reviewed the police file before that name had been entered into the registry. He knew about as much as could be expected of someone who'd been retained just forty-eight hours earlier, having picked up bits and pieces from the file and a brief talk with Jack after the arraignment. Jack had a lot to tell him, and he was eager to hear Manny's assessment of the case. But after a brief overview of the salient facts, and at the risk of sounding like so many of his guilty clients at the Institute who were so quick to assert their innocence, Jack couldn't help but get to the bottom line.

"I've been framed," he said.

"Whoa," Manny half kidded. "Turning paranoid on me already, are you?"

"It's not paranoia. It's a fact, Manny. Somebody

wanted me to think Goss was stalking me. Why else would they have given me a map to Goss's apartment? Why else would they have left the chrysanthemum under Cindy's pillow the night I stayed at Gina Terisi's townhouse? That was when I, of all people, should have known it wasn't really Goss who was harassing me. Goss never left flowers anywhere. His signature was *seeds*. He had this perverse connection between chrysanthemum seeds and his own semen. He was a nut case, but he was consistent about his signature."

"So, somebody wanted you to think Goss was after you," said Manny, moving the theory along. "Why?"

"I don't know exactly why. I guess because they planned to kill him. And they planned to make it look like I did it. That's why the silencer showed up in my car at the repair shop. Somebody planted it there."

Manny stroked his chin, thinking. "And why would someone want to pin you with the murder of Eddy Goss?"

"Again," Jack said with a shrug, "I don't know. Maybe to retaliate against me for getting Goss acquitted. Friend of the victim, or somebody like that. Maybe even a cop. All the lawyers from the Freedom Institute have lots of enemies on the force. And we already have that nine-one-one call about a cop being on the scene right after Goss was killed."

That much was true. They did know about the cop. The prosecutor had disclosed that information under rules established by the Supreme Court, which required the government to disclose helpful information to the defense. "We have a recorded phone message," said Manny, putting the evidence on the cop in perspective, "but we don't have a witness, because we don't have a name and we don't know who the caller is." Then he sighed, swiveled in his leather chair, and looked out the window.

Jack studied his lawyer's face, trying to discern his thoughts. It was important to Jack that Manny believe him, not just because Manny was his attorney, but because he was the only person other than Cindy to whom Jack had proclaimed his innocence—and he was a man whose judgment people valued. That was obvious, Jack thought as he admired the way income from praiseworthy clients had helped Manny furnish his oversized office. Primitive but priceless pre-Columbian art adorned his walls and bookshelves. Sculptured Mayan warriors lined the wall of windows overlooking the glistening bay, as if worshiping the bright morning sun. A touch of sentimentality rested atop his sleek marble-top desk: a glass vase with a white ribbon around it, containing the black soil of a homeland the Cardenal family had left more than three decades ago, fleeing a Cuban revolutionary turned despot.

"Let me say this, Jack," Manny said as he turned to face his client. "I *do* believe you're innocent. Not that guilt or innocence is relevant to whether I would defend you. I want you to know it, though, because it's important you continue to tell me *everything*.

"That said," he continued, "I hope you'll understand if I don't appear overly enthusiastic about your frame-up theory. I've been doing this for twenty years. Every client I've ever represented claimed he was framed. Juries are skeptical of these kind of claims, as I'm sure you're aware. That makes it a tough defense to prove."

"Tough—but not impossible."

"No," Manny agreed. "Not impossible. And I think we already have a couple of very important leads to follow, which may prove key to your theory. One is this Richard Dressler. Who is he, and why is he snooping in your file? And second, we need to find out who made that nine-one-one call and reported they saw a police officer leaving the scene of the crime. Obviously, we need to get on both these leads immediately. It could take some time, especially tracking down the nine-one-one caller."

"We don't have time," said Jack.

"Well, we have a little time. Trial is two months away."

"The trial isn't our deadline."

"I know, but—"

"I think you're overlooking something," said Jack in a polite but serious tone. "We don't have two months. We may not even have two minutes. Whoever framed me, Manny, is a cold-blooded killer. Which means one thing: We have to find the nine-one-one caller— before *he* does."

If the newspapers Jack read over lunch were any indication, the public couldn't hear enough about the brilliant young son of the governor who'd wigged out and blown away his client. Jack was a veteran when it came to bad press, but still, it helped when he called home and picked up messages on his machine from Mike Mannon and Neil Goderich, both offering any help they could.

One newspaper story in particular had Jack concerned. After summarizing the evidence against him, it made prominent mention of the anonymous 911 call. "A little something," the article observed, "that a lawyer of Jack Swyteck's ability could seize upon to blow the case wide open."

The article made Jack feel uneasy. It was bad enough that anyone who'd looked at the police file could have learned about the 911 caller. Now, anyone who read the newspaper would know about it, too.

Jack drove the five minutes to the police station and requested the recorded 911 message. He played it over and over, until the caller's voice was one he'd recognize. The man had spoken partly in English, partly in Spanish, a hybrid that made it easier to remember.

From the station he drove to Goss's apartment building and checked the mailboxes. There were seventeen Hispanic surnames, which he wrote down. He walked to the corner phone booth, confirmed there was a telephone book, then matched the names and addresses to numbers. He then went back to his car to make the calls. He posed as a pollster from a local radio station seeking views on U.S. immigration policy, as a salesman, as someone just getting a wrong number—anything to get the person on the other end of the line to speak long enough so that he could compare his voice to the one on the 911 recording.

A few of the people weren't home. One line had been disconnected. Those people Jack did reach had clearly not made the call. After thirty minutes of calling, he still didn't have a match. *Damn*.

Sitting there outside Goss's apartment building, watching the last rays of the setting sun glint off the Mustang's windshield, he wondered if it might already be too late.

28

The next morning, a Thursday, Jack and Manny were scheduled to meet in Manny's offices with their first potential witness: Jack's alibi, Gina Terisi.

From the moment he'd called Gina to arrange the meeting, Jack had been ambivalent. He considered the frame-up theory his best defense, and as the minute hand on his watch drew closer to their eleven o'clock appointment, he found himself wanting to drop the whole idea of an alibi, rather than deal with her. Manny, however, had a different point of view.

"Humor me, Jack," said Manny, seated behind his desk. "Just for the moment, let's put this frame-up and grand-conspiracy theory of yours aside. It may sound like a good defense. But even if my investigator makes headway on this Dressler lead, a frame-up is very hard to prove. Your best defense is always going to be an alibi. Because no human being—framed, or unframed—can be in two places at one time."

"I understand that."

"And I understand your reluctance about Gina. It certainly won't sound good when the tabloids print that kinky hot sex with girlfriend's roomie is your alibi. But it will sound a lot worse if a jury comes back and says you're guilty of murder in the first degree. So," he said as he reached for his desktop telephone, "let's not keep Ms. Terisi waiting. All right, Jack?"

Jack took a deep breath. There were so many reasons he would have liked to leave Gina out of this and just forget using her as an alibi. But it was too late for that. "All right. Let's see how cooperative she is."

Manny hit the intercom button and spoke to his secretary. "Shelley, send in Ms. Terisi, please."

"Yes, Mr. Cardenal."

The office door opened, Manny's secretary stepped aside, and Gina Terisi entered the spacious corner office. Manny politely rose from his chair to greet her, and Jack followed suit, though with considerably less enthusiasm.

"Good morning," said Manny, his face alight with the expression most men wore when they first laid eyes on Gina Terisi. She was wearing a cobalt blue dress, not tight, but flattering in all the right places. Her long brown hair was up in a twist, tucked beneath a black, broad-brimmed hat, revealing sparkling diamond-stud earrings, two on the left ear, one on the right. At least a karat each, Jack observed, and undoubtedly "gifts" from one of her admirers.

"Nice to see you, Jack," she said through a forced smile.

He nodded courteously as Manny flashed a chiv-

alrous smile and stepped forward to greet her. "Please,"
he said, offering her the winged arm chair in which
Jack had been seated.

"Thanks," said Gina, making a production out
of taking her seat. Jack moved to the couch beneath the window, and Manny returned to the black
leather chair behind his desk. Both men faced their
guest. Gina crossed her long legs comfortably, as if
constructing a barrier between her and her interrogators.

"Can I get you some coffee?" Manny offered.

Gina didn't acknowledge the question. She was
busy checking her makeup in the reflection of the
glass-top table beside her.

Manny was completely unaware that he was staring as Gina applied her lipstick slowly and seduc-
tively to the bottom of her pouty lip. "Nothing for
me," she said finally. "This will be a short meeting.
I assure you of that."

"What do you mean?" asked Manny.

"It means that although I tentatively told Jack on
the phone that I'd support his alibi, I need to have
some questions answered before I commit to anything."

"That's fair enough," answered Manny. "I'll do my
best to answer them."

Gina narrowed her eyes, stressing the import of
her question. "What I need to know is this: Exactly
what time of the morning was Eddy Goss shot?"

"Why do you need to know that?" asked Jack.

Gina ignored him and looked only at Manny.
"Never mind why. Just answer my question."

Manny leaned back in his chair. He, too, was curious about the reason for the question. "We don't know exactly. But some time after four A.M. is the medical examiner's preliminary estimate, based on the fact that the blood had not yet dried by the time the police arrived on the scene."

"Four o'clock, then, was the earliest possible time he could have been shot," Gina pressed.

Manny shrugged. "If you accept the medical examiner's report, yes. There's not much doubt that death was instantaneous."

Gina seemed satisfied. "That's all I need to know," she said to Jack. "I can't testify for you. And I *won't.* The time of Goss's death changes everything."

Jack's gut wrenched. Manny shot him a glance, but he just looked away uncomfortably. "How does it change things?" Manny asked her.

"If Goss was shot after four A.M., then that makes me a very flimsy alibi. Granted, if I were to say that Jack and I went to bed, it might help Jack explain how he got his"—she smiled with false modesty—"scratches and bruises. But that's as far as it goes. It's not like I can place him somewhere else at the time of the murder."

"But you slept together," said Manny.

"No. We fucked each other. Nobody got any sleep. And, most important, he *didn't* spend the night. Jack left my townhouse before three. I'm certain of that."

Manny again glanced at his client, but Jack wouldn't look him in the eye.

Gina rose from her chair and headed for the door. "Sorry, fellas," she said as she reached the door. "I'm not going to tell the world I betrayed my best friend and went to bed with her boyfriend, when the truth really isn't much help."

Manny leaned across his desk to make his point in a firm but not quite threatening manner. "You realize we can subpoena you. We can make you testify."

"You can make me show up at the courthouse. But you can't *make* me say Jack was with me. Not unless I want to say it."

Manny knew she was right. He tried another angle. "You *should* want to," said Manny. "You should want to help Jack."

"That's just the point: I *don't* want to. Good day, gentlemen," she said coolly, then left the room, closing the door behind her.

The two men sat in uncomfortable silence, until Jack looked into Manny's piercing black eyes and said, "I warned you about her."

Manny seemed concerned, but not with Gina. "I don't think she's lying," he said sharply. "And now I understand why you were having second thoughts about the alibi. I think *you* lied to me, Jack. You told me you spent the night with her. *All* night. That was a lie, wasn't it?"

Jack sighed and averted his eyes, then responded in a quiet tone. "It happened almost exactly the way I told you before, Manny. While we were making love or having sex or whatever you want to call it, somebody *did* sneak into the townhouse and smear ketchup on the sheets and put a chrysanthemum under Cindy's pillow. And whoever it was called me and tried to get me to go back to Goss's place—which I *definitely* wasn't going to do at that point. But I didn't stay either. I honestly didn't want to leave Gina by herself—especially after seeing that some lunatic had taken a knife to my convertible. But I didn't want to wake up the next morning with Gina by my side, either. Cindy and I were technically split up at the time, but that didn't seem to matter. I just had to get the hell out of there. So I left."

"Before three o'clock."

"Right."

"At least an hour before Goss was killed."

Jack sighed. "I'm afraid so."

"Unbelievable," Manny groaned, shaking his head. "Or maybe it's not unbelievable. I suppose it's understandable that someone charged with murder might try to reach for something that's not there. But honestly, Jack: What the hell were you thinking? Did you think she was going to have amnesia about what time it was when you left her apartment?"

"I don't know," Jack grimaced. "I guess I just hoped she wasn't going to be so damn certain about the time. After all, we'd had a lot to drink. I thought she might be a little fuzzy on the time. Or maybe even she'd be wrong about the time and say I left at four-thirty."

"You were hoping she was going to lie for you."

"Not lie, no. I mean—I don't know. I don't know what I was thinking, Manny."

Manny's face showed deep disappointment. Then his eyes narrowed with suspicion. "Are there any more lies, Jack, and more important, is your alibi the *biggest* lie you've told me?"

Jack became indignant. "Are you questioning my innocence?"

"Not based on what I've heard so far. But I can't live with deception from a client who, at the very least, was willing to put himself in a position where he might *have* to kill Eddy Goss."

"I resent that. I'd never kill *anyone*."

"Really? Then why did you go inside Goss's apartment that night—before you went to Gina's? And just what were you planning to do with that pistol you were packing?"

Jack paused. It was a difficult question. "Maybe I don't know *what* I was going to do with it."

Manny looked his client straight in the eye. "You can do better than that," he said, speaking in a tone that forced Jack to search his own soul. Manny's look was not accusatory. It was not judgmental. But it still made Jack uncomfortable.

"Look, Manny. The bottom line is this: I didn't kill Eddy Goss."

"Then don't kill your chances for an acquittal," he said, "and don't manipulate your lawyer."

Jack looked him in the eye. He said nothing, but they'd reached an understanding. Then he rose from his chair and stepped toward the window. "We're really better off without Gina anyway. Better this blew up now than at trial."

Manny leaned back in his chair. "One thing still bothers me, though. When I told Gina she should help you, she said she didn't want to. That disturbs me."

"That's just Gina."

"Maybe. But when she says she doesn't want to help you, is that all she's saying? Or is she saying she wants to *hurt* you?"

Jack froze. His throat felt suddenly dry. "I don't think so. But with her, you really never know."

"We *need* to know."

"I suppose I could talk with her. I think she'd say more if it were just the two of us."

"All right," Manny nodded. "Try the personal approach. The sooner the better. Let's talk again as soon as you've had a conversation with her."

"I'll call you first thing." He shook Manny's hand, then started across the room.

"Oh, Jack," Manny called out as his client reached the door. Jack stopped short and looked back at his lawyer.

"This Gina is a key player," said Manny. "Don't get into it with her. Be polite. And if it's not going well, just ask her if she'll meet with me. Then let me handle her. And don't worry. I'm good with witnesses. Especially women."

"Thanks," Jack replied, his expression deadpan. "But you've never known a woman like this one."

29

Seventy-three-year-old Wilfredo Garcia stood in his kitchen before his old gas stove cooking dinner, *bistec palamillo* and *platanos fritos*—flank steak and fried plantains. A Cuban who'd come to the United States with grown children in 1962, he had never become completely conversant in his adopted tongue, often shifting to Spanish to get his point across. He was a likable sort, though, and even his English listeners easily forgave his linguistic limitations.

Wilfredo was pudgy, with warm, deep brown eyes and chubby cheeks. He loved to eat, and most nights he dined at home, since the area of Adams Street wasn't really safe after dark.

Tonight, just as he was smothering his steak with chopped onions and parsley, the phone rang. He glanced up, but he didn't answer. He'd been ignoring his phone calls for the past couple days, ever since he'd read that article in the newspaper about how important the 911 call could be in the case against Jack Swyteck. He knew it was only a matter of time before they'd come looking for the man who'd been so ambivalent about getting involved that he'd called from a pay phone to keep the police from tracing it. He still didn't want to get involved. So until things blew over, he'd decided to live like a hermit.

But the phone kept on ringing—ten times, and then more than a dozen. It had to be important, he figured. Maybe it was his daughter in Brooklyn. Or his bookie. He turned off the stove and picked up the phone.

"*Oigo*," he answered in his native Spanish.

"Wilfredo Garcia?"

"*Sí.*"

"This is Officer Michael Cookson of Metro-Dade Police. How you doin' this evening, sir?"

Wilfredo's heart sank. He instantly wished he hadn't answered. "Am fine." He answered in English, though his heavy accent was detectable even in his two-word response.

"Mr. Garcia, I'm just doing some routine inquiries about the murder of Eddy Goss. I understand you live on the same floor as Mr. Goss used to live on."

"Same floor, *sí*. But—*por favor*. I know nothing. I no want me involved."

"I can understand that, sir. But this is important. We're looking for the man who dialed nine-one-one from a pay phone outside your building the night Mr. Goss was killed."

Wilfredo grimaced. "I no want—"

"Hey, listen, my man," the officer said, speaking in a friendly tone, "I understand where you're coming from. Between you and me, I don't care if they ever catch the guy who killed this Goss character. But it's my job to follow up on all these things. So if you know who made the call, you might just want to pass it along to him that it's really much better to talk to the police before all the lawyers come looking for him. Will you do that for me?"

Wilfredo had a lump in his throat. "All right."

"In fact, let me make it real easy for you, Mr. Garcia, because I know how people hate to get involved in these things. I don't want you or anyone else to have to come down to the station, or even make a phone call to the station. Let me give you my personal beeper number. If you hear anything, or if one of your friends knows anything, just beep me. All I want is information. I promise I won't use your name unless I absolutely have to. Sound fair, my man?"

"*Sí.*"

"Write this down—five, five, five, two, nine hundred. Got it?"

"Uh-huh."

"Excellent. Thanks for your time, sir."

"Good-bye." Wilfredo was short of breath as he hung up. It surprised him that he'd actually written down the beeper number. He really did hate to get involved, but the same instincts that had prompted him to dial 911 in the first place were gnawing at him again. It was a long time ago that he'd been naturalized as a citizen, that he'd sworn an oath to support his country and be a good American, but his memory of it was still vivid.

He glanced at the number he'd just scribbled down.

The policeman had seemed nice enough. Maybe it wouldn't be as bad as he feared. Maybe it was time to come forward and get the monkey off his back.

Wilfredo drew a deep breath. Then he picked up the phone. His hand was shaking, but he managed to dial the number.

30

Jack put the top down and took a long drive along the beach after leaving Manny's office. Cindy had called him a couple of nights before—just to chat, but they'd talked about being apart, and suddenly he heard her saying she'd move back in. Unfortunately, the euphoria he'd felt then had been severely dampened by the past two days' events. They'd settled on tonight for her to bring her stuff over, and he knew she'd be at the house, unpacking, when he arrived. He needed time to think before facing her.

The meeting today with Gina had been a real reality check. Any prior illusions about keeping his "evening" with her a secret were beginning to dissipate. He kept looking for a way to steer a course with her that would help his case and not affect his relationship with Cindy, but nothing was coming to him.

It was shortly after six o'clock when he finally pulled into the driveway and turned off the engine, and by then he'd received a call from Manny in his car that made him even more ill at ease. He thought about the call as he got out of the Mustang and walked up the wood-chip path.

The front door opened before he'd even mounted the stairs. "Hi there," Cindy said. She stood smiling in the doorway, and although he felt miserable it was impossible for him not to throw his arms around her.

"How's the unpacking going?" he asked, closing the door behind them.

"Getting there," she said, taking his hand as they walked into the living room. "It's mostly just clothes, but I spent most of my time sifting through Gina's closet, looking for things she borrowed from me."

As they sat down on the couch, she noticed that he was brooding about something. "You're not having second thoughts, are you?"

He sighed. "Cindy, as much as I want us to be together, after today I wonder if it's such a great idea for you to move in."

"What do you mean?"

"It's not a question of loving you. I'm crazy about you. It's just that I'm not sure it's safe for you here."

"Why not?"

He exhaled, then launched into a selective summary of the events of the past two days, focusing on the Tampa real estate attorney by the name of Richard Dressler.

"So why is Dressler so interested in this?" she asked.

"He's not. I got a call from Manny driving back here. His investigator met with Dressler in Tampa. Turns out his wallet was stolen two months ago. Somebody got all his identification. Including his Florida bar card."

"So somebody's been using his bar card to pose as an attorney?"

"Exactly. This somebody used his name to check out the police file in my case *after* Goss was dead. I think the guy, whoever he is, is trying to frame me. If I'm right, it was *him* who was hassling me all along, not Goss."

Her eyes widened. "Are you saying—"

"I don't know exactly what I'm saying. I haven't thought it all the way through yet. But I'm pretty sure there's still a killer on the loose. Whoever was after me is still out there."

She took a step back. "Who is it, then? If it wasn't Eddy Goss, who could it be?"

"I don't know. But I'm going to find out. And until I do, I think it's best if you take a vacation or just get out of town for a few—"

"No. I'm staying with you, Jack. I'm not going to leave you at a time like this. We'll deal with this together."

He took a deep breath, then put his arms around her again. "We still can't call the police. I can't tell them that whoever was after me is still out there. Because the minute they find out I thought Goss was threatening me, the prosecution goes from no evidence of motive to iron-clad proof."

Cindy bit her lip. It was bad enough that a stalker

was still out there, but not being able to tell anyone was against common sense. Yet everything Jack had said seemed logical. "All right," she said with a sigh. "No police. We'll look out for ourselves, and we'll look out for each other."

That same Thursday evening, Governor Harold Swyteck checked into a room on the thirty-second floor of Miami's Hotel Intercontinental. He was scheduled to speak at a fund-raiser later that evening, but first he had to give away some money of his own. The bouquet of chrysanthemums he'd ordered was waiting for him in his room. He took the money from his briefcase—fifty thousand dollars—and placed the bills in the oversized pot. Then he took his shoes from his suitcase, all the while fighting to keep his anger under control. It was demeaning, really—like stealing a man's clothes and leaving him stranded on a street corner. But if that was the kind of cheap power trip this lunatic needed, so be it. At this point, Harry would have given much more than fifty grand to be rid of his blackmailer, once and for all.

He checked his watch. Six-thirty. With traffic, it would be about a twenty-minute drive to Memorial Cemetery. For perhaps the hundredth time that day, the governor mentally ran through his options, trying to find some way out of this ludicrousness. But both of his alternatives—calling the police or letting his tormentor do what he'd threatened—seemed unacceptable. At least, by following his blackmailer's instructions, he had a *chance* of holding on to the life he'd struggled so hard to create.

He grabbed the pot and the keys to his rental car and he was off, wondering with a growing dread if the grave he was about to visit was his own.

31

Jack and Cindy were in bed by 9:00 P.M., and they didn't stop making love to the sounds of "Love Jazz" on the radio until well after the deejay said, "Thank God it's Friday." Afterward, Jack decided he *had* to find some way to tell Cindy the truth about Gina. She was risking too much for him to be dishonest with her. Before breaking the news, however, he wanted to confirm Gina's position. He wanted to be able to tell Cindy that Gina wouldn't be telling their sordid story to the world—as a witness for the prosecution.

The following afternoon Jack was deep in thought as he headed to Gina's townhouse, driving so slowly that even carloads of tourists zoomed by him on the expressway.

Gina had just returned from jogging when Jack knocked on her door. She wore orange nylon shorts, Nike running shoes, and a skimpy tank top that had been pasted to her body by a good hard sweat. Her long brown hair was pulled back and tied behind her head.

"Can I come in?" he asked, standing in the open doorway.

Gina sipped her Gatorade Lite, her expression as cool as the ice in her glass. "Sure," she said with a shrug.

He stepped inside and closed the door, then followed her to the kitchen. "I realize this isn't your favorite subject, Gina. But the way you left Manny's office yesterday, I felt like we should talk."

Gina went to the refrigerator for a refill on her drink. "I've pretty much said it all, haven't I?"

"That's what I'm here to find out. That crack you made yesterday about not wanting to help me. That worried me."

"Well," she said with a wry smile, "maybe I did lay it on a little thick. But you got the point of my performance: I don't want to get involved. That shouldn't surprise you, Jack. I honestly don't think it even upsets you. I could see it on your face. The *last* thing you wanted was for me to be your alibi."

"You don't know what I want, Gina."

"Oh, no?" she said coyly, switching to a low, sexy voice. She suddenly felt challenged. She moved closer to him, so close that he could feel her breath on his cheek and smell the sweat that reminded him of things he should never have done. She reached behind her head and tugged on the sweatband, letting her hair down. "Let me put it another way, Jack. Did you actually *want* me to say I touched this body," she said, gliding her open hand lightly over his chest, a half inch away from touching him, but never making physical contact. "That I felt the weight of it on top of me. That we tangled and sweated and screamed in the night, that with each thrust I dug my nails into your back and sunk my teeth into your chest, crying out for more, even though you were more than enough for any woman. Is that *really* what you wanted? And if you did," she whispered, now looking deeply into his eyes, "did you want Cindy in or out of the courtroom when I said it?"

Jack pulled himself away from her. "What happened between you and me was a mistake. I think we both regret it. And you certainly could have been my alibi without making it sound so lurid."

Gina emptied her Gatorade into the sink and opened the liquor cabinet. She filled her glass with Campari and ice. "Are you negotiating with me?"

"Negotiating for what?"

She arched an eyebrow, then sipped her drink. "Do you want me to say you didn't leave my townhouse until after four o'clock?"

Jack knew her serious look, and she was definitely being serious. "Just hold it right there, Gina. You've totally got the wrong idea. I didn't come here for that."

"I didn't say you did. But, then again, think about the last time you came here. You didn't come here to make love to me. But you did."

"And I wish it had never happened."

"Do you? Or do you just wish Cindy would never find out about it?"

He looked away, trying not to lose his temper. He brought his emotions under control, then gave her a very lawyerly look. "Listen, Gina, I didn't come here to talk you into being my alibi. I just wanted to make sure you weren't going to testify *against* me."

Her eyes widened. "Don't be absurd, Jack. I would never do that."

"And as far as what happened between you and me—no, I haven't told Cindy yet. But she'll know everything. Just as soon as I find the right time to tell her."

"There is no *right* time, Jack. I know Cindy. I know her better than you do. If she finds out about us, you can bet that neither one of us will ever see her again. The only reason there'd ever be to tell her anything is if I were going to be your alibi. And I'm not. So it's final. I won't have you shooting your mouth off to Cindy in some juvenile attempt to soothe your conscience. I won't allow it."

"It's not up to you."

"Oh, yes, it is. Because I'm taking back what I said earlier. I can't say I would *never* testify against you. Because there *is* one way I would. If you tell Cindy about us, I swear I'll tell the police everything— including how you came to my apartment thinking Eddy Goss was after you and Cindy.

"And that's only the half of it. I'll tell the world what really happened between us—how you *really* got your scratches and bruises. I'll tell them how I invited you inside my townhouse because you had scared me to death about Eddy Goss. How I trusted you when you said you'd sleep on the couch. And how I scratched and bruised you only after you snuck into my room, tore off my nightgown, and forced yourself on me." She took a long sip and finished the rest of her drink. "It's your choice. Just grow up and keep what happened between us to yourself. Or face the consequences."

Jack stared with disbelief. "Why are you doing this? Why not just live with the truth?"

"Because the truth helps no one. If I tell the truth to the police, it hurts you. If you tell the truth to Cindy, it hurts us both. So those are my terms. Neither of us talks. Or we both talk. Take your pick."

He would have loved to tell her to butt out of his relationship with Cindy, but he couldn't. Maybe she was bluffing—he certainly couldn't believe she would fabricate a rape claim. But he was in no position to take that kind of risk. "All right," he said with resignation. "I'll take your terms, Gina. And just be glad I don't have a choice."

"Smart boy," she said, smiling. She raised her glass. "Can I offer you some Campari?"

He didn't bother to answer as he let himself out.

At 5:30 A.M., Wilfredo Garcia was awakened by a loud knock on the door. He'd been up most of the night, his mind racing. It had been almost thirty-six hours since he'd beeped Officer Cookson, but he still hadn't heard back. He was beginning to worry.

The knocking continued. Wilfredo rolled from his mattress, which lay on the floor.

"*Un momento.*" He put on his robe and stepped into his slippers, then shuffled toward the door.

There was a place for a peephole in the door, but the little window had been removed and replaced with a wad of putty. Wilfredo removed the putty and peered into the hallway. It was dark, as usual, but he could see well enough to recognize the midnight blue uniform.

"It's Officer Cookson," came the voice in the darkness.

The old Cuban gentleman opened the door just a crack and peered through the opening. He was a foot shorter than the policeman and nearly twice as old.

"Can I come in, sir?"

Wilfredo felt a mixture of relief and anxiety. He didn't know what to expect, but he certainly didn't expect a cop to show up at this hour. Nonetheless, he nodded his head obediently and opened the door the rest of the way. The officer stepped inside and closed the door behind him. Wilfredo switched on a lamp with no shade, then turned and faced his visitor.

The old man froze at the sight. He hadn't been able to make out the features in the dark hallway, but in the better lighting it was clear. The build, the complexion, the sweeping dark eyebrows. A thousand different things were hitting him at once, and each screamed out the similarities between this man and the man he'd seen on the night Goss was murdered. His hands trembled and his heart hammered in his chest as he suddenly realized he was staring into the eyes of a killer. He turned to run, but the man in the uniform grabbed him by the shirt and pulled him back. Wilfredo opened his mouth to cry out for help, but before he could utter a word, the deadly hand of a trained killer came up from below and delivered a powerful jolt to the base of his chin. His head snapped back with the force of a rear-end collision, cracking the frail old vertebrae in his neck until the crown of his head met the middle of his back. In an instant Wilfredo went limp.

The killer released his grasp of the old man's nightshirt, and let the body fall to the floor. He bent down and felt for a pulse. There was none. His job was done.

He straightened his stolen uniform, put on his dark glasses, and then quietly left the apartment, closing the door behind him. Once again, he left behind his handiwork at 409 East Adams Street. Once again, his footsteps echoed through the empty hallway—like just another beat cop making the rounds.

Part Four

Tuesday, October 11

32

"All rise!" were the words that set everything in motion, like the blast from a starter's pistol. After nine weeks of preparation, the stage was finally set. On one side of the courtroom sat a publicity-craving prosecutor, cloaked in the presumption of validity that came with his office. On the other sat a beleaguered defendant, clinging to the presumption of innocence that came with his predicament. Wilson McCue would go it alone for the government. Jack and his lawyer would see this through together, a joint defense, unified in their resistance.

Judge Virginia Tate emerged from her chambers through a side entrance to the courtroom. She was black and white in motion, with pasty white skin, salt-and-pepper hair, steely dark eyes, and a long, double strand of pearls swaying against her black robe. The thunderous clatter of reporters and spectators rising to their feet only added to the effect of her entrance. As she sat in a black leather chair, she looked first at the lawyers and then at the reporters, momentarily shedding her dour expression for a pleasant but tough smile.

"Let's get moving," she said and with those distinctly unceremonial words began the first of what would be nine days of jury selection, the phase lawyers referred to as voir dire. It was during this phase that opposing counsel would summon their best psychoanalytic powers, divining who should serve and who should be rejected. Jack could only feel helpless in these circumstances. Manny called the shots, displaying his finely honed skills for all to admire; Jack sat in silence, passing an occasional breath mint or a scribbled message, at once useless yet indispensable to the performance, like a page turner for a concert pianist. And it would remain that way for weeks. He would speak only through Manny. Wear clothes approved by Manny. Take his place at the polished walnut table beside Manny. He was on display as much as he was on trial.

Judge Tate had been apprehensive throughout jury selection. She was well aware of Wilson McCue's reputation for abusing voir dire—for using it to present his case to the jury or to prejudice his opponent, his questions doing less to elicit information than to advocate his position. McCue had behaved himself, for the most part—until Friday of the second week of selection, when they were finally on the verge of empaneling a jury.

"Do any of the jurors know Mr. Swyteck personally?" McCue began innocently enough. The prospective jurors simply shook their heads. "Surely you have *heard* of Mr. Swyteck," was his follow-up, eliciting a few nods. "Of course you have," he said with a smirk. "Mr. Swyteck was the lawyer who defended the infamous Eddy Goss, the man he is now charged with having murdered." Then that gleam appeared in his eye as he put his first drop of poison into the well. "Let me ask you this, ladies and gentlemen: Would anyone here be less inclined to believe Mr. Swyteck because he's a slick lawyer who was able to persuade twelve jurors to find a confessed killer not guilty?"

"Objection," said Manny.

"Sustained."

"Your Honor," McCue feigned incredulity. "I'm a little surprised by the objection. I'm just trying to ensure a fair panel. I mean, there are people who might even want to hold Mr. Swyteck responsible for all those grotesque murders his guilty clients committed—"

"That's enough!" the judge rebuked. "You are much more transparent than you realize, Mr. McCue. Move on. *Now.*"

"Surely," he agreed, having already made his point.

"I mean it," the judge said sternly. "I'll have no more of that."

Like a man testing fate, McCue seemed to get more outrageous with Manny's repeated objections, each of which was sustained and followed by increasingly stern reprimands from the judge. His antics pushed jury selection well into that Friday afternoon. But by the middle of that ninth interminable day the judge finally had some good news.

"We have a jury," she announced with relief.

A burly black construction worker who carried his lunch every day in the same crinkled paper sack; a retired alligator poacher with cowboy boots, tobacco-stained teeth, and a crew cut; and a blue-haired widow whose juror identification number, fifty-five, might have been half her age were just three of the twelve "peers" who would decide whether Jack Swyteck would live or die.

It was nearly four o'clock in the afternoon, and normally Judge Tate would have called it a day at that point, recognizing that there wasn't enough time for both the state and the defense to present opening statements. But in light of McCue's conduct during jury selection, she had a plan that would allow her to finish opening statements and still have plenty of time to watch herself on the six o'clock news.

"Mr. Cardenal," the judge said with a nod, "please proceed for the defense."

Manny rose slowly, giving the judge a confused look.

McCue also rose. "With all due respect," he interjected in his most folksy manner, "the govuhment usually gives the first opening statement."

The judge glared, then spoke explicitly, so that the jury would understand exactly what she was doing.

"We know the government *usually* goes first," she said. "But we warned you repeatedly—you were making your opening statement while selecting a jury. So now the defense gets its turn; you've had yours."

McCue was dumbstruck. "Your Honor, that seems

pretty draconian, don't you think? I mean, if I could just have a couple of minutes. That's all—"

"Very well. You have two minutes."

"Well," he backpedaled, "I mean two min—"

"You've just wasted ten seconds of your two minutes."

At that, McCue scurried across the room, putting on his jury face. His big, dark eyes were full of life as they peered over the spectacles that he wore low on the bridge of his prominent nose, Teddy Roosevelt-style. Even in a serious moment like this, a trace of a smile lit up his happy, round face, making it clear why people said Wilson McCue was simply an overgrown good ol' boy at heart.

"Ladies and gentlemen of the jury," he said, pacing as he spoke, "this case is about murder, about power . . . the power over life and death. By the will of the people, we *do* have capital punishment in this state: We recognize the power of the government to put convicted killers to death. What we don't recognize, however, are the misguided efforts of private citizens to exercise that power at will. We do not allow vigilantes to take the awesome power of the state into their own hands. We do not permit men to carry out their own private executions, whatever their motive.

"As the evidence in this case unfolds, ladies and gentlemen, you will come to know a man who did indeed take that power into his own hands. This man was a lawyer. A lawyer who had devoted his professional life to defending men and women who were accused of some of the most violent murders this community has ever seen. Most, if not all, of his clients were guilty. A few were convicted. Now, there's nothing wrong with that. Some lawyers would say it's even admirable to defend the rights of the guilty. It's in the public interest, they might argue."

McCue moved closer to the jury, addressing each of the twelve as individuals, as if it were just the two of them sitting on his front porch, sipping lemonade and watching the sun set. "But it's not the public interest or even this lawyer's public service that is at issue here," he said in a low but firm voice. "You are here as jurors today because this lawyer," his voice grew louder, "the defendant in this case, has a private side—a very dark private side. The evidence will show that on August second, at roughly four o'clock in the morning, he burst into an apartment—another man's *home*—and made himself judge, jury, and executioner. He took out his thirty-eight-caliber pistol, fired off two quick shots, and slew his own client. And ladies and gentlemen, the defendant—the man who did this deed—is sitting right here in this courtroom," McCue said solemnly, scowling as he pointed an accusing finger. "His name is Jack Swyteck."

Jack suddenly felt the weight of the government's case, as if McCue's pointed finger had brought it to rest on his shoulders at that very moment. *How true it all sounds!* he thought morosely as the hallowed courtroom seemed to transform even this blowhard state attorney into something dignified, the way dirt becomes soil just because it's in a nursery, or spit becomes saliva when in a dentist's office.

"You have fifteen seconds left," the judge intoned.

"My time is short," McCue grumbled, "and I don't have nearly enough to lay out all the evidence against Mr. Swyteck. But you will see and hear all of it over the next several days. And at the end of the case, I will come back before you—and then I will ask you to find Jack Swyteck *guilty* of murder in the first degree."

McCue paused, the silence in the room seeming to reinforce his words. Then he headed back to his seat.

Manny rose and stepped toward the jury, exchanging glances with McCue as he passed. Manny stood comfortably before the jury, made eye contact with each of the jurors, and then held up the indictment in one hand and read loudly: "*The State* versus *Jack Swyteck.*" He let his hand fall to his side, still clutching the indictment. "*The State,*" he repeated, this time with emphasis, "versus *Jack Swyteck*. Now, *that*," he said, his resonant voice making his audience shiver, "is power. And Mr. McCue is right in one respect: This case *is* about power. And what you have seen so far is simply the power to accuse," he said as he flipped the indictment irreverently on the prosecutor's table, then faced the jury squarely. "Because that's all an indictment is, ladies and gentlemen: an accusation. In a criminal case, the government has no *power*. It has only a burden. It has the burden of proving its case beyond a reasonable doubt. Over the next few weeks, the testimony, the evidence, the *facts*," he hung on the last word, "will show you that the government is powerless to meet that heavy burden . . . because Jack Swyteck is an innocent man."

Jack's gut twitched. Just how innocent did he have to be, he wondered. Just how much would this jury make McCue prove? Jack knew that his lawyer would address all those things in his opening statement, and he wanted to hear every word of it. But he was having trouble focusing. McCue hadn't said anything that he hadn't expected him to say, but finally hearing the accusations directly from the prosecutor's mouth had deeply affected him. It was as if Jack had convinced himself that the prosecutor didn't really have any evidence, and now he had to deal with the fact that McCue just might have all the evidence he needed.

"And when you evaluate the testimony of the government witnesses," Manny told the jurors, "remember that not a single one of these witnesses *saw* my client commit a crime. The government's case is based entirely on circumstantial evidence: Not a single government witness will say they saw Mr. Swyteck do *anything* illegal with their own two eyes."

Jack scanned the courtroom. All eyes were on Manny except . . . What was it? He looked around again, more slowly this time, focusing. There it was. A man seated in the last row of public seating was staring at him—not the way a curious observer would stare, but in a penetrating, communicative way. He looked familiar. Tall and broad-shouldered. A very round, clean-shaven head. The sparkle of a diamond stud on his left earlobe. And then the image of the man merged with another. Jack could see himself standing outside Goss's apartment on the night Goss was killed. He was pounding on the door. A man had stepped into the hall, a few doors down from Goss's apartment, and shouted, "Cut the racket." Without question, this was that same man.

Jack quickly looked away from the man. He tried to listen to Manny's opening statement but couldn't keep his concentration. *What the hell's that guy doing here?* he asked himself. It seemed odd that Goss's neighbor would be in the courtroom. He could have been a compelling witness for the prosecution. He could identify Jack and place him at the scene of the crime. But he obviously wasn't going to be a witness. As a lawyer, Jack knew that the rules of court prevented potential witnesses from being in the courtroom at any time before they testified. He glanced again at the man. The cold, unnerving look in his eye was definitely one of recognition, which only increased Jack's confusion.

The next thing he knew he was hearing Manny say "Thank you very much," to the jury. He couldn't believe it! He pried his tight, starched collar from his throat and sighed. After weeks of anticipation, he'd missed his own lawyer's opening statement. But it didn't seem to matter. Curiosity now consumed him. Who *was* that guy?

"Ladies and gentlemen," said the judge, "we will break for the weekend now. But due to the inordinate amount of publicity attending this trial, I am exercising my prerogative to sequester the jury. The jurors should check with the clerk about accommodations. Thank you. Court's in recess until nine o'clock Monday morning," she announced, banging her gavel.

Jack rose quickly as the shuffle and murmur of spectators and reporters filled the courtroom. He didn't wait for Manny to offer him a ride home. "I gotta get out of here," he said, his eye still on the man in the last row. "Can you keep the press busy while I duck out and find a cab?"

"Sure," said Manny as he closed his briefcase. "But what's the rush?"

"There's something I have to check out," he said, giving Manny no time to ask what. He quickly stepped away and passed through the swinging gate that separated the lawyers from the audience, pushing his way through the crowded aisle and ignoring calls from reporters. Manny was a few steps behind. With his height Jack could see over the crowd just well enough to keep a bead on the back of the man's shaved head.

"I'll take all your questions right over here," Jack heard Manny announce as the crowd poured from the courtroom into the lobby. Most of the reporters moved in one direction, and Jack immediately went the other way, toward the elevator, where the clean-shaven head was just then passing through the open doors of a packed car, going down. Jack dashed through the maze of lawyers, reporters, and spectators, trying to keep his target in sight. A couple of reporters tagged along, persisting with their probing questions. He was just ten feet from the closing elevator doors when he broadsided a blur of pin-striped polyester, a five-foot-tall personal-injury lawyer with files tucked under both arms. The collision sent papers flying and bodies sprawling, like the violent end of a bowling lane.

"You jerk!" the man cried from the floor.

"Sorry," said Jack, though he was sorry only that the elevator had just left without him. He left the man on the floor and his manners behind as he sprinted toward the stairwell and barged through the emergency door. He leaped down two and three steps at a time, covering five flights in little longer than it would have taken his hundred-and-ninety-pound body to fall down the shaft. He burst through the metal door at the bottom, catching his breath as he scanned the main lobby. The place was bustling, as it always was, but the crowd was scattered enough for him to see that he'd been too slow. The elevator had already emptied, and the man with the clean-shaven head was nowhere to be found. Jack charged out of the courthouse and stood atop the granite steps, searching desperately. The sidewalks were full of rush-hour traffic, but the man had disappeared. Dejected, Jack lumbered down the steps, hailed a cab, and jumped into the backseat.

"Where to?" asked the driver.

Jack started to give his home address, hesitated, then replied, "Four-oh-nine East Adams Street."

Adams Street was twenty long blocks from the courthouse, each block representing a geographic uptick in the crime rate. The sun was setting as the taxi entered Eddy Goss's old neighborhood, steering past mountains of trash and vandalized buildings. The driver left Jack off at the curb right in front of Goss's apartment building. Jack passed a twenty through the open car window for a ten dollar fare, and before he could ask for change the driver was gone.

Once inside, Jack retraced his journey of eleven weeks earlier up to the second floor, to a very long, graffiti-splattered hallway with apartments on either side. It was just as dark as the last time; not even the murder of tenant Wilfredo Garcia had prompted the landlord to replace a single burned-out or missing bulb.

Jack walked briskly down the dimly lit hall and came to a halt before number 217, Eddy Goss's old apartment. Yellow police tape barricaded the doorway, but Jack had no intention of going inside. He stood in front of the door just long enough to look down the hall and determine the apartment from which the neighbor had emerged that night. It was only a second before he was certain: four doors down— apartment 213, the one with a swastika spray-painted on it. He walked the thirty feet, knocked firmly on the door, and waited. There was no reply. He knocked a little harder, and the force of his knock pushed the door halfway open.

"Hello?" he called out. But no one answered. With a gentle push, the door swung all the way open, revealing a dark efficiency that had been completely ravaged. Huge holes dotted the plasterboard walls like mortar fire. Newspapers, bags, empty boxes, and other trash covered a floor of cracked tile and exposed plywood. Broken furniture was piled up in the corner. The room's only window had been boarded up from the outside. He checked the number on the door to verify he was in the right place. He was, so he stepped inside, sending a squealing rat scurrying to the kitchen. He looked around in confusion and disbelief.

"What the hell you doing here?" demanded a man in the doorway. Jack wheeled around, expecting to see Goss's neighbor. But it was an old man with yellow-gray hair and a scowl on his pasty white face. He was wearing a T-shirt stained with underarm perspiration, and a toothpick dangled from his mouth.

"The door was open, so I came in. I'm looking for someone. Tall guy. Shaved head. He was living here on the second of August."

"The hell he was," the old man said, the toothpick wagging as he spoke. "I'm the manager of this dump, and there wasn't *nobody* livin' here on no second of August. Ain't nobody lived in this rat hole goin' back more than a year."

"But—he said he had a two-year-old kid."

"Kids?" the manager scoffed. "Here?" Then his look soured. "I'm puttin' the padlock back on the door one more time. And if it's broken off again, I'm gonna remember you, mister. We've had two murders in three months in this building—both of them on this floor. So get your butt outta here, or I'm callin' the cops."

Jack didn't argue. He lowered his head and left the way he had come, down the hall, down the stairs, and out the front door.

It was nearly dark outside when he stepped out of

the building, but the streetlights hadn't yet come on. From the top of the steps he saw someone on the sidewalk across the street, standing in the shadows of what little daylight remained. Jack looked at him carefully, and the man glared back. He felt a chill of recognition: *It's him.*

Suddenly the man bolted, running at an easy pace back toward the courthouse. Jack instinctively gave chase, sprinting across the street and down the sidewalk as fast as he could in his business suit and black-soled shoes. The man didn't seem to be trying to pull away. He was taunting Jack, as if he wanted him to catch up. Jack came within fifteen feet, and then the man pulled away, effortlessly disappearing into the Greyhound parking lot two blocks down the street. Jack tried to follow, stopping and starting again and again, catching a glimpse of him every second or two as he weaved between coaches bound for New York, Chicago, and Atlanta. Revving engines filled the air with window-rattling noise and thick exhaust. Thoroughly winded, Jack stopped between two coaches and looked frantically for his target. He scanned in one direction, then the other. Nothing. The door to the empty bus beside him was open. Cautiously, he stepped inside and peered down the aisle.

"I know you're in here," Jack called out, though he was far from certain. There was only silence. He took one step down the dark aisle, then thought better of it. If his man were crouched down between the seats, he had to come out sometime. Jack decided he'd wait for him outside.

He turned to leave, but suddenly the door slammed

shut. He wheeled around to see that someone was standing behind him, but a quick blow to his head and then another to the gut doubled him over in pain. Another blow to the back of the head and he was face-down on the floor. His attacker threw himself on top of him from behind and pressed a knife to his throat.

"Don't even *think* of moving."

Jack froze as the blade pinched at his neck.

"I'd really *hate* to have to slit your throat, Swyteck—after all the trouble I've gone to."

Jack clenched his fist tightly. "Who are you?"

"Think back. Two years ago. The night before Raul Fernandez was executed."

Jack felt a chill as the voice came back to him. "What do you want from me?"

"I want justice. I want you to die like Raul died—in the chair for a murder you didn't commit."

"That's not justice," he struggled to say. "This is sick. And it won't work."

"It'll work," the man said, laughing as he drew a little blood with a slight twist of the knife. "Remember: You're alive only because I let you live. You might think you're safe. The locks on your doors. The alarm on your car. All that's just bullshit. It's like that warm, safe feeling people get by closing the drapes in their house at night, when for all they know there's a guy with an axe outside their window with his face up against the glass. There's no protection from that, Swyteck. All you can do is play by the rules. *My* rules."

"Such as?"

"There's only one. This trial is me against you,

one-on-one. You try to turn it into anything else, and I promise you, innocent people are gonna get hurt."

"What does that mean?"

"You're smart. Figure it out, asshole."

"Why—"

"Why must you die?" The man leaned forward until Jack felt his breath on the back of his neck. "Because there's a killer on the loose," he said in a cold whisper. "And the killer is *you.*"

Jack gasped as he felt the knife press harder against his throat. Then his attacker sprung to his feet and vanished into the night. Jack just lay there, his face resting on the gritty floor, feeling like he did when he was five years old. Like he was all alone.

33

Ten weeks had passed since Harry Swyteck followed his blackmailer's instructions and left the final payoff at Memorial Cemetery. Thankfully, the dark forebodings that had plagued him that night turned out to be false apprehensions. The journey to the cemetery passed without incident—though the governor did experience profound discomfort as he looked down at Raul Fernandez's final resting place.

Harry had not been in the courtroom today for opening statements. But he'd received a full report from one of the young lawyers who served as governor's counsel. The purpose of opening statements was for each side to give the jury a road map identifying the evidence that they intended to present during trial. After analyzing the direction the defense seemed to be taking, it struck Harry as odd that Manny hadn't made a reference to the 911 caller's report of a man in a police uniform leaving the scene of the crime.

The governor had promised Manny that, although he was paying the bills, the legal strategy would be up to Manny and Jack. Therefore, he was reluctant to second-guess Manny's opening statement. But he feared the lawyer might have gotten the wrong idea. Perhaps Manny hadn't brought up the 911 call because Harry had once been a police officer. If that was the case, Harry needed to set Manny straight. He caught the next flight from Tallahassee, and by eight o'clock that evening he was sitting across from his son's attorney.

"Thanks for meeting me on such short notice," Harry said as he studied the exotic decor of Manny's office.

"My pleasure," Manny replied. "You mentioned on the phone that you had some concerns about my strategy."

"Yes," Harry said. "Well, not concerns really, just areas that I needed clarified."

"Such as?"

"Well, the nine-one-one call, for one. I'm told that you didn't mention it in your opening statement today." The governor looked at him appraisingly. "I don't mean to insult you, Manny, or question your integrity. But I want to make it clear that I hired you to represent Jack for one reason only: because you're the best in the business, and because I think that if anyone can get my son acquitted, you can. *How* you go about it is up to you and Jack. If that means making the police look bad—well, so be it. I'm a former cop. But I'm a father first."

Manny nodded slowly, seeming to measure his response. "I understand what you're saying. And I'm not insulted. You're not the first concerned parent who's walked into my office. You are, however, the first concerned parent to leave a footprint outside the door of the murder victim's apartment."

The governor went rigid. All expression ran from his face. "What are you talking about?"

Manny was a master at reading reactions. He was testing Harry, and Harry had flunked. "Please, don't say anything. Let's just say I know you didn't come here because I decided not to mention the nine-one-one call. You're here because I didn't mention the footprint."

"What *footprint?*" Harry was genuinely confused—and concerned.

Manny frowned, sat up straighter in his chair. "I honestly don't think we should discuss this any further, Governor. Rest assured, I'll use the footprint at trial, if it's necessary to win Jack's case. That I didn't mention it as a matter of argument doesn't mean that I won't offer it later as a matter of *evidence.*"

"But Manny, I honestly have no idea what footprint you're talking about."

"And that's precisely the response I would expect from you. Like I said. I don't think you and I should discuss this any further. I'm Jack's lawyer, not yours. And you should have a lawyer."

"Me?" he chuckled nervously. "Why do *I* need a lawyer?"

Manny leaned forward, not to threaten him, but to convey the import of what he was about to say. "Let me spell it out for you. You've told me some things about the night Raul Fernandez was executed—about what happened between you and Jack. But I don't think that's the end of the story."

"What do you mean?"

"Well, I'm sure you heard about that old man in Goss's apartment building who got his neck snapped a few weeks ago. Tragic thing—a real mystery. The police don't even have a motive, yet. Can you think of one, Governor?"

Harry's face showed irritation. "No, except that there are lunatics out there who like to kill innocent people."

"There's more to it than that, I think. I reviewed the investigative file in that old man's case. There were extraneous footprints in his apartment. Turns out that the lunatic who snapped the old man's neck in apartment two-oh-one was wearing wing tips. Wiggins wing tips. The *same* Wiggins wing tips that left a very clear footprint outside Eddy Goss's door on the night *he* was killed."

The governor went cold. He'd been wearing the same brand the night he'd gone to Goss's apartment. And now he realized the purpose of the seemingly silly "souvenir" he'd left on the grave of Raul Fernandez, along with the money and flowers—right before the old man had been murdered.

"Now," said Manny, "you're the former cop, Governor. Maybe it's time for you to remind yourself of your right to remain silent. And of your right to an attorney. Your *own* attorney."

The governor shook his head slowly, but said nothing more than "thank you" and "good night."

34

·

A taxi took Jack from the bus station and dropped him at the end of his driveway just before nine. He was still shaken from the attack, but fortunately he had time to recuperate. It was Friday night, and there was a weekend between opening statements and what would surely be the worst Monday of his life—the day the first witness for the prosecution would take the stand against him.

He stepped slowly up the stairs of his front porch and reached out wearily with his key, but the front door flew open and Cindy greeted him with a smile.

"I hope you have a reservation," she said.

"What?"

"All right," she said, pretending to give in. "I'll let you in this time, but no complaints about the evening's menu."

She looked great in her short black skirt and paisley blouse.

As he walked into the house, he was met by the mixed scent of her perfume and a tangy, buttery smell coming from the kitchen. A quick glance at the dining room table revealed flickering candles.

Okay, I get it, Jack thought to himself. To take some of the edge off my first day in court, she's knocked herself out and prepared a candlelit dinner.

As he passed into the bright light of the front hall, she noticed the scratches on his face and his soiled clothes. "What happened to you?" she asked.

He swallowed hard. "I met him tonight. The guy who's been stalking me."

She froze. "You *what?*" Eyes wide with fright, she took him by the arm and led him into the living room. She switched on the lamp and took a closer look at his scratches. "It doesn't look serious," she said. "But what happened?"

He lowered himself onto the couch. She sat beside him and listened as he told her everything, beginning with the night Goss was killed: Jack's banging on Goss's door, the man stepping out of the apartment down the hall to complain about the noise, the same man staring at Jack in the courtroom, the return to East Adams Street, and finally the attack on the bus.

With some difficulty he also told her about the night Raul Fernandez was executed, and his inability to persuade his father to grant a stay.

After listening to his monologue, she felt like she'd finally met Jack for the first time. "I'm glad you told me—about you and your father. But this attack. What does it mean?"

He took a deep breath. "It confirms that Eddy Goss was never after me. And it confirms that I'm being framed. This guy killed Goss, and then made it look like I did it. It's poetic justice in his eyes. Raul Fernandez died an innocent man. I'm his killer. So I have to die, too—for a crime I didn't commit."

"But that doesn't make sense. Why you? After all, you pleaded with your father to stop the execution. If this guy is trying to avenge Fernandez's death, why are you the target, instead of your father?"

Jack shook his head. "I don't know. I don't know how his crazed mind works."

"And what's his motive? I understand that he's punishing you for the execution. But why's he so attached to Raul Fernandez? What's the connection?"

Jack sighed. "I don't know that either."

"Oh, Jack," she said, holding him close. "Why would anyone hate you this much? It scares me that he *enjoys* hating you so much. He's taunting you, Jack. He's playing with you like this is a game."

Jack nodded in agreement. He looked into her eyes, then repeated the suggestion he'd made to her weeks ago. "I really think you should get out of Miami. The man put a knife to my throat, Cindy. I still can't tell the police about it. I need to call Manny, but I'm sure he'll agree with me. It's no different now than it was before: I still can't give the prosecutor proof of my motive to kill Eddy Goss."

A knock at the door interrupted them.

"Did you invite someone else for dinner?" he asked.

"Of course not."

The knocking continued. "I'll get it," he said.

"What if it's *him?*"

"I know what he looks like now. I'll know if it's

him before I open the door." Jack walked briskly through the living room and stopped in front of the door. A third round of harsh knocking began, then it stopped as he flipped on the porch light. He peered out through the peephole and saw a man staring back at him with a dour expression. He wore a beige short-sleeve shirt, chocolate-brown pants, and black patent-leather shoes that glistened in the porch light. And he had a gun with a pearl-white handle tucked in to a heavy black shoulder holster. His official license to bear a sidearm—a shiny gold badge—was pinned to his chest. Jack opened the door.

"Evenin'," the officer said in a polite but businesslike tone. "I'm with the county sheriff's department. I'm looking for Miss Cindy Paige."

A lump came to Jack's throat, followed by second thoughts about opening the door.

"I'm Cindy Paige," she said, standing behind Jack.

"This is for you," the sheriff announced as he handed her an official-looking document.

Jack intercepted the delivery.

"What is it?" Cindy asked.

"It's a subpoena."

"A trial subpoena," the sheriff clarified.

"What's it for?" she asked.

"Be at the courthouse, Monday, nine A.M.," the sheriff commanded. "You're the government's first witness in *State* versus *Swyteck*."

"The *government's* first witness?"

"Don't say another word," Jack advised her. He quickly closed the door on the sheriff.

"I can't believe this," she said as her eyes welled

with tears. "Why me? Why do they want *me* to go first?"

"Maybe because you're honest," he said. "The prosecutor probably thinks he can get you to say something to hurt me."

She pulled back and looked into his eyes. "Never."

"I know you wouldn't," he said as he pulled her close. As he pulled her close, he noticed that smoke and the smell of their burning dinner had begun to seep in from the kitchen. *At least not intentionally*, he thought.

35

The air seemed electric with possibility that Monday morning as the players in the drama of *State* v. *Swyteck* assembled for the opening act. The script called for the prosecution to present its version of events first. After Jack's character was thoroughly impugned and his actions given the most sinister interpretation, the defense would come on and try to reverse the brainwashing. It seemed almost amazing, really, that juries so often reached the right result. But the lofty notion that this was the best system in the world was little consolation for an innocent man who might well be put to death.

"Call your first witness, Mr. McCue," the judge ordered.

"The State calls Cindy Paige," McCue announced.

Jack's heart sank. It was no bluff.

A sea of heads turned in unison toward the rear of the courtroom as Cindy emerged through the twelve-foot swinging doors. She looked nervous, but only Jack could detect just how nervous she truly was. He knew the little signs—the tightness in her lower lip, the stiffness in her walk, the way she pressed her thumb against her forefinger.

She wore a beige skirt and matching jacket, with a powder-blue blouse. "Look soft and sympathetic," Manny had told her last night. And she did.

"Do you swear to tell the truth, the whole truth . . ." the bailiff said, administering the familiar oath. Jack looked on from across the courtroom, watching Cindy's raised right hand tremble just slightly. It was ironic, he thought, that she appeared so anxious. If ever there was a person who could be counted on to tell the truth, it was her.

Wilson McCue allowed the witness to settle into the old Naugahyde chair, then began innocuously enough. "Please state your name," he requested.

Cindy shifted in her chair, as if even this easy question caused discomfort. "Cindy Paige," she replied in a soft voice.

"Miss Paige, how long have you known the defendant?"

"A year and a half," she said.

"How well do you know him?"

She shrugged. "Better than anyone, I suppose."

"Is it fair to say you two are romantically involved?"

"Yes. We live together."

"You're not married, though," said McCue, sounding more than a little judgmental.

Cindy glanced at the jurors. She saw grandmotherly disapproval from a blue-haired retired schoolteacher in the second row. "No, we're not married."

"And how long have you two lived together?"

"About a year. Except for a couple of weeks a while back."

"Let's talk about that little hiatus," said the state attorney. "When was that?"

She sighed, not because her memory failed her, but because it was a time in her life she'd rather have just forgotten. "Almost three months ago."

"It was right after the trial of Eddy Goss, wasn't it?" he asked, sounding a little less friendly now, more like an interrogator. "Right after Mr. Swyteck defended him and got him off."

"Objection as to characterization," said Manny as he rose from his chair.

"Sustained," groaned the judge. "I won't tolerate cheap shots, Mr. McCue. The jury is reminded that Mr. Swyteck is on trial for the alleged murder of Eddy Goss," she instructed the jurors, "and not because he represented Mr. Goss in another trial."

A few jurors exchanged glances, as if they were torn as to which of the two was the real crime.

"The witness may answer the question," said the judge.

"Jack and I split a couple of days after the Goss trial," Cindy responded. "But that trial had nothing to do with our breakup."

"It was your decision to move out, wasn't it."

"Yes, it was my decision."

"And Mr. Swyteck was pretty upset about that."

She hesitated, surprised at how personal the questions were, and suspicious of where this was leading. She glanced at Jack, then looked the prosecutor in the eye. "It was hard on both of us."

"Well, let me be a little more specific. The two of you had a nasty fight before you left him, didn't you?"

"Objection," said Manny. "Judge—"

"Overruled."

Cindy shifted nervously in her chair. "We had a disagreement, yes."

McCue smirked. "And I suppose the battle of Gettysburg was also a disagreement."

"Objection!" said Manny.

The judge frowned at McCue. "Sustained. I'm warning you for the last time about the cheap shots, Mr. McCue."

McCue was unfazed. "Isn't it true, Miss Paige, that the defendant literally threw you out of his house?"

"He never laid a hand on me. We had an argument. Every couple I know has arguments."

"But this wasn't just like any other argument," McCue said, moving closer to the witness. "On the morning you left him, Mr. Swyteck really lost control," he said in a low, serious voice. "He was a different person. Wouldn't you say?"

"Objection," said Manny. "Your Honor, this line of questioning is getting ridiculous."

The judge glared at the prosecutor. "I'd tend to agree."

"If we could have a sidebar," said McCue, "I think I can explain the relevance."

"Make it brief," the judge said as she waved them forward.

The lawyers stepped quickly toward the bench and huddled beside the judge, out of earshot of the jury.

"I've been patient," Manny argued quietly, "waiting to see where Mr. McCue is going with this. But lovers' spats between my client and Miss Paige are completely irrelevant to the issues in this case. This is simply humiliating and improper."

"It goes right to the heart of the government's case," McCue countered, his expression deadly serious. "We have an all-American defendant who looks like the last person on earth who'd kill another human being. But on the inside, Your Honor, Mr. Swyteck is wound a little too tightly. He snapped after the Goss trial. And when he did, he killed his own client. I need the testimony of this witness to prove that he snapped. To prove that *stress* made him into a different person—someone capable of murder."

"Miss Paige is not a psychiatrist," Manny said with sarcasm.

"I don't want a medical opinion," McCue fought back. "I want to know what this woman perceived— the woman who has lived with the defendant for the last year, and who has already testified that she knows him better than anyone."

The judge wasn't completely persuaded, but she deferred to the state attorney. "I'll allow it," she muttered. "But not for much longer."

"Judge," Manny groaned, "I—"

"I've ruled," she said sharply.

"Thank you," said McCue. Manny shook his head, then returned to his seat beside Jack. The prosecutor resumed his position in front of the witness, a little closer than before, almost close enough to touch her.

Cindy tried to be ready for anything as she stared back at McCue. She wondered what the judge had said to him. She hoped he'd move on to another topic, but knew from the gleam in his eye that he wasn't finished yet.

"How about it, miss?" McCue continued. "On that morning you left your boyfriend—right after Eddy Goss was acquitted, and right before he was murdered—would you say you saw a side of Jack Swyteck that you'd never seen before?"

She looked at Jack, then back at McCue. "I wouldn't say that . . . exactly."

"He scared you though, didn't he?"

Cindy reddened. "I don't know. He could have."

"*Could* have, huh? Well, let me clarify a few things. The morning you left him, you didn't bother to kiss him good-bye, did you?"

"No."

"You didn't even shake his hand, did you?"

"No."

"In fact, you didn't *walk* out on him. You *ran* out."

"Yes, I ran."

"You ran out so fast you didn't even have time to dress."

"No."

"You ran out half-naked, wearing nothing but a T-shirt."

She gulped, her eyes welling. "It's what I sleep in."

"You ran out because you were scared for your own safety, weren't you?"

She was flustered. She licked her lips, but her mouth was desert-dry.

"Isn't it true," he said, "that you *told* Mr. Swyteck that the Goss trial had changed him?"

Cindy shook her head with confusion. "I don't remember anything like—"

"Miss Paige!" McCue bellowed, his voice filling the courtroom like a pipe organ. "You thought Jack Swyteck had changed so much, that you told him he was no different from the scum he defended. Isn't that right!"

"I—" Cindy gasped.

"Isn't that right, Miss Paige!"

"No, not exactly. I said, 'You are the scum you defend,' but—"

"He *is* the scum he defended!" McCue exclaimed, pouncing on her words for having dared to equivocate. "Thank you, Ms. Paige. Thank you very much for clearing that up for us. I have no further questions," he announced as he turned away from the witness and headed back to the prosecutor's table.

She sat limply in the witness chair, her head down and shoulders rounded. Manny approached slowly, to give her time to compose herself before his cross-examination. "Good morning, Miss Paige," he said in a conversational tone, trying to put her at ease.

Jack listened as Manny tried to rehabilitate her. She explained that she'd spoken purely out of anger on that ugly morning, that she'd never meant a word of it, and that they were now back together. But

Jack couldn't listen. He knew Cindy had told McCue the truth, and nothing could change the truth. The best strategy was to minimize the importance of her testimony, and the longer Manny kept her on the stand, the more important her testimony would seem. Thankfully, Manny didn't keep her long.

"That's all the questions I have," said Manny, dismissing the witness. "Thank you."

Cindy stepped down and headed for the swinging gate that separated the players from the spectators. As she laid her hand atop the polished mahogany banister, she paused and gave Jack a look that asked for forgiveness.

"We got a problem," he whispered to Manny.

"It's only round one," Manny said, shrugging it off.

"No, you're missing the point," Jack said. "It was just me and Cindy in my bedroom that morning she left me. We were *alone*."

"So? Why is that a problem?"

"If Cindy and I are the only two people who know what went on in that room, how did McCue know how to ask her all the right questions?"

For a moment they just stared at each other. Then Jack's eyes shifted from Manny to Wilson McCue, who was seated at the prosecutor's table across the room. The state attorney looked up from his notepad and returned the glance, as if sensing the weight of Jack's stare. He was smiling, Jack noticed, albeit just around his eyes. Jack fought a rising tide of anger. He was ready to leap from his chair and drag it out of him if he had to: *How did you know, you bastard? How did you know what to ask her?*

"Is the State ready to call its next witness?" asked the judge.

Jack was so engrossed he didn't hear the words. Then it came to him. Of course McCue had an informant. *Who else could it be?*

"Your Honor," the prosecutor announced to the hushed courtroom, "the State calls Miss Gina Terisi."

36
·

The big mahogany doors in the back of the courtroom swung open, and Gina Terisi strode down the center aisle like a model on the runway. Though her dazzling beauty attracted stares, she didn't have her usual seductive air. Her makeup was understated. Her navy-blue suit and peach silk blouse were stylish but conservative.

"Do you swear to tell the truth, the whole truth, and nothing but . . ."

Please, God, Jack prayed as the oath was administered. The truth was bad enough, but "the *whole* truth"? He wasn't sure he—or his relationship with Cindy—could survive it. "Please state your name," the prosecutor began.

Jack watched carefully as she testified, searching for some sign that she resented McCue's questions. A downturned lip, clenched teeth, lowered eyes. But, to his consternation, she seemed articulate, cooperative, willing.

"Do you know the defendant?" McCue asked.

"Yes, I do." Jack listened impassively to the interrogation, trying not to panic as Gina told the jury how she'd met Jack and how long she'd known him.

"Now, Miss Terisi," the prosecutor shifted gears, "I'd like to turn to the night Eddy Goss was murdered. Did you see Mr. Swyteck on the night of August first?"

"Yes, I did," she answered. And from that point forward her testimony moved from a wide-angle view to a punishing close-up. Wilson McCue was no longer eliciting bits of background generalities; he had Gina poring over every detail about the night Jack showed up at her door. He wanted specifics, from how Jack looked and what he was wearing, to what he said and how he said it. Jack's fear that he was being stalked by Goss, and his outrage when he discovered that an intruder had broken into Gina's townhouse received particular attention. Reporters in the gallery scribbled down every word as Gina's damning story unfolded and Jack's motive to kill Eddy Goss became clear. Strangely—*very* strangely, Jack thought—Gina didn't mention that Jack had had a gun in his possession.

By late afternoon, though, the damage to his defense was clear. The State had plugged the gaping hole in its case: The defendant's motive to kill Eddy Goss had been the weakest part of the prosecution's case, and Gina's testimony had transformed it into the strongest. Jack tried to show no reaction, but he wondered whether things would get worse. Though Gina had been on the witness stand nearly four hours, she had yet to breathe a word of their "indiscretion."

With Cindy sitting right behind him, he could only hope she never would.

"Now, Ms. Terisi," McCue continued, "did you call the police after all this happened?"

"No," she replied, "I didn't."

"I see," said the prosecutor as he stroked his chin. "That may seem a little odd to some of our jurors, Miss Terisi. After someone broke into your house, you say you didn't call the police. Can you tell us *why* you didn't call the police?"

Gina glanced at Cindy, then looked back at the prosecutor. "I really don't have an explanation."

McCue did a double take. He hadn't expected that answer. Indeed, it was far different from the answer Gina had given him several times before, when they'd rehearsed her testimony. "Are you saying you don't remember?" he asked politely. "Because I can refresh your recollection if—"

"I'm saying I don't have an explanation," she said firmly.

McCue narrowed his eyes and stepped out from behind the podium. If he was going to have to impeach his own witness, he needed to let her feel his presence. "Miss Terisi," he said, his tone decidedly less friendly, "when I interviewed you in my office, you told me that Mr. Swyteck had insisted that you not call the police. Isn't that correct?"

Gina shifted nervously in her chair, but she remained firm. "Yes. I said that. But I wasn't telling you the truth when I said it was Jack's idea. *I* was the one who insisted on *not* calling the police. Not him."

Wilson McCue stood in silence. He'd hoped to

convince the jury that Jack had prevented Gina from calling the police because he wanted to take care of the problem himself—that Jack had intended to murder Goss. Gina's sudden switch had thrown him a curve. McCue didn't know the reason for the change. But he had to make at least one attempt to put his witness back on course.

"It's okay, Miss Terisi," he said in a sympathetic tone. "I understand that Mr. Swyteck is the boyfriend of your best friend. And I can understand how you might be reluctant to hurt her and her boyfriend. But come on, now, level with us. You have to admit that it's a little hard to believe that *you* were the one who didn't want to call the police after some stranger had just broken into *your* apartment."

Manny rose from his chair. "Is that a question?" he asked sarcastically.

"Objection sustained."

"My question is this," the prosecutor said to his witness. "Did you want to call the police, or didn't you?"

Gina swallowed hard. "Of course I wanted to."

McCue felt a rush of satisfaction. It had taken a little maneuvering, but he'd placed his witness right back on track. Or so he thought. "Then tell us, please: Why didn't you call the police?"

"I wouldn't let myself."

"Excuse me?" Again he'd received an unexpected answer.

"I refused to call the police because—" Gina stopped herself. She looked away and wrung her hands in her lap. "I didn't call," she said, lowering her head in shame, "because I didn't want to have to tell the police that Jack and I had slept together."

The prosecutor's mouth fell open, and a murmur of disbelief filled the courtroom. Reporters feverishly flagged their notes with stars and arrows. Jack felt like a man impaled, but he couldn't allow himself the slightest reaction. He didn't dare look behind him, knowing that if he did, he'd lose all self-control.

"Order," said the judge with the bang of her gavel.

Jack couldn't fight the impulse any longer. He looked over his shoulder at Cindy. Their eyes met for just a split second—long enough for him to see something he'd never seen before. It wasn't anger or embarrassment or heartbreak or disbelief. It was *all* of those things.

"All right, miss," McCue said to his witness. He took a deep breath. Gina had diverted widely from the script, and at the moment his chief fear was that her admission about having lied was something the defense would seize on in cross-examination. He had to prevent that from happening. If ever there was a time to turn lemons into lemonade, this was it. "That was a very painful admission you just made, and I'm glad you made it. It shows that you're an honest person—you tell the truth, even when it hurts."

"Objection," said Manny.

"Sustained," the judge said. "Let's not vouch for our witnesses, Mr. McCue."

"Sorry, Your Honor. But I'm just trying to elicit a very simple point." He turned and faced the witness. "Ms. Terisi, when you and I talked in my office and you told me that little falsehood about it being Mr.

Swyteck's idea not to call the police, you were not under oath, were you?"

"No, I wasn't."

"Today, however, you are under oath. You *are* aware that you're under oath?"

"Yes."

"Very well. So, tell us, Miss Terisi. What about all the other things you've testified to today, under oath: Are those true, or are they false?"

"They're true," she said resignedly. "All of them are true."

The prosecutor nodded slowly. "And tell us one more thing, please, if you would: Did Mr. Swyteck voice any objection when you told him that you did *not* want to call the police?"

"He didn't fight it," she said.

"What *did* he do?"

Gina shrugged. "He left."

"What time did he leave?"

"I don't know exactly," she said shaking her head. "Sometime before three o'clock."

"Before three," he repeated, as if to remind the jury that Goss was not murdered until four. The point seemed to register with most of them. "Was he drunk or sober?"

Gina's mouth was getting dry. She sipped some water, then answered, "He still appeared to be a little drunk."

"Did he take anything with him?"

"His car keys."

"Anything else?"

She nodded. "He took the flower with him—the

chrysanthemum he found under Cindy's pillow. The one he said was from Eddy Goss."

"And did he say anything at all before he left?"

Gina took a deep breath. "Yes, he"—she looked into her lap—"he said, 'This has got to stop.'"

McCue turned and faced the jury, looking as if he were about to take a bow. "Thank you, Miss Terisi. I have no further questions."

McCue buttoned his jacket over his round belly and returned to his chair. The courtroom filled with the quiet rumble of spectators conferring among themselves, each seeming to confirm to the other that the accused was most definitely guilty as charged.

"Order," said the judge with a bang of her gavel. The courtroom came to a hush. The judge checked the clock on the wall. It was almost five o'clock. "I see no reason to keep the jury any longer today," she said. "We'll resume tomorrow morning with defense counsel's cross-examination of this witness."

"Your Honor," Manny politely interrupted. He had to do something to keep the day from ending on this devastating note. "If I might just begin my cross-examination. Perhaps just twenty minutes—"

"The defense will have all the time it needs—tomorrow. This court is in recess," she announced as she ended the day with another sharp bang of the gavel.

"All rise!" shouted the bailiff, but his instruction was totally unnecessary. Everyone in the courtroom immediately stood and sprung into action. Television reporters rushed to meet five o'clock deadlines. Print journalists ran for the rail, hoping to get an interview with the prosecutor, the defense—or maybe even the government's star witness.

Jack jumped up, too, immediately looking behind him. He needed to say something to Cindy, but she was already gone. She'd darted from her seat the instant Judge Tate's gavel had landed on the block.

He stood beside his chair as he scanned the buzzing courtroom. *Where is she?* He flinched as he felt Manny's hand on his arm. "You and I have to talk," his lawyer said.

Jack sighed. He could barely speak. "Cindy and I have to talk," he said quietly.

37

J ack raced home as quickly as he could, weaving in and out of rush-hour traffic. He was relieved to see Cindy's car in the driveway. She hadn't left him—at least not yet. He rushed into the house, then froze as he heard the sound of dresser drawers slamming shut in the bedroom.

"What are you doing?" asked Jack as he appeared in the bedroom doorway.

Her half-filled suitcase was lying open across the bed. "What's it look like I'm doing?" she said as she dumped a drawer of panty hose into her suitcase.

He sighed. "It looks like you're doing exactly what I would do. Looks like you're giving me exactly what I deserve. But I'm asking you not to."

She wouldn't even look at him. She just kept packing. "Why shouldn't I leave?"

"Because I'm sorry. You just don't know how sorry I am. You don't know how much I love you."

"Stop it," she glared. "Just *stop* it."

"Cindy," he pleaded, "it's not what you think.

You've got to remember: This all happened right after the Goss trial, when everything was so crazy. I was being stalked by some guy who had tried to run me over and who'd just killed Thursday. I'd just come from Goss's apartment after stabbing myself in the hand. And then Gina managed to convince me that I was being naive to think you'd ever come back to me. She told me you and Chet were definitely not going to be 'just friends' over there."

"Hold it," she said, looking at him with utter disbelief. "Are you listening to what you're saying? Less than twelve hours after I left for Italy, you were in bed with my best friend because *you* were afraid that you couldn't trust *me*. That makes a lot of sense, Jack," she said with sarcasm, then resumed packing.

"You don't understand, I was drunk—"

"I don't care. Have you been drunk for the past two months, too? Is that why you didn't tell me about it? Or maybe you just thought it was best for me to hear about it for the first time in a crowded court-room, so I could be humiliated in front of the entire world."

"I was going to tell you," he said weakly.

"Oh, *were* you? Or did you just think you could sweep this problem under the rug, like you do with all the problems between you and your father? Well, that obviously hasn't worked very well with *that* relationship, has it? And it won't work with me anymore, either. What you and Gina did is bad enough. But keeping it from me is unforgivable," she said, then closed up her suitcase and bolted out the bedroom door.

He stepped out of the way, then followed her down the hall. "Cindy, you can't leave."

"Just watch me," she said as she opened the front door.

"I mean, you can't leave town. You're still under the trial subpoena. It's possible you could be recalled as a witness. And if you don't appear, you'll be in contempt of court."

She shook her head in anger. "Then I'll just move into a hotel."

"Cindy—"

"Good-bye, Jack."

He searched desperately for something to say. "I'm sorry," he called as she headed down the front steps.

She stopped and turned around, her eyes welling as she looked back. "I'm sorry, too," she said bitterly. "Because you *ruined* it, Jack. You just ruined *everything*."

He felt completely empty inside, like a lifeless husk, as he watched her toss her suitcase into the car and pull out of the driveway. He tried to feel *something*, even anger at Gina. But another voice quickly took over. He could hear his father repeating that lesson Jack had never seemed to learn as a boy, probably because Harold Swyteck had tried so hard to teach it to him. It was the same lesson Jack had fired back at his father the night Fernandez was executed. "We're all responsible for our own actions," Jack could hear his father telling him. The memory didn't help Jack with his sense of loss. But somewhere deep inside, he felt a little stronger because of it.

"I'll always love you," he whispered over the lump in his throat as Cindy drove away. "Always."

38

Harry Swyteck received a full report on the day's events in his Tallahassee office. Gina's testimony was the first he'd heard of Jack's stalker. While the rest of the world took the story as Jack's motive to kill Eddy Goss, he saw it differently, because he also had been harassed before the murder—and he, too, had believed it was Goss.

His first instinct was to make a public statement, but it was quite possible that going public with what had happened to him could *strengthen* the case against Jack. From the jury's standpoint, evidence that both Swytecks were being threatened would only double Jack's motive to kill Goss. And even telling Jack wouldn't be wise, because he'd have to divulge everything he knew when he testified in his own defense.

A knock on the door interrupted his thoughts. "This just came," his secretary said as she entered his office, handing him a large, sealed envelope. "I didn't want to interrupt, but the courier said it relates to your son's trial."

"Thank you, Paula." It was a brown envelope, with no return address. He was immediately suspicious. He waited for her to disappear behind the closed office door, and then he cautiously slit the seal with his letter opener and peered inside. He paused. Photographs—again. He feared it was more of the same horrible photographs his blackmailer had shown him after his carriage ride in the park. But there was only one photo this time. Slowly, he removed the large black-and-white glossy, then froze. He'd never seen the shot before, but the subject was certainly familiar. It was taken on the night of the murder. It was a photo of the governor walking away from Goss's apartment, after he'd chickened out and decided not to go inside, toting the shoe box full of cash his blackmailer had told him to deliver to apartment 217 at four o'clock in the morning.

His hands shook as he laid the photograph face-down on his desk. Only then did he notice the message on the back. It was a poem—brief, but to the point:

One word to your son,
one word to the cops,
we double the fun,
the other shoe drops.

The governor went rigid in his chair, disgusted by the way he was being manipulated. But he knew exactly what "shoe" would drop. This was one last threat—a solemn promise that if he came forward in defense of his son, the police would shortly come into possession of the wing tips that could connect the governor and his extraneous footprints not only to the murder of Eddy Goss, but to that of Wilfredo Garcia as well. And there was more still: The tape recording of the bribe, the payoff for the victim's photographs—all of it would bring into public focus that this entire tragedy was rooted in the execution of an innocent man.

The governor held his head in his hands, agonizing. He felt compelled to act, yet at the same time paralyzed. He had to make sure he didn't play into the hands of the enemy. He had to figure out a way to help his son—without self-destructing.

39

Jack didn't want to stay in the empty house after Cindy had left, and he'd lost all appetite for din-ner. So he drove to Manny's office to prepare for the next day of the trial.

The first thing he mentioned to his lawyer was Gina's glossing over that he'd had a gun that night he came to her apartment. The question was never asked, and so Gina never answered it. Perhaps she'd sensed that saying anything about the gun would be driving the last nail into Jack's coffin? Maybe that was too much even for Gina.

Manny was as perplexed as Jack. What she *had* said, though, had been devastating. He wanted a powerful cross-examination of Gina, and by ten o'clock that night, the two lawyers had mapped out an impressive assault. Jack feared, however, that it was the kind of legal warfare that could impress only a lawyer. Manny couldn't disagree. They both knew the bottom line. Gina had told the truth. And there was only so far a criminal defense lawyer could push a truthful witness on cross-examination before the jury would start to resent the lawyer *and* his client.

To say the least, Jack wasn't feeling very optimistic when he got home—until he checked his answering machine.

"Jack," came the familiar voice. "It's Gina."

There was a long pause. He turned up the volume, then stood frozen as he listened.

"I think we should talk," she said finally. "Face-to-face. Come by tonight, please. I'm sure I'll be up."

He took a deep breath. He detected no gloating in her tone. No animosity. No seductiveness. Just honesty.

He picked up the phone, then put it down. If he called her, he was afraid she might change her mind. But if he showed up at her door, he was certain she'd talk to him. He grabbed his car keys and rushed out.

Twenty minutes later, Gina opened her front door. She was dressed in soft slippers and a white bathrobe. Her chestnut hair was wet and a little tangled, as if she'd washed it an hour ago, started combing it out, then lost the energy to finish the job. She wore no makeup, and in the same strange way that her toned-down appearance in the courtroom had made her more attractive, she was even prettier now, Jack thought—except for one thing. She looked sad. Very sad.

"Come on in," she said in a subdued voice.

"Thanks." He stepped inside, and she closed the door behind him.

"Something to drink?"

"No, thanks."

"A Jagermeister, maybe?" A smile briefly bloomed on her face, then withered. She crossed the room to a hammock-style chair, sat down, and brought her knees up to her chin. She kept her back to Jack as she enjoyed the balmy breezes that rolled in through the open sliding-glass doors.

Jack took a seat on the couch, on the other side of the cocktail table. They said nothing until Gina turned her head and looked at him plaintively.

"You don't have to tell me if you don't want to," she said. "But what happened with Cindy?"

He hesitated. For a second he felt as if she were intruding. But this wasn't just idle curiosity. She really seemed to care.

"She packed up and left."

"I'm sorry," she said. Then she rolled back her head, closed her eyes, and sniffled. "I don't know why I do the idiotic things I do," her voice cracked. "I really don't."

Jack moved to the edge of his seat. The last thing he'd expected tonight was to be consoling Gina. But he found himself doing it. "Everyone makes mistakes."

She shook her head and suddenly snapped out of her malaise. "Mistakes? Do you have any idea how *many* mistakes I've made? You don't know me, Jack. Nobody knows me. Not even Cindy. Everyone thinks that a great body has gotten me anything I've ever wanted in life. And it did, for a while. When I was sixteen years old, I made over a hundred grand modeling for the Ford Agency. But then the next year I gained twenty pounds and was all washed up—out of work. A real wake-up call, that was. 'Use it while you got it' is what I learned. But then I learned something else: The more you use it, the more you *get* used. And believe me, there's no shortage of users out there."

He nodded slowly.

"Anyway," her voice quivered. "That's why I called you. I'm through being used. I'm through feeling like shit even when I *try* to do the right thing. Like today. All I did was tell the truth on the witness stand. Yet I feel like *I've* done something wrong."

"You *didn't* mention the gun. I wondered about that."

"Yeah, well, maybe it's because they were licking their chops too much over everything else I told them. I didn't feel like volunteering it, you know?"

"But why volunteer anything? I'm confused."

"Welcome to the club," she said, running her hands through her hair. "They want you to play the game, but they don't tell you the rules."

Jack was confused. "What game?"

She started to speak, then stopped. Finally she said, "The whole charade that landed me in that courtroom—*that's* the game. I've been playing it ever since you asked me to be your alibi. Everything I did and said was designed to make you think that I didn't want to get involved—or that if I did get involved, it would be to help you, and not to hurt you. The whole idea was to make sure you'd be totally shocked when I took the stand and testified against you. That was part of my deal."

Jack's eyes narrowed with suspicion. "Your deal with who?"

"With that cop, Stafford," she said, then looked away in shame. "The truth," she said with a lump in her throat, "is that right after you were indicted, he came over to question me. I let the creep use my bathroom, and he comes out saying he just saw enough amphetamines sitting out in plain view to put me away for years. I use them to lose weight. It's not smart, but I do it. Anyway, he said he wouldn't bring any charges if I'd help him out. And all I did was tell him the truth. It's just the sneaky way he made me do it that has me so disgusted. I mean, how do you think the prosecutor knew every little detail about the morning Cindy left you? She told me all about it. And I told Stafford. And then Cindy got creamed on the witness stand."

Jack felt a rush of anger, but he kept cool—because a tremendous opportunity was within his grasp. "Gina," he said in a calm, understanding tone, "this is important. What Stafford made you do isn't just sleazy. It's illegal. The prosecution has violated the law by failing to tell Manny and me that Stafford cut a deal with a government witness. This could get the whole case against me dismissed. The trial could be over tomorrow. I could go *free*."

"What do you want me to do?" she asked cautiously.

"All I want you to do is to get on the witness stand tomorrow morning and say exactly what you told me. That's it. Just tell the truth."

"And then what happens to *me*? I'll go to jail on drug charges?"

He thought fast. "The state will have to honor its deal with you. Stafford made the promise. You've already lived up to your end. You told the truth. It's Stafford's fault if it blows up in his face, not yours."

"I don't know—"

"Gina," he pressed. "You've told the truth so far. I respect you for that. But if you told the truth for Stafford, the least you can do is tell the truth for me."

She sighed. "This is so crazy. But in the last twenty-four hours, it's like I've suddenly got this feeling that it's time to start making up for all the lies I've told my entire life. I just feel like it's time to tell the truth."

"The truth is best," he said. "Even when it hurts."

She swallowed hard. "All right. I'll do it."

Jack's heart was in his throat. "In fact, why don't I call Manny now, and we can go over some things—"

"No. I don't want to do this according to a script."

"I understand," he said, sensing that he shouldn't push too hard.

Gina rose. "I'll see you at the courthouse at eight-thirty," she said, leading him out. "Right now, I need some sleep."

He nodded in agreement. "I'll see you then," he said as they reached the door.

She laid her hand on his shoulder and stopped him. "I'm sorry about you and Cindy," she said. "I really am."

"Thanks," he said.

As he drove home, he was barely conscious of the tires gripping the road. He felt like he was floating on air. His conversation with Gina had made him feel alive again. Suddenly he felt hope.

40

At 3:30 A.M., just as Jack and Manny had finished planning a case-saving cross-examination of Gina Terisi, bare-breasted women were dancing one last set at Jiggles, a rundown, smoke-filled strip joint where stiff drinks came as cheap as the thrills. A buxom black woman wearing only spike heels and a holster was lit by an orangey-red spotlight as she strutted up and down the long bar top, thrusting her hips to the delight of the drunk and howling crowd each time the rap vocalist on the jukebox screamed "I like big butts!" Around the room women danced on little round tables, each wearing only boots or bow ties or maybe a Stetson, and all of them wearing a garter on one thigh so the men they teased could stuff them with cash and extend their fantasies.

Just before closing, a tall, broad-shouldered man with a clean-shaved head and a diamond-stud earring presented himself at the entrance. A bearded bouncer who looked like he was moonlighting from the pro wrestling tour stepped in front of him. "We close in fifteen minutes," he said.

"That's all the time I need," the man replied as he started inside. The bouncer grabbed him by the shoulder.

"Ten-dollar cover, chief."

"Shee-it." But he was in a hurry, so he paid it and stepped inside. He looked around the room, first checking the bar top and then each individual table for the woman he knew as Rebecca. She knew him as Buzz, a name she'd given him not simply because of his shaved head, but because of his whole look. She said his hook nose, folds of leathery skin, and skinny neck made him look like a buzzard. Especially at night, when his eyes were bloodshot. Rebecca usually worked until closing, but Buzz didn't see her anywhere. Then his eyes lit up as he saw her standing by the cigarette machine, having a smoke.

She had short, wavy hair—black, this week—and the best body of all the dancers. She was dressed tonight, or as dressed as women ever got here. A sleeveless V-neck undershirt with the neck-line ripped down to her navel revealed ample cleavage and a long chain necklace as thick as a dog leash. Tight black leather shorts with silver studs on the pockets were cut up to the middle of her round rear end, and shiny patent-leather boots rose up to the butterfly tattoo on her inner thigh. He caught her eye from across the room and walked over to her.

"I'm done for the night," she said, blowing smoke in his face.

He shook his head, as if he knew better. "How much?"

"Three hundred."

"Fuck you."

"That would be extra."

He emptied his pants pockets. "I got a hundred sixty dollars. Take it or leave it."

"Deal." She snatched the money and stuffed it into the top of her boot. "But I ain't goin' back to the car with you for no hundred sixty. We do it in here."

"Here?" He winced.

"Over there," she said, pointing to a dark and isolated corner. "Meet you there."

He nodded in agreement, then headed for the corner. Rebecca stepped up to the bar. "The crazy-man's usual," she told the bartender. "Margarita, just salt." The bartender smirked and handed her a glass filled only with margarita salt, moistened with a squirt of lemon juice. "Thanks," she said, then strutted toward the darkest corner of the bar.

"I missed you," he said when she returned.

Rebecca put the glass on the table, threw her shoulders back, and placed her hands on her hips. "Don't talk shit," she barked like a drill sergeant.

"You're right," he said in a husky whisper. "I've been bad."

"Just as I thought," she spat, her voice growing menacing. "You know what happens when you're bad."

He nodded hungrily.

She raised her index finger, stuck it in her mouth, and sucked it sensually, from base to tip. She immersed it in the glass of lemony margarita salt and stirred, then removed it and held it before his eyes. The crystals stuck to her moistened finger. "How bad were you?" she demanded.

He got down on his knees and looked up sheepishly. "Very bad," he assured her.

Slowly, she lowered her coated finger and rubbed the salt deep into his eye. He cringed and moaned, his head rolling back with perverse pleasure. His intermittent cries of pain were drowned out by the loud music. She knew he liked her to remain tough, but she had to fight to keep a look of fear from crossing her face. She'd seen men approach ecstasy in the bar before, usually the creeps who got tossed out for masturbating. But he was beyond ecstasy. This was utter rapture.

He regained his composure, still on his knees. He looked up at her through his one good eye. The other was puffy and closed. Lemon and salty tears streamed down his cheek. For a hundred sixty bucks, he knew he'd have her for at least another song. "Put the salt away," he said. "I've been very, very bad."

Rebecca sighed; she knew what that meant. She lit up another cigarette. "What did you do?"

He took a deep breath, then with his left hand he reached deep inside his pocket and discreetly squeezed a handkerchief that contained two bloody nipples. "Nothing I haven't done before," he whispered, a thin smile coming to his face. Then his body jerked and his head rolled back in another fit of ecstasy, as Rebecca crushed out the glowing end of her cigarette in the burn-scarred palm of his right hand.

41

Jack and Manny arrived in the crowded courtroom just before nine that morning. Jack was a bit worried that he hadn't been able to spot Gina in the courthouse lobby earlier, but he told himself that she must have been delayed. She'd show up, he was sure. Something in her eyes the night before convinced him that she was determined to set the record straight.

Quite quickly, though, he sensed something was wrong. McCue, who normally arrived early, was conspicuously absent from the courtroom, and the bailiff seemed to have disappeared as well.

Ten minutes passed. The murmur of the spectators built as there was still no sign of the prosecutor. Finally the bailiff appeared, showing no expression as he stepped up to the defense table. "Mr. Cardenal," he said politely, "Judge Tate would like to see you and Mr. Swyteck in her chambers."

Jack's heart sank as he and Manny exchanged glances. This was not standard procedure. Something had to be wrong. "All right," said Manny, and they followed the bailiff to a side exit.

The judge's chambers had the air of a funeral parlor. Judge Tate sat in the leather chair behind her imposing desk, framed by the state and American flags. Wilson McCue sat in an armchair to her left, before a wall of law books. Their expressions were somber.

"Good morning," said Manny as he entered the room.

"Please sit down," the judge said formally, her tone suggesting that this was *very* serious.

Jack and Manny sat in the Naugahyde chairs facing McCue. Jack swallowed hard, fearing the worst— perhaps some wild accusation that he had threatened Gina. The judge folded her hands on her desk and leaned forward to speak.

"Mr. McCue has just informed me that Gina Terisi is dead," she said.

"What?" Manny uttered with disbelief.

"She was murdered," said the prosecutor.

"That can't be," Jack said, stunned.

"Mr. Swyteck," said the judge, "you would be advised to remain silent."

He sat back in his chair. The judge was right.

Judge Tate glanced at Manny, then at McCue. "I am not trying to be cold or unsympathetic, gentlemen, but I didn't assemble this group to discuss the how and why of Ms. Terisi's murder. The purpose of this meeting is to decide what impact the murder will have on Mr. Swyteck's trial. Fortunately, we have a sequestered jury, so they won't hear anything about it."

"But, Your Honor," said Manny, "the jury has already heard the witness's testimony, and now I won't have an opportunity to cross-examine her. My client can't get a fair trial under these circumstances. The court has no choice but to declare a mistrial. We have to start all over again—without Gina Terisi."

McCue slid to the edge of his chair, unable to contain himself. "Judge," he implored. "I knew they'd try to pull this. You *can't* grant a mistrial. You'd be playing right into their hands. Look at the sequence here, Judge. And look at the motive. This is no coincidence. The government was building an ironclad case. Gina Terisi devastated Mr. Swyteck on the witness stand. And then a few hours later she turns up dead. Now, you don't have to be a genius to see—"

"That's an outrageous suggestion!" said Manny.

"The hell it is!" McCue fired back. "Swyteck's car was spotted at Gina Terisi's last night."

Jack's jaw dropped. "Now wait just a minute—"

"Gentlemen!" the judge barked. "That's enough."

There was silence. The prosecution and defense exchanged glares. Jack glanced at the judge, then looked away. Judge Tate was no easy read, but her suspicious eyes had revealed a glimpse of her feelings. And Jack didn't like what he saw.

"I will not declare a mistrial," she announced, shaking her head. "Mr. Swtyeck's trial will proceed. However, Miss Terisi's testimony will be stricken. I will instruct the jury that it must disregard her testimony, and I will further instruct them that they are to draw no inferences whatever from the fact that she has not returned to the courtroom."

"Judge," Manny argued, "a curative instruction isn't going to help anything. The jury has already heard her testimony. You can't tell them to ignore it. That's like telling a shark to ignore the blood."

"Mr. Cardenal," she said sternly, "I've made my decision."

McCue's face was aglow. "It may go without saying, Judge," he said in his folksy manner, "but I presume that Ms. Terisi's disappearance would be fair game on cross-examination, assumin' Mr. Swyteck were to take the witness stand in his own defense. The court's instruction will not curtail my ability to question him about that, will it?"

The judge leaned back in her chair, thinking. "I hadn't thought about that. But I would have to agree with you, Mr. McCue. If Mr. Swyteck takes the witness stand, the door is open. You're free to question him."

Manny shook his head incredulously. Even the judge, it seemed, had concluded that Jack was guilty. "Your Honor, you have just made it impossible for Mr. Swyteck to testify on his own behalf. I can't put him on the stand if you're going to allow the prosecutor to suggest that my client murdered the government's star witness. Your ruling is a death sentence. I strenuously object and urge you to reconsider—"

"That's all," said the judge, heading off any further argument. "You understand my position. Now, I'm giving both the prosecution and defense twenty-four hours to regroup. We shall reconvene at nine o'clock tomorrow morning. Mr. McCue, be prepared to call your next witness. Thank you, gentlemen," she said with finality.

"Thank *you*," McCue told the judge.

The lawyers rose and turned away. Jack stood more slowly, in a state of disbelief. He followed his lawyer down the hall, past the water cooler. Neither said a word until they reached the exit and McCue caught up with them.

"Better circle your wagons, Swyteck," the old prosecutor said sarcastically, all trace of his good-old-boy accent having vanished. "Because if you don't get the electric chair for killing Eddy Goss, you can bet I'll be coming after you for the murder of Gina Terisi." He nodded smugly, like a gentleman tipping his hat, then headed out the door.

Jack stood in the open doorway, looking at his lawyer with dismay. "This can't be happening," he said quietly. But it was. Innocent people kept getting killed. Fernandez, Garcia, now Gina—and Jack, it seemed, was next in line. The only thing more unfathomable was the *reason* it was happening—why his life, like Gina's, might end before his thirtieth birthday. Never to be a husband or a father . . . never to achieve his dreams—for the first time since the trial began, the weight, the enormity of what was at stake pressed down on him, nearly crushing him with its load.

Being convicted. A death sentence. The electric chair. All those things had seemed so abstract before, but suddenly they were palpable, real. A memory came to him—of lying in bed as a young boy and trying to scare himself, trying to imagine what death felt like. He'd picture himself crouched over a hole in the earth, a dark hole. And then he'd see himself falling into it. It was a descent that never ended. Nothing could stop it . . .

He shook off the memory and tried to focus. What had the stalker said when he attacked Jack on the bus? Something about "innocent people" getting hurt if he turned to others for help. He looked at Manny with apprehension, then sprinted down the hall to a bank of pay phones near the rest rooms. He quickly dialed Cindy's work number.

He nearly fainted with relief as the sound of her voice came on the line. "Thank God you're all right."

"I just heard about Gina," she said. "Her brother called me."

"They're saying I did it."

"They're liars," she said. "The things that animal did to her . . ." She shuddered. "No sane human being would *do* that."

He didn't know the details, but he didn't have to ask. "*Please*, be careful," he said, "I'm worried about you. If there's anything you need or want, just call me."

"I'll be all right," she said. "Really, I will."

He wanted to say something else, anything, to keep her on the line, but words eluded him.

"Good luck," she said, meaning it.

"Thanks," he said softly. "Cindy, I—"

"I know," she said, "you don't have to say it."

"I love you," he blurted out.

He heard what he thought was a sob on the other end of the line, and then she said, "Good-bye, Jack."

42

"Call your next witness, Mr. McCue," Judge Tate announced from the bench.

Trial had reconvened at nine o'clock, Wednesday. As promised, the judge had instructed the jurors that they were to disregard Gina Terisi's testimony and that they were to infer nothing from her failure to return to the courtroom to complete her testimony. The instruction, of course, had evoked nothing but suspicious glares from the jury—all of them directed at the defense. With that, the government spent the morning with some technical witnesses, then moved directly after lunch to its final big witness—an experienced fighter who could hardly wait to take his best punch at Eddy Goss's staggering lawyer.

"The State calls Lonzo Stafford," said McCue.

The packed courtroom was silent as Detective Stafford marched down the center aisle, the click of his heels on the marble floor echoing throughout. After taking the oath and stating his name and occupation, Stafford allowed himself to be guided by McCue in a summary of the physical evidence against Jack Swyteck.

Stafford's testimony unfolded like a script: The defendant's fingerprints matched those on the steak knife in Goss's kitchen; twenty-seven footprints matched the tread on his Reeboks; his blood type matched the blood on the blade; Mr. Swyteck appeared nervous and edgy the next day, when Detective Stafford interviewed him; he had scratches on his back and a bruise on his ribs, as if he'd been in a scuffle; and Swyteck knew that Goss had been killed by gunshot before the detectives had mentioned anything about a shooting. And, just as McCue had planned, the witness saved the best for last.

"When you say Goss was killed by gunshot," asked McCue, "what kind of gun do you mean, exactly?"

"It was a handgun. A thirty-eight-caliber, for sure. And there was definitely a silencer on it."

"Was the murder weapon ever found?"

"Not the gun, no. However, we did locate the silencer."

"And where did you find the silencer that was used to kill Eddy Goss?"

Stafford's eyes brightened as he looked right at Jack. "We retrieved it from Mr. Swyteck's vehicle."

A murmur filled the courtroom. The jurors glanced at each other, as if the case were all but over.

"No further questions," said the prosecutor. He turned and glanced at counsel for the defense. "Your witness," he said, dripping with confidence.

Manuel Cardenal was at his best in the spotlight, and this one was white-hot. His client, the jurors, the packed gallery, and especially the witness were filled with anticipation, everyone wondering if the skilled defense counsel could rescue his client. Manny stepped to within ten feet of the government's final witness and stared coldly at his target. "Detective Stafford," he began, "let's start by talking about the alleged victim in this case, shall we?"

"Whatever you want, counselor."

"Anyone who is alive and breathing in this town has heard of Eddy Goss," said Manny. "We all know the awful things Mr. Goss was alleged to have done. And we all know that Mr. Swyteck was his lawyer. But there's one thing I want to make clear for the jury: You were personally involved in the investigation that led to Mr. Goss's arrest, were you not?"

"Yes," he replied, knowing he was being toyed with. "I was the lead detective in the Goss case."

"You personally interrogated Mr. Goss, didn't you?"

"I did."

"In fact, you elicited a full confession from Mr. Goss. A confession on videotape."

"That's right."

"But that confession wasn't used at Mr. Goss's trial."

"No," he answered quietly. "It was ruled inadmissible."

"It was ruled inadmissible because you broke the rules," said Manny, his tone judgmental.

Stafford drew a sigh, controlling his anger. "The judge found that I had violated Mr. Goss's *constitutional rights*," he said, spitting out the words sarcastically.

"And it was Mr. Swyteck who pointed out your violation to the court, wasn't it?"

Stafford leaned forward, his eyes narrowing. "He *exploited* it."

Manny stepped to one side, closer to the jury, as if he were on their side. "That must have been very embarrassing for you, Detective."

"It was a travesty of justice," replied Stafford, using the words the prosecutor had coached him with the night before.

Manny smirked, sensing that he was getting under Stafford's skin. Then he approached the witness and handed him an exhibit. "This is a copy of a newspaper article from June of this year, marked as Defendant's Exhibit 1. It reports certain pretrial developments in the case against Eddy Goss. Could you read the bold headline to us, please? Nice and loud," he added, gesturing toward the jurors, "so we all can hear."

Stafford scowled at his interrogator, then cleared his throat and reluctantly read aloud: "Judge throws out Goss confession."

"And the trailer, too," said Manny. "Read the little trailer underneath the headline."

Stafford's face reddened with anger. "Seasoned cop botched interrogation," he read. Then he laid the newspaper on the rail in front of him and glared at Manny.

"And that's your photograph there beneath the headline, isn't it, sir?"

"That's my picture," he confirmed.

"In forty years of police work, Mr. Stafford, had you *ever* gotten your picture on the front page of the newspaper?"

"Just this once," Stafford grunted.

"In forty years," Manny continued, "had you ever screwed up a case this bad?"

"Objection," said McCue.

"I didn't screw it up," Stafford said sharply, too eager to defend himself to wait for the judge to rule.

"Overruled," said the judge.

"I'm sorry," Manny said, feigning an apology. "In forty years, had you ever been *blamed* for a screw-up this bad?"

"Never," he croaked.

"Yet, there you are, page one, section A, in probably the least flattering mug shot the newsroom could dig up: the 'seasoned cop' who 'botched the interrogation.'" Manny moved closer, crouching somewhat, as if digging for the truth. "Who do you blame for that?" he pressed. "Do you blame yourself, Detective?"

Stafford glared at his interrogator. "At first I did."

"But you don't blame yourself anymore, do you," said Manny.

Stafford fell silent—he knew exactly where Manny was headed. "Come on, Detective. We *know* who you *really* blame. *This* is the man you blame," said Manny, pointing toward his client, his voice much louder now. "Isn't it!"

Stafford glanced at Jack, then looked back at Manny. "So what," he scoffed.

Manny locked eyes with the witness. "Yes or no, Detective. Do you blame Mr. Swyteck for your own public disgrace?"

Stafford stared right back, hating this lawyer almost as much as he hated Jack. "Yeah," he said bitterly. "I do blame him. Him and Goss. Both of them. They're no different in my eyes."

Manny paused, allowing the answer to linger. A quiet murmur passed through the courtroom as Manny's point struck home.

"But that doesn't make it okay for Swyteck to kill him," Stafford blurted, seeming to sense that he was in trouble.

"Let's talk about that," replied Manny. "Let's talk about just who *did* kill Eddy Goss. The time of Mr. Goss's death was about four A.M., right?"

"Yes," replied Stafford.

"What time did you get to the police station that morning?"

"Five-fifteen," he answered, "same as always."

"Can anyone corroborate where you were before then?"

"No. I live alone."

Manny nodded, as if to emphasize Stafford's response, then forged ahead. "Now, after you arrived at work that morning, an anonymous phone call came in to the station, right?"

"I don't know what you mean," Stafford played dumb. "We get lots of calls—"

"I'm not talking about *lots* of calls," Manny bore

in. "I'm talking about the caller who reported that someone in a police uniform was seen leaving Goss's apartment about the time of the murder."

"Yes," he answered. "Someone did call and report that."

"You used to be a patrolman, didn't you?"

"Yes. Twenty-eight years, before I became a detective."

"And I'll bet you still have your old police uniform," said Manny.

Stafford fell silent. "Yes," he answered quietly.

"I thought so," said Manny. "Now, Eddy Goss was shot twice in the head, at close range, was he not?"

"That's right."

"Thirty-eight-caliber bullets."

"Correct," said Stafford.

"You carry a thirty-eight-caliber, don't you, Detective?"

"Eighty percent of the police force does," Stafford snapped.

"Including *you*."

"Yes," he grudgingly conceded.

Manny paused again, allowing time for suspicion to fill the jury box, and then he continued his roll. "Now, after Mr. Goss was killed by not just one, but two gunshots, you interviewed all the neighbors in the apartment building, didn't you?"

"I did."

"And not *one* of those neighbors heard any gunshots."

Stafford was silent again. "No," he finally answered, "no one heard a gunshot."

"And that was one of the reasons you suspected that a silencer had been used to kill Goss."

"That's correct," he said. Then he took a free shot. "And we found a silencer in your client's car," he added smugly.

Manny nodded slowly. "How convenient," he said sarcastically, his eyebrow arching. "But let's take a closer look at that incredible stroke of luck, Detective. Let's talk about how, incredibly, you seemed to have found the one man in the world who was smart enough to be graduated summa cum laude from Yale University, yet stupid enough to leave a silencer under the front seat of his car."

"Objection," McCue groaned.

"Sustained."

Manny pressed on, unfazed. "You, personally, did not find that silencer in Mr. Swyteck's car. Did you, Detective?"

"No."

"You got it from a patrolwoman, isn't that right?"

"Yes."

"And she got it from the owner of Kaiser Auto Repair—the shop where Mr. Swyteck's convertible top was being fixed."

"That's right."

"And the owner of the shop got it from one of his mechanics."

Stafford's eyes narrowed. "Yeah."

"Am I leaving anybody out, Detective?"

Stafford just glared. "No," he said angrily.

"What do you mean, *no*," Manny rebuked him.

"You didn't stand guard over Mr. Swyteck's car while it was in the repair shop, did you?"

"No."

"So," said Manny, pacing before the jury, "as far as you know, scores of people could have come and gone from Mr. Swyteck's car over the two-day period it was in the shop."

"I don't know," he evaded.

"Precisely," said Manny, as if it were the answer he wanted. "You *don't know*. Or, to put it another way, maybe you have a reasonable doubt."

"Objection," McCue shouted.

"Overruled."

"I don't know who went into his car," Stafford snarled. "That's all."

"Isn't it possible, Detective, that any one of the people walking by or fixing Mr. Swyteck's car could have put the silencer there?"

"Objection," McCue groaned. "Calls for speculation."

"Let me ask it another way," said Manny. He stepped closer, moving in for the kill. "Detective Stafford: Do you happen to own a silencer for your own thirty-eight-caliber pistol?"

"I object!" shouted McCue. "Your Honor, this is insulting! The suggestion that Detective Stafford would—"

"Overruled," said the judge. It wasn't the first time she had seen a defense lawyer turn a cop inside out. "Answer the question, Detective Stafford."

The courtroom fell deadly silent, awaiting the detective's answer. "Yes," he conceded. "I do."

Manny nodded, checking the jurors to make sure the response had registered. It had. He started back to his chair, then stopped, pointing a professorial finger in the air. "Just one more question, Detective," he said as he turned back toward the witness. "When I asked you who you blamed for your own public disgrace, you did say *both* Jack Swyteck *and* Eddy Goss—didn't you?"

"Objection," shouted McCue. "The question was asked and answered."

"Withdrawn," said Manny, smiling with his eyes at the jurors. "I think we all heard it the first time. No further questions. Thank you, sir."

"The witness is excused," the judge announced.

Stafford remained in his chair, his face frozen with disbelief. He'd been coveting this moment—his opportunity for revenge against Jack Swyteck, the lawyer who'd humiliated him. The last laugh was supposed to have been his. But a lawyer had humiliated him again. He'd been more than humiliated. This time he wasn't just the stupid cop who'd botched the investigation. He'd been painted as the *bad* cop who'd done the deed. He'd been pushed too far—and he wasn't going to just sit there and take it.

"It's irrelevant, you know," he groused at Manny, as if no one else were in the courtroom.

"You are excused," the judge instructed the witness in a firm voice.

"It wasn't my silencer that was used to kill Goss," he said angrily.

"*Detective*," the judge rebuked him. But Stafford was determined to have his say.

"It was the silencer we found in Swyteck's convertible!"

"Detective!" The judge banged her gavel.

"Swyteck's silencer was used on Goss," he shouted, "and he used a silencer to kill Gina Terisi, too!"

"Your Honor!" Manny bellowed, rising to his feet. "Your Honor, may I approach the bench? I have a motion to make."

The judge held up her hand, stopping Manny in his tracks. She knew what he wanted—that she declare a mistrial. And if all the other evidence against Jack Swyteck hadn't been so strong, she would have done it. But she was not going to throw out the state's entire case just because one witness had lost his temper and spouted something he shouldn't have.

"Save your motion, Mr. Cardenal," she said. Then she turned toward the jurors. "Ladies and gentlemen of the jury," she said in a very serious tone, "I am instructing you to disregard that last outburst. Those remarks are not evidence in this case. As I instructed you earlier, you are not to draw any inference whatsoever from the fact that Ms. Terisi did not return to the courtroom to complete her testimony against the defendant."

Jack's heart sank as, yet again, he listened to the judge deliver the dreaded "curative instruction." It was any criminal defendant's nightmare. In theory, the instruction was supposed to "cure" any mistake at trial by telling the jury to disregard it. In reality it was, as lawyers often said, like trying to "unring" a bell. Jack knew the bottom line. Manny's beautiful cross-examination had been ruined. The *only* thing the jury would remember was what the judge insisted they forget.

"As for you, Mr. McCue," the judge's reprimand continued, "Detective Stafford is your witness, and I'm holding you responsible, at least in part. Five-hundred-dollar fine!" she barked. "And Detective Stafford, you're an experienced officer of the law. You know better. Why don't you spend a night in the county jail to think about what you've done. And next time," she warned, pointing menacingly with her gavel, "I won't be so lenient. Bailiff," she said with finality, "take the witness away."

The bailiff stepped forward and led Stafford from the witness stand. He should have been ashamed, but he was looking at Jack and smiling. Jack looked away, but Stafford wasn't going to let him off easy. He stopped, rested his hand on the table at which Jack was seated and looked him right in the eye. "I'll save a seat for ya, Swyteck," he whispered, loud enough only for Jack and the bailiff to hear.

"Detective," the judge said sternly. "On your way!"

Jack looked up at Stafford but said nothing. The detective flashed a thin smile, then the bailiff tugged his arm and they headed for the exit.

"Mr. McCue," the judge intoned, "do you have any more witnesses?"

McCue rose slowly, resting his fists on his chest with contentment, his thumbs tucked inside the lapels. "Your Honnuh," he said, speaking like a Southern gentleman, "on that note, the State most respectfully rests."

"Very well," she announced. "We'll reconvene

tomorrow, nine o'clock sharp. Mr. Cardenal: If you plan to put on a defense, be prepared to proceed. If not, we'll conclude with closing arguments. Court's in recess," she said, then banged her gavel.

The crowd rose at the bailiff's instruction and stood in silence as the jury filed out of the courtroom. Jack and Manny exchanged glances as the judge stepped down from the bench. The irony of her comments wasn't lost on either of them. The fact was, as they both so painfully knew, that it wasn't at all clear the defense *had* a defense.

43
.

At six o'clock the next morning, Governor Harold Swyteck was in his robe and slippers, shaving before a steamy bathroom mirror, when he heard a ring on the portable phone in his briefcase. It was the same phone he'd been given in Miami's Bayfront Park. Realizing who was calling, the governor gave a start and nicked himself with the blade.

Annoyed, he dabbed his shaving wound with a washcloth, then dashed from the bathroom, grabbed the phone from his briefcase, and disappeared into the walk-in closet, so as not to wake his sleeping wife. "Hello," he said, sounding slightly out of breath.

"Me again, Governor," came the thick but now familiar voice.

Harry bristled with anger, but he wasn't totally surprised by the call. Clever as this maniac was, he seemed to thrive on letting his victims know how much he enjoyed their suffering, like a gardener who planted a rare seed and then had to dig it up to make sure it was growing.

"What do you want now?" he answered. "A pair of argyle socks to go with your wing tips?"

"My, my," came a condescending reply. "Aren't we testy this morning. And all just because you're gonna have to sign your own son's death warrant."

"My son is *not* going to be convicted."

"Oh, no? Seems to me that his last chance at getting off is lying on a slab in the morgue. I'm sure you've heard that the fox who testified against him had him over for a little chat—and then ended up a bloody mess on her bedroom floor. Too bad, because if you happened to be the eavesdropping type"—he snickered, remembering how he'd perched outside her sliding-glass doors—"you'd know that she was going to get back on the stand and bail him out of trouble."

"I knew it was you," Harry said in a voice that mixed frustration with outrage. "You butchered that poor girl."

"Jack Swyteck butchered her. I told him the rules. It's just me against him. I warned him that whoever tried to help him was dead meat. He went and asked for the bitch's help anyway. That son of yours did it again, Governor. He killed another innocent person."

Harry shook with anger. "Listen to me, you sick son of a bitch. If you want your revenge for Raul Fernandez, go ahead and take it. But don't take it out on my son. *I'm* the one responsible."

"Now, isn't that noble—the loving father who's willing to sacrifice himself for his son. But I'm not stupid"—his voice turned bitter—"I know Jacky

Boy didn't even make an effort. If he had, his own father would have listened to him in a heartbeat."

Harry sighed. *You'd think so, unless that father were a pigheaded fool.*

"You're not going to get away with this," Harry said firmly.

"And just who's gonna stop me, Governor?"

"I am."

"You *can't*. Not unless you want to turn the case of *State* versus *Swyteck* into *State* versus *Harold Swyteck*. And not unless you want the whole world to know you've been paying off a blackmailer to cover up the execution of an innocent man. Didn't you get the point of my poetry, my man? You're as powerless to save your son as I was to save Raul."

The governor's hands began trembling. "You bastard. You despicable *bastard*."

"Sticks and stones—well, I think now you get the point. Gotta go, my man. Big day ahead of me. Should be a guilty verdict coming down in the Swyteck case."

"You listen to me! I won't allow my son—" he said before stopping midsentence. The caller had hung up.

"Damn you!" He pitched the phone aside. He was boiling mad, but he was feeling much more than that. He was scared. Not for himself, but for Jack.

He turned and saw his wife standing in the doorway.

"It was him again, wasn't it?" she asked.

Sensing her fear, he took her in his arms and held her close. "Agnes," he asked with a sigh, still holding her, "would you still love me if I weren't the governor of Florida?"

"Of course I would, Harry," she replied without hesitation. "Why would you ask such a silly question?"

He broke their embrace and stepped back, pondering his next move. "Because I think I've made a decision."

44

At twenty minutes past nine, Judge Tate's cavernous courtroom was packed with thirty rows
of spectators, yet quiet enough to hear the scratch of
a reporter's pencil on his pad. Trial had been scheduled to begin at nine, but the jury had yet to be
seated. Judge Tate presided on the bench with hands
folded, her dour expression making it clear she was
infuriated by the delay. The prosecutor sat erect and
confident at the table closest to the empty jury box,
pleased that the judge's wrath would soon befall his
opponent. Jack was seated at the other side of the
courtroom—nervous, confused, and alone.

"Mr. Swyteck," Judge Tate demanded from the
bench, her tone more threatening than inquisitive,
"just *where* is your lawyer?"

Jack rose slowly. Manny had phoned him a few
minutes before nine and told him to stall until he got
there. That made Jack the sacrificial lamb, for he
knew the one thing that absolutely incensed Judge
Tate was a lawyer who kept her waiting. "Your

Honor," he said apprehensively, "I'm sure there's an excellent explanation for Mr. Cardenal's tardiness."

Judge Tate scowled, but before she could tell Jack just how excellent his lawyer's explanation had better be, the double mahogany doors in the back of the courtroom flew open and Manny walked down the center aisle. The steady tap of his heels echoed over the quiet murmur of the crowd.

"You're late, counselor," the judge said severely.

"I apologize, Your Honor," Manny said as he passed through the swinging gate on the rail, "but there was a last-minute development—"

"Two-hundred-dollar fine, Mr. Cardenal! Bailiff, call in the jury!"

"Your Honor," he pleaded, "could I please have a word with my client? Just a couple minutes is all I need."

"All rise!" came the bailiff's announcement, and with it Manny's plea was drowned out by the shuffle of six hundred spectators rising to their feet. The jurors filed in and took their seats. The bailiff called the court to session, proclaiming "God save this honorable court." The judge bid a pleasant "good morning" to everyone, then turned to the defense.

"Mr. Cardenal," she said with an unfriendly smile, "will you be putting on a defense?"

Manny swallowed hard. He'd been meeting with his witness all morning, but Jack still knew nothing about it. It was Manny's duty to inform his client what was going on. "Your Honor, if I could have just a brief recess."

"Obviously you didn't hear me," she interrupted.

"I asked you a question, Mr. Cardenal: Will there be a defense?"

He nodded. "I may have one witness, Your Honor, but—"

"Call your witness, or rest your case. And I mean it. You've kept us waiting long enough."

Manny took a deep breath. He wanted Jack's approval, but there was no time for discussion.

"Mr. Cardenal," the judge pressed, "we're waiting."

Manny paused, his eyes locking with Jack's for a moment. Jack gave a quick nod, as if he instinctively sensed that whatever Manny had planned was the right thing to do. Manny smiled briefly, then looked up at the judge. "If it please the court," he announced in a resounding voice, "the defense calls Governor Harold Swyteck."

A wave of surprise hit the courtroom like a huge breaker on the beach. The heavy wood doors in the rear of the courtroom swung open, and in walked a tall, handsome man whose gold cuff links and graying around the temples added color and distinction to a dark suit and crisp white shirt. Harold Swyteck never just appeared. He was the kind of man who made an appearance. Being governor amplified that trait. Being both governor *and* the surprise witness in his own son's murder trial made *this* the appearance of a lifetime.

The courtroom was electric yet silent as the governor came down the aisle. As he passed, heads turned in row after row like a wheat field bending in the breeze. Everyone knew who he was, but no one knew what he would say—not even Jack. A strange sensation filled the courtroom as he stepped to the witness stand and swore the oath. It was as if the bailiff had stood up and officially announced that the young man on trial was indeed the governor's son. The prosecutor's gut wrenched. The jurors stared in anticipation. Jack's heart filled with hope and with something else, too—something pleasant, if unfamiliar: genuine pride.

"Good morning," Manny greeted the distinguished witness from behind the lectern. "If you would, sir, please introduce yourself to the jury."

The governor swiveled in his chair and faced the jurors. "I'm Harold Swyteck," he said cordially. "Most people call me Harry."

A few jurors showed faint smiles of familiarity. If it were possible for one man to look at twelve people simultaneously and make each one of them feel like the only person on the planet who mattered, Harold Swyteck was doing it. He responded directly to them after each of Manny's introductory questions, as if the jurors, not the lawyer, were eliciting the testimony.

"Now, Governor," said Manny, marking the transition from introductory questions to more substantive testimony, "I want to focus on the events that took place immediately after the trial of Eddy Goss. Did anything out of the ordinary happen to you?"

The governor took a deep breath, glanced at Jack, and then looked back at the jury. "Yes," he replied solemnly. "I was attacked."

"You were *what*?" the judge asked. The stunned reaction was the same throughout the courtroom.

Jack watched with concern as his father explained not just the attack, but also the reason for it. Harry admitted that his attacker had blackmailed him and that he had paid the man thousands of dollars.

And then he explained why.

"The man threatened to reveal that I'd executed an innocent man," he said. His voice was low and subdued. His eyes filled with remorse. "A man named Raul Fernandez."

A buzz of whispers filled the courtroom. Reporters scribbled down the new name, some of them recalling it from the outburst at the governor's press conference. Every word was another nail in the governor's political coffin.

"Order," said the judge, banging her gavel.

Jack went cold. Long ago, he'd come to the conclusion that he and his father would never discuss Fernandez again, not even privately. His public confession was overwhelming—and a bit confusing, really, until Manny's next line of questioning brought it all into focus.

"Did you come to any conclusion, Governor, about the identity of the man who was threatening you?"

"Yes," he said with conviction. "I firmly believed it was Eddy Goss."

The whispering throughout the courtroom became a quiet rumble. Jurors exchanged glances. No one seemed quite sure whether to feel sympathy or suspicion.

"Order!" the judge intoned, more loudly this time, and with a few more cracks of the gavel.

Manny waited for the courtroom to settle, then proceeded, still standing behind the lectern. "Governor," he asked gently, though pointedly, "why did you think it was Eddy Goss who was blackmailing you?"

Harry took a deep breath. "I first thought it was Goss when one of the messages I received was accompanied by a bouquet of chrysanthemums. I'm sure you recall that Goss was known as the Chrysanthemum Killer. But what really convinced me was when I learned that the address the blackmailer had told me to deliver the ten thousand dollars to—four-oh-nine East Adams Street—was where Goss lived."

"And did you in fact go to Goss's address?"

"Yes, I did—at four o'clock in the morning, on the second of August."

The courtroom exploded once again in a torrent of whispers—followed immediately by the rapping of Judge Tate's gavel. "Order!"

"Judge," the prosecutor croaked. "I move to strike all of this testimony. It's—it's," he stammered, searching desperately for some way to stop this assault on his ironclad case. "It's prejudicial!"

The judge frowned. "I don't doubt it's *prejudicial*, Mr. McCue. I hardly think Mr. Cardenal would call a witness to *help* your case. Overruled."

McCue grimaced as he lowered himself into his chair.

Manny smiled briefly, then continued. "Just a few more questions," he told his witness. "Governor, is there any way you can prove you were at Eddy Goss's apartment on the night he was murdered?"

"Yes," he nodded, "because on the night I went there I was wearing the same kind of shoes I'm wearing now. The same kind of shoes I've worn for twenty-five years. I was wearing—"

"Hold it!" McCue shouted, seemingly out of breath as he shot to his feet. "Just one second, Your Honor."

"Is that an objection?" the judge groused.

"Uh, yes," McCue fumbled. "I just don't see the relevance of any of this. Governor Swyteck is not on trial. His son is."

"Your Honor," Manny countered, "this testimony is highly relevant, and for a very simple reason. We now have not just one, not just two—but *three* people with the means and motive to kill Eddy Goss. We have Detective Stafford. We have Governor Swyteck. And we have the defendant. Ironically, it's the man with the weakest motive of all who's been charged with the crime. We submit, Your Honor, that under the evidence presented in this case, it is impossible for any reasonable juror to decide which, if any, of these three men might have acted on his motive and killed Eddy Goss. If it could have been any one of them, then it might not have been my client. And if it might not have been my client, then there is reasonable doubt. And if there is reasonable doubt," Manny said as he canvassed the jurors, "then my client must be found not guilty."

The judge leaned back in her chair and pursed her lips. "Very nice closing argument, Mr. Cardenal," she said sarcastically, though in truth she was more impressed than annoyed by Manny's speech. "The objection is overruled."

The prosecutor's round face flushed red with anger. He felt manipulated, and he feared that clever lawyering was stealing his case from under him. "But, Judge!"

"*Overruled*," she rebuked him. "Mr. Cardenal, repeat your question, please."

Manny nodded, then turned toward the governor. "My question, Governor, was whether you can prove you were at Eddy Goss's apartment on the night he was murdered."

"Yes, because I was wearing my Wiggins wing tips."

Manny stepped toward the bench, waving an exhibit as he walked. "At this time, Your Honor, we offer into evidence as defendant's exhibit two a copy of the footprint that was left outside Mr. Goss's apartment on the night of the murder. This document was prepared by the police. It is an imprint from a Wiggins wing tip."

The judge inspected the exhibit, then looked up and asked, "Any objection, Mr. McCue?"

"Well, no. I mean—yes. I object to this whole presentation. I—"

"Enough," she groaned. "Overruled. Do you have any further questions, Mr. Cardenal?"

Manny considered. He was sure the governor's testimony had planted the seed of doubt, but with Jack's life hanging in the balance, he owed it to his client to pursue *every* avenue of inquiry—even if it cast further suspicion on the governor. "Just one more question, Judge." He turned back to Harry.

"Tell me, Governor, how did your life of public service get its start—have you always been a politician?"

McCue rolled his eyes. Where was Cardenal heading now?

Harry smiled. "Well, my mother would say I've been a politician since birth." A few of the spectators tittered. "But no, my first years of public service were as a police officer. I spent ten years on the force," he said proudly.

"And do you still have your patrolman's uniform?"

"I do," the governor conceded.

Over a loud murmur, Manny called out to the judge, "I have no further questions, Your Honor."

Jack felt a lump in his throat. He was nearly overcome by his father's selfless act. The governor was a destroyer on the witness stand. He was destroying the prosecution's case against Jack—as well as his own chances for reelection.

"Mr. McCue," the judge queried, "any cross-examination?"

McCue sprung from his chair. "Oh, most definitely," he said. He marched to within a few feet of the witness, his stance and expression confrontational, if not hostile. "Governor Swyteck," he jabbed, "Jack Swyteck is your only son. Your *only* child, is he not?"

"That's true," the governor replied.

"And you love your son."

There was a pause—not because the governor didn't know the answer, but because it had been so long since he'd said it. "Yes," he answered, looking at Jack. "I do."

"You love him," McCue persisted, "and if you had to tell a lie to keep him from going to the electric chair, you would do it, wouldn't you!"

A heavy silence lingered in the courtroom. The governor leaned forward, his eyes narrowing as he spoke from the heart. "Mr. McCue," he said in a low, steady voice that nearly toppled the prosecutor, "if there's one thing I always taught my son, it's that we're all responsible for our own actions. Jack even reminded me of that once," he added, glancing over at the defense table. "My son didn't kill Eddy Goss," he said, looking each of the jurors right in the eye. "Jack Swyteck is innocent. That's the truth. And that's why I'm here."

"All right, then," McCue said angrily. "If you're here to tell the truth, then let's hear it: Are you telling us that *you* killed Eddy Goss?"

The governor looked squarely at the jurors. "I'm not here to talk about me. I'm here to tell you that Jack did *not* kill Goss. And I'm telling you that *I know* he did not."

"Maybe you didn't hear my question," McCue's voice boomed. "I am asking you, sir—yes or no: Did *you* kill Eddy Goss?"

"It's like you said earlier, Mr. McCue. I'm not the one on trial here. My son is."

McCue waved his arms furiously. "Your Honor! I

demand that the witness be instructed to answer the question!"

The judge leaned over from the bench. "With all due respect, Governor," she said gravely, "the question calls for a yes or no answer. I feel compelled to remind you, however, of your fifth amendment right against self-incrimination. You need not answer the question if you invoke the fifth amendment. But those are your only options, sir. Either invoke the privilege, or answer the question. Did you or did you not kill Eddy Goss?"

Time seemed to stand still for a moment. It was as if everyone in the courtroom suddenly realized that *everything* boiled down to this one simple question.

Harold Swyteck sat erect in the witness stand, calm and composed for a man facing a life-and-death decision. If he answered yes, he'd be lying, and he'd be hauled off in shackles. If he answered no, he'd be telling the truth—but he'd remove himself as a suspect. Invoking the privilege, however, raised all kinds of possibilities. His political career would probably be over and he might well be indicted for Goss's murder. And, of course, there was the one possibility that truly mattered: Jack might go free. For the governor, the choice was obvious.

"I refuse to answer the question," he announced, "on the grounds that I might incriminate myself."

The words rocked the courtroom. "Order!" the judge shouted, gaveling down the outburst.

The prosecutor stared at the witness, but the fire was gone. He knew it was over. He knew there was reasonable doubt. This witness had created it. "Under the circumstances," he said with disdain, "I have no further questions."

"The witness may step down," announced the judge.

Governor Swyteck rose from his chair, looking first at the jurors and then at his son. He wasn't sure what he saw in the eyes of the jurors. But he knew what he saw in Jack's eyes. It was something he'd wanted to see all his life. And only because he'd finally seen it did he have the strength to hold his head high as he walked the longest two hundred feet of his life, back down the aisle from the witness stand to the courtroom exit.

"Anything further from the defense?" the judge asked.

Manny rose slowly, feeling the familiar twinge that all defense lawyers feel when it's time to either put their client on the stand or rest their case. But the specter of Gina Terisi gave Jack and Manny no choice, really—and, more important, the governor had given Jack all the defense he needed. "Your Honor," Manny announced, "the defense rests."

The judge looked to the prosecutor. "Any rebuttal, Mr. McCue?"

McCue sighed as he checked the clock. "Judge, it's almost one o'clock, and the governor has shocked everyone—including me. I'm simply not prepared to rebut something as unforeseeable as this. I would like a recess until tomorrow morning."

The judge grimaced, but this *was* a rather extraordinary development. "All right," she reluctantly agreed. "Both sides, however, should be ready to deliver closing arguments tomorrow. There will be no further delays. We're in recess until nine A.M.," she announced, then banged the gavel.

"All rise!" cried the bailiff. His words had the same effect as "There's a fire in the house!" Spectators flooded the aisles and exits, jabbering about what they'd just seen and heard. Journalists rushed in every direction, some to report what had happened, others to pump the lawyers for what it all meant, still others to catch up with the governor. A few friends—Mike Mannon and Neal Goderich among them—shook Jack's hand, as if the case were over.

But Jack knew it wasn't over. Manny knew it, too. And one other man in the courtroom knew it better than anyone. He lingered in the back, concealing his shiny bald head and diamond-stud earring beneath a dark wig and broad-brimmed hat.

He glared at Jack through an irritated eye.

"Should have been Raul," he muttered to himself, "not you, Swyteck." He took one last look, imagining Jack telling his pretty girlfriend the good news. Then he stormed from the courtroom, determined to give the Swyteck family something else to think about.

45

The parking lot at Jiggles strip joint was full from the Thursday evening crowd, so Rebecca had to find an empty spot on the street. She was wearing baggy jeans and a sweatshirt, her usual attire on her way to and from the bar. There was just one cramped dressing room inside for all the dancers, which was a hassle—but it was safer changing in there than walking the parking lot in some skimpy outfit that was sure to invite harassment or worse. Rebecca checked her watch. Ten after ten. "Damn," she muttered, realizing she was late for her evening shift. She locked her car and started across the parking lot. In one hand she carried a gym bag, which held her dancing clothes and makeup. In the other was her mace, just in case.

"Hey, Rebecca," came a low, husky voice from somewhere to her left.

Her body went rigid. Her name wasn't really Rebecca, which meant that it had to be a customer calling. She quickened her walk and clutched her can of mace, making sure it was ready. She jerked to a halt as a man jumped out from between cars.

"Get back!" she shouted, pointing the mace.

"It's Buzz," he said.

She took a good look, then recognized him beneath his hat and behind the dark, wraparound sunglasses that he wore, even after dark, to conceal his irritated eye. "Let me by," she said sternly.

"Wait," he replied, his tone conversational. "I have a proposition for you."

"Not *now*," she grimaced, her jaws nervously working a wad of chewing gum. "I'm supposed to punch in by ten, or I can lose my job. Come inside."

"Not that kind of proposition," said Buzz. "This is something different. I want your help."

"Why should I do anything for you?"

"No reason. But I'm not asking you to do it for me. I want you to do it for Raul."

Rebecca averted her eyes. The name clearly meant something to her. "What are you talking about?"

"I'm talking about revenge. I'm gonna nail the fuckers who put Raul in the chair."

Her shoulders heaved with a heavy sigh, then she just shook her head. "That's history, man. Raul was a punk. He treated me like dirt, even when I was giving it to him for free. Shit happens to punks."

Buzz stifled his fury. He would have liked to put her in her place with the hard truth that to Raul she was just a free blow job, but that wouldn't advance his purpose. "Fine," he said with a shrug. "Just go on pretending you weren't nuts over him. Don't do it for him. Just do it for the money."

Her interest was suddenly piqued. "How much?"

"Ten percent of my take."

Rebecca rolled her eyes. "I've heard that one before. Ten percent of nothin' is still nothin'."

"Yeah. But ten percent of a quarter million is more money than you'll ever make sucking cocks."

She flashed a steely look, but she was more interested in the proposition than in refuting the insult. "Don't bullshit me. Where you gonna get that kind of money?"

"I'm not bullshittin' you. I'm serious. We're talking high stakes. And all you gotta do is make one phone call. That's it. A cush job."

She paused. "I don't believe it."

"*Believe* it. I've already conned sixty grand out of him. I'll show it to you. Count it, if you want. It's all right in my van. And that's just the tip of the iceberg. So what do you say? You in?"

Rebecca pressed her tongue to her cheek, mulling it over. "Sure," she said with a crack of her gum. "But I want ten percent of the sixty grand you already got, up front. Then I'll know you're for real."

Buzz flashed a thin smile. "I'm for real. You can have your six thousand. But you gotta come with me now."

She twitched, practically kicking herself for not having asked for the whole sixty thousand. "I can't come now. I gotta go to work."

"Six thousand dollars," he tempted her. "You can come now. Fuck work."

She cracked her gum, then sighed. "All right. I'll go. But I *want* my money."

He smiled and nodded toward his van. "Just get in."

"And I want to know more about what I'm getting into," she said as she heaved her gym bag over her shoulder and started walking. "I want to know *everything*."

He focused on the wiggle in her rear end as she reached the other side of the van, his eyes narrowing and a smirk coming to his face. No way you *really* want to know everything, he thought.

46

•

Cindy received a bouquet of flowers when she arrived at the studio that Friday morning. They were from Jack.

"Please be there for me today," the card read. "I need you."

She wanted to pretend that the message didn't affect her, but it did. Leaving Jack hadn't made her stop loving him. In fact, leaving him was the easy part. It was staying away that was the test. Tuesday morning, after attempting to be cool and distant with him, she'd felt her resolve eroding. Gina's death had reminded her of how little time there is to do anything in life—of the purposelessness of grudges and resentment. Gina had probably died believing that Cindy hated her. Cindy didn't want the same thing—God forbid!—to happen to Jack.

By the time she received the phone call, at ten o'clock in the morning, she'd already made up her mind to go over to the courthouse.

"Miss Paige," a woman said over the phone. "This is Manuel Cardenal's paralegal. Sorry to bother you, but he asked me to call you right away."

"Yes," she said with trepidation, afraid the trial had already accelerated to a verdict.

"Both Mr. Cardenal and Mr. Swyteck are in court right now, so they couldn't call you themselves. But they need you to come down to the courthouse. Mr. Swyteck needs you to testify for him. It's extremely important."

Cindy was confused. How could anything she had to say help Jack's case?

"I was about to go over there." She looked at her watch. "I can be there by ten-twenty—will that be in time?"

"Yes, I believe so," the woman said, "but *please* hurry."

Once Cindy heard the click on the other end, she sprung into action. She picked up her bag and rushed out of the office to the parking lot. The tires of her Pontiac Sunbird squealed as she accelerated out of the lot. She weaved in and out of traffic as she raced toward Frontage Road—the quickest route to the courthouse.

Ordinarily, Cindy was no speedster, but now was the time to see just how fast her Pontiac could go. She jammed down the accelerator and squeezed the steering wheel tightly, glancing intermittently at the speedometer as it pushed its way toward uncharted territory, past eighty-five miles per hour. The road was nearly deserted, and she was covering the distance in record time until she rounded a wide turn and suddenly the engine started to sputter. She was quickly losing speed.

"Come *on*," she urged as she pumped the accelerator. The car lunged forward a little, but the engine just gasped, then died. She coasted to a stop and steered off the road to the gravel shoulder. She pressed the pedal to the floor and turned the key. The ignition whined, but the engine wouldn't fire. She tried again. Same response.

"Not now," she groaned, as if she could reason with the vehicle. She didn't see a single car on the road, and she suddenly wished she had a car phone. She glanced in her side-view mirror and gave a start as she was suddenly staring into the face of a stranger.

"Can I help you, miss?" he said—loud enough to be heard through her window.

Cindy hesitated. The man's voice sounded pleasant enough, but the way he'd suddenly appeared out of nowhere seemed strange. She looked in the rear-view mirror and saw an old gray van parked a short distance down the road. She looked at the man but couldn't read his expression, since most of his face was covered by the brim of his baseball cap and big dark sunglasses. Then she remembered: *Jack needs me.* She cracked the window half an inch. "My car—"

"Has sugar in the carburetor," he finished for her.

Cindy gulped. "I need—"

"To get to the courthouse," he interrupted again.

Her eyes widened with fear, but before she could react, the window suddenly exploded, and she was covered in a shower of glass pellets. She screamed and pounded the horn, but her cries for help quickly turned to desperate gasps for air as the hand of a very strong man came through the open window and wrapped tightly around her throat.

"Ja—ack!" her strangled voice cried.

"It ain't Jack, baby," came the snide reply. Then he reached for his sheath and showed her the sharp steel blade that had grown very cold since it had been used on Gina Terisi.

47

J ack had wanted to see his father before return-
ing to the courtroom on Friday morning, but
Manny insisted that father and son have absolutely
no communication until the trial was over. Since
McCue had reserved the right to call rebuttal witnesses, the possibility remained that he'd recall the
governor, and anything Jack and his father discussed
would be fair game for cross-examination.

As it turned out, McCue called no further witnesses, and closing arguments were finished by one
o'clock. Manny was brilliant, expanding on the speech
he'd delivered during the governor's testimony. He
reminded the jurors that the law did not require Jack
to prove he was innocent—that it was the government's heavy burden to prove him guilty "beyond a
reasonable doubt."

McCue did the best he could, then retreated to
his office. Jack and Manny waited in the attorneys'
lounge, down the hall from Judge Tate's courtroom.

At five-fifteen, the courtroom deputy stuck her head into the lounge and gave them the news.

"The jury has reached a verdict," she told them.

In a split second they were out the door, walking side-by-side as quickly as they could without breaking into a dead run down the hall and into the courtroom. The news of a verdict had traveled fast, and the expectant crowd filed in behind them. Wilson McCue was already in position. Manny and Jack took their places at the defense table. Jack glanced behind him, toward the public seating. Ten rows back, Neil Goderich gave him a reassuring wink. On the opposite side of the aisle, Mike Mannon looked worried but gave him a thumbs up. Cindy, Jack realized with a pang, wasn't in the courtroom. Not even the flowers had worked.

"All rise!" cried the bailiff.

Judge Tate proceeded to the bench, but Jack gave her only a passing glance. He was focused on the twelve jurors who were taking their seats for the final time. He was trying to remember those indicators jury psychologists relied on to predict verdicts. Who had they selected as foreman? Did they look at the defendant, or at the prosecutor? At that moment, however, he couldn't think clearly enough to apply any of those tests. He was consumed by the feeling of being on trial—of having twelve strangers hold his life in their hands.

"Has the jury reached a verdict?" Judge Tate asked.

"We have," responded the foreman.

"Please give it to the clerk."

The written verdict was passed from the foreman to the clerk, then from the clerk to the judge. The judge inspected it, then returned it to the clerk for public disclosure. The ritual seemed to pull everyone to the edge of his seat. Yet the courtroom was so deathly quiet that Jack could hear the fluorescent lights humming thirty feet overhead.

This is it, he thought. *Life or death.* He struggled to bring his emotions under control. Everything had seemed so encouraging moments ago, when he and Manny had assessed his chances. But odds were deceiving. Like a year ago, when Cindy's mother had been diagnosed with breast cancer. They'd all taken comfort in the doctor's assurance that her chances of survival were 80 percent. Those odds sounded pretty good until Jack had started thinking of the last hundred people he'd laid eyes on—and then imagined twenty of them dead.

"The defendant shall rise," announced the judge.

Jack glanced at Manny as they rose in unison. He clenched his fists tightly in anticipation.

"In the matter of *State* versus *Swyteck*, on the charge of murder in the first degree," the clerk read from the verdict form, "we, the jury, find the defendant: *not* guilty."

A roar filled the courtroom. On impulse, Jack turned and embraced Manny. Never had he hugged a man so tightly—not even his father. But had the governor been there, Jack would have cracked his ribs.

"Order!" said the judge, postponing the celebration. The rumble in the courtroom quieted. Manny and Jack returned to their seats, smiling apologetically.

"Ladies and gentlemen of the jury," the judge intoned, "thank you for your service. You are discharged. A judgment of acquittal shall be entered. Mr. Swyteck," she said, peering over the bench, "you are free to go. This court is adjourned," she declared, ending it all with one last crack of the gavel.

Happy cries of congratulation flew across the courtroom. Neil and Mike and the other friends who'd never stopped believing hurried forward and leaned across the rail that separated players from spectators, slapping Jack's back and shaking the hand of an innocent man. Jack was elated but dazed. He canvassed the buzzing crowd, still hoping for a glimpse of Cindy. Then he thought of the other person who was missing.

"Where's my father?" Jack asked Manny. His voice was barely audible in the thundering commotion of the crowded courtroom.

Manny smiled. "We've got a special celebration planned," he said with a wink. "Back at my office."

Jack was overcome with a sense of euphoria. He felt like a death-row prisoner released into the bright light of day. He'd never been so eager to see his father. As he and Manny started toward the gate, they were stopped abruptly by Wilson McCue.

"I'd lose the smiles if I were you," the prosecutor said bitterly. He spoke in a low, threatening voice that couldn't be overheard by the noisy crowd on the other side of the rail. "This is only round one, boys, and round two is about to begin. It's just a matter of how fast I can assemble the grand jury and draft the indictment, that's all. I warned you, Swyteck. I said I'd come after you for the murder of Gina Terisi, and I meant it. Right now the only question is whether I'll do it before or *after* I indict your old man for the murder of Eddy Goss."

Jack's eyes flared with contempt. "You just won't take those blinders off, will you, McCue?"

"Jack," Manny stopped him. "Say nothing."

"That's right," McCue countered. "Say nothing. Take the fifth. It runs in the family." He shook his head with disgust, then turned and stepped through the swinging gate, into the rabble of reporters clamoring at the rail.

Jack desperately wanted to rush after McCue and set him straight, but Manny held him back. "Just take it easy, Jack," he said, pulling him toward the bench, away from the media frenzy. "McCue can afford to talk out of anger, but you can't. So for now, just let me handle the press. The best thing you can do is to say nothing and go back to my office. We need to regroup and talk with your father."

"My father . . ." Jack said slowly, as if tapping into a source of strength. Then he nodded. "All right, I'll meet you there." Then he opened the gate and pushed his way into the swarming press. He kept his head lowered, ignoring all questions until he reached the elevators. Less than three minutes later, he was behind the steering wheel of his Mustang, ready to pull out of the courthouse parking lot.

He'd just put the car into gear when he heard the ringing of his car phone. *Cindy*, he hoped. But why would she use this number? Could she have already heard the verdict? It didn't seem possible.

He moved the shift back into park and picked up the phone.

"Jack," he heard her voice. "It's me, Cindy."

He started to say something, but words wouldn't come. "Cindy," he said finally, just wanting to say her name. "Where are you?"

"Balcony scene's over, Romeo," came the ugly reply. It wasn't Cindy's voice anymore. It was the same voice he'd heard while on his belly in the bus. "She's with me."

Jack's hand shook as he pressed the phone to his ear. Some part of his brain that wasn't absolutely terrified directed his other hand to turn off the ignition. He moved slightly forward in his seat. "What have you done with her!"

"Nothing," the caller said coolly. *"Yet."*

"It's me you want, you bastard! Just leave her out of it."

"Shut up, Swyteck! I'm through fooling around. Your legal system has fucked everything up again. This time we'll play on my turf. And this time I want real money. I want a quarter million. Cash. Unmarked fifties."

Jack's head was spinning. He tried to focus. "Look, I'll do whatever you want. But that's a lot of money. It'll take time to—"

"Your girlfriend doesn't have *time*. Talk to your father, asshole. He's so eager to help you."

"Okay. Please, just don't hurt her? Just tell me how to get you the money."

"Take it to Key West. Just the two of you."

"The *two* of us?"

"You and your father."

"I can do it myself—"

"You'll do it the way I *tell* you to do it!" the caller snapped. "I need to know where everybody is who knows anything about this. I'm not gonna be ambushed. No police, no FBI, no National Guard—not even a meter maid. Any sign of law enforcement and your pretty girlfriend's dead. If I see any roadblocks on U.S. 1, any choppers in the air, any news reports on television, anything that even *looks* like you called in the cavalry—she's dead, *immediately*. It's me against the Swytecks. End of story. You got it?"

"I got it," Jack said, though he could barely speak. "When do you want us there?"

"Saturday night, October twenty-ninth."

"That's tomorrow," Jack protested.

"That's right. It's the Key West Fantasy Fest weekend. Nice, big Halloween street party. Like the Mardi Gras in New Orleans. Everyone's going to be in costume. And so will I. No one could possibly find me in that mess, Swyteck. So don't even try."

"How will we contact you?"

"I'll contact you. Just check into any one of the big resort hotels. Use your name. I'll find you. Any questions?"

Jack took a deep breath. "No," he replied.

"Good. Very good. Oh—one other thing, Swyteck."

"What?"

"Trick or treat," he taunted, then hung up the phone.

It should have been a night of celebration, beginning with him and his father sipping Dom Perignon, then blossoming into a fairy-tale reunion with Cindy. Instead, the nightmare was continuing.

Jack went to Manny's office as planned, where he met up with his father. They sat alone in Manny's conference room, considering their options.

"Agnes and I can certainly come up with the money," the governor assured his son. "That's not a problem. And, naturally, I'm in a position to bring in the best law enforcement available. All I have to do is make a phone call. I can do it right now."

Jack shook his head. "We can't," he said emphatically. "He'll kill Cindy, I know it. He'll spot anything we try to do."

The governor sighed. "You're probably right. He may be crazy, but he's brilliant-crazy. I'm sure he's monitoring a police radio even as we speak. And if there's anything I learned in my ten years on the force, it's that police departments are sieves."

Father and son sat staring at each other. "All right," the governor finally said, "we don't bring in the police. But I have lots of friends in the private sector— retired FBI agents, retired Secret Service. They can help. They can at least give advice."

Jack wrestled with it. "That makes sense, I guess. But any advisers have to be just that—advisers. Ultimately, it comes down to me."

"No," the governor corrected him. "You *and* me."

Jack looked at his father across the table. The governor gave him a reassuring smile that was meant to remove any doubt that he could count on his old man.

"Let's do it, then," said Jack. "We'll nail this bastard. Together."

Part Five

Saturday, October 29

48

Jack and Harry Swyteck reached the end of U.S. 1 and the city limits of Key West at about noon the next day. They followed the palm trees along the coastline and parked Harry's rented Ford Taurus near Duval Street, the main thoroughfare that bisected the tourists' shopping district. Both sides of Duval and the streets leading off of it were lined with art galleries and antique shops housed in renovated white-frame buildings, booths advertising snorkel tours, T-shirt emporiums, bicycle rental shops, and open-air bars blaring a mélange of folk, rock, and calypso.

At the north end of Duval was Mallory Square, a popular gathering spot on the wharf where magicians, jugglers, and portrait artists entertained crowds and turned sunsets into a festival every day of the year. During Fantasy Fest, the square was simply an extension of a ten-day party that stretched from one end of Duval to the other.

Fantasy Fest was already in its ninth day when

the Swytecks arrived, and the party in the streets was still nonstop. Some tourists were buying their feathers, beads, and noisemakers for the annual but hardly traditional Halloween parade on Saturday night, others were just people-watching. Many were already in costume. Men dressed as women. Women dressed as Martians. A brazen few were undressed, covering their bare breasts or buttocks with only grease paint.

"Check that out," Jack said from his passenger seat, pointing to a man outfitted in a lavender loincloth and a pink bonnet.

"Probably the mayor," the governor deadpanned.

Harry parked the car in the covered garage near their hotel. They grabbed their overnight bags and a briefcase from the trunk and headed up the old brick sidewalk, grateful for the shade of hundred-year-old oaks and a cool ocean breeze. Hotel rooms were hard to come by during Fantasy Fest—especially if requested at the last minute—but the governor had a few connections. They checked in at the front desk and carried their own luggage to a suite on the sixth floor.

The sliding-glass doors offered a stunning, eight-hundred-dollar-a-night view of the Gulf of Mexico. Jack walked out onto the balcony and looked at the Pier Point, one of those outdoor waterfront restaurants where the food was never as good as the atmosphere. It all seemed so surreal, he thought. He wanted to think that at any moment Cindy would join them, and then they'd get caught up in the party, walk on the beach or head over to the original Sloppy Joe's and find the table Ernest Hemingway used to like. But they had business to tend to—someone to meet. And at 1:00 P.M., the man they wanted to meet was at their door.

"Peter Kimmell," said the governor, "meet my son, Jack."

Jack closed the balcony's sliding-glass doors and pulled the curtains shut. "Glad to meet you," he said, reaching out to shake the man's hand.

Kimmell was tall, about six feet four inches, with a lean body that moved with catlike grace. His face registered little emotion, but his eyes seemed to be constantly assessing, processing information. They gave Jack the uncomfortable feeling that he was being evaluated, measured against some personal set of standards.

Old habits die hard. Kimmell was a twenty-year veteran of the Secret Service who'd burned out two years before and retired to his bass boat in the Florida Keys. But he'd quickly grown bored with fishing, so he took up cycling, then swimming, then running—and before he knew it, the same energy that had made him a top agent made him one of the top competitors in the age-fifty-and-above Ironman triathlon. He still did some work as a private investigator when he wasn't training, and Harry Swyteck used him as a consultant on special events that raised thorny security problems. The governor considered Kimmell the best in the business. And, most important, he was the only man Harry trusted to give Jack and him the expertise they needed without any danger of a leak to the press or police.

"So *you're* Jack," Kimmell said, smiling. "Your dad's told me a lot about you—all good." He shifted his gaze from son to father. "You ready to get right to it, men?"

"Ready," they both answered.

"Good. Now let me show you some toys I've brought along for you," he said with a wink. He hoisted onto the bed a gray metal suitcase that was nearly as big as a trunk. "Voila," he said as he popped it open.

The Swytecks stood in silence as they peered at the cache inside. "What did you do," asked the governor, "mix up your bag with James Bond's?"

"You won't need half this stuff," said Kimmell. "But whatever you will need is here. I got everything from voice-activated wires to infrared binoculars."

"I think we should keep it simple," said Jack.

"I agree," he replied. "First, let's talk weapons. You ever fired a gun, Jack?"

Jack smiled at the irony. How would Wilson McCue have answered that question for him? "Uh-huh"—he nodded—"back when I was in college. I had a girlfriend who didn't feel safe at night without a gun in the apartment, so I learned to use it."

"Good. Now, for you, son," he said as he removed a sleek black pistol from the holster, "I recommend this baby—the Glock Seventeen Safe Action nine-millimeter pistol, Austrian design. It's completely computer-manufactured of synthetic polymer. Stronger than steel, but weighs less than two pounds even with a full magazine, so you can hold it nice and steady. Deadly accurate, too, so you don't have to be right in this lunatic's face to blow him away. And it's got a pretty soft recoil, considering the punch it packs: You got seventeen rounds of police-issue hollow-point para-ammunition that'll drop a charging moose with an attitude dead in its tracks." He handed it to Jack. "How's that feel, partner?"

Jack laid it in his hand and shrugged. "Feels like a gun."

"Like a part of your hand, Jack. *That's* what it feels like." He took the pistol back, then dug into his suitcase. "Now, let's talk real protection: body armor. It's gonna be hot as hell, but you gotta wear a vest. This is the top of the line in my book. Made of Kevlar one twenty-nine and Spectra fibers. Full coverage. Protects your front, back, and sides, and the shirttails keep it from riding up on you. Stops a forty-four-magnum slug at fourteen hundred feet per second— that's point-blank range. Excellent multihit stopping power, too"—he winked—"but I think I'd still hit the deck if he pulls out an Uzi. Best of all, it weighs less than four pounds and gives you full range of motion. Beneath your baggy black sweatshirt, your kidnapper won't even know you got it on. Governor, got a Glock and body armor for you, too. I know you never used to like to wear the vest, but—"

"I'll wear one," he said without hesitation.

"Good," replied Kimmell. "Now—the plan. If I'm gonna help you men get ready to meet this character face-to-face, I need to get a fix on who he is. I need to know everything *you* know about him. So let's start at the beginning. Tell me about the murder he confessed to. Who was the woman he says he killed?"

"A teenager, actually," Jack answered. "She got herself into a nightclub with a phony ID, then she was abducted in the parking lot on the way to her car. The next morning, they found her on the beach. Her throat had been slit."

"What else—" Kimmell asked, but he was interrupted by the shrill ring of the telephone. "You guys expecting a call?"

"No," answered the governor.

The phone was on its third ring. "Answer it, Jack," Kimmell directed.

"Hello," he answered, then listened carefully. "No, thank you," he finished the conversation, and then hung up. His father and Kimmell were staring expectantly. "There's a package at the front desk for us."

"From who?" asked Kimmell.

"No name on it. But it must be him. When he called me yesterday, he said we should just check into one of the big hotels and that we'd hear from him. There's only a handful of possibilities on the Key. Looks like he found us."

Kimmell nodded. "Tell them to send it up."

Jack phoned the manager and asked him to deliver the package to their room personally. The manager was glad to accommodate. In two minutes he was at their door with the delivery. Kimmell answered, then brought the shoe-box-sized package inside and lay it on the bed. He took a metal detector from his suitcase and ran it across the package.

"There's metal inside," said Kimmell.

"You think he sent us a bomb?" asked the governor.

"Can't be," Kimmell answered. "If he was going to blow you up, he would have done it two years ago. Open it."

Jack carefully removed the string and cut the tape with the care of a surgeon. He lifted the lid. Inside the bubble wrap was a cellular phone. Across the top lay a business-sized envelope with a handwritten message on the outside. "Switch on the phone at midnight," it read.

"At least we know your kidnapper hasn't lost his nerve," said Kimmell. "He's still in the game. Which means there's still hope."

"What's in the envelope?" asked the governor.

Kimmell opened it and unfolded its contents. "It's a certificate of death," he said.

"Not Cindy?" the governor asked with sudden fear.

"'Raul Francisco Fernandez,'" he read from the first line. "It's from the County Health Department. An exact duplicate, except for Box thirty—the cause of death. You can still make out the original, type-written entry. 'Cardiac arrest,'" he read aloud, "'as a consequence of electrocution.' But someone has crossed out the coroner's entry and penciled in a different cause of death." He handed it to the governor.

"'Jack Swyteck,'" Harry read aloud, his voice cracking.

A heavy silence permeated the room. Then Kimmell took a closer look at the certificate. "Why'd he do this?" he asked.

"That's been his message all along," Jack said. "He's blamed me from the beginning."

"I'm talking about something different," said Kimmell. "There's another message here—one that's a little less obvious. Maybe even unintended. Box seven," he said as he pointed to it, "is the space for the 'informant.' That's the person who provides personal data for completion of the certificate. The named informant here is Alfonso Perez."

"Who's that?" asked Jack.

"There are lots of men named Alfonso Perez. But from my days in law enforcement I know that at one time it was also one of the aliases used by a guy known as Esteban. Every federal agent based in Miami in the eighties knew about this character. Brilliant guy. Speaks English as well as he does Spanish. Every so often he changes his name and identity. The feds can't keep up. I heard they almost nabbed him two years ago, but he took off to somewhere in the Caribbean. Anyway, he's a suspect in at least five murder-kidnappings in this country alone."

"He's wanted in other countries, too?" asked Jack.

"Came here from Cuba. He was a thug in Castro's army, years ago. Trained with the Russians during the war in Angola, then distinguished himself by torturing political prisoners—a merciless bastard. Earned himself a nice promotion to the Batallon Especial de Seguridad, Castro's elite military force. But when they cut off his daily routine of driving nails into molars and bashing heads with bayonets, they say he snapped. He craved the violence. Went on a killing spree. Raped and murdered about a dozen women in Havana—all prostitutes. The Cubans threw him in a booby hatch for a couple years. Then Castro sent him over to Miami in 1980, when he opened the jails and asylums and turned the Mariel boat lift into a Trojan horse. Esteban just snuck in with the hundred and fifty thousand other Marielito refugees. FBI and Immigration have been looking for him ever since."

"Raul Fernandez came to Miami in the Mariel boat lift too," said Jack.

"Probably not a coincidence," Kimmell speculated. "That doesn't mean Fernandez was a criminal, though. Only a small number of the Marielitos were."

Jack and his father sat in silence. "You think it could be him?" Jack asked.

Kimmell sighed heavily. "I really can't say for sure. But for your sake," he added, "I sure as hell hope not."

Jack rose and stepped toward the window, pulling back the drapes just enough to peer out at the vast ocean. "It's not *me* who I'm worried about," he said with more than a touch of fear.

49

On the other side of Key West, near the tourist landmark designated "The Southernmost Point in the Continental United States," beneath the rotting pine floorboards of an abandoned white frame house, Cindy Paige blinked her eyes open. She wasn't sure if she was awake. Although her eyes were open, her world was total blackness. She tried to touch her eyes to make sure she wasn't blind, but her hands wouldn't move. They were bound. She struggled to get loose, but her feet were bound too. She screamed, but it didn't sound like her. She screamed again. It was muffled, as if a hand were covering her mouth. Was someone there? Was someone *with* her? Suddenly it came back to her—the last two things she could remember: a sack being thrown over her head and then a jab in her arm.

She heard a pounding above her. Her heart raced. More pounding, and then a blinding light was in her eyes. A wave of fresh air hit her face, making her painfully aware of how stifling hot her hell really was. Her blurry vision focused, and then her eyes widened with fear. The image had returned—the man in the cap and wraparound sunglasses who'd attacked her in the car.

"Quiet, angel," Esteban said softly. He was seated on the floor and speaking down into the hole. "No one is going to hurt you."

She'd never been so frightened in her life. Her teeth clenched the gag in her mouth. Her chest heaved with quick, panicky breaths. *Please*, she cried out with her eyes, *don't hurt me!*

"If you'll promise not to scream," he said, "I'll take off your gag. If you'll promise not to run, I'll take you out of your hole. Do you promise?"

She nodded eagerly.

Esteban's mouth curled into a sinister smirk. "I don't believe you."

Cindy whimpered pathetically.

"Don't blame *me*," he said. "Your boyfriend is to blame. Swyteck *forced* me to do this. I didn't want it to be this way. So many times I could have hurt you, had I wanted to. But I never did. And I won't hurt you . . . so long as Jack Swyteck does what I tell him to do. You do believe me, don't you?"

Cindy's eyes were still wide with horror. But she nodded.

"Good," he replied. "Now, I can't let you out of your little hiding place. But I'll make a deal with you." He displayed a syringe. "This is secobarbital sodium. It's what made you sleep so deeply. I must have gotten the dosage right. But now I've got a problem. You see, I don't know how much of it is still in your system. Which means that I don't know how much to give you. If I give you too much, you're not gonna wake up. So promise me you'll lie real quiet, and we can skip the injection. Deal?"

Cindy nodded once.

"Smart girl." He stood up and put one of the loose floorboards back in place. At the sound of Cindy's muffled cry, he stopped and wagged his finger at her. "Not another peep," he reminded her, like a loving parent telling a four-year-old she can't sleep with Mommy and Daddy tonight.

Cindy swallowed hard. Somehow she managed to stop crying.

"Good girl. Now, don't you worry, I've already found better accommodations for us. You'll be out of there before long."

She quivered as she lay in the hole, hoping for a miracle as he reached for the other floorboard. Her world went dark as he laid it in place.

"Night, angel," she heard him say through the wooden barrier.

Esteban got up off his knees and pulled off his cap and sunglasses. The humidity in the boarded-up house was nearly as sweltering above the floor as it was below. He was in a living room of bare wooden floors and water-stained walls. A few trespassing transients had left behind their aluminum cans, cardboard blankets, and cigarette butts. Esteban had brought only what he absolutely needed: a couple of lounge chairs, a fully stocked ice chest, his ham radio, and three battery-operated fans that pushed stale air around the room. He didn't dare open the boarded-up windows, for fear of being detected. But the chances of that were slim. The old house was so overgrown with tropical foliage that he'd practically needed a machete to reach the front door. And so far as he could tell from the police band on his radio, no one was searching for him.

"What's this *angel* crap?" Rebecca groused from across the room, startling him. She'd been standing in the doorway, listening.

He gave her a quick once-over. She was wearing very short blue-jean cutoffs, a loose tank top, no shoes, no bra, and no makeup. She had the deep suntan of a woman who worked nights, yet her skin didn't look all that healthy.

"Something a whore like you wouldn't know anything about," he snarled.

"Right," she said indignantly, then walked across the room to the ice chest and grabbed a Coke. "If she's such an angel, then why you got her under the floorboards? Huh?"

His expression went cold. "She's *alive*, isn't she? And you know why she's alive?"

"Because she's no good to you dead."

"No," he spat, "because I've been watching her for months. Because I *know* she's not a slut like her girlfriend—or like *you* and all the other cocksuckers who dance on tables."

Rebecca leaned against the wall, shifting her weight nervously. She was afraid but tried not to show it. "Listen, I don't know what your problem is. If anyone should be complaining, it's me. I said I'd make the phone call, and I did. I called the bitch. You paid me the six thousand dollars, and that's fine. But you didn't tell me I was going to have to come all the way to Key West with you to collect the rest of my stinking twenty-five grand. You didn't tell me we were going to have Sleeping Beauty in the back of the van. And you sure as hell didn't tell me we'd have to hole up in this dump, or in this other place you're bringing us to. So maybe I deserve a little more. Or maybe I walk out right now."

He glared at her. "You'd do *anything* for money. Wouldn't you, Rebecca."

"Oh," she said, "and you're not doing this for the money."

"I'm doing this for Raul! Because Raul was fucking innocent!"

Beneath the floorboards, Cindy shuddered with fear. She could overhear everything, and the tone in the man's voice made her wish she was still unconscious.

Inwardly, Rebecca also trembled at his tone. "Just cool your jets," she said, feeling a lump rising in her throat. "I just want my fair share, all right?"

Esteban stepped toward her slowly, looking as though he were deliberating. He reached into his pocket. "You'll get your share," he assured. "But you gotta earn it. Here," he said as he crumpled up a twenty and threw it at her. He stopped a foot away from her and stared into her eyes. "Here's twenty bucks, bitch. Do it."

Rebecca stepped back in fear, her back to the wall. "Do *yourself.*"

He slapped her across the face. "Do *me.*"

She tried to slide away, but he grabbed her by the wrist and squeezed hard. "Do *it.*"

She was about to scream, but was silenced by the look in his eyes. She had been in bad situations before. Men who pulled knives on her. Men who urinated on her. She was streetwise enough to sense whether a scream would make him stop or make him snap. This time, she didn't *dare* scream.

Rebecca lowered herself onto her knees, her hands shaking as she unzipped his pants. His head rolled back and he moaned with pleasure. She worked fast and furiously to finish the job as quickly as she could. "Quickies" were her trade, with hundreds or maybe even thousands of them under her belt. But she didn't swallow for any of her customers, for fear of the deadly virus. She heard Esteban groan, signaling that he was near. She prepared to pull away, but this time the routine was different. She felt his hand clasp the back of her neck, pressing her head down further, forcing her to take in much more than she could. His groaning grew louder. She gagged. He was in so deep she was unable to breathe. She tried to back off, but he forced even harder. She needed out. So she bit him.

Esteban smacked her across the head, knocking her to the floor. "Watch the fucking teeth!"

Rebecca gasped for air, looking up in fear. "I couldn't breathe!"

He grabbed her by the hair, jerking her head back. "That's the *least* of your problems," he said, his eyes two vacuous pools.

Beneath the floor, Cindy began to shake uncontrollably. She closed her eyes tightly to shut off the tears, but no matter how hard she tried, she couldn't shut her ears.

"I got plans for you, Rebecca," Cindy heard him say—and the laugh that followed chilled her to the bone.

50

Kimmell, Jack, and Harry spent the rest of that
Saturday going over everything—main plans,
backup plans, contingency backup plans. Each plan
revolved around the same basic triangle. Jack and
his father would be out in the field, following the
kidnapper's instructions. Kimmell would remain in
the hotel suite, a kind of central command station
operator who could be reached by phone or beeper
in case of emergency.

By 10:00 P.M. they'd about reached the point of
information overload. They ordered room service
and ate dinner in total silence, save for an occasional happy scream or blast of fireworks from the
burgeoning Halloween crowd on nearby Duval
Street. The increasing level of noise was a steady
reminder that the midnight phone call was just two
hours away.

When he finished eating, Kimmell tossed his nap-
kin to his plate and rose from the table. On average,
he smoked two, maybe three cigarettes an entire

year. Already tonight he'd exceeded his annual quota. He grabbed the ashtray and retreated to the adjoining room to take another look at the photographs and notes sent by the kidnapper, as if by absorbing all available information he could get into his mind.

Jack and Harry sat across from each other at the dining table. The governor watched as Jack picked at his food.

"I'm sorry, Jack," he said sincerely.

Jack wasn't sure what he meant. "We both are. I just pray we get Cindy back. Then there'll be nothing for anyone to be sorry about."

"I pray we get her back, too. No question—that's the most important thing. But there's something else I'm sorry about," he said with a pained expression. "It has to do with pushing a kid too hard when he was already doing his best—and then pushing him away when his best wasn't good enough. I mean, hell, Jack, sometimes I look back on it and think that if you'd been Michelangelo, I probably would have walked into the Sistine Chapel and said something like, 'Okay, son, now what about the walls?'" He smiled briefly, then turned serious again. "I guess when your mother died I just wanted you to be perfect. That's no excuse, though. I'm truly sorry for the pain I've caused you. I've been sorry for a long time. And it's time I told you."

Jack struggled for the right words. "You know"— his voice quivered with emotion—"in the last two days, the only thing I've been able to think about besides the kidnapping is how to thank you for what you did at the trial."

"You can thank me by accepting my apology," Harry said with a warm smile.

Jack's heart swelled. Of course he'd accept it; he felt like *he* should be the one to apologize. So he expressed it another way. "You're gonna love Cindy when you get to know her."

The governor's eyes were suddenly moist. "I know I will."

"Hey," said Kimmell as he entered the room, "time to get dressed."

Jack and his father looked at each other with confidence. There was strength in unity. "Let's do it," said Jack. The governor gave a quick nod of agreement, and they marched off to the adjoining room, where Kimmell helped them get ready. Both wore dark clothing, in case they had to hide. Sneakers, in case they had to run. And both wore the Kevlar vests Kimmell had brought them, in case they couldn't hide or run fast enough.

"What's that?" Jack asked as Kimmell wired a battery to his vest.

"It's a tracking device," he answered. "The transmitter sends out a one-watt signal. It's on intermittent-duty cycle, so it'll be easy for me to recognize your signal—and the battery will last longer, too, just in case this takes longer than we think. Any time I need a location on you, I can do it in an instant from my audio-visual indicator here in the room."

Kimmell went ahead and rigged the antenna and

was tucking the pistol into Jack's holster when the portable phone rang.

It was exactly midnight.

Jack took a deep breath, then reached for the phone. Kimmell stopped him.

"Be cooperative," Kimmell reminded him, "but insist on hearing Cindy's voice."

He nodded, then switched on the receiver. "Hello," he answered.

"Ready to trick or treat, Swyteck?"

Be cooperative, Jack reminded himself. "We've got the money. Tell us how you want to do the exchange."

"Ah, the *exchange*," Esteban said wistfully. "You know, no kidnapper in the history of the world has ever really figured out the problem of the exchange. It's that one moment where so many things can go wrong. And if just *one* little thing goes wrong, then *everything* goes wrong. Do you understand me, Swyteck?"

"Yes."

"Good. Here's the plan. I'm splitting you up. Your father will deliver the money to me in a public place. You'll pick up the girl in a private place. Brilliant, isn't it?"

"What do you want us to do?"

"Tell your father to take the money to Warehouse E off Mallory Square and wait outside by the pay phone. When I'm ready for the money, I'll come by in costume. Believe me, he'll recognize me."

"What about Cindy? How do I get her?"

"When we hang up, take the portable phone with you and start walking south on Simonton Street away from your hotel. Just keep walking until I call you. I'll direct you right to her. And so long as your father hands over the money, I'll direct you to her in time."

"What do you mean *in time*?" Jack asked.

"What do you *think* I mean?"

"I need to speak to Cindy," he said firmly. "I need to know that she's all right."

The line went silent. Ten long seconds passed. Then twenty. Jack thought maybe he had hung up. But he hadn't.

"Ja—ack," Cindy's voice cracked.

"Cindy!"

"Please, Jack. Just do what he says."

"That's all," said Esteban. "If you want to hear more, you gotta play by my rules. No games, no cops, nobody gets hurt. Start walking, Swyteck." The line went dead.

Jack breathed a heavy sigh. "No fear," he added, speaking only to himself.

51

After some last-minute advice from Kimmell, Jack and his father told each other to be careful. Then they left the hotel and headed in separate directions. The governor went west toward Mallory Square, an assortment of big, wide piers that had once been a waterfront auction block for wine, silks, and other ship salvage hauled in by nineteenth-century wreckers. During Fantasy Fest, the square was more or less a breaker between the insanity on Duval Street and the peaceful Gulf of Mexico. Jack walked south on Simonton, a residential street that ran parallel to Duval. The neighborhood was a slice of wealthy old Key West, with white picket fences and one multistory Victorian house after another, many of them built for nineteenth-century sailors, sponge merchants, and treasure hunters, many of them now bed-and-breakfasts.

He walked two blocks very quickly, then slowed down, realizing that he had no official destination. The Flintstones danced by on their way to the festival, singing their theme song. Others in costume streamed by on foot or on motor scooter, since cars were useless during Fantasy Fest.

Jack's portable phone rang, startling him. "Yes," he answered.

"Turn left at Caroline Street," said Esteban, "and stay on the phone. Tell me when you hit each intersection."

Jack crossed Simonton and headed east on Caroline Street. The noise from Duval was beginning to fade, and he saw fewer pedestrians on their way to the party. It was darker, too, since there were fewer street lamps, and the thick, leafy canopy blocked out the moonlight. The sidewalk was cracked and buckled from overgrown tree roots. Palm trees and sprawling oaks rustled in the cool, steady breeze. Majestic old wooden houses with two-story porches and gingerbread detail seemed to creak as the wind blew. Jack just kept walking.

"This is not about your girlfriend," said the voice over the phone.

Jack exhaled. The phone obviously was not just for directions. "I'm at Elizabeth Street."

"Keep going," said Esteban, and then he immediately picked up his thought. "This is *all* about Raul Fernandez. You know that, don't you?"

Jack kept walking. He didn't want to agitate, but after two years of wondering, he had to keep him talking. "Tell me about Raul."

"You know the most important thing already." His tone was forceful but not argumentative. "It wasn't Raul's idea to kill that girl."

"Tell me about *him*, though."

There was silence on the line—one of those long, pivotal silences Jack had heard so many times when interviewing clients, after which the flow of information would either completely shut down or never shut off. He heard the man clear his throat. "Raul had been in prison in Cuba for nine years before we came over on the boat. And after nine years in jail, what do you think he wanted most when he got to Miami?"

Jack hesitated. The story about the boat fit Kimmell's theory that the kidnapper was Esteban. But he wasn't sure whether this was meant to be a monologue or a dialogue. "You tell me."

"A *whore*, you dumb shit. And he was willing to pay for it. But there are so many whores out there who just won't admit what they are. Just pick one, I told him. He did, but he still needed encouragement. So I went with him, to show him how easy it was."

"You and Fernandez did it *together*?"

"Raul didn't *kill* anyone. The knife was just to scare her. But the stupid bitch panicked and pulled off his mask. Even then, Raul *still* didn't want to kill her. I was saving his ass by doing it. So how do you think it felt when *he* was the one arrested for murder? I did everything I could to keep him from getting the chair. I even confessed! But you didn't do *your* part, Swyteck. The governor, the man who could stop it all, was your father, and you did *nothing*."

Jack resisted the temptation to educate the kidnapper, but he felt a certain vindication—not for himself, but for his father. Since the murder had begun as a rape or attempted rape by Raul Fernandez, Fernandez was as guilty as the man who had slit her throat. By law, anyone who committed a felony that brought about an unintended death was guilty of murder, even if the murder was committed by an accomplice. It was called "felony murder." It was a capital crime. And most important, it meant that his father had *not* executed an innocent man after all.

"So you and Raul were prison buddies. Is that it?"

"Prison buddies," he said with disdain. "What do you think—we were a couple of fags, or something? Raul was my brother, you son of a bitch. You fucking killed my little brother."

Jack took a deep breath. It didn't seem possible, but the stakes had suddenly risen. "I'm approaching William Street."

"Stop now. Face south. Do you see it?"

"See what?"

"The house on the corner."

Jack peered through the wrought-iron fence toward a stately old Queen Anne-style Victorian mansion that was nearly hidden from view by thick tropical foliage and royal poinciana trees. It was a three-story white frame house with a widow's walk and a spacious sitting porch out front, due for a paint job but otherwise in good repair. Blue shutters framed the windows, purely for decoration. But the windows themselves and even the doors were covered with corrugated aluminum storm shutters— the kind that winter residents installed to protect their property during the June-to-November hurricane season.

"I see it," said Jack. "It's storm-proofed."

"Yes," replied the voice on the other end of the line. "But your girlfriend's inside. And she's not coming out. You have to go in and get her. And don't even think about calling the police to go in and get her for you. It's a big old house, and she's very well hidden. Maybe she's in the attic. Maybe she's under the floorboards. The only way you'll find her alive is if you stay on the phone and listen to me. I'll direct you right to her. But you have to move fast, Swyteck. I fed her arsenic exactly five minutes ago."

"You bastard! You said you wouldn't hurt her!"

"*I* didn't hurt her," he said sharply. "The only one who can hurt her is *you*. You'll kill her, unless you do as I say. She can last twenty minutes without an antidote. The sooner you find her, the sooner you can call the paramedics. The back door is open. I took the storm shutters off. So go get her, Jacky Boy. And stay on that phone."

Jack felt anger, fear, and a flood of other emotions, but he realized he had no time to consider his options. He yanked open the squeaky iron gate, sprinted up the brick driveway, and leaped over a three-foot hedge on his way to the back door—the only way into the desolate Key West mansion.

52

Harold Swyteck was pacing nervously outside the waterfront warehouse where he'd been instructed to deliver the ransom. He was alone, but the noise from the nearby festival made it sound like he was in the Orange Bowl on New Year's night. He was as close as he could be to the madness on Duval Street and still be in relative seclusion. Occasionally someone in costume passed by, coming or going to the dimly lit parking lot behind the old warehouse to have sex, take a leak, or smoke a joint.

The governor checked his watch. It was almost 1:00 A.M., and he still hadn't heard from Jack or the kidnapper. Strange, he thought. He was alone in the dark with a suitcase full of money, and he wasn't the least bit concerned about himself or the cash. He was worried about Jack. He stopped pacing and lifted the receiver on the pay phone to make sure it was still working. He got a dial tone, then hung up.

He sighed heavily. He was trying to stay alert, but the noise from the festival was impossible to block out. Laughter, screaming, and every kind of music, from kazoos to strolling violins, had him constantly on edge. A rock band was blasting from the nearby Pier House Hotel. He could hear the bone-rattling bass and the beat of the drum. It was annoying at first, like a dripping faucet in the night. Then it became a thunder in his brain. He wished it would stop, but the pounding continued. He shook his head—and then he froze as he realized that the bass and drum were coming from one direction, but the *real* pounding was coming from the opposite direction. He wheeled and checked behind him. The pounding was right there, coming from somewhere near the pay phone.

"Who's there?" he called out. No one replied. The pounding grew louder and more frantic by the second, like the palpitations of his heart. He took two steps forward, then stopped. There was an old, rusted van parked just beyond the telephone. The rear doors bulged with each thudding beat. The pounding was coming from inside. It was like a kicking noise. Someone was trying to get out! The metal doors flew open. The governor drew his gun.

"Freeze!" he shouted. "Who's there?"

The violent motion stopped, but there was no reply. The governor stepped closer to the van. He knew it would do no good to ask again. If he wanted an answer, he'd have to go in and get it.

53

Jack threw open the back door of the old mansion and rushed into a pitch-dark kitchen. He ran his hand along the wall and found a light switch. He flipped it on, but the room remained dark—*totally* dark, since every window in the house was covered by hurricane shutters.

"There's no power!" Jack shouted into the phone.

"It's off," said Esteban. "Take the flashlight from the kitchen table."

Jack bumped into a chair and found the table, then snatched up the flashlight and switched it on. His adrenaline was flowing, but he suddenly realized that he was terrified. His white beam of light cut like a laser across the room, and he felt like an intruder—not just in this house, but in another world. The old wooden house seemed to come alive, creaking and cracking with each breath it drew. The Victorian relic had a musty, shut-in smell, and everything in it was ancient—the furniture, the wallpaper, even the old hand pump by the sink. It was as if no one had lived here in a hundred years. No. It was as if the same people who'd lived here a hundred years ago were still living here now.

"Where's Cindy?" he screamed into the phone.

"Go through the door on your right. Into the dining room."

Jack shined the light ahead of him and walked hurriedly toward the door. The floorboards creaked with each step. He turned the crystal doorknob and entered the dining room. His flashlight's bright beam skipped across the long mahogany dining table, chair by chair. Cindy wasn't there. He searched higher, but the crystal chandelier only scattered the light. He scanned the walls, fixing on a hundred-year-old portrait of some crusty old sea captain who'd probably lived and died here. He almost seemed to scowl at Jack.

"Where *is* she!" he demanded.

"Easy," said Esteban. "You've got time. You've got as much time as *you* gave *me* to convince you that Raul should live. And now," he said, "it's *your* turn to convince *me*."

Jack felt a sinking dread. It was dawning on him that he was way out of his depth, that he was a pawn being manipulated at will. Sweat poured from his brow as he pressed the portable phone to his ear. "Listen, please—"

"I said *convince me*! Convince me she shouldn't die!"

"I'll give you anything you want. Just name it— whatever you want."

"I want *you* to feel what I felt. I want *you* to feel as

helpless as I did. Let's start with groveling. Beg me, Swyteck. Beg me not to execute her."

Jack stood speechless for a second, fearful that precious time was wasting. He shined the flashlight into the living room and down the long hall. He wanted to sprint away and search for Cindy. But the house was huge. He could never find her in time. "Please," his voice shook, "just let her go."

"I said *beg!*"

"*Please*. Cindy doesn't deserve this. She's never hurt anyone."

"Try the cabinet. Beneath the breakfront."

Jack darted across the dining room, tripping over the Persian area rug. He pulled open the cabinet and shined the light inside. "She's not—"

"Of course she isn't. Begging and pleading gets us nowhere—remember? Try something else."

Jack rose to his feet, taking short, panicky breaths as he squeezed the portable phone in his hand. "You miserable son of a bitch. Just tell me where she is."

"*Anger*," he taunted. "Let's see where *that* takes us. Try the living room—the closet at the base of the stairway."

Jack pointed the light across the room, revealing a grand stairway worthy of Scarlett O'Hara. It curved majestically up to the second floor, then curled in tight, smaller steps all the way to the third.

"The closet!" ordered Esteban, as if he somehow sensed that Jack hadn't moved.

Jack felt the seconds ticking away. He was a puppet, but following orders was his only hope. He darted toward the stairway, leading with the flashlight as he zigzagged through a maze of antiques in the living room. He found the closet and yanked open the door. Nothing. "You bastard!" his voice echoed in the dark, cavernous stairwell.

"Time is short," came the voice over the phone. "What are you going to do now?"

"Just stop the game! I'm the one you want. Take me. Just take *me*."

"Yessss," said Esteban, hissing with satisfaction. "A confession. It's your last chance. That's exactly the conclusion I reached, Swyteck. See if it works *this* time. Confess to me."

"I'll confess anything. I'm the one you want."

"Why?" he played his game. "What did *you do*?"

"Whatever you say I did. Whatever you say. I did it—"

"No!" he said bitterly. "You have to mean it. Confess to me and *mean* it!"

"I did it!"

"You killed Raul! Tell it to me!"

"Where is she?"

"Confess!"

"Yes! Yes!" he shouted into the phone. "I killed Raul Fernandez, all right? I did it! Now *where is Cindy*?"

"She's right behind you."

Jack wheeled, looked up into the stairwell and saw a body plunging like a missile through the stale air. "Cindy!" he cried out. But the next awful sound was the cracking of a neck at the end of a rope. Her feet never hit the ground. Jack screamed in agony. He recognized the clothes. A black hood covered her head—execution-style. "Oh, God, no . . ." he cried, all of his senses recoiling in horror. He dropped the portable phone and rushed halfway up the stairs to try to pull her down. But he couldn't reach her. He climbed a couple more steps and stretched out as far as he could. He still couldn't reach. He ran to the living room to grab a chair on which to stand, then rushed back toward the stairs.

"It's no use," came a deep, booming voice from somewhere in the pitch dark stairwell. "She's dead."

Jack's body went rigid. He was not alone.

He dropped the chair and drew his gun. He shined the flashlight behind him, then swept it forward and above. He didn't see anyone. "I'll kill you!" he shouted into the darkness.

"Revenge!" came a thundering reply that rattled the stairwell. "Now we *both* want it! Come get me, Swyteck!"

Jack thought only of Cindy hanging from her neck, and for one crazy moment he was willing to trade his own life for her killer's. He ran up the stairway with no conscious thought of his own safety, his gun in one hand, the flashlight in the other. He was at full speed when he reached the top of the steps. But as he turned the corner and started down the hall, a deafening blast sent him flying backward. *Pain . . . feet leaving ground . . . falling back . . . out of control.*

His gun and flashlight flew out of his hands as he crashed through the wooden banister. He was falling in what felt like slow motion. He heard himself cry out as he crashed onto a table and tumbled to the living-room floor. Then he sensed himself lying on his back. *Can't breathe . . . God, the pain.*

Seconds passed. The room was total blackness. Then a bright beam of light hit him in the eyes.

Esteban stared down from the top of the stairs. A smile crept onto his face at the sight of the body squirming and writhing on the floor. It pleased him that Jack was still alive. He pointed his flashlight up into the towering stairwell, as if admiring his work. The limp, lifeless body dangled overhead, twirling slowly on the rope. He tucked his gun into his belt, then pulled out his switch-blade. "Let the games begin," he said dryly. Then he shined the flashlight back down the stairway toward Jack—and his satisfied smile disappeared. In the few seconds he'd taken to savor the moment, his prey had quietly vanished.

Esteban scanned the living room floor with the flashlight. A look of confusion crossed his face. He saw no blood. No blood at all—anywhere. He grit his teeth in anger, realizing that his quarry must have been wearing a vest. Quickly, he jerked the flashlight from downstairs to upstairs. Jack's gun and flashlight were lying on the floor.

Esteban's smile returned. Jack was unarmed, and he couldn't have gone far. The house was completely dark, yet he'd snuck away without a sound. To do that, he had to have stayed within the glow from Esteban's flashlight. Esteban laid the flashlight down on the floor right where he stood at the top of the stairs, so as to mark the outer limits of Jack's escape. The dim, eerie glow extended all the way across the living room, into the parlor on one side, down the hall that led to the library on the other. It was large enough to make this *fun*. Esteban put his knife away, then pulled out his pistol. This time, Jack Swyteck would *not* get away.

54

·

Outside the warehouse four blocks away, Governor Harold Swyteck stepped cautiously toward the wide-open doors of the old Chevy van. His gun was drawn and his heart was racing. He froze ten feet from the van when he saw that a sack the size of a body bag was lying across the van's floor, jerking back and forth.

"Don't move!" he shouted.

The motion stopped, but a steady whimpering followed. It was a muffled, desperate sound. The governor stepped closer and focused on the license plate. It was a Dade County tag—from Miami.

"This is Harold Swyteck," he announced as he reached the back of the van.

The whimpering grew louder, more urgent.

"Lie perfectly still," he ordered. "I have a gun." He stepped up into the dark van and knelt down beside the body. He pointed the gun with one hand and quickly untied the strings on the sack with the other.

"Cindy!" he said, recognizing her from Jack's description.

She stared up at him with wide, horrified eyes.

"It's okay," he tried to calm her. "I'm Jack's father." He began to open the sack, then stopped, realizing she was naked. The monster had taken her clothes. He untied the gag.

She drew a deep breath and tried to move her stiffened jaw. "Thank God," she cried in a trembling voice.

"Are you all right?"

"Yes, yes!" she answered. "But you have to call the police. He's going to kill Jack! He told me he would, right before he knocked me out with some injection. He was moving to another house, said you'd find me in this van. I'm his messenger to you." She raced on without catching her breath. "He said he's going to kill Jack, and he wants *you* to find the body. We may already be too late to save him. He said Jack would be dead by the time I woke up."

"Where are they?"

"He didn't tell me. He's not looking for a showdown with you. He wants you to search for your son, hoping you can save him. He wants you to be too late. He just wants you to find Jack's body."

The governor snatched a portable phone from his vest and punched the speed dial. "Code red, Kimmell! I've got Cindy. She's okay. Jack's in trouble. Need a location."

"Roger," replied Kimmell. He punched a button on his terminal. In seconds, it would pick up the signal from Jack's pulsating transmitter. At least it should have picked it up. He punched it again. Still nothing. Again. Nothing.

"Dammit, I'm not getting a reading," he said.

"What?"

"It's not coming through."

"How can that be?"

Kimmell shook his head, trying to think. "I don't know—maybe, maybe he lost the transmitter? I'm sorry, Governor. I can't find him."

The words cut to Harold Swyteck's core. "God help him," he uttered. "Dear God in heaven, please *help* him."

55

A determined Esteban stepped quietly down the staircase, beneath Rebecca's dangling corpse. He'd left the flashlight on the top step, pointing into the stairwell. He needed light, but he didn't want to reveal his whereabouts by being its source. In the eerie yellow glow, his tall, lean body cast a lengthy shadow into the living room. His movements were quiet as a snake's. The gun felt warm in his hand. His heart actually beat at a normal pace—just another day at work for an experienced killer. He could either wait for Jack to come out of hiding, or he could go and get him. The choice was easy. Esteban *loved* flushing his quarry out of the bush.

Behind the staircase, at the end of the long, dark hallway, the heat in the tiny bathroom was nearly suffocating Jack. Sweat poured from his body. The bulletproof vest cloaked him like a winter parka, but he didn't dare take it off. It had saved his life once already—though a constant sharp pain told him the blow from the bullet had probably cracked a rib. He

drew shallow breaths to minimize the pain. But pain
was the least of his problems. He had no gun, no
flashlight, and no contact to the outside world. He'd
lost everything in the tumble down the stairs, and
the gunshot had destroyed Kimmell's transmitter.
Surprise was his only weapon. He stood perfectly
still, hiding behind the open bathroom door with
his back against the wall. He listened carefully for
his stalker and accepted the brutal fact that only one
of them would walk out of the house.

Leading with his gun, Esteban crept down the
hall behind the stairway, one slow and silent step at
a time. The fuzzy light from the stairwell grew
dimmer with each step, but this was familiar territory. He had walked the entire house several times
before Jack's arrival. He knew that just a few feet
ahead, just beyond the faint glow from the flashlight, there was a bedroom on the right and a bathroom straight ahead. He moved closer to the wall
and stopped just five feet away from the open bathroom door.

Jack was in total darkness, but his eyes were adjusting. From behind the open door he peered with
one eye through the vertical crack at the hinges.
There was light in the living room at the other end
of the hall, but the hallway itself was barely illumi-
nated. Jack's night vision improved with each passing second. Finally, he could see Esteban—a black
silhouette with a gun in its hand.

Jack could feel his hands shaking and his heart
pumping even more furiously. He could taste his
own blood from a cut on his lip. The shadow slowly

inched closer. He couldn't see his eyes or the features of his face. But there was enough light in the background to know he was right there. He was staring into the face of the enemy—but the enemy was a shadow. He wondered whether Esteban—or whoever he was—could see *him*, whether he was toying with him, knowing that his prey was unarmed and defenseless. Jack would find out in a moment. Esteban had two doors from which to choose—the bedroom or the bathroom. Jack held his breath and waited.

Go into the bedroom, he prayed.

Time stood still. Then Esteban moved—just a few inches. He was coming closer. He'd chosen the bathroom.

Jack could hear Esteban breathing. Jack's own lungs were about to explode, but he didn't dare take a breath. He was frozen against the wall. The open door was in his face. Esteban was at the threshold. His hand had crossed the imaginary plane. Another step and he'd be inside.

Suddenly, Jack pushed against the door with all his might, slamming it shut. Esteban cried out. His wrist was caught in the door, and his hand with the gun was in the bathroom. A shot roared in the pitch-dark bathroom, shattering the mirror. Another shot exploded the basin. Esteban was firing wildly. Jack put all his weight behind one last shove, and then he heard the sound of metal crashing on ceramic tile. The gun was on the floor. And Esteban was pinned.

Still braced against the door, Jack groped with one foot in the darkness, searching for the gun. He found it. His foot was right on it. He heard a piercing sound above his head, like a nail puncturing wood. Another piercing sound, and Jack cried out with pain as the point of Esteban's switchblade passed through the door and punctured his forearm. Jack dove to the floor and grabbed the gun, expecting Esteban to come crashing through. He pointed and shot twice in the darkness. But no one fell. Through his terror, he registered the sound of footsteps in the hall. Esteban was running. Jack opened the door and fired another quick shot, but his target had already turned the corner.

Jack dashed from the bathroom and followed in Esteban's footsteps. He heard a crash in the kitchen. The killer was escaping. Jack sprinted to the kitchen just as the back door slammed shut, then ran out to the porch. He looked left, then right. He saw a man dressed in black running down the sidewalk toward Duval Street. Jack knew Esteban would disappear forever if he made it back to the madness at Fantasy Fest. Jack's ribs were sore from the gunshot, his forearm had a puncture wound, and he was bleeding badly from the forehead, but his fall hadn't broken any bones in his legs. So he tucked the gun into his belt and began sprinting.

He was running faster than he had ever run, despite the vest, and he was gaining ground. As they drew closer to Duval, they started passing peacocks, tin men, and drunks who'd spilled over from the crowded street festival. Rock music rumbled in the night. A sudden burst of firecrackers drew piercing screams and a round of laughter.

"Hey, watch it!" a woman dressed as Cleopatra

shouted, but Esteban plowed through her like she didn't exist, then plunged into the safety of a shoulder-to-shoulder parade of costumes on Duval. Jack followed right behind, trying desperately to keep his target in sight as he weaved his way through the heaving mass. He could hardly breathe. All at once the sea of beads and feathers and painted faces swallowed him up, and when he broke free Esteban was gone.

"You stupid jerk!" he heard someone shout. He looked ahead in time to see Esteban dashing through the middle of a long and twisted Chinese dragon, ripping it right in half. Esteban wasn't just trying to vanish in the crowd, Jack realized. He was *going* somewhere specific. He was headed north, toward the marina off Mallory Square. Jack had a sudden flash. A *boat!* Esteban was going to escape by boat. Jack hesitated only a second—just long enough to think of Cindy. Then he darted in the same direction, bumping into the Beatles and Napoleon, pushing aside Gumby and Marilyn Monroe.

Esteban was untying a sleek racing boat from its mooring just as Jack reached the long wooden pier at the end of Duval. The triple outboard engines cranked with a deafening blast. Jack stopped short, pulled out his gun, and took aim. A clown screamed and the crowd scattered, since Jack's gun looked too real, even for Fantasy Fest. A caveman suddenly turned hero and whacked the pistol from Jack's hand with a quick sweep of his club.

"No!" Jack shouted as his weapon skidded across the dock and plunked into the marina.

Esteban's boat drifted away from the dock, slowly at first, until it was clear of the other boats. Instinctively, Jack sprinted ahead and leaped from the dock to the covered bow of the boat just as Esteban hit the throttle. The powerful engines roared, and the bow rose from the water, knocking Jack off balance as he landed. He scrambled to his feet on the wet fiberglass as the boat cut through the darkness.

Realizing that Jack was aboard, Esteban kept one hand on the steering wheel and with the other slashed at his unwanted passenger with a long fishing gaff. The engine noise grew deafening as the needlelike boat shot from forty, to sixty, then seventy miles per hour, bouncing violently on the waves. Jack fell to his knees as the hull slammed through a big whitecap. With a quick jerk of the wheel, Esteban shifted the boat to the right and Jack tumbled across the bow. In a split second he was overboard, head over heels, bouncing like a skipping stone across the waves at seventy miles per hour.

He emerged dizzy and coughing up salt water. He was trying to swim when his foot hit bottom. In less than ninety seconds the speeding cigarette boat had taken them nearly a mile offshore, where they'd reached a coral reef. He could stand flat-footed with his head above water. He cursed as he stood in the middle of a zipper of white foam that was Esteban's wake, forced to watch as the boat grew smaller in the distance. Then he froze as he saw that Esteban was turning around. He was coming back—at full throttle, headed right at him.

The bastard is going to flatten me.

Jack dove beneath the surface and pressed himself against the reef. He cut his hands and knees on sharp coral that projected like huge fingers and fans from the floor, but it saved his life. He held fast as the boat zipped overhead. The churning propeller missed him by less than a foot. He emerged for air, saw the boat coming back for another pass, and went under again. This time, though, the boat approached more slowly. Esteban wanted to check his work. After two years of waiting, he *had* to see the blood.

"Are you fish food, Swyteck?" he called into the darkness. He was nearly certain he'd cut the miserable lawyer in half. He'd felt the thud. But the water was so shallow it was possible the boat had hit bottom rather than pay dirt. He looked left, then right, searching intently as the boat slowly arrived at the spot where he'd last seen his prey.

Jack clung to the reef, struggling to stay underwater. But he desperately needed air. The boat was right overhead, puttering at no-wake speed. A few seconds passed, and he couldn't stand it any longer. He broke the surface and grabbed onto the diving platform on the back of the boat. He looked up. Esteban hadn't seen or heard him. The triple engines still rumbled loudly, even at a slow speed. Carefully, Jack pulled himself onto the platform and peered up over the stern. Esteban was studying the waves, longing to see little pieces of floating flesh.

Jack moved silently across the diving platform, toward the outboard engines. He was after the fuel lines. Without them, Esteban might get another mile from shore, but then he'd be stranded at sea. Jack reached for them and tried to muffle his cry as he scorched his hand on the hot engine block—but Esteban heard the stifled groan.

"Die!" he screamed, bringing the gaff down like an axe across Jack's back.

Jack cried out in pain, but he grabbed the gaff and pulled as he tumbled into the water, taking Esteban with him. They plunged into just three feet of sea water, both hitting the jagged coral bottom simultaneously. Esteban emerged first, thrashing like a marlin on the end of a line as he struggled to hold Jack underwater. Jack tumbled over the coral, trying to find his footing so he could get his head above water. But Esteban's powerful fingers found Jack's throat before he could plant his feet. Jack kicked and swung with his fists, but the resistance of the water made his blows ineffective. His nostrils burned as he sucked in more salt water. He gasped for air but drew only the sea into his lungs.

He reached frantically on the shallow bottom for a rock to use as a weapon. There were none. But there was the coral that projected from the bottom like a fossilized forest. It was hard and sharp, and it cut like a knife. He groped and found a formation that felt like the stubby antler of a young buck. He grabbed it, snapped it off, and swung it up toward Esteban's head. It hit something. Jack was blinded by the churning foam, but he sensed the penetration upon impact. He jabbed again, and finally the death grip around his throat loosened somewhat. He broke free and shot to the surface, coughing as he emerged.

Jack spit out the last of the salt water just in time to see Esteban, less than fifteen feet away, once again raising the gaff, which had floated back into his grasp. As he lifted it overhead, Jack could see the blood pouring from his throat.

"You bastard!" Esteban cried out. "You fucking bastard!" His arm shot forward in an attempt to impale, but Jack jinked to his left and grabbed the gaff's wooden shaft. By now, Esteban's eyes were glassy and his grip insecure. The loss of blood was taking its toll, but Esteban was still coming at him.

"No more!" Jack called out fiercely.

He drove forward, shattering the Cuban's teeth with the blunt end of the gaff and pushing it into his throat. The force of the movement jerked Esteban's body backward, then headfirst under the waves as Jack leaned forward and maintained steady pressure on the pole. Only after a full minute, when the bubbles had stopped floating to the surface, did he unclench his hands and swim toward the boat.

Once aboard, he watched intently, still unwilling to believe that the fight was over. He sat for ten minutes, staring at the spot where Esteban had gone under, half expecting him to rise again like the mechanical shark in *Jaws*. But this was real life, where people paid for their actions. The full moon hung like a big bright hole in the darkness. A shooting star appeared briefly on the horizon, and the gentle lapping of the waves against the hull reminded Jack that even this drama had done nothing to disturb nature's rhythms.

He heard a flutter behind him and looked up.

A Coast Guard helicopter was approaching from shore. Jack sat perfectly still as the warm, gentle current washed across the reef and dispersed the dark, crimson cloud of Esteban's blood. It was ironic, he thought. Hundreds, maybe thousands of oppressed refugees had fled Cuba in little rafts and inner tubes, only to be caught in the Gulf Stream and lost somewhere in the Atlantic. Finally, one of the oppressors was on his way to the bottom. And with God's grace, the sea would never give him up.

Jack looked up as the pontoon helicopter hovered directly overhead, then came to rest on the surface. The glass bubble around the cockpit glistened in the moonlight, but he could see his father inside. Jack waved to let him know he was all right, and the governor opened the glass door and waved back.

"She's okay," his father shouted over the noise of whirling blades. "Cindy's okay!"

Jack heard the words, but couldn't assimilate them. *She can't be alive.* He'd seen her with his own eyes. Seen her hanging there. The part of his soul where she'd resided had been ripped out of him. Still, he wanted to believe. Oh, how he wanted to believe . . . He looked at his father intently, allowing himself some small measure of hope.

"She is *definitely* okay," Harry said, seeing the confusion on his son's face. "I just saw her. I just held her in my arms."

The governor threw him a line, but Jack was too stunned to move. Slowly, the realization sank in. Cindy was *alive.* His father was with him. And the danger was behind them. He reached for the lifeline and swam toward the helicopter. The swirling wind from the chopper blades blew water in his face, but he didn't mind. All the cuts and scrapes, the bruises— even his cracked rib—were glorious reminders that he was alive—alive with something to live for.

That much was obvious from the face that greeted him. As he looked up, Jack saw tears of joy in his proud father's eyes.

Epilogue

B efore Esteban's body was borne by currents out to sea, his story had washed ashore with the force of a tidal wave. The media blitz began that Sunday morning and lasted for weeks, but the essential elements of the story were out within twenty-four hours. It was front-page news in every major Florida newspaper. It was the lead story on local and national network newscasts, and CNN even ran several hours of continuous coverage.

By Monday afternoon the Swytecks had revealed all to the media, and the truth was widely known about Esteban's two-year campaign to avenge his brother's execution. The public knew that neither Jack nor his father had killed Eddy Goss. Esteban had, as part of his plan to frame Jack and have him executed for a murder he'd never committed. The public knew that Esteban, not Jack, had murdered Gina Terisi, in a last-ditch effort to ensure Jack's conviction. And the public knew that Governor Swyteck had not executed an innocent man. As Esteban had admitted to Jack, Raul Fernandez was in the act of raping the young girl when Esteban had killed her; both Esteban and Fernandez had gotten what they deserved.

By Monday evening the Swytecks were heralded as heroes. They'd eliminated not just a psychopathic killer, but one of Castro's former henchmen. The governor received congratulatory telegrams from several national leaders. A petition started in Little Havana to create "Swyteck Boulevard." Amidst all the hoopla, a cowardly written statement was issued quietly from the state attorney's office, announcing that Wilson McCue would promptly disband the grand jury he'd empaneled to indict the Swytecks.

And on the following Tuesday—the second Tuesday in November—the voters went to the polls. Florida had never seen a larger turnout. And no one had ever witnessed a more dramatic one-week turnaround in public opinion.

"The second time is sweeter!" Harry Swyteck proclaimed from the raised dais at his second inaugural ball.

Loud cheers filled the grand ballroom as three hundred friends and guests raised their champagne glasses with the re-elected governor. The band started up. The governor took Agnes by the hand and led her to the dance floor. It was like a silver wedding anniversary, the two of them swaying gracefully to their favorite song, the governor in his tuxedo and his bride in a flowing white taffeta gown.

Couples flooded onto the dance floor as Jack and Cindy watched from their seats at the head table. It had been a long time since they were this happy. They had their wounds, of course. Cindy had nightmares and fears of being alone. Both she and Jack constantly remembered Gina and what she'd gone through. Slowly, though, they regained some semblance of normalcy, and their love for each other became the source of their strength. Cindy returned to work at her photography studio. Jack started his own criminal-defense firm and enjoyed the luxury of picking his own clients. By Christmas, their lives had vastly improved—psychologically, emotionally, and most of all, romantically.

Jack couldn't hide his look of wonder and admiration as he stared at Cindy across the table. She was spectacular in a deep purple gown that featured an elegant hem and sexy décolletage. Her hair was up in a swirling blonde twist; her face was a radiant portrait framed by dangling diamond earrings that Agnes had loaned her.

"Come on," he said as he took her by the hand. "There's something I want you to see." They walked arm-in-arm away from the crowded ballroom to one of the quiet courtyards that had made this classic Mediterranean-style hotel so special since its opening in the 1920s.

Soft music flowed through the open French doors, making it even more romantic beneath the moon and stars on this cool, crisp January evening. They strolled arm-in-arm amidst trellised vines, a trickling fountain, and potted palms on a sweeping veranda the size of a tennis court. Jack rested their champagne glasses on the stone railing where the veranda overlooked a swimming pool forty feet below. He took Cindy in his arms.

"What's that for?" she asked coyly, enjoying the hug.

"Forever," he answered. Then, covertly, so she wouldn't notice, he took a diamond ring from his pocket and dropped it into Cindy's glass.

"Well, *here* you are," said the governor with a smile as he came around the corner. "I've been trying to have a word alone with you two all evening."

Jack wasn't sure how to handle the untimely interruption.

Cindy returned the smile. "And we've been waiting for a minute with you, too, Governor. To drink our own private toast to another four years."

"A wonderful idea," he replied, "except I'm out of champagne."

"Well, here," she offered, "have some of mine."

"Wait—" Jack said.

Cindy reached for her glass but knocked it off the railing.

"Oh, my God," Jack gasped, looking on with horror as it sailed over the edge and plunged forty feet down, exploding on the cement deck by the pool.

"Oh, I'm so clumsy," she said, looking embarrassed.

Jack continued to stare disbelievingly at the impact area below. Without a word, he turned and sprinted down the stone stairway that led to the pool, then began furiously searching the deck. Hunched over and squinting beneath the lanterns by the pool, he scoured the area with the diligence of an octogenarian on the beach with his metal detector. But he found only splinters of glass. He got down on his knees for a closer look, but the ring was gone.

"Looking for this?" Cindy asked matter-of-factly. She was standing over him, extending her hand and displaying the sparkling ring on her finger.

Jack just rolled his eyes like a guy caught on "Candid Camera." "You saw me drop it into the glass?" he asked, though it was more a statement than a question.

She nodded.

"You had the ring all along . . . it didn't go over the edge?"

"I fished it out when you were looking at your father," she said, smiling.

He laughed at himself as he shook his head. Then he looked up and shrugged with open arms. "Well?"

"Well," she replied. "So long as you're on your knees . . ."

Jack swallowed hard. "Will you?"

"Will I *what*?"

"Will you *marry* me?"

"Mmmmmm," Cindy stalled, then smiled. "You *know* I will." She pulled him up by the hand and threw her arms around him.

For one very long, happy moment, they were lost in each other, oblivious to their surroundings. But a sudden round of applause reminded them that they were in public. Perched on the veranda and smiling down on them were the governor and Agnes, and perhaps ten other couples the governor had rustled together after Cindy had shown him the ring.

Jack waved to them all, then took a quick bow.

"Your father's proud of you," Cindy said, looking into Jack's eyes. "And when we have a little Jack or Jackie running around our house, you can be proud, too."

"'Jackie' sounds good," he said with a shrug, "if it's a girl. But if it's a boy I'd like to call him 'Harry,'" Jack said thoughtfully. "For his grandfather."

She drew him close. "I'm happy he'll have a grandfather," she said.

"I am, too," Jack said.

He'd finally earned the governor's pardon. And the governor had earned his.